also by Gray Lightfoot

THE MALTHOUSE FALCON

The First Humphrey Boggart novel

and

A VIEW FROM A CAB

(the poetry and musings of a bus driver in Cornwall)

THE SEER'S TALE

At the highest point of Screamers Cliff, a party of hand-picked observers hunched themselves against the wind. They waited as a small donkey cart made slow progress towards them. The driver hauled on the reins before clambering onto the back of his cart. As he brushed the straw off a newly-inscribed gravestone, three people of very dissimilar appearance left the group and drew near to it. The most interested of these was a female elf who ran forward to look at the stone. The inscription read...

Here Lies

J.C. BIGG

HONOURED SEER

OF THE ALL-SEEING EYE

Born - 979 SA Died -

A tiny bald man, smaller even than the elf, had to wrestle with his wind-tossed white coat before he could approach the back of the cart. "Now will you jump off the cliff?" he said. His hands, pushed deep into his pockets, rose with frustration only as far as the material would allow.

"It's not finished!" said the elf, still busy checking the spelling.

"Of course it's not finished!" said the man on the cart. "These things take time, you know. Dragging me all the way up here just so the intended can have a look doesn't help matters. I'm a busy man!"

"Well we thank you very much for that, Mr Winslade," said Avis Davies, by far the tallest of the three. Her long black cloak was an indication of her status; she was a witch. "And of course you will be duly paid for your trouble." The monumental mason, careful not to overstep the mark, nodded in deference. The witch, satisfied order had been restored, continued, "Right, Seer Bigg, you've seen the stone and you also have my word. People are getting cold. Now will you kindly throw yourself off the cliff? Then we can all go home."

JC Bigg had never liked the names her parents had given her. From the day she found out Jennet and Cowslip were actually girl's names she would answer to nothing other than her initials.

Content in her own mind that posterity would not now mark her out as just another soppy girl, JC focused once more on the job she had chosen to do. With an exaggerated rock back on her heels she set off as fast as she could towards the edge of the cliff. Her tough toned body, despite having to clutch a folded silk sheet to her chest, ate up the ground between her starting point and the cliff's edge. Behind her the group of onlookers held their breath as she approached the point of no return. Then, with a braking manoeuvre any cannonball hurler would have been proud of, she brought herself to a halt inches from possible oblivion. She risked a glance over the edge. Five hundred feet below her, a larger crowd of probably-more-interested-than-they-ought-to-be onlookers stared right back up at her. A question needed answering. She marched back to the party behind her and singled out the tiny man in the white coat. He was now cradling a large ginger cat.

"Doctor Thumb? Tell me why we need the hole again."

The little man sighed. "Well…when we did the trials before, we noticed the parachute tended to oscillate wildly as it descended. By putting a hole or vent in the parachute, it seems to stop this problem," said Thumb, all the while stroking the cat.

"Hang on! I thought you said I was the first person to test this thing."

"You are." Thumb ceased stroking and the cat opened its eyes. The first thing it focused on was the folded up sheet JC was holding.

"Then who…?" The cat yowled and scrambled over Thumb's head in a desperate attempt to escape.

"Oww!" cried the little man, his face already beading with blood. After regaining a little composure and re-siting his glasses, he puffed out his chest like a lovelorn pigeon. "Kipper must have recognised the parachute. Still, he's been with The Eye for five years now and he's still got all of his nine lives intact."

"And just how do you know that, Doctor Thumb?" said JC.

The little man lowered his gaze as the elf watched the ginger blur getting smaller and smaller in the distance.

"I guess it's just the 'being-catapulted-over-a-cliff' bit he doesn't like", he said.

JC caught a disapproving look from Avis Davies. It had been The Massy Witch herself, in her role as Commander of the All Seeing Eye, who had taken her to one side some weeks ago. The two of them walked together away from the others.

"Are you scared, Seer Bigg?" said Avis Davies.

"No!" JC was stung her courage had been called into question.

"I didn't think so. That is why I chose you."

"It just seems silly to jump all that way when I could fly-"

"That's just it, Seer Bigg. We don't know whether the rush of the wind at such a height would allow you to open your wings? Dr Thumb doesn't seem to think so. Or at least, he wouldn't let you risk it. He believes the parachute is the safer option."

"But-"

"There is no alternative, Seer Bigg. Where you will be expected to go, your magical powers will be useless to you. I don't want to explain the situation until I am sure you are up to the task."

"With respect, Commander, if you tell me to jump over that cliff, I will." JC saluted and waited for the order.

A couple of seconds passed by before Avis Davies said, "Are you ready, Seer Bigg?"

JC felt the eyes of everyone upon her; Avis Davies, Doctor Thumb, her colleagues...even Kipper the cat watched from a safe distance. Mindful of the weight of expectation hanging over her she turned and faced the cliff.

"OK...let's do it!" Digging her heels into the soft turf to get maximum purchase she was off and running. Once more her body felt good. She knew in her head, she was made to do such things. As her foot hit the edge of the cliff she screamed and threw her body into the star shape they had shown her in training.

A KNIGHT'S TALE

Carl Knight's parents had once been proud of their eldest son's achievements. Having left school without any qualifications, he started work in the construction industry. Within five years he was running his own company. At thirty, he won the contract to build Gilsland's bijou new shopping centre and it seemed to him that everything he touched turned to gold…that's when he started gambling.

He first got involved with the Domania project some seven years ago. Times were hard and in a small town like Gilsland, an ex-convict found it hard to get work. He'd served his time but people don't forget. His father had hardly been cold in his grave when Carl, struggling to pay off gambling debts, had robbed the local post office and accidentally hospitalised the town's popular postmaster. Carl blamed himself for his mother's death. She never quite got over the shame of it all and his brother Dan reacted badly to her passing. The last Carl had heard of him had been the news that he'd joined the French Foreign Legion.

Carl knew he had to get away from the unforgiving town of Gilsland. His job as a woodsman in the Forest of Elphinstone provided him with some kind of peace but he knew he was underachieving. It was always easier to drown his sorrows in one of the local pubs than it was to think about starting something new. Normally a solitary drinker, Carl got talking to some guy in a smart suit who actually seemed interested in his problems. When the man found out about Carl's career in construction, he seemed delighted…although Carl couldn't help feeling that it wasn't exactly news to the guy.

"I think what you need is a fresh start, Carl" said the man who had introduced himself as Rutger. He was about thirty years old with blonde hair. "Do you feel you're capable of working at a higher level? Say a multi-million pound building project? Do you believe in yourself? " Carl swallowed before answering. It was now or never.

"Yeah, I think I could pull something like that off."

"Only *think*?"

"I *know* I can do it!"

"Good man, Carl! If you *know* you can do it, I *believe* you can do it."

"Hang on…just hold fire a minute…am I right in thinking you are asking me, a bloke you just met in the pub, to take charge of a multi-million pound building project, when there are already people out there who are experienced in doing that kind of thing? Maybe I've had too much to drink…" Rutger put a firm hand on Carl's shoulder.

"I believe in you, Carl. It is now time that you believed in me. The project we are talking about requires someone with no ties of family or relationships of any kind. It has to be a total commitment. If you take on this project, I can guarantee within a year you will have made your first million."

Carl pondered on this for a minute or so while Rutger paid a visit to the men's room. On his return he suggested a further meeting.

"OK, Carl. It's up to you. But I think you're more than capable of running this project for us. If you really want to make a difference to your life and show these people round here just what they missed out on then I suggest you meet up with my elder brother and me at 10.30 am in the café across the road in a week's time. Oh and Carl, wear a sharp suit, eh?" said Rutger, "Wilkie is impressed by sharp suits."

A week went by in which Carl had his hair cut, his nails done and bought himself a rather expensive suit. He paid a visit to his Mum and Dad's grave and told them he was going to make them proud of him. He only wished his brother Dan could be here to make the whole thing perfect.

His talk with Rutger had instilled a new sense of self-belief in him. There was a still a small part of Carl that worried that the whole thing might be a huge set-up at his expense but he decided to 'accentuate the positive'…as that old song his father sang went. After all if the whole thing did fall through, Carl had decided that the suit and the new look would be moving to another town to start all over again.

In the cafe, a week later, Carl met Rutger and his elder brother, Wilkie. The pair looked nothing like each other and Carl was amazed at the age difference between them. The man was, quite frankly, old enough to be Rutger's father. All the time they were talking Carl could feel the older man watching him through his powerful spectacles with a marked intensity. He only asked Carl the one question which was how he felt about offering such complete commitment to the project. Carl, inspired by the fact that the whole thing hadn't been a dream, exuded his passion from the outset.

Rutger then began to outline the project which involved creating a theme park inside the huge cavern that lay beneath Elphinstone Crag. Carl hit the ground running and started coming up with ideas that seemed to impress Rutger much more than his brother. He noticed that Wilkie had become distracted and was constantly looking at his watch. In the middle of Carl's suggestion that they re-introduce steam engines as a means of entering the theme park, the old man struggled to his feet and announced it was time they went and took a look at the site itself. Wilkie seemed to look even older than he did an hour ago. Rutger helped his brother to his feet and Carl was somewhat relieved that their car was outside. The two of them manoeuvred Wilkie into the back seat before they drove to a small lay-by quite near the railway line.

The Elphinstone railway tunnel was the only way they could get into the cavern although the line had closed down many years ago when the lead mines had become uneconomical. Rutger took a couple of torches from the boot of the car and the three of them walked across a field and entered the tunnel. A good way down it was blocked by a wooden wall with a small padlocked door built into it. As Rutger unfastened the padlock, Carl noticed that Wilkie was becoming quite agitated. Even in the torchlight, he could see that the old man was perspiring. Carl and Rutger helped Wilkie down the tunnel making hurried progress until they reached the huge cavern. Redundant railway fixtures and fittings from the old mining days surrounded them as they helped him over to a pile of railway sleepers so that he could sit down. The man was clearly not well.

"Is he all right?" Carl asked Rutger. "He was almost bent double in the tunnel."

"He'll start to feel better once we get into the light." Carl looked at Rutger as if he was mad.

"Perhaps we should get him out of there before something serious happens?" Just as he had finished speaking, a bright light began to fill the cavern and a small patch of sky appeared in front of them. It was almost as if the wall of the cavern had started to open to reveal the daylight outside. Carl felt that he should have been frightened but Rutger and Wilkie seemed unsurprised so he relaxed a little.

"What do you think?" said Rutger. Carl just stood there shaking his head in disbelief as more holes of skylight began to reveal themselves. As soon as a hole big enough to crawl through appeared, Wilkie was on all fours and scrambling into the daylight. He collapsed onto the green grass beneath him. Carl rushed through to help him but the old man waved him away.

"I'll be all right in a minute!" he groaned. "But it's the last time, Rutger. I'm not doing it again."

"Look!" shouted Rutger over the noise created by these strange openings, "Over there!" Carl looked to where Rutger was pointing despite being spooked by the man's callous attitude to his brother's misfortune. He stared at the huge palatial building that stood in the distance.

"Where is this?" asked Carl. "Are we at the other side of the crag? I didn't know there was a stately home around here. Me and our Dan often explored over the Crag but I don't recall…"

"This is the palace that will form the basis of our theme park. Welcome to our world! Welcome to *your* world!" Carl was struggling to come to terms with the conflict of Rutger's guided tour and the lack of concern for the old man who was crawling behind them. Rutger sensed this and linked his arm with Carl's.

"The magic of this place is that we are still inside the Elphinstone Crag." Carl looked up at the sky above him and saw the clouds passing by.

"But…how?" was all he could say.

"Who is this…Dan, who you mentioned?" Carl felt relief at hearing Wilkie's voice again but when he turned round he was surprised that it wasn't the old bent man who he had seen writhing in pain a few seconds earlier. He seemed…younger. His eyes almost sparkled behind his thick lenses.

"He's my brother."

"I thought you had no family." Wilkie's recovery was amazing. "I hope for your sake, he's no longer with us."

Troubled by Wilkie's reaction to his brother, Carl said. "Yeah, he's no longer with us." He decided it would be best not to jeopardise this new opportunity. It wasn't really a lie.

"Come, Mr Knight…Mother's looking forward to meeting you." Wilkie gestured towards the palace.

"Mother?" said Carl.

"Wilkie likes to think that he is the brains behind it all but in truth it is our Mother."

"Is that where she lives?" said Carl, indicating the palace.

"Oh, Mother lives in lots of places", said Wilkie. The three of them set off walking and by the time they reached the palace Carl was quite disconcerted at the change in the older man. He couldn't take his eyes off Wilkie who now appeared to be much younger than Carl had ever understood him to be.

12

Back in Gilsland he had been a bent old man but here he was transformed. By the time the three of them entered the palace, Wilkie appeared to be barely ten years older than his brother. It was a strange world that Carl had arrived in and just as he was coming to terms with the strangeness, he met Rutger and Wilkie's mother.

"Good Morning, Mr Knight or perhaps I should call you Carl. Actually I do like that name; I might allow you to keep it. Rutger has told me quite a bit about you." Carl tried hard to close his mouth but the woman who had been introduced as his new friends' mother was thirty if she was a day.

*

It turned out that the woman was Rutger and Wilkie's metaphorical mother rather than a biological one to them. She explained to Carl the miracle that he had just been witness to… 'A world within a world' was how she described it. She outlined her plans to create a pleasure ground for children much like she had heard of elsewhere. A place where children could come and play; where their parents needn't worry about them.

"I've even thought of a name for it" she said, "…Domania. What do you think, Carl?"

"Sounds fantastic" Carl replied.

"But are you the man to make this 'fantastic' place a reality?" Carl couldn't believe his luck. Seizing his big chance, he started bouncing ideas off her as though Domania had been all he had thought about for a year. She seemed impressed...Rutger and Wilkie seemed impressed.

"Of course it'll take quite a bit of money." Carl had come to the tricky bit and he braced himself for a setback. The woman clicked her fingers and another man brought in a large casket and set it on the table. He flipped the lid and lifted it.

"This is my eldest son, Hans-Christian" said the woman. Carl gazed on the casket full of gold coin but the name Hans-Christian started ringing alarm bells. This is a fairy tale, he thought. Would he wake up in a minute and find that it had all been a dream? Hans-Christian shook his hand.

"Is that really gold?" said Carl

"Indeed it is", said Mother, "...but I still need my original question answering...are you the man to make this a reality?' You see for this to work I have to have your utmost devotion...just like I have from all my other sons." Carl looked at her and then at her three 'sons'. Two more men came into the room and Carl was introduced to both Jakob and Arnold. "I am offering you the opportunity of a lifetime. If you fulfil this dream of mine I will make you rich beyond all expectation. For reasons you will later discover, neither I nor my sons can make this work. Rutger and Arnold can assist you up to a certain point but neither of them has the contacts or ability to build the project I have envisaged. If you are that man, Carl Knight, then I need some kind of assurance from you...but remember that there is a price to pay...there is always a price to pay."

THURSDAY MARKET WEDNESDAY

"So tell me again, Will…why are they called Thursday Market Wednesday? It just seems strange that other football clubs are called something dynamic like Rovers, Wanderers or Athletic."

Will sighed. "Thursday Market Wednesday Football Club was founded by local stallholders and shopkeepers…"

"So why aren't they called Thursday Market Thursday?"

"If you let me finish…they couldn't play football on Thursday because that was market day…the busiest day of the week…so they played on Wednesday which was half day closing…they had the afternoon off on Wednesday so they became known as The Wednesday Football Club…which was fine when they just played local matches. When they formed the national Football League and started playing against other towns and cities they became Thursday Market Wednesday F.C. Have you got that?" I nodded. "…because I'm not going to explain it again."

The Wednesday were top of the league and playing well. This was a special day, not only because they were playing their local rivals Fleetpool Athletic, but Avis Davies, the Massy Witch herself, was at the game. Half an hour earlier she had opened the new wooden grandstand and was now sitting in the State Box waiting for the match to kick off.

Will Spargo was a big man. He was a coach driver and not frightened to speak his mind. So when the tall guy with the broad-brimmed black hat stood in front of us Will wasn't backward at coming forward. He tapped him on his shoulder.

"Oi, Lofty! How about you find somewhere else to stand?"

When the object of Will's ire turned around and stared into his eyes, my friend seemed to lose some of his bravado. "Did you say something?" said the guy, like myself an ironised sprite, having relinquished his magic to make a new life for himself in this magic-free city.

"Well you could at least take your hat off," said Will, with uncommon compromise.

"Perhaps you would like me to take my head off for you? I could do that if you want me to." There was a formidable build-up of anger coming from the i-sprite who then gripped both the cheeks of his rather small head. He looked about to fulfil his suggestion when Will put both his hands up in deference.

"Now there's no need to get all upset about this. It's just my mate here can't see."

The tall i-sprite dropped his hands, looked down at me and smiled. His violet eyes as cold as tripe left out in the rain, took me in. "Ex-boggart, like myself. For you, my friend, I will move." And with that he ventured further into the crowd.

Will puffed his shoulders like a lovestruck pigeon. "Bit speciesist that, wasn't it? Only moving because you're one of his lot..."

I watched the i-sprite make his way through the crowd towards the new grandstand. I got the feeling that he wasn't here for the football.

THE ASSASSIN'S TALE

He passes through the throng eager to kill. His target is the Massy Witch herself. She is opening the new grandstand. He doesn't like crowds, they get in his way. His mistress seems to think it will help him. 'The more the merrier', she said. He doesn't like her interfering with his work. She thinks she knows about killing people but most of her killing is reactive. Proactive killing is a very different business.

He was still annoyed by the big red-haired man asking him to move. Had he not been on a kill, he would have made him rue that big mouth of his. The appearance of another boggart had provided him with a get-out clause. He remembers a time when he himself was a boggart but that was before he met his mistress. Now he's no longer sure what he is.

Thinking back to the first time he ever met her, he recalls a bitter-sweet memory. Back then he was satisfied with just frightening people. It had been such a joy to scare the lights out of someone. In fact, if he was honest (and despite everything he prided himself in his honesty), he still found the instillation of fear much more enjoyable than the actual killing. All the power was in the terror, the act itself was merely functional. His favourite trick had been to go for a walk in the forest disguised as a little old woman. The forest was a primeval place that instilled a fear borne of childhood memories and loneliness. The trick was to disarm the natural fear a person carried with them into the forest; to make them so relaxed that any terror they later experienced would be the greater because it had travelled further across the spectrum of emotions. Dressed in a poke bonnet and carrying a large basket with a cover over it, he was the very essence of vulnerability. Once the unsuspecting person saw a frail old woman with a picnic basket, they would take comfort from her lack of fear. After all, if she felt safe enough to wander through these woods then what harm could befall them?

He would hear them calling out to her; eager for comfort; eager not to be the most vulnerable in the forest. It was best to ignore them and carry on walking. The pursuer would presume the old woman to be deaf and come after her. Once they reached her shoulder they would put a hand there, knowing that such a touch would frighten the old woman but they would be quick to assure her they meant no harm. If only they could. As the old woman turned around they would gape into the black void that filled her poke bonnet. The scream was wonderful, so satisfying. After all what could be more frightening than accosting a headless old woman while out walking... the realisation that you really are out of your depth? But he was not finished. He would remove the cover of his basket to reveal the missing head, screaming with laughter at their terror. The memory still gave him a rush of pleasure.

It didn't work with his mistress though and for that reason she still commands his respect. He remembers that she did scream - he would defy anyone not to - but it was the speed at which she regained control of the situation that caused his admiration. He recalls with a half-smile she poked both the eyes in the basket and told him he was a dead boggart. A dead boggart.

She bound him with a spell and took him back to her cottage. Far from being angry with him, she enjoyed his company. He began to understand that despite her power she was lonely. She gave him the name Deadboggart from that first meeting. He often objected to it but her only concession was that she would change the way his name was pronounced.

"You remain Deadboggart but I will call you Deedboggart until the time shall come when I think of another name more appropriate." He became her servant and faithful companion and has been since that day. He might be a ruthless killer, but he knew on which side his toast was buttered.

He remembers the days spent with his mistress in that cottage all those years ago. She had inherited it from an old witch who, in exchange for help in old age, had taught her well in the black arts.

One day his mistress asked him what his dearest wish would be and he told her he would like to be human in some way and have his head reconnected to the rest of his body. She laughed at this and said even with her powers she knew of no way of fixing heads or making a sprite human and perhaps he should take comfort in his carefree life. When he asked her why she didn't seem to age at all in the time he had known her, she tapped the side of her nose and told him she alone had the secret of everlasting life.

His mistress must have been mulling over his predicament as a few days later she sat him down and told him a story. It seemed when she was captured by the old witch, whose cottage she now lived in, she was treated very cruelly at first. She was starved half to death while the old woman ate all too well. A special treat for the old woman would come whenever a child was lost in the woods. The child would be killed, put in the big iron oven and served for supper.

His mistress confessed that the first child the old woman cooked was shared between them, and half-starved as she was, she was not ashamed to say there were no qualms over eating human flesh. After all, it was dead meat when it was put before her.

The old witch was no fool in this matter because his mistress would only enjoy a full and satisfying meal whenever a child was caught. The rest of the time she was half-starved and had to get by on vegetables and roots.

On the day the first child was caught, the witch told his mistress to clean out the old iron oven as she couldn't remember the last time she had used it. His mistress wasn't stupid and waited for the old witch to go out before embarking on cleaning the oven. After all she didn't want to be shut inside it herself. On opening the oven door she was struck by a horrible smell coming from within. She tied a kerchief round her mouth, climbed inside and was horrified to find the remains of a full-grown body curled up in the far corner. Much to her disgust, she dragged the corpse out of the oven and buried it in the midden behind the cottage.

When the old witch returned, his mistress asked why there was a rotten human body inside the oven. The witch had looked thoughtful for a minute or two before remembering she had once come upon an elf in the forest and, as they were mostly a nuisance, she had cracked him over the head and carried him home. Shutting him inside the iron oven, she had soon learned to ignore his pleas for food. Then one day he stopped making any noise.

His mistress asked the old witch two questions. First, why did she not eat the elf and second, how come the elf was the size of a full grown man?

The witch answered by saying that the iron of the oven destroys the magic of a sprite and turns them funny; they begin to grow. They don't taste too good either... 'magic never tastes good'.

And so it was his mistress became the inventor of the process that so many people make money out of these days - although she is shrewd enough to take her cut out of every 'ironed out' sprite.

His own claim to fame, one he never shouted about (not that he ever shouted about anything) was that he was the first sprite to purposefully undertake the process. It had been his dearest wish to be human but it had grieved him that his mistress had not been around to supervise the procedure. Called away to a council of witches, she had left him in the hands of the oldest of her sons. He was still not sure whether he could ever forgive her for that, but he knew he would never forgive him. One day when he was free from his mistress' service, he would administer retribution... after all; it was what he was good at.

He was kept in the oven for three weeks. The son ignored his screams at first but the mistress had told him to expect that. On the day that words were exchanged between the two of them through the oven door; the mistress's son waited until he had fallen asleep before exacting his revenge. After the ironisation his body came out as human as he possibly could be but he knew he would always remain a freak of nature.

And now he was on yet another assignment. It was a simple matter. The Massy Witch would sit back down after undertaking her official engagement. It was not a straightforward execution, he knew she had her protective hard air spell but there were ways and means of getting around it. Once she was dispatched, he would easily disappear into the crowd and be away before the Massy Witch gurgled her last breath.

THE DISTRACTION

The roar of the crowd announced that both teams were making their way out onto the pitch. It was a feelgood moment. The sun was shining and the city of Thursday Market was booming. The new steam-powered rail-way to Quickbridge was almost complete but best of all our football team had started playing really well again. All this seemed to have happened since I moved here. I take no credit.

It was Will Spargo who had taken me along to my first game. He'd bought me the orange and white barred scarf, I now wore with pride. As the two teams started knocking the numerous balls about as a warm-up for the game, it became noticeable, even to my limited knowledge of the game, that the players in the orange and white stripes of Thursday Market Wednesday didn't look very adept at kicking a ball around. The crowd started muttering in disbelief...

"That's not The Wednesday!" shouted Will. "Who's the goalkeeper? It's certainly not Shanksy!"

Another supporter peered myopically before commenting, "I think number eleven is a woman!" The incredulity of the crowd built-up to a braying crescendo as they witnessed the unthinkable. Their beloved football team were unrecognisable to them...and they were about to do battle with their mortal enemies from the nearby port of Fleetpool.

At this point a familiar figure edged his way past me. "Sorry, mate...excuse me" said a young man with a mop of ginger hair who was making his way to the main stand. The first time, I had met Arnold Grimm, the youngest of the notorious brothers, was back home in the place of my birth, when he had just attempted to make off with Avis Davies' broomstick, her symbol of power. Since coming to ThurMar our paths had crossed again but this time with my hat pulled down over my eyes he hadn't recognised me. Knowing full well that he probably wasn't up to any good, I told Will I was off to get us a pie and a beef tea each and set off to follow him.

As the pair of us headed towards the main stand, the game kicked-off and the fury of the crowd was rising as the unfamiliar figures on the field struggled to make a passing resemblance to professional footballers. The crowd was in turmoil; people looked at their matchday programme with disbelief and pointed accusatory fingers at the usurpers on the pitch. Arnold Grimm approached the place where you paid extra to get into the main stand. I watched as he handed money to the man at the turnstile and instead of receiving a ticket, like those who had passed before him, Arnold had something pressed into his hand. Moving along the side of the stand, the smell of fresh paint betraying the newness of our surroundings, I followed him until he reached a door that allowed access underneath the new stand. I took up a place in the queue at the pie stall across the way. Arnold Grimm unlocked the door and then headed off back to the guy at the turnstile and handed back the key. It was then the familiar figure of the tall i-sprite loomed out of the brightness. I pulled my hat down over my eyes and watched as he approached the door, pushed it open and slid inside.

I asked myself why the Grimms would want to get access beneath the new stand and then I remembered. I ran back to the turnstile and, fumbling in my pocket for change, I paid the half-mark to get in. Moving along the rows, I ignored the 'tuts' and muttering of people having to rise from their seats to let me get past...until I got to the point that meant that there was no time for politeness. I dragged people out of their seats until I got near enough to the Massy Witch for her to hear me. The abject performance happening on the pitch as the home team were being outclassed by their biggest rivals brought those in the stand to their feet whose anger was so much that they didn't notice me walking between them over the bright orange seats. At the point that Avis Davies saw me coming towards her waving my arms and screaming at her to get out of her seat, Fleetpool Athletic scored a goal and the groan of despair and the tide of rising anger was accompanied by a volley of gunfire up from underneath the stand. The crowd dispersed away from the splintered seat like a hole burning in paper. I beckoned Avis Davies towards me and we panicked with the rest of the crowd getting as far away as we could, teetering over the backs of the seats until we reached the relative safety of a gangway. There were people who had fallen down between the seats and a few were nursing possible broken arms but the incident was over in a matter of seconds. Avis Davies pulled me down into a couple of now-vacated seats. Her staff were close by awaiting instructions. I quickly told her about the gunman, Arnold Grimm and how he had obtained the key. She dispatched two men to arrest the turnstile operator but surmised that Grimm and the tall i-sprite assassin would be well away by now.

On seeing the commotion in the stand, the referee had abandoned the game. Something quite clearly wasn't right about the whole event. Down on the pitch the manager of Fleetpool Athletic was remonstrating with the referee he was livid that his team's one-nil advantage had been wiped out but appeared to calm down when things had been explained to him.

26

I found Will more or less where I left him and told him how I had just managed to save the Massy Witch's from being assassinated. He ruminated on this for a few seconds before saying…

"So you didn't get the pies, then?"

*

Avis Davies, the Massy Witch stood at the table making two cups of tea. "Thanks for coming, Humphrey. I've brought you in, firstly to thank you for saving my life…and I do appreciate that without your intervention I would most probably be lying in state today. The people who want me dead…"

"The Grimms."

"It seems likely…they found that as they couldn't get around the hard air spell that protects me in public places they would take the one chance they had…"

"To get underneath you."

"Quite. The second reason I called you in is to fill you in on what happened yesterday." Avis Davies handed me a cup of tea and then returned to her chair.

"Hmm…a de-briefing. Does this mean I'm part of the All-Seeing Eye now?"

"I think you and I both know that your independence from the ASE allows us the freedom to look at things from the outside. I appreciate your co-operation in these matters."

"So what did happen yesterday?"

"The whole Thursday Market Wednesday team were kidnapped for an hour or two."

"So the team that took the field were reserves?"

"No, that's just it. The team that took the field firmly believed they *were* the Thursday Market Wednesday first team."

"Even the young woman on the left wing?"

Avis Davies nodded her head. "Totally convinced!"

"Their performance would suggest otherwise."

"What about the real first team?"

"Two men with guns forced them into an outbuilding at the training ground. They were released an hour after the game kicked off. No ransom required or anything…they just let them go."

"So you think this as the distraction required to set up your assassination?"

"It certainly stirred up the crowd."

"And these people who thought they were Thursday Market Wednesday…what's to become of them?"

"That's just it, they're not the first. We keep coming across people who seem to be stricken with a form of amnesia…but it's not just that they forgotten who they are as much as they're convinced they're somebody that they're not…somebody who doesn't exist…if you get my drift."

"Have you any idea where they are coming from in the first place?"

"We've got people in the field who are working on it…"

JC Bigg wished she was back in the field now. Ten minutes earlier, she had been standing in a lush sweet-smelling meadow in the dead of night waiting to climb into a large basket. Now, as she peered over the edge of her wicker world, she presumed the tiny lights below her were the few brave souls who had witnessed the take off. High above her head the large black hydrogen balloon rose steadily. For the first time in her life, she was sort of scared.

She had considered it an honour to have been chosen to fly this mission into what might be hostile territory. Mixed feelings of both trepidation and pride had been her constant companion over the last few weeks, while her contemporaries looked on with what she hoped was envy and not pity.

JC had joined The Eye as a Seer almost fifteen years ago. She knew that if she had played the game like many of the others had; 'kept her nose clean and her head down' as her first commanding officer was fond of saying, she might have been in charge of her own unit by now. However, always one to act first and think later, JC had managed to deconstruct her own career path with a number of high profile mistakes (although she herself preferred to think of them as misinformed choices). She saw this assignment as her big chance to prove a few people wrong. The question of her courage had never been in doubt to any of her superiors and it was Avis Davies herself who had recognised that this mission needed someone capable of acting on their own volition.

When it came to her own ability, JC had no cause for concern. It was Dr Thumb, the scientist in charge of this operation, that she had doubts about. JC lived in a world where magic could provide so much and science was still the poor relative. Now she needed to place her faith in a thin sheet of silk and a rudimentary steering mechanism. For the first time in her memory, her life depended on the crude mechanics of mankind and she wasn't happy.

She checked the time on her wristwatch. Dr Thumb had made numerous calculations on how fast the balloon would rise and at what point JC was to evacuate the module. That was the trouble with scientists, thought JC; they always used words like 'evacuate the module' instead of 'jump out of the basket'. It wasn't so much that scientists told lies; they just gave the truth umpteen coats of varnish.

She recalled the briefing Avis Davies had given her soon after JC's first leap from Screamers Cliff. The Massy Witch had arranged for a swift carriage to whisk them both back to The Druid's Palace.

"Recent events have necessitated an investigation into what might be happening beyond the Wall of Thorns" said Avis Davies. A moment passed as she waited for the information to sink in. "From your blank look, I surmise you are unfamiliar with the place." The Massy Witch made herself comfortable before resuming. "Over one hundred years ago a spell was cast by a powerful witch called Dorothy Garland. She created a huge impenetrable barrier that protected the Palace of Fotherghyll. It consists of vicious thorns that replenish themselves faster than anyone man can cut them down."

"Then surely I can fly over it!"

"The curse precludes any use of magic to overcome it. She was a very powerful witch. We have already lost two seers who tried to fly over it. They remain impaled on the thorns. Their deaths were not swift. Those of us who heard their screams will not forget them in a hurry. The need to use scientific methods is paramount. Dr Thumb has worked it out that with a favourable wind and a high enough starting point, someone, particularly someone as light as an elf, could float over the Wall of Thorns. Being dropped into the grounds of the Palace of Fotherghyll will mean losing all contact with the outside world."

That carriage journey seemed like a lifetime ago. After a few more test jumps she had slipped back into the schedule of a Seer of the All-Seeing Eye - paperwork and more paperwork. Yesterday she had been in the middle of a routine customs check in the port when she was swept up in a whirlwind of commotion; today she was rising up through the night sky. The prevailing wind had to be just right. The mission had to be timed to take place at night time so her arrival in the grounds of the Palace of Fotherghyll would occur before anyone might have woken up. She laughed at the very idea. If what she knew about this place was true; waking people up was the least of her worries.

JC shook her head as she fought the urge to fall asleep. Dr Thumb had warned her this would be her greatest battle and she knew what the consequences of losing it would be. The balloon was never going to come back down again.

Curled up in the basket and shivering in her black fur cloak, JC had decided to fight the desire to sleep by reciting aloud the incredible story of the Palace of Fotherghyll. She had been given a report, one compiled by the Wisdom Wardens for those seers working on the Fotherghyll Project. It made use of both primary and secondary sources and a great deal of supposition. Avis Davies was a great believer in information - "Those with the most information will have the greatest success" she had once said. "Seers are expected to make the most of the information given them. After all it might save their life at some stage." JC, who normally committed to memory all the information she was given, thought this was definitely one of those occasions. So, pulling her cloak tightly around her to make the most of its warmth, she stood with her hands gripping the edge of the basket and addressed her imaginary audience. One day she fully expected to be named Seer of the Year…she saw this as good preparation…

"The Palace of Fotherghyll had been under a spell for over 100 years and most people, apart from those in the local tourist trade, had forgotten about it…until recently. The people of the nearby village of Without-the-Wall have reported seeing lights, apparitions, magical creatures and hearing strange noises when the wind is coming in over the Wall of Thorns.

"Well over one hundred years ago, the Palace of Fotherghyll was the home of King Cole, a monarch noted for his puritanical ways. One suggestion for his lack of joyfulness was that he and his wife, the Queen, had failed to produce a child from their many years of marriage. The pair of them had called up all the greatest doctors, astrologists and even the local witches all to no avail. One witch, new to the area, called

Dorothy Garland (these, of course, being the days before the Naming of Witches Act), made a suggestion that the King take a special potion that she had prepared every night for a month until the Queen should find herself with child. The potion worked although the King complained he never remembered anything about his night-time activities as he always seemed to fall asleep very quickly, but still he was happy when his wife announced that she was with child. (The rumour that the same witch arranged for a virile young woodsman to pay the Queen a visit each night while the King was asleep was a popular one with the common-folk of the nearby villages of Without-the-Wall and Within-the-Wall).

"From the day that he realised he was going to be a father, old King Cole's character changed somewhat and consequently the Palace of Fotherghyll became quite the place to be. Highest among those favoured at court was Dorothy Garland, the young witch whose magic had brought about the prospect of a child for the King and Queen.

"When the child was born, the herald's proclaimed that the King was the proud father of a lovely daughter. A great party was held to honour and name the young princess. Invitations were sent out to all the most important people in the region. Street parties were held by all those who weren't invited to the Palace because they were so pleased that the old King was at last happy. King Cole wanted all the known witches of his kingdom to be invited to the celebration so that they might bestow wonderful gifts on the young princess. He sent out his messages to contact all the kingdom's witches and all were found but one. Old Meg Stoker, the kingdom's oldest witch was presumed to be dead for no one had seen her for many years now. The messenger returned with the news that there were now seven witches who should be invited to the celebration and the King decided that each witch would be presented with a gold plate and gold cutlery which was set with emeralds, rubies and diamonds. After the meal, the plate and cutlery would be theirs to keep as a memento of the child's arrival.

"Of course the great day soon came round and all the guests began to take their seats at the table and one by one the witches, happy with their wonderful gold plate and cutlery, would rise and bestow a wonderful gift on the young princess. The oldest witch present declared that the princess would be beautiful and one by one the witches bestowed the gifts of wit, grace and the ability to dance, sing and play music upon the baby girl. When it was time for the youngest witch, Dorothy Garland, to present her gift to the baby princess, she rose and approached the child in her mother's arms. At that point the door of the hall was thrown open and Old Meg Stoker, long suspected of being dead, burst into the Great Hall. She was angry that she had not been told of the princess' birth and had only found out by overhearing two swineherds discussing the celebrations. Of course King Cole was beside himself with fear because in those days an angry witch was a loose cannon and something to be wary of. He apologised profusely to her and begged forgiveness, all the while getting his servants to make room at the high table for her. This seemed to appease her anger for a while until she realised that all the other witches were eating with solid gold, jewel encrusted cutlery. She roared in anger because she was having to make do with mere silver like the other guests and as the King could not arrange for solid gold cutlery to appear from thin air, he could do nothing more than apologise. Old Meg Stoker, in her anger, rose to her feet and approached the sleeping child.

"When the child is become a woman she will prick her hand while spinning wool and die of the wound!" And with that she stamped her way out of the great hall in a state of hysterical anger. Of course this put a great dampener on the mood of all those in attendance here to celebrate the life of the young princess. They now knew full well that the child would die if she wasn't careful. Fortunately for the royal family, the arrival of Meg Stoker had prevented Dorothy Garland from bestowing her gift upon the child. It was not within her power, she said, to undo the mischief that Old Meg Stoker had done, but she could do something to soften the curse. Her gift to the princess was that should the princess ever be unlucky enough to cut her finger while spinning wool, her death would not be a permanent one, but a symbolic one. She would merely fall asleep for a hundred years until she is woken by the kiss of a stranger. The King was pleased with how Dorothy Garland had taken control of the situation and she was always part of his counsel from that day.

"Over the intervening years, the King did his best to prevent the curse from being fulfilled. He banned all spindles and the spinning wheels, not only from his own palace but from the surrounding villages and countryside as well. Woollen yarn could not be spun so all clothes had to be brought in from outside. All seemed well as reports of Meg Stoker's death were confirmed and witnessed and with the palace completely spindle-free there seemed no chance that the princess would succumb to the witches terrible curse. By way of further protection, the King appointed Dorothy Garland as his daughter's governess and tutor. The two of them became inseparable.

36

"The princess knew nothing about the curse that had been put upon her all those years ago and it was thought that all the other witches gifts had become a part of her character. She could sing, dance and play music divinely; she was both graceful and witty and many remarked that she was surely the most beautiful young woman they knew. The courtiers and servants of the palace all loved their beautiful princess and would do anything for her.

"One day she chose to wander into a part of the palace she had never been to before and there she met an old lady who was busy singing away as she spun woollen yarn on a rough-fashioned spinning wheel. The young princess was intrigued by what she saw as the old woman spun the wheel and pulled at the distaff with her hand. The spinning wheel was almost mesmerising to the young princess and she asked the old woman what she was doing. It has been surmised that the old woman was attempting to make the most of the gap in the market for quality hand-made woollen goods and possibly didn't think the King would mind as he often spoke about how he admired the entrepreneurial spirit in his people. The princess, it is assumed, would have been less interested in the old woman's business acumen and more inclined to learn how wool was spun. No doubt eager to try her hand at it herself, she must have pricked her finger on a splinter of wood in the flax or something, as spinning wheels and spindles are not known for their sharp edges.

"Whatever the cause the princess slumped to the floor in a deep faint. When she was discovered by the side of an old spinning wheel, the worst was feared. Doctors were summoned by the King and they pronounced that she was not dead but merely asleep, indeed her soft breathing could quite clearly be heard. The old witch's curse had come to fruition.

"The King and Queen summoned Dorothy Garland to the Great Council Chamber to see what could be done. The witch said she was powerless to break the curse but after some deliberation, suggested that, with the King's permission, she could put a spell over the whole of the Palace of Fotherghyll that would put everyone else asleep for a hundred years so that the young princess would not wake up alone. The King and Queen were not sure about this and were fearful that as they were now quite old they might never wake up again. However, they thought that it might be a good idea if everybody else in the Palace was put to sleep so that their child might recognise friendly faces when she awoke. The King also felt that it might be prudent if his servants were not informed about what was to happen to them. He and the Queen (and a retinue of their most faithful servants) packed up their belongings and moved to a small single level palace near to the seaside. It had apparently been something they had been hoping to do anyway.

"A few days later, everyone and everything in the palace fell asleep. The young princess' maids of honour, ladies of the bedchamber, gentlemen, officers, stewards, cooks, undercooks, scullions, guards, pages, footmen and the gardeners; all the horses in the stables, the great dogs that guarded the courtyard and all the inhabitants of the village of Within-the-Wall. Only one man, a middle-aged woodsman (who may or may not have been the princess' real father) was allowed to leave the palace to explain just what had happened to the outside world. Then because no one ever saw her again, it has to be assumed that Dorothy Garland must have succumbed herself to the spell so that she too might be of service to the waking princess in a hundred years time.

"Within a few short days a great Wall of Thorns grew around the palace engulfing all its surrounding walls. This impenetrable growth also claimed the little village of Within-the Wall thus further dividing it from its sister town Without-the-Wall for over one hundred years."

JC shivered as she thought about the enormity of it all. The callousness of how a whole village and a palace full of people could be put to sleep without their consent; yet how unselfish it was of Dorothy Garland to tie herself to the life of this young princess whose name still remained a mystery. Her parents were by now dead, the middle-aged woodsman too and anyone who could recall the Palace of Fotherghyll would surely be long gone. If all went well she would be the first to set eyes on it in a hundred years.

As the first light of the day glowed in the distance, JC checked her watch. It was time. With the cold biting into her joints, she struggled to steady herself; gripping the edge of the basket with her gloved hands. Her eyes watered in the cold thin air. She put on her goggles: all she could see was greyness. Next she checked her two packs, one containing food, equipment and a plan of the Palace of Fotherghyll; the other, more importantly, held her parachute. She fastened the harness to her body and gathered the neatly folded silk to her chest. Everything seemed in order. She needed to jump to the east, the direction of the rising sun. This she double-checked by the means of a compass fished from the pocket of her coat. Holding off the terrible moment in which she would hurl herself out of the basket was not an option; to stay in the basket was also certain death. She pulled herself up by the balloon's restraining ropes and swayed in the wind; her feet struggling to find their purchase on the edge of the basket.

And then it was done. A rush of air rose up to meet her, buffeting her body for a second, before she began to fall. Sure that she was clear of the basket she released the parachute as if she was giving a bird its freedom. She was once again in the hands of science and she shuddered at the thought. To be fair to Dr Thumb, he did seem to know what he was talking about. He had even come round earlier in the evening to re-check the parachute for himself and to reassure her that it would work. As the parachute opened and she began to rise in her own grey world she took some comfort from his confidence. After all, the dry runs had all been successful (she wouldn't have been here if they hadn't) and once her initial fears had been overcome she had found the experience to be quite exhilarating. Whether her confidence was borne on the presence of her colleagues waiting to catch her as she landed, she wasn't sure. This time there would be no one waiting; this time she was on her own.

The area she was aiming for was big enough and she had been successful in all the previous trials in hitting her target, but still she could see nothing. Her only ally was the prevailing wind bearing her east towards the palace. Estimates of the area of the Wall of Thorns were speculative at best. No one knew whether it engulfed both the village of Within and the original palace walls or not. All they did know was that no one had been able to pass through the lethal thorns on the ground.

At last the cloud cleared and JC recognised the village of Without below her. The Wall of Thorns dominated the background and she began to make adjustments with the steering mechanism that Dr Thumb had devised. JC called upon her one-to-one training with the scientist and made the correct adjustments. In the distance she could now see the extent of the Wall of Thorns; a clearing beyond it remained steadfast grey in the half light. Below her she tried not to think of the murderous thorns that waited to embrace her or of her long dead colleagues pinioned upon them. On and on she went, guiding the great silk sheet into roughly the right direction; wary that all the time she was losing height. Beneath her the thorns were hurrying along waiting to catch her when she fell to earth. She peered into the dreary distance hoping to clearly define a place to land as she fell closer and closer to what seemed like her certain death. For the first time she began to dwell on what it might be like to be impaled on top of the Wall of Thorns. Waiting for death in the sun or the rain, stuck like a butterfly specimen in a collector's display. Then up ahead she discerned a definite outline of shapes. Small lights twinkled – the eyes of waiting creatures? Something ahead was different. Her speed in the wind meant she approached too quickly to do much about it. There it was, definitely an end to the forest. She was almost on top of it when she was yanked hard across the sky as if something had caught her. She wondered whether one of the great flying insects that had been reported had plucked her out of the sky. Another lurch pulled her back and she began to fall to earth. Then she stopped with a shudder and hung in the air, spinning round and round like a caterpillar on a silk. When her world finally stopped turning she looked up and saw that her parachute had been caught on something. Up above her a long dark shape hung on the end of a long chain. Following it up she gasped as she saw the dark outline of what – a huge bird or animal rigid against the lightning sky? She looked down; it was a long way, perhaps too far to fall. Her only chance was to climb out of her parachute and chance the fall with her real wings. The curse prevented magic over the forest but technically she wasn't over it now. She wriggled to free herself of her trappings when the most amazing thing happened.

All around her huge great lights came into life. JC, unprepared for such intensity, could only squint as she hung from her parachute. Below her the palace grounds came alive as row after row of brilliant lights illuminated huge buildings and large machines. She felt almost honoured; as if this whole show had been arranged just for her benefit as she dangled high above it. In the distance, the old palace stood highlighted and JC was amazed to see it surrounded by much smaller buildings, all giving off lights brighter than anything she had ever seen before. She watched as tiny, helmeted workmen began, like worker ants, to invade the open spaces beneath her and she recognised how vulnerable she was to being seen. Hanging by one hand from the parachute she flexed her wings; the fact she had never flown this far off the ground before prevented her from letting go. A sudden shout from below and a pointing finger helped make her decision. Within moments a spotlight had picked her out and realising she was now an easy target for an arrow or a bullet, JC let go. Plummeting to earth, she was out of the light but every attempt for her wings to open was prevented by the onrush of air. The hard earth below came hurtling towards her until a huge cart moving under its own power broke her fall.

JC had landed in a vast pile of sand in the back of what she would not have known was a large tipper wagon. Unconscious and a few feet deep in the sand she could do nothing as the wagon lurched across the palace grounds and prepared to tip its load into the artificial beach that bordered the heated swimming pool. The rear of the wagon took an age to reach tipping point. Fighting gravity with a mouth full of sand and a strange feeling of nausea, JC and the sand were disgorged onto the ground. Dragging herself to her unsteady feet, she looked up to see a huge machine fronted by a vast metal scoop heading towards her. With seconds to spare she scrambled out of its way and dived into a clump of bushes. As the machine passed by it was with a certain amount of detachment that JC noticed it had her initials written on the side of it.

All she wanted to do now was sleep but she knew her parachute would alert the enemy of her presence. Hiding in the bushes she watched as the humans huddled together to discuss what was to be done with the dangling evidence.

"What the bloody hell is that?" said the first man to arrive. Soon he was surrounded by others all wearing the identical blue overall bearing the name DOMANIA.

"Looks like a parachute or something," said another.

"Whatever it is, we best get it down. Have a word with George and get the girder lowered," this was the foreman, signified by his green overall. "I'd best have a word with the gaffer about this. Looks like it might be a journalist or something. What with the grand opening being next week. Probably wants a sneak preview or something. Get some of the lads to have a look round; he can't be far." JC, already in a state of invisibility plunged deeper into the ornamental bushes just to be on the safe side. Now wasn't the time for flight, she decided, but she did have to think about what she had discovered. These humans were different to the ones she was used to. They were far better groomed for a start; they betrayed a certain confidence that was lacking in the humans she knew. She thought about the enormity of it all as she watched them search the site. A mile or two from the village of Without was a place the like of which she had never seen. A place of wonder with bright lights that were powerful enough to illuminate the night sky; with lights inside the buildings that were far brighter than the gas lights that were becoming fashionable in ThurMar. Huge machines that could knock down a whole village in less than a minute were beginning to stir into life. As she looked up into the dawning sky she could see her parachute was being lowered to the earth and the waiting crowd of humans. It was then she noticed it. Her back pack, the one that contained the plans to the old Palace of Fotherghyll, had been caught up with the parachute. She had to get it back if she was ever going to be successful in her mission. The question she asked was – how?

Her invisibility gave her an advantage and the knowledge that her elfin magic was no longer compromised by the Wall of Thorns curse. Her wings were working perfectly well so she guessed the only thing for it was to wait until they had freed the bag and then to just grab it and get out of there as fast as she can. JC, confident they didn't know she was there, approached the group of men as near as she could. Watching as the great machine dropped the huge steel bar to the ground she waited while two of the men untangled the parachute and extracted the backpack. Trained in the art of surprise attack, JC threw herself at the bag just as one of the men was handing it to the foreman.

"What the-!" The group of men stood open-mouthed as they watched a large brown bag flying through the air and into the distance. As the men wrestled with their own disbelief, another man was watching from less than a hundred yards away. He was dressed in a smart designer suit the like of which had not been seen in JC's world.

"So," he said, "it seems the elfin bitch managed to make it through. Mother won't be too pleased about that." A scowl appeared on Hans-Christian Grimm's face and he turned back towards the Palace itself.

*

Days passed and because JC was concerned her enemy would know she had infiltrated the Wall of Thorns, lying low was the sensible option. The land she had discovered within the Wall of Thorns was much bigger than she had anticipated. It had been quite easy to lose herself for a few days while she worked out a plan of action. Despite her ability to become invisible, JC thought it might be better to avoid the palace for the time being. Ever one to do it by the book, she decided to find herself a bolt-hole to escape to, should the need arise. Until she discovered the way into this land behind the Wall of Thorns she had no way of escape or of ever notifying Avis Davies.

Surviving on a diet of berries and the small animals she could trap, JC had sheltered in the caves that overlooked what seemed to be an old mine. She had observed the comings and goings from below her with interest. Workmen had arrived in strange mechanical vehicles similar to those she had seen at closer quarters. More interesting was her first sighting of one of the Grimm Brothers which confirmed her suspicions. Arnold, being the youngest, was not regarded to be the most dangerous of the Grimm brothers although he had once escaped from custody for a crime that had threatened the stability of the state itself.

She noticed that work more or less ceased when nightfall came so she made her investigations after dark and returned to her cave to sleep in the mornings. The mine revealed little to her other than some sort of office near the entrance and a huge silver box which lay much further down the mine. Its purpose mystified her. It was empty on the inside even to the point of not having a door handle. It seemed to have little purpose other than for storage.

"…or a prison!" she said out loud, much to her own embarrassment.

After a week without success in her search for a conventional way in or out of this land, she resigned herself to the fact she would now have to concentrate on the palace and its more immediate surroundings. This meant coming into closer contact with the humans on the site. There had been the odd sprite wandering about but these had all been ironised and, having lost their magic, they were incapable of seeing her. She took some kind of comfort from the fact she had yet to see a sprite that hadn't been ironised. Of the humans she had already come across they seemed far more confident and sure of themselves than they should have been in such a modern and alien environment. Yet when she first arrived here the men who had seen a canvas bag jump out of their hands and make its way across the manicured lawn were simply awestruck. She had observed them from the nearby shrubbery. It was clear to her that not one of them had even considered that an invisible sprite might have stolen the bag. Although she knew that wasn't true, there was a man who seemed far from mesmerized by the whole event. Tall and about forty years of age, this man was more elegantly dressed than those around him. Without doubt, JC suspected him to be yet another of the Grimm brothers. He alone had been familiar with the concept of magic. He alone looked for tell-tale signs of her whereabouts. They knew she was here and now she had to get closer to them.

A ROYAL VISIT

I looked in the mirror. It was something I had got into the habit of doing since my ironisation. Becoming more human had increased my vanity but with the long nose and pointed ears of my boggart past all remaining, I was never going to play the romantic lead. I ran my hand across the stubble on my chin, comforted by the strangeness of it. Shaving - that was another new one for me. I ran some water and mixed soap into the palm of my hand with the brush. As I applied the lather, my diminutive neighbour Jonty Thumb walked in to the office. With his wire spectacles and the fluffy white hair that half-circled his head Jonty might have been mistaken for a dwarf…had he been about a foot taller.

"Morning Humphrey! I can't stop long, I've much to do. Sphagnum is having a lie-in."

"He still got that night job then?" I asked. Jonty nodded. "Do you mind if I…?" I pointed to the soapy beard that covered my face.

"How are you getting on with this shaving lark then?"

"Actually, I find it quite relaxing…gives me time to think."

"You'll soon get fed up of it. Day after day of it…staring at your face."

"When you think that a month ago, I would have had to stand on a chair to do this."

"Not really! You wouldn't have put the mirror up so high in the first place, would you?" Jonty didn't like to be reminded of his lack of height. The only sound for a while was the careful scrape of blade against skin until he broke the silence. "Did it hurt?"

"Did what hurt?"

"When you went through the ironisation process…I've never really discussed it with a sprite before. How long does it last?"

"Two weeks…"

"So you're shut away in an iron tank and…

"The magic sort of leaches out of you into the metal and your body grows taller. You get withdrawal symptoms…headache, vomiting, stomach cramps and then it gets worse…the growing pains."

The little man watched me finish my shaving before asking…

"Do you miss your magic? I expect as a boggart you were able to become invisible?"

"Actually I had two magical abilities, due to my mixed parentage. Mum was a water sprite so I could become as one with any water I found myself in. It was very handy for the job I was in."

"Hmm…" said Jonty. "I suppose it would; you being a…'stepping stone mischief maker'. I never understood why 'so-called' jobs like that need to carry on in the sophisticated world we find ourselves in…" At that moment the cry of a rag and bone man could be heard from the street outside."

"I can't believe you're saying that, Jonty. Of all people, you know how important it is for magic to be regulated. If your bosses at The All-Seeing Eye could hear you talking like this. If you have magic it must be used in a practical-"

"What's practical about tipping people into a river?"

"You've been living in the big city too long. Out in the country where there's far more magic than is needed, it has to be channelled in some way…and registered. That's the way the witches like it and who's going to argue with them?"

We both knew that it was a different matter in the city. Thursday Market was full of ironised sprites eager to make their way in this new industrial age. Like me, they had paid to lose their magic. There was good money to be earned in the new factories, but employers wouldn't consider a sprite who hadn't been ironised. Close proximity to iron machinery would bring about a lethargy and nausea in them which made them a danger to themselves. Stories of sprites falling into machinery hadn't shocked the city as much as when it had been children, but cleaning out their remains still cost time and money in the factory owners' eyes.

Ironisation almost became a necessity as any regular sprite, be they elf, dwarf or goblin, had to register their magical ability and apply it to a service for the city. The witches had more than enough to fill the ranks of the Guardians, who enforced the law in Thursday Market, and the All-Seeing Eye, who were their intelligence agents.

Any other unregulated use of magic, was seen as anti-social and clamped down on by the witches. Crimes that made use of invisibility, such as breaking and entering, bought a heavy punishment - enforced ironisation, prison and even death in some circumstances. The witches were so paranoid about the power that magic could achieve that they even imposed a spell upon themselves, one involving running water, which could be used to keep any rogue witches in check.

"So, did you hear about what happened at the big game the other day?"

"I've been busy, Humphrey and you know I can't get excited about twenty-two men kicking a bag of wind around a field."

"No...but..."

"I can't sit here chatting all day," said Jonty "I've got things to do!"

"Me too!" I shouted, more to have the last word as anything else. I began rummaging through my paperwork before opening one of the desk's drawers and dropping the lot of it in there. I pushed back my chair, hiked my feet up onto the desk and pondered on the lack of business that Humphrey Boggart, Private Investigator was pulling in. I didn't like not having things to do...I wasn't one of those people who could sleep all day.

*

A hard knock on the door woke me from my catnap. The door opened and a big burly guy blocked out the sunlight. He grunted and threw a suitcase into my office.

"The lady says you'll pay for the cab!"

It took me a moment or so to get my bearings. "Er...right. How much will that be?"

"Two marks." He held his hand out as I fished a two mark piece out of my purse. Pocketing the money, he raised his eyebrows. "Whaddabout a tip?"

By now I was holding the saw at both ends. "Ask for your money back from the charm school!"

"Yahh...sting bum!" He dismissed me with a wave and passed a beautiful woman in the doorway. She was tall, blond and in tears - a damsel in distress.

I invited her to take a seat and had to stop myself from falling in love with her. Be professional I thought...this might just be your next case. It was all new to me...having to comfort a weeping woman. I would have offered her my handkerchief but she already had one and besides I remember blowing my nose earlier and well...too much information, I suppose. Gradually she composed herself and I asked her why she was crying. This started her off again, so I played the genial host and poured her a couple of fingers of whiskey.

As she gulped down the first glass, I gave her the once over. She was rich and pretty. Her coat was expensive and displayed enough precious stones to reconstruct a chandelier. My first deduction, that she was married to a jeweller, turned out to be wrong. She opened up by telling me that contrary to her appearance she was really not very posh at all. The blowing of her nose with all the gusto of the Fleetpool fog horn sort of gave that one away. I listened as she told me about her humble beginnings as a miller's daughter.

"The trouble with my father was that he was always boasting to everyone about me. He told so many people about my beauty that eventually it got to the ears of the King."

"Which one?" I asked.

"Both of them of course!"

"No I didn't mean which ear…I meant which king." Here we go, I thought.

"What do you mean – which king?" She gave me the look that I once got from my Auntie Nellie when I did my white-eared elephant impression. "*The* King! The one and only!"

"Look Mrs-"

"Your majesty would be appropriate!"

"Look Mrs King, you're in the big city now. Here in Thursday Market we get people like you coming in every day claiming to be King this or Queen that. The truth is there are that many little kingdoms out there in the sticks that here in the city they don't amount to a hill of cabbages. You see lady, I've got three kings on my books already and they all live on the same street." Of course I was lying but when she eventually unfolded her story and what with the whopper her father told, I didn't feel too bad.

"You see Daddy was always boasting about how wonderful I was. Clever… beautiful…virtuous…a world authority on all aspects of spinning…oh, and a master of the martial arts…"

"And are you? The last one I meant." Never underestimate a client.

"Not really, Daddy was just scared someone might try and burgle the mill. I suppose it's a bit like having a big painting of a fierce looking dog by the door with the words 'I Live Here' written underneath it. "

"I get your drift."

"Anyway, one day he was telling the King just how beautiful I am when he got a bit carried away. You see our King was famous for his greed."

"That knocks him down to about twenty we know." She looked a bit hurt but, she'll thank me in the long run.

"So, when my father realised extolling my beauty and virtue wasn't getting him anywhere, he got a bit carried away."

"And?"

"He told the King I could spin straw into gold! Can you believe that?"

"Of course I can. And I bet that suddenly the King had more ears than a cheap sausage."

"'Bring her up to my palace and we'll see what she can do', he said. Of course my stupid father had not considered the fact I might have to actually spin straw into gold. He told me not to worry… 'The King will take one look at you and fall madly in love.' Of course, what my father didn't know was women were ten a penny to the King whereas gold…well that was…er…"

"Worth considerably more?"

"Exactly. Anyway I spent all day making myself look beautiful…a girl has to look her best, you know? So off I go to the castle and I had hardly time to flutter my eyelids at the King before he has me in a locked room with a big pile of straw and a spinning wheel. Not only that, Mr Boggart, but he told me if I was wasting his time, I would be put to death the next day. Of course I tried but all I managed to make was a set of six place mats with coasters to match. It was useless, I just broke down into tears and cried my heart out when suddenly I looked up and there before me was a strange-looking man… not unlike you Mr Boggart…and he asked me why I was crying. When I told him I had been commanded to spin straw into gold he just laughed and asked me what I would give him if he did it for me. Of course I told him he could have the lovely pearl necklace my father had given me. He accepted and said I was to close my eyes and sleep and in the morning the gold would be there…but if I was to peek then all the gold would turn back into straw. I have to tell you Mr Boggart I kept my eyes tightly shut. I was clutching at the very thing I was expected to spin into gold. I ignored all the strange noises that were going on in that room and in the morning when the King unlocked the door, there in the corner of the room, was a pile of gold ingots. You could have knocked the both of us down with a feather. Of course the King was delighted and I thought 'Wow, I'm going to end up as Queen of this mighty kingdom all for the price of a pearl necklace'."

"I guess you'll not be the first," I spluttered, amused at her delusions of grandeur. "So, what is it you want me to do?"

"Well, it didn't end there, did it, Mr Boggart? The King, as I have already told you was one greedy so-and-so and,

55

delighted as he was with my work, he decided I needed to prove myself again…only with more straw this time. As you can imagine, I was distraught. What was I going to do?

"The following night I was locked in with this even bigger pile of straw. Of course I started to weep again and after a while I looked up and the strange-looking man was there again. Are you sure he isn't a relation of yours, Mr Boggart. There is a sort of resemblance."

"I assure you, Mrs King, I have no relatives who would have the remotest idea of how to spin straw into gold."

"Well anyway, the strange-looking man asked me what the trouble was and I told him. This time when he asked me what I could give him, I offered him the ruby ring my father had presented to me on my eighteenth birthday. Once again he told me to close my eyes and sleep and the gold would be there in the morning, but if I opened them then the gold would be spun back into straw. I was so terrified I might lose my life that I did as I was bid. Sure enough I woke as the King put his key into the lock and there in place of all the straw was an even bigger pile of gold ingots. The King was so pleased he offered to marry me, despite my low birth, *if* I could manage to spin straw into gold one more time. Of course if I was to fail he said I would forfeit my life."

"Not the most romantic of men was he?" I said.

"So the following night the King filled up the room with as much straw as he could find. This night I was even more distraught as I had managed to achieve the impossible two nights running. My only hope was the reappearance of the strange-looking man. You weren't adopted, were you Mr Boggart? You do look an awful lot like him."

"Mrs King, I think we can safely assume we are looking for an ironised sprite…most likely a boggart, like me. Now will you continue please?"

"So anyway, I sobbed as loud as I could, knowing that my only chance rested with the str-…this ironised boggart. Sure enough while I was weeping on the mattress, he turned up once more. He asked me what I could give him this time and it was then I realised I had nothing else to give. Of course I was desperate so I asked him whatever he wanted and I would do my utmost to give it him. Do you know what he said, Mr Boggart? He asked that should I become Queen, when he next visits, I should give him my first baby*. He even brought a little contract for me to sign. Well, you can imagine what I thought of that but the alternative was certain death. I can cross that bridge when I come to it, I thought. So, true to his word the boggart spun all the straw into gold while I lay there asleep. In the morning the King came in to see the room filled with an even bigger pile of gold ingots. He was overjoyed and announced I was now the richest Queen a man could have, despite my low birth, so I became his wife. As you can imagine, I wasn't too keen on him by now. He wasn't much of a looker…old as well, which meant there was little chance of me giving birth to a baby. The old sod died six weeks later so I was laughing, I didn't need a king as I was quite capable of ruling the country of my own. Around this time, of course, there were many suitors for my hand, for now I was both rich and beautiful.

"And modest with it," I muttered under my breath.

"One of my suitors presented me with a gift so wonderful that I instantly fell in love with it. It was a little white bull terrier who I called Barry. I loved him like I'd loved nobody else. I

57

smothered him in trinkets, he had a little jewel-studded collar and a fine coat made out of ermine that he wore on state occasions. He even had a little crown made for him by the royal jeweller. Then one day, I was sitting in my chamber playing with my darling Barry when the boggart turned up.

"Time to pay your debt," he said brandishing the contract I had signed, "I've come for your baby*." Of course at first I laughed at him.

"I haven't got a baby to give you. My husband and I never had children."

"Well then I will have to refer you to the small print." He showed me the contract and pointed out the asterisk. *In the event of the King and Queen remaining childless then an equivalent will be taken of similar emotional value. So I suppose that means Barry here. He's your baby as much as any child. I'll have him." I begged for him to take any amount of gold or jewels but he insisted on taking my Barry. "Don't you see," he said, "something I can love is dearer to me than all the gold and jewels in the world." I was distraught and got down on my knees and pleaded with him not to take my Barry; but to his credit, the boggart showed me a little compassion by giving me three months grace; and at the end of each month I had to try and guess his name. He said I could keep Barry until the end of the third month when, if I hadn't guessed his name, he would take Barry away forever.

At the end of each month he turned up at my palace so I might try and guess what he was called. At first I thought how difficult can it be? When he came at the end of the first month, I just sat there and guessed every name I could ever think of and each time he just laughed at me. At the end of the second month I had become better prepared. I bought a copy of

Blaskett's Compendium of Common and Uncommon Names and read each entry out feeling sure I would eventually come across the right one. Once again I was unsuccessful and the boggart took great delight in confounding me. This time, however, I was a bit smarter; I managed to capture a likeness of him."

The woman began to rummage in the large bag she had brought with her. With luck, a picture of the boggart would make it easy for me to find him. I suppose I should have known better, the science of photography was in its infancy here in the city. Out in the sticks, it was still in the womb. She handed me what I hoped would be a little pocket-sized sketch of my target…what appeared from the bag was a great big life-size drawing. I sighed.

"Just the face would have been enough"

"It *is* just the face!" she said with some delight as she turned it around so I could see it. "I called in our country's finest lightning sketcher." Knowing the country she referred to probably amounted to two villages and the football pitch between them, I braced myself to be disappointed.

"Did he have to draw it so big?" I moaned. "I *am* going to have to carry it around all the bars and taverns."

"That's the size of paper he always uses." The drawing, despite its lack of portability, did at least give me something to go on. It would also keep the rain off.

"Of course, I also had the strange-looking man followed by one of my most trusted soldiers. That's why I'm here, Mr Boggart."

"I see; your man has failed you, so you wish to make use of ThurMar's Number One P.I."

"My man hasn't failed me; he has led me to your door. He seems to think *you* are the person I am looking for because…"

"…Because I'm a *boggart*. Really, Mrs King, I see you're still going down that line, aren't you? There are other boggarts in this city, you know."

At this point, my visitor started crying again. "Well you all look alike to me!" she sobbed. I poured her another large whiskey. She knocked it back as if she was used to it. "I'll be totally honest with you, Mr Boggart. I'm desperate! I've got to find out the name of the boggart before he comes to take away my Barry forever. Anyway, what's a P. I.?"

I explained the definition of a private investigator to her and she seemed to take some reassurance from the fact that I was the *number one* in ThurMar. The fact I was the *only* investigator in ThurMar I decided to keep from her. I looked at the huge drawing of the boggart and straight away pointed out that he looked nothing like me…his hair was bluer than a night sky and his eyes were blacker than an even darker night sky. It was at this point that I myself became enlightened.

"This lightning sketcher…" I chewed my lip. "Would I be right in supposing he only uses blue and black in his drawings because he only actually sketches lightning?"

"It always looks better at night, Mr Boggart" I decided I was getting nowhere fast, so I accepted the drawing. "If this fellow does live round here then I'm the man to find out his name…or mine isn't Humphrey Boggart."

Carl couldn't believe Mother's reaction to his news. She had torn up the letter he'd received from the detective. Just like that. Why couldn't she just be happy for him? Hadn't he done everything she had asked of him to deliver Domania to her? What was her problem? Still angry, he watched as she disappeared into the next room; the room she always kept locked.

He picked up the shreds of the letter and placed them into his jacket pocket. The detective had found his brother Dan, the only family he had left now. The thought of seeing his kid brother once again almost made up for the loss of his Mum and Dad. Surely she could recognise how much it meant to him? He wouldn't let her reaction spoil the moment.

"Could you come in here, Carl?" Mother stood in the doorway. Her smile had returned. "I'm sorry about the way I reacted. It's just that I look upon you as my son and…I sometimes forget that you are not wholly mine." She crooked her finger and disappeared into the room. Carl felt happier now that she had at least come round a little.

Inside the room, Mother was standing in front of a voile curtain. Carl outstretched his arms to embrace her.

"I will always be your son. No one understands or appreciates how much you have done for me more than I." Her smile was beatific and she held him close. "That is why I wanted you to know of my news. I wanted you to be happy for me." Carl was unaware that, over his shoulder, the smile was as lost as a child in the forest.

Behind the curtain, Carl could make out the form of a woman lying on some kind of bed. "Who is that?" he asked.

"Ah…" said Mother, "I've been waiting a long time for this moment. That is Rosebud."

Carl pushed the curtain to one side and took a closer look. The woman was young, probably in her late teens. Her hair was a burnished auburn and it was loose around her face. Her clothes were like something out of a costume drama. He bent down close to her and listened for her breathing.

"Is she dead?"

"Just sleeping…"

"But why is she here?" Carl turned around and Mother was no longer there. He turned back to the young woman and took hold of her hand. It was cool, but not cold. Looking once more upon her face, despite it being a strange notion to him, he felt the urge to steal a kiss…

Rosebud opened her eyes and saw a strange man leaning over her. Carl, despite feeling ashamed at being caught in such a compromising position, smiled at her waking. The beautiful face wrinkled in confusion as myriad questions bombarded her waking thoughts. Where is she? Who is she? Who is this man? Is he a doctor? Has she been ill? Is it serious? *Had he just kissed her?* She got the feeling that he might have. She licked her lips as if the very action might have answered the question in her head. It didn't.

She tried to speak but it was almost as if she had to think how to do it. Her throat felt as though it was full of cobwebs. Carl handed her a drink of water.

"Are you all right?" he asked. Her tired arms reached for the glass and she drank all of the water in one go.

"Have I been ill?" said Rosebud in a cracked voice.

"I don't think so."

"You don't think so? You *are* a doctor, aren't you?" Carl shook his head.

"Before I woke up, I dreamt I had been kissed. Was that you?" Carl couldn't hide the guilt in his eyes. He looked at the door behind him as if waiting for Mother to come in and explain. "Do you know who I am?" Carl was surprised by the change in attitude in Rosebud's voice. Behind him the door opened and Mother came into the room. A look of relief swept across Carl's face.

Rosebud turned her head and studied the new arrival. A minute passed before she said, "Hi." Complete with a childlike wave.

"Hello, Rosebud. Do you remember what I told you to do if someone ever kissed you without your permission?"

"Now wait a minute..." said Carl.

"I would have to kill that person," said Rosebud.

In the half-light of early morning, JC took her first proper look at the centre of this strange new world she had infiltrated. Up to this moment she had remained content in searching for an access point around the edge of Domania. Now she needed to investigate the beating heart of the operation. The further into Domania she plunged the less control she felt she had.

People were thin on the ground at this hour and her invisibility allowed her access to all areas of the site. Marvels of architecture and technology surrounded her, but JC was not the type to be impressed by things she could not understand. She was here to do a job and any gushing admiration for these modern day wonders would do little to help her complete it. The wafting smell of cooked food however was another matter and she fought the urge to investigate it further. A nearby clock struck the hour and JC was brought to a puzzled halt as hundreds of ironised sprites began to spew out of the large unremarkable building that faced her. She was thrown by this revelation. Up to now she had seen one or two disinterested sprites wandering about but wherever there was money to be earned there were always i-sprites to take it. JC had assumed that whatever enterprise was taking place here at the Palace of Fotherghyll, it had nothing to do with her fellow sprites. Now she was witnessing vast numbers of them pouring into the buildings all around her. Every one of them had lost their magic so she knew they could not see her. The faces of all the goblins, elves and dwarves, filed past her, each dressed in a similar uniform. There was something about them, as if they had been struck by a malaise of some kind; a certain deficiency of spirit. One by one they passed her on their way to some set task like so many ants. Many went into the kitchens close by and JC, ruled by her rumbling stomach as much as professional interest, did not need much encouragement to follow them.

It was the sound of gunfire from the palace building that stopped her furthering her progress. JC turned on her heels and ran round the corner. She was knocked clean off her feet by a man who was running away from the gunfire. He stopped for a second, surprised by the contact he had made with the invisible elf. Fear over-ruled his curiosity and he was soon on his way again. JC was up and after him as he headed away from the palace. She followed the man alongside what she understood to be a railway line. Another shot was fired and JC felt the whirr of the bullet as it passed her ear. Turning to see the man's pursuer she was surprised to see a young woman dressed in a rather glamorous but outmoded ball gown. A man who was all too familiar arrived at the young woman's side and spoke to her. JC was too far away to hear but the woman handed the gun to Jakob Grimm, who took up the pursuit on her behalf. JC waited until he passed her before she set off flying behind him. In the distance she could see the fugitive running for his life. Both men were dressed in the same clothing, matching jacket and trousers of a design she was unfamiliar with. Jakob Grimm divested himself of his jacket and flung it behind him. Had he not been so hell-bent on his target he might have noticed that his jacket had found a home on the trailing elf. With the jacket both blinding her and fouling her wings, JC came to a ungraceful halt. The chase carried on without her as she struggled to remove the jacket from her head. Another shot was fired. Up ahead the hunted man seemed to be heading for the small building that lay at the end of the railway line. His pursuer, a much larger and less mobile man, seemed to be losing ground. JC was back on track and closing on him. There seemed to be nowhere for the hunted man to go. If it had been JC herself being pursued she would have headed up towards the caves above the mine but obviously this man was running blind. He could only outrun the bigger man for so long before he came up against the Wall of Thorns.

JC flew low behind Jakob Grimm and tapped his ankles as she passed him. He clattered to the ground in a confused heap behind her. When she caught up with the fugitive she found that he had arrived at the small building at the end of the railway line. He stopped just long enough to look at his watch. Shaking his head in frustration he set off to his right and ran alongside the Wall of Thorns. JC came to a halt and checked the progress of Jakob. He was still on all fours and coming to terms with his fall. On and on went the hunted man. He was obviously much fitter than his pursuer but there was nowhere for him to go. His only recourse now was to work his enemy so hard that a heart attack might be imminent. If only she could engineer enough time to talk to him.

Jakob Grimm was relentless despite his lack of athleticism. JC wondered if there was a way she could stop him long enough for her to get to the bottom of things. As she watched the hunted man duck under a low-growing branch up ahead it gave her an idea. She flew to the branch and bent it back as far as she could, waiting for Jakob to arrive. Struggling with all her might to hold the branch, she willed him to come around the corner. Just at the point she felt it was going to slip from her grasp he arrived and she let the branch go. It caught him full in the chest and knocked him flat onto his back. JC hovered over him for a second or two to see if he was all right. He was conscious but she felt he wouldn't be

67

running for a minute or two. Behind her a harsh grating sound filled the air. She flew on up ahead and was surprised to see a man she hadn't seen before. He was sat on a rustic bench nursing his chin. The fugitive was nowhere in sight but the loud grating sound was coming from within the Wall of Thorns.

"What happened?" asked JC

"I tried to stop him pinching my chainsaw," said the man with his back to her.

"He's gone in there." He pointed to the Wall of Thorns in front of him. Already the thorns were beginning to grow back. The man turned and was surprised to see that the woman who had just spoken to him was no longer there.

Two minutes later Jakob Grimm arrived. "Which way did he go?"

"It was Mr Carl. He hit me and pinched my chainsaw. He went through there, Mr Grimm."

"Have you got another?"

"I've one in the van, Mr Grimm, if you give me a minute." Grimm nodded, pulled his mobile phone out and made a call. "Hi, it's Jakob, he's taken a chainsaw and set off through the Wall of Thorns...do you want me to follow him?" JC almost admired the cold detachment of the man. His quarry had chosen to breach the Wall of Thorns in desperation at keeping his life. This man had been given a job to do.

"Hurry man, I haven't got all day!"

"Here, Mr Grimm...you didn't see a woman round here, did you?"

Jakob Grimm screwed his face up. "Shut up!" Then he yanked the chainsaw into life and plunged into the Wall of Thorns.

BREAKFAST AT MANKY'S

Before it was bombed out of existence, Jonty and I were living as paying guests at Enid Brazenose's guest house. Order was in the process of being restored and despite winning a fortune on the Windblown Lottery, Enid was more than happy …well Enid never really seemed happy…so let's say she was determined to continue as before. Dunlaying was being rebuilt and the pair of us couldn't wait to return to her freshly-made beds and tasty home-cooked breakfasts. In the meantime we were sleeping in our respective offices on camp beds and having to make do with far less wholesome repast to start our day.

Jonty had been away for the weekend trying out some new invention of his so I had missed the routine the pair of us got into each morning. Once washed and brushed I would call at his office and together we would make our way over to Manky Knowles's place for a fried breakfast, a mug of tea and a read of the paper. The two of us would usually have a good old natter before our day began in earnest. Well, I say a good old natter but I always felt Jonty was holding back about what he was up to. I suppose working for The All-Seeing Eye it went with the nature of his job.

This particular morning we were both enduring 'A Big Manky Breakfast' (r.r.p. M1.25) when I asked him how his little break had gone. This brought about a lot of harrumphing. Clearly he wasn't too pleased about the whole thing.

"It turned out to be quite a waste of time. I did manage a bit of cycling around the Wall of Thorns.

"The what?" I asked.

"The Wall of Thorns…out by the village of Without. Surely you've heard of it?" I shook my head. "Without is the village I was born in. Its full name is Without-the-Wall." My eyebrows raised enough for Jonty to proceed. "The wall surrounds the old Palace of Fotherghyll…let me start again…there are two villages…one is Within-the-Wall and one is Without…"

"Without what?" The question needed answering, I thought. Flustering to the point I could easily work with, Jonty continued.

"Without-*the-Wall*! One village is within the wall and the other is with…*outside it*!" I nodded in understanding, more as a courtesy to Jonty's blood pressure than anything else.

"So this wall you're going on about…it's made of thorns right?"

"No! That's another wall…much later in the story. The first wall around the Palace of-"

"-Fotherghyll" I was getting the hang of it now.

"That's right." Jonty still seemed a bit tetchy. "Well that wall is of stone and when they built it at first, hundreds of years ago, it split the old village of Fotherghyll in half."

"Why did they build it?"

"The King-"

"Not another King!"

"The King got a bit worried about being invaded by a neighbour and he didn't really trust his subjects."

"It must have cost a bit."

"That was the clever part, he asked his citizens to contribute…those that could afford it got to live within the wall and those that didn't…had to stay outside it. Once the wall was built there was little contact between the two villages…"

"Seems a bit harsh."

"…Both kept their own company and barring the odd forkful of horsemuck being thrown over the wall every now and again, contact ended from that point…although there are stories of connecting passages and secret trysts between young lovers separated by the fact that one set of parents were rich and the other poor."

"So where does this Wall of Thorns come in?"

"Ah, well that all came about due to a curse from a witch, years later. She had been snubbed by the King at that time. There had been a great celebration for the birth of his daughter and anyway this old witch turned up uninvited and there was a right kerfuffle. She put a curse on the child; said that if the princess pricked her finger then she would die. Luckily, one witch had not bestowed a gift on the young princess yet and she used her gift to change the spell to 'she would fall asleep for a hundred years' instead of dying, you see. Of course the child grew up and despite all the necessary precautions, the silly thing managed to prick her finger. Consequently she fell asleep for a hundred years. They say that in order to protect her, all the people in the palace were put to sleep as well so that when she woke up…she wouldn't be on her own. Don't know if it's true or not. The witch placed the Wall of Thorns around the palace to protect it and nobody ever got through it to find out."

"So what were *you* looking round there for?"

"Er…nothing really, I was just hoping to meet up with a young lady I know over that way…but she didn't show."

"Pity, that." It seemed Jonty was more of a dark horse than I'd given him credit for.

"Yes, it was. Still, it gave me the chance to give my bicycle a test drive." Jonty had become tired of all the jokes made whenever he rode his tiny bicycle so he had set about building himself a regular-sized bike with specially adapted pedals. He was touchy about his size.

"OK, was it?"

"Well that's one of the things that irked me. Some chap ran straight into me near the Wall of Thorns and stole my bike."

"Surely he wouldn't be able to use it?"

"Oh yes…he'd obviously cycled before."

"But didn't he find the special pedals a bit difficult to use?" I asked.

Jonty began to turn red. "Yes…well obviously when I said I redesigned the bike…"

"Well how did he cope with the big pedals?"

"Look, I didn't actually change the design, OK? It worked out cheaper. I mean, why fix something that isn't broke? I decided it might be more practical to redesign my footwear."

"What do you mean?"

"Well…I've decided to call them platform shoes…"

"OK…so what did you do when he cycled off with your bike?"

"Well there wasn't much I could do." By now Jonty was quite angry. "What you fail to understand, my dull-witted friend is that twelve inch platform shoes are easy to put on but trying to stand up from a prone position is an operation that requires an element of assistance!"

"So you didn't do anything, then?" I did like to tease Jonty. "So…what did he look like?"

"Well it was hard to say really…on account of him being covered in cuts."

"Cuts?"

"Yes, it was quite remarkable really. His clothes, which I discerned to be somewhat different from the norm, were almost shredded. What parts of his body I could see, i.e. his face and hands, were covered in nasty cuts and grazes."

"So you think he might be a stranger? Did he say anything?"

"Well he was obviously somewhat distressed. To be fair to the chap, he did apologise. He muttered something about being sorry but that he needed to get to the nearest village and…I have been pondering on this for sometime…but I think he said…he had to tell the police."

"The police? That's interesting."

"Is it?"

"Yes. My guess is they are some kind of law-enforcing agency in the land where he comes from."

"You mean like the Guardians?" said Jonty. Manky came over with a huge tea-pot and asked if we would like a top-up. We gratefully accepted.

"Oh well, detecting will have to wait for a while," as I held out my mug.

"I could do with you putting a tail on that nephew of mine. He's been acting weird lately," said Jonty.

"What do you mean?"

"Well you know he's had this night job over the last few weeks…" I nodded. "…which I don't mind as he sleeps all day and is out from under my feet. But he's being very secretive about it. Well you know Sphagnum. He doesn't do 'secretive' very well. It seems to be upsetting him." Jonty looked a little pained himself.

"You never did tell me how come he's so much bigger than you?" I half expected a reaction from Jonty in the implicit reference to his shortness but clearly his concerns for his nephew took prevalence.

"He's the son of my sister, Thumbelina and her husband Jack the Giant."

"Killer?"

"What, Jack Carn? He's as gentle as a lamb's wool cushion."

"No, I meant is your brother-in-law Jack the Giant Killer?" I said. Jonty looked somewhat confused.

"No, don't be silly…Jack *is* a giant. I don't know why anyone would want to kill him. He's as gentle as…"
"Yeah, I get the picture. But if your sister is…how can I put this…like you. How did she…er…you know…Sphagnum is a big fellow." I was struggling to put it mildly. Jonty got my gist.

"Oh! I see…no…Sphagnum is Jack's son by his marriage to his first wife, Granita." I felt the blood rush from my face as the tricky subject had been sidestepped.

"Ah!" I said. "She would be a giant I expect?"

"No, no…she was a dwarf! Sphagnum is some sort of throwback. Granita died when Sphagnum was a baby. My sister has been a wonderful mother to him. For that reason it's been hard to tell him about his real mother."

"You mean he doesn't know?" Just on cue the giant lad came in to the café carrying a tea tray.

"Here you are, Uncle Jonty, I made you a mug of tea and a sandwich." The big lug looked pleased with himself.

"But Sphagnum, I'm in an eating house!" Jonty looked across at the scowling Manky Knowles who was heading this way. "If we all brought our own food and drink into Mr Knowles' establishment, how would he make any money?"

Manky who had now arrived on the scene seemed to be thinking the same way but with more swearwords.

"Oi! What are you jeffing doing with that mug?" said Manky whose career as an ex-prize fighter was well-documented around the walls of the eatery.

"That's no way to talk about Uncle Jonty!" said Sphagnum, picking Manky off the floor with one hand. The look of fear that came across the proprietor's face was not one he often used. Jonty, flustered to the point of apoplexy, commanded his nephew to put the proprietor down. While the little man did his best to smooth Manky's ruffled grease-stained clothing, I looked up and smiled at the huge young man. He studied me for a while before returning what could only be described as a grimace. Well…at least he tried, I thought. As Jonty accompanied Manky to behind the safety of his counter, I thought I would do a little digging on his behalf.

"So…what are you doing with yourself these days?" I asked. A guarded expression passed across the young lad's face.

"It's a secret."

"Let me guess."

"I'm not telling you."

"You're working for The Guardians."

"No."

"The All-Seeing Eye?"

"No."

"The Witches?"

"No."

"Not the Druids?"

"No, I'm not telling you."

"Are you on the coaches…the night-soil…the canals?"

"No…no…and no!"

"Did a bloke in a tavern give you the job?" Sphagnum's confidence took a hit here. Then his face lit up.

"No!"

"*Are you sure*?"

"Yes!"

"How come you're so sure?"

"Because there were two of them! Hah!"

"You outsmarted me there, Sphagnum." The big guy was congratulating himself as Jonty came back from his rescue mission.

"What are you so happy about, nephew?"

"Mr Boggart was trying to find out what I was doing at nights and he couldn't?" Jonty looked across at me and I feigned a beaten look.

"Tell Mr Boggart what you used to do back home in Without-the-Wall", said Jonty.

"I was the village idiot," crowed the giant.

"Sphagnum became ambitious," continued Jonty, "the village wasn't big enough for his ego. He wanted to move to the city so he could enter for the King of Fools." I looked bemused. "It's a sort of City Idiot competition."

"How come he didn't go for it?"

"He didn't know about the residency clause. He has to wait a year or so but he's keeping his hand in. Aren't you, Sphagnum?"

Any response from Sphagnum was put from my mind by the sound of gunshot outside. Numerous screams followed as the inhabitants of Manky's place swarmed to the dusty window that fronted the eating house. What we saw was not something you wish to see everyday…

THE SECRETARY

"That's my bicycle!" shouted Jonty as we gazed open-mouthed at the scene before us. Sure enough Jonty's bike lay abandoned by the kerb but next to it, in a state of some distress, lay the man who Jonty had described to me only minutes before.

"Well at least he's brought it back!" I said. We were both out onto the street before Manky could shout, "Hey you haven't paid for your breakfast!" and I was at the mystery man's side witnessing what would surely be his last moments on this earth.

"Seems to be all right!" said Jonty, setting his bicycle up on its wheels..

"Never mind the flaming bike! Get your arse over here!" Jonty scurried over to where I was cradling the man's head. The gunshot wound to his chest looked fatal, so I guess the first thing to ask him was… "Who did this to you?"

He coughed up some blood and struggled to breathe. Dying is never a pretty sight. I watched him trying to control the rising blood in his throat. The last word that he uttered in this life was…

"Rosebud?"

No sooner had I closed the dead man's eyes than the familiar ring of the Guardians' hand-bell broke the silence. Six well-built Guardians arrived accompanied by a witch, who going off her appearance, had quite a high profile. Her arrival made sure that people were quick to disappear from the scene of the crime. Not having been a citizen of ThurMar for very long, my curiosity overcame any fear I might have for her. As the Guardians picked up the dead man and bundled his body into a convenient coffin, the witch scanned those that remained, none of whom would return her eye contact. When her gaze reached me, I watched her size me up and down.

"You there in the unusual clothing. Listen to me carefully, sprite, you will pay no heed to what happened here today…or you will have me to answer to." With that she twirled her great black cape and strode off down the street. It was the action of someone accustomed to other people making sure they never got in her way. I turned to see what the Guardians were doing. They and the dead man's body had gone.

I returned to the Manky's place to settle the bill and found Jonty cowering at his table.

"Has she gone?"

Ten minutes later, a much recovered Jonty skipped alongside me as we headed down the street.

"What did she say to you?" he asked. "She didn't want to know where he got the bicycle from, did she?"

"You're really frightened of her, aren't you?"

"Isn't everyone? You do know who she is, don't you?" I knew perfectly well who she was but I did like winding Jonty up.

"Some witch…that much I could tell. It's the low self-esteem that gives it away, I guess." Jonty looked amazed.

"Some witch?! That was Doris Morris!"

I shrugged my shoulders. "You forget I've only just moved here from the country. We've got our own witches without worrying about city witches with a thing about black." Jonty began a sustained rant about how foolhardy it was to rub important witches up the wrong way. We walked alongside one of the nicer canals of the city, turned through the gates of Caravan Park and headed for the rose garden.

"Doris Morris is *only* second in command to the Massy Witch herself," said Jonty.

"Then why are you so scared of her. Avis Davies is a very nice woman." Jonty harrumphed as the two of us sat down on a park bench. He was so easy to wind up. The delicious scent of the roses reminded me of the last word that the dying man had spoken. I picked a small red rose and sniffed it. Another case for me, perhaps?

"Whither Rosebud?" I muttered under my breath. Jonty looked at me beneath his furrowed brow.

"It should keep for days if you put it in water as soon as you get home."

*

When a guy comes cycling into your street and is shot at, you start to wonder. When you go over to have a look at him and notice his body is covered in a thousand tiny cuts, you start to ask questions. And when he mumbles the name 'Rosebud' you start to think, "Hey, perhaps this could be an interesting case!" When he doesn't come round...ever...then you start to worry about just who it is you're going to send the bill to...

I was back at the office, and taking Jonty's advice, I swilled out the glass that Mrs King had used the other day (OK, so I'm not the most domesticated person...give me a break...I was living in a river a few months ago!) and popped the rosebud in it. Intrigued by what I had been witness to this morning, I stared out of the window, focusing on the empty space in front of me rather than the busy street below. This was the kind of case I had been looking for and if I could solve the mystery of the dead man and this Rosebud then I would prove myself worthy of the name Humphrey Boggart Private Investigator. The dead man's answer when I asked who did this to him had been 'Rosebud?'...there was a distinct rising inflection at the end of the word...it wasn't an answer but a question. I picked up the rosebud and held it to my nose, filling my nostrils with nature's bounty. I repeated his last word aloud.

"Rosebud?"

"Very good, but it would be more impressive if you wore a blindfold!" I put down the flower and for the second time since I opened for business a beautiful woman was standing in my doorway. "Hi, my name is Scarlett Alewife...the door was open...so I just came in." With a smile like that I could

83

forgive her everything. Her hair was the colour of burnished copper and her lips were as red as a well-sucked sarsaparilla tablet. I closed my mouth before asking if I could help her.

"Actually it could be me who can help you," she said, "I've heard you're looking for a secretary." This came as something of a surprise to me as I hadn't even thought about paperwork. I supposed I would have got round to it at some point. Maybe I'd mentioned the fact to Jonty?

"Did Jonty send you?" For the first time she looked unsure of herself but still remained stunning.

"It might have been, I overheard someone in one of the taverns saying you were looking for a secretary." The possibility that Jonty might gossip to someone else about my business was not implausible. "I've just arrived in the city and I need some kind of work. Accommodation isn't cheap here."

"Tell me about it?"

"Well firstly, I went to the place around the corner that has the price of all the lodgings in the shop window…"

"No, you misunderstand…when I said 'tell me about it'…I meant that I understand exactly what you're saying." For a split second she was ruffled again but I got the feeling that once she had taken this information on board she was again in complete control.

"So, when do I start?" Beautiful as she was I wasn't stupid enough just to take her on without seeing what she could do.

"Can you read and write?"

"Can I read and write? I wouldn't be coming for a secretarial job if I couldn't, now would I? I can write poetry, music and romantic stories; I can do thirty words a day…"

"Now I'm no expert but I'm sure thirty words a day isn't very impressive."

"…in embroidery? As you can imagine, I'm much faster when it comes to penmanship."

I was impressed but I wasn't letting on. "Perhaps you're overqualified for this job," I suggested. She bristled, which was quite something to see. Being a bit of a plodding country bumpkin I was never one for stereotyping but her red hair was a warning that she possessed quite a temper. Perhaps it was time to cool things down. "How about I give you a month's trial? What did you say your name was again?" Everything about her softened and she turned into the beautiful young lady I had seen only minutes earlier. I was going to have my work cut out with this one."

"Scarlett…Scarlett Alewife." I smiled. "What's so funny?" she asked. I sensed another bristle coming.

"I couldn't think of a less appropriate name for someone who looks…er…as pretty as you do." The bristle arrived in full sweep mode.

"Listen sir, I'm not here to make your office look nice, though it could do with refurbishment, I'm here to offer you my clerical services. Incidentally, have you ever thought of bringing in decorators? If I am to work in these surroundings at least they could be made to look a little more stylish. Have you ever considered chandeliers …or? " It was my turn to bristle.

"Look lady, this is my office and I like it like this, OK. I'm a private investigator and we're supposed to have offices like this. Haven't you ever seen *The Big Sleep*? Of course you haven't." Sheesh, I could be dumb sometimes.

"So when do you want me to start this month's trial. It should be long enough…if I like you I may even stay longer." I flashed her a look but she just smiled and winked at me. I smiled back…she was the nice one again.

"Don't you want to know how much I pay?" It seemed strange that money had never been mentioned.

"The going rate, I suppose?"

"Which is?"

"You tell me, you're the boss."

"Three marks a day?"

"Yep, fine by me."

"See you tomorrow morning…don't be late." Scarlett grinned and pointed her fingers at me like a gun.

"Just try and stop me." And as she blew the smoke away from her imaginary gun, I couldn't help feeling I had just hired one incredible woman…at an incredibly cheap rate of pay.

*

Scarlett dragged her beautiful self into the office the next morning. She was a few minutes late, but I was never that bothered about things like that. I probably made my first mistake by telling her this. She took off her expensive but rather old-fashioned coat and sat herself down at the large desk.

"Right, where do I start?" A big beaming smile filled her glorious face. I settled into the role of boss rather well, I thought.

"Take a letter, Miss Alewife."

"Who to? And please call me Scarlett."

"Not who to, Scarlett…but where to?"

"Sorry?"

"I want you to take it to the Post Office."

"Oh…right." She got up, snatched my letter (a progress report to Avis Davies) out of my hand and flounced through the door.

"Oh and can you pick up a newspaper while you're out? The Thursday Market Barker will do nicely!" While she was gone, I set to thinking what she could do all day. I think I might have fallen in love with the idea of having a secretary, but if I was being truthful, I only had two cases on the go at the moment and one of them wasn't actually a paying job. Then I remembered the book that Avis Davies had found in Arnie Grimm's bag. Since it had been investigated by the Wisdom Wardens and proved to be of no value, Avis Davies had been happy to let me keep it.

Scarlett came back with the paper and I sent her along the corridor to organise some stationery from Jonty. She was just about to open her mouth.

"As long as it's for Humphrey Boggart, Private Investigator, I don't care what it looks like, Scarlett. You choose." The door closed a little hard for my liking but I suppose I was going to have to get used to that kind of thing. I picked up the Thursday Market Barker and read the front page.

RAILWAY: THE AGE OF THE IRON HORSE IS HERE!

...said the main headline. Now that the new line to Quickbridge had officially been open the suggestion was that this new means of transport would revolutionise the world using a steam-driven engine that could run on rails of iron and carry both goods and passengers. Now that I had seen the world of *The Big Sleep* nothing really surprised me anymore. I realised how far we still had to go. In the paper the representatives of the canal companies were passing the railway off as a mere fad and showing no concern for the threat to their business. I guess that one day the railway will say the same thing about cars.

I perused the rest of the paper for its usual tales of good deeds and bad ones. On page two I read about a pack of dogs that had appeared from nowhere and was now running wild in

ThurMar. At the bottom of the page my eye was caught by a report of strange happenings across the city.

WHO ARE THESE SLEEPERS?

Four people had been admitted to the Druidsgrove Hospital suffering from memory loss. It appears that each one had claimed to have woken up in different locations around the city unable to identify just who they were. In each case the person concerned had only been able to identify themselves by labels that were found attached to their clothing indicating their name, age, place of birth and occupation. None of the four people seemed easy with their identities least of all one woman who had been told by two people and her label that she was John o'Woods, a night-soil remover. Later in the day a man was charged at one of the guardian stations for causing a public nuisance by singing and dancing while dressed as a woman. He claimed that his name was Lettice Dodgin, an out-of-work music hall entertainer and in his defence produced a similar label to prove his identity. The Guardians are investigating the case further.

I was intrigued enough by the story to ask Scarlett what she thought about it when she returned from Jonty's.

"How would I know, Mr Boggart? I'm just a secretary. Now what have you got lined up for me?"

"Yeah, but imagine waking up and not knowing who you were…and then…here's the best bit…finding out your name from a little label tied to your wrist." Scarlett looked almost bored.

"You have got something for me to do, haven't you?"

"Right, you'll like this…it'll be like you're getting to read the story before it hits the shops." Scarlett looked nonplussed as I handed her the book. I waited while she read the first few lines aloud.

"When Mr. Bilbo Baggins of Bag End announced that he would shortly be celebrating his eleventy-first birthday with a party of special magnificence, there was much talk and excitement in Hobbiton… - What *is* this, Mr Boggart?" Scarlett held the book in her fingers as though it was a very dirty housebrick.

"Really, Scarlett. That's my new serialised novel you're insulting. Did you really think that I would need a secretary when I am working on only two cases at the moment. I need to make money to keep this job going and *The Digest for Readers* are very interested in my new work. They're going to print five thousand copies of the first instalment."

"But it's already printed out…"

"Yes and if I hand it to the printers already printed out they're going to wonder where I got it from. Aren't they?"

"Where did you get it from?" I tapped the side of my nose.

"Remember, Scarlett my dear, that you are working for a very resourceful man." For once, Scarlett looked totally bemused.

"But, I didn't know you were a writer. It's going to take me ages to write out all this in longhand. I mean, look at all these pages…"

"One thousand two hundred and sixteen pages to be exact. Scarlett read on before asking…

"What in the name of Druid Duguid *is* a hobbit anyway?"

"It's a licence to print money." I replied struck by her archaic turn of phrase.

THE BUSINESS OF PEEPING

After a couple of days of trailing around all the taverns and bars of Thursday Market searching for a boggart with a penchant for bull-terriers, I had got nowhere. Not only was it difficult to get people to talk to me in front of others, it was also embarrassing having to unroll the huge sketch that Mrs King had provided me with. Whenever I showed people the picture of the boggart, the response was negative. It was making me feel uncertain whether I was cut out for this role. Fortunately, thanks to Jonty, I was at least making things a little easier for myself. He had laughed at my huge drawing and asked why I hadn't reduced it. When I responded with a blank look, he invited me into his workshop to offer his services.

"Copying is what we do!" he said as he unlocked the door. A huge clanging metal sound greeted us as we entered. I froze.

"Burglars?" I whispered.

"Sphagnum," said Jonty. "He'll be just getting his things ready. This new job seems to keep him out of mischief and it certainly gets him out from under my feet during the day...and night!" I smiled at the paradox of his analogy. The clanging continued as Jonty marched around his workshop. "Sphagnum! It's only me...and Humphrey. Are you about ready to go now?" The huge man poked his head around the door.

"Oh, hi Uncle Jonty! I'm just getting ready. I hope you haven't told Mr Boggart about my new job...you know it's top secret." Jonty winked at Humphrey.

"Of course I haven't told him. We don't want you getting into trouble, do we?" Sphagnum came out into the room with a large briefcase. It's contents were the cause of the clanging noise.

"What's in the case, Sphagnum?" I asked. The big lad just touched the side of his nose with his forefinger. Don't you just hate it when somebody else does that?

"That's for you to know and me to find out. Bye Uncle Jonty…Mr Boggart." He slammed the door behind him, more through over-exuberance than anything else. From what I had seen of Sphagnum, he didn't have an angry bone in his body.

"What's he doing?" I asked his Uncle.

"To tell the truth, Humphrey, I don't really know…but it keeps him out of my hair." Jonty sure could pick analogies. "Only trouble is, I miss having him around the place for the heavy stuff. He's not the brightest button in the box, but he can't half shift boxes of stationery. Still, he seems happy…that's the main thing. He's not a bad lad." I nodded my head. Just as I had settled down for the demonstration of modern copying, Sphagnum came back into the room.

"Sorry, it's only me! I forgot something!"

"I don't know," said Jonty, "I 'm always saying you'll forget your head one day." Sphagnum stopped dead in his tracks and furrowed his brow at his uncle.

"How did you know that, Uncle Jonty? Have you been peeking?" He rushed into the back room and came out with a large heavy sack of something. With a smile once more planted on his face, he slung the bulky sack over his back and set off once again. I got up and held the door for him and pulled my face at the disgusting smell that accompanied him out of the room. Jonty waited till I returned to my seat.

"What was in the sack?" I asked.

"Cabbages" he shrugged before rubbing his hands together. "Now then, prepare to meet the cutting edge of image copying technology."

*

Now, armed with a much smaller black and white copy of the drawing of the boggart-with-no-name, I made my way into Fleetpool. Jonty had reduced the image by use of a pencil attached to a small wooden framework. As he traced over the original picture a smaller drawing was created on an adjacent piece of paper. I had been suitably impressed. It was not only witches who could weave magic. Even the snapping of the pencil's point couldn't dampen my enthusiasm. I was just glad I didn't have to unfold that blasted picture ever again.

I had decided to try Fleetpool, the old fishing village that now found itself as ThurMar's port, simply because I was desperate. I had hawked the boggart's image all around the city but no one seemed to know him. I took the barge down the Great Canal into Fleetpool. All ports seem to attract the casualties of life and there was also a high proportion of sprites living and working there. Maybe I'd get lucky here. Many people didn't. There were some dubious types in the port. I walked past the fish market, which, in the late

94

afternoon, was not the hive of activity it was in the morning. The dominant sound was that of hose-pipes swishing water over the marble slabs. I was heading for the taverns around the fish quay where, in the next few hours, they would be getting ready for the evening catch. The first place I dropped into was The Three Pilchards. All manner of life existed and drank in these places, men whose nerve and sinews were wound up tight…and women who were markedly more loose. As soon as I pushed open the door an old buxom women with bright red hair threw her arms around me and tried to put her tongue in my ear. All she received for her trouble was a mouth full of hat as I ducked under her flaccid grasp. She sounded hurt.

"Oh come on lovey! I could show you a good time!" I very much doubted it but decided a polite refusal wouldn't offend. "Please yourself, you miserable git! I didn't fancy you anyway!" Her raucous laughter drowned itself in a pint glass of brown ale, but I took it in good spirit. After all, I didn't want to intimidate anybody…yet. I walked up to the bar where a huge bald man covered in nautical tattoos grinned like a graveyard gate.

"Whaddaya want?" he roared like a sea captain in a force nine gale. I ordered my usual whiskey. He slammed the drink on the counter and spat the price at me. I paid and showed him the drawing of the boggart.

"Have you seen this man recently?" The bald barman straightened up.

"Hey you aren't a Guardian, are ya?" He looked around the tavern nervously. An immediate hush filled the room. I turned to find thirty pairs of eyes fixed upon me.

95

"No", I assured him, "I'm merely a private detective trying to find a missing person." The noise took up again but I sensed that at least half of each pair of eyes were still watching me.

"I've never seen him in his life. Relative of yours, is he?" I sighed, picked up my drink and shuffled over to an empty table in the corner. To my left an elderly barrel of a man stared into space while cradling a pint of beer with his shovel-like hands. I sipped my drink and prepared to watch the comings and goings of the tavern. After a few minutes the man turned and spoke to me.

"Did you say you were a private detective?" he asked. I nodded. "Does that mean that you try and detect things for people?" I nodded again. He turned away and stared into space once more. I noticed two men entering the tavern. One was tall and had the posture of a stork while the other was small and stocky. They approached the bar but the tall one noticed the man sat next to me; a few words passed between them and they turned and left the pub.

"You see those two," said the old man, "they used to be my best friends."

"What happened?" I was curious. It came with the job.

"You tell me…you're the detector. Not long back I woke up on the breakwater and I couldn't remember a thing. Apparently, I'm Hamble Titchmarsh, a 59 year old fisherman." His story had me hooked.

"And aren't you?"

"I don't know… I don't feel like a fisherman. I haven't got the first clue about how to cast a net or gut a fish. Nobody speaks to me. Don't you think that's strange? Those two men who were in here before… one of them greeted me like a long lost friend, he was the first person I met after I woke up on the breakwater. The other one, the shorter one, Scuzzer, he paid me thirty marks for my boat. This is for a boat I can't describe, a boat I've never seen."

"And he paid you thirty marks?" Hamble Titchmarsh nodded. "Is that a good price?"

"You tell me-"

"-I'm the detective, yeah." I offered to buy the man a drink and he accepted. I brought the drinks back to his table and sat down opposite him. He finished the flat beer that was still left in his glass and pulled the fresh pint closer to him. He pulled a large iron key from under his shirt.

"What's that for?" I asked. He shrugged his heavy shoulders. "So why is it that no one speaks to you?"

"I don't know," said the old man, "it's just that if I had lived here all my life, why doesn't anyone know me? I swear that the only two people who have spoken to me since that day are Scuzzer and Tranter and now whenever they see me, they make themselves scarce."

I remembered the newspaper story from the other day and wondered whether this old man was one of the so-called 'sleepers' that the journalist had referred to.

"When you woke up on the breakwater… what made you think you were a fisherman?"

"I had a little label in my pocket that told me."

I explained to Hamble about the other similar cases that had appeared in the paper, but it did little to raise his spirits. I showed him the drawing of the boggart I was looking for and got my first positive result.

Taking the picture in his big calloused hands, he said, "I have seen him…in here. But I don't know who he is or where he goes. I've hardly been out of this place since I 'woke up'. This is my home till the money runs out."

"What'll you do then?" I asked. The fellow just shrugged his big round shoulders.

"I suppose I'll have to find some kind of work."

"Fishing?"

A grin cracked his face. "Probably, I've been doing it all my life…apparently" I went to the bar to get two more drinks. I felt sorry for the guy; he seemed like a fish out of water if you pardon the pun. When I returned, he handed me back the picture.

"I'm not much help to you but I bet if anyone knows who this fellow is, then it's Scuzzer and his mate." I've seen them in here, they're wheeler-dealer types…always got their nose to the ground."

I pushed the two drinks across to him. "Have them both; I'm going to see if I can find them." I took a business card out of my pocket and handed it to him. "Here, I can't promise you a job but maybe I know a person who could use someone who's not frightened of hard work. Come and see me at this address in Thursday Market if you're interested."

"Where's Thursday Market?"

"It's the big city just up the Great Canal from here."

"There's a canal?" I clapped him on his shoulder and said goodbye.

*

Finding the two men called Scuzzer and Tranter wasn't too difficult. Some of the people I asked were suspicious and kept quiet but I sensed that a lot of the inhabitants of the port weren't too keen on this couple. It was in The Jolly Sailor that I caught up with them. Tranter, the tall lanky one was stood at the bar chatting to a drunken goblin sailor. I looked around for his colleague but couldn't see him until he came out of the jakes. I stepped up to the bar, ordered a whiskey and shuffled my way into the corner of the room. I decided it might be best to watch these two to see how they operated rather than confronting them straight away. I thought it strange at first that the guy called Scuzzer didn't go over and join his friend. He just sat down with someone else and began chatting away. I noticed that he was continually watching Tranter and the goblin who by now was quite drunk. Tranter appeared to be buying the goblin sailor one drink after another. After about an hour, I saw Tranter turn and nod his head to his colleague. Scuzzer made his excuses to the person he was chatting with and then made for the jakes again. I was intrigued and as nature was calling anyway, I decided to follow him outside.

In the darkness of the outhouse, I walked up to the channel and was surprised to find that the man called Scuzzer was nowhere to be seen. The gate out of the back yard was left ajar, so I peered out in the hope of seeing something. Scuzzer was waiting at the corner where the back alley met the harbour front. I inched out through the gateway to get a better view. As I suspected, the goblin sailor came swaying out of the tavern and as soon as he reached the back alley, Scuzzer raised what looked to be a truncheon and whacked the poor goblin over the head. He whistled between his fingers. I froze, if I blew my cover, he would be on to me, so I slipped back into the tavern and shouted that someone had just been slugged out in the back alley. I was almost surprised that my cry for help was not met with total indifference. What did surprise me was that most of the people who got up to see what was happening were sprites, the humans stayed put. A crowd of them were outside before I knew it, goblins, dwarves and elves and when I followed them out I fully expected the goblin sailor to be spark out on the floor. But Scuzzer and the goblin were nowhere to be seen. The crowd turned rather ugly and a fat dwarf mumbled something into his beard. The others looked at me and I expected I was in for a bruising for disturbing their drinking time. To my surprise one of the goblins came up to me.

"Dwarf, elf or goblin?"

"It was a goblin, I'm not making it up, you know?"

"No mate, we know you're not. It's happening all the time; they're only kidnapping sprites for some reason. Press gangs are back, we reckon."

"But I think he already *was* a sailor."

He lifted the brow of my hat and looked at my face. "Better watch out, boggart. They'll be after you as well." I readjusted my hat and turned to follow them in. In the doorway behind all the disgruntled sprites, was Tranter. He was staring straight at me.

WHO IS HAMBLE TITCHMARSH?

Returning to the tavern I finished my drink and decided to make my way up to the Great Canal for the last barge back to the city. I was not looking forward to it. The last barge was also the last resort; a feeding frenzy full of drunks and pick-pockets. I reckoned that if I walked on to the stop where the barge turned round up by the breakwater I could at least get myself a seat before it picked up most of the lairy passengers at the harbour itself. It started to rain as I walked along the poorly lit quayside so I pulled down my hat and huddled inside my coat. I hadn't walked more than a few hundred yards when I bumped into somebody. I looked up and there in front of me was a tall thin man.

"Why don't you look where you're going, sprite?" It was the man Tranter and he towered over me. Despite his height he looked as though he would have trouble punching his way out of a wet paper bag. I looked into his eyes and I don't know what it was but something about him changed. It was as though he was expecting something else to happen. Then I remembered how they had dealt with the drunken goblin and I knew that his partner must be somewhere around. Bracing myself for a sap on the back of the head I turned and saw Scuzzer...but this wasn't the confident man I had seen ducking and diving in the tavern. This Scuzzer had a glazed look in his eyes...this Scuzzer fell sideways onto the wet stone floor. I turned to face Tranter but he was long gone, the dark alleyways that had brought him to me had swallowed him back up again. I bent down to examine Scuzzer and caught the movement of a shadow from the alleyway.

102

"Lucky I was just passing!" chuckled Hamble Titchmarsh as he appeared out of the darkness. "I'd been thinking what you'd been saying and I thought I might be able to catch you up in one of the taverns. I saw you leaving the Jolly Sailor and right behind you, though not that you'd have noticed it, was Tranter." I stood up and clapped him on the shoulder.

"Thanks, mate, I owe you one."

"Well how about I take you up on your offer of help."

"Come on, help us get this one sorted out and you can sleep in my office until we get you fixed up." The both of us rolled Scuzzer into the dim light of a gas lamp and I decided to go through his pockets. His wallet was crammed full of marks and he also had a small pocket book that listed numerous accounts. There on the pages were payments made for various kidnappings…dwarves, elves, goblins. It seemed that Scuzzer and Tranter had a good little business going on between them. They were paid twenty marks per head and that night three more names had gone into the book already…the last one of which must have been the drunken goblin at The Jolly Sailor.

"I'll bet that's what happened to that fellow you were looking for. They seem to be picking on sprites", said Hamble.

"I've been thinking on those lines myself; I witnessed a similar event earlier on."

"The locals reckon that none of them ever come back? That's the strange thing. …they just disappear. And they say that there's no point calling The Guardians because they just aren't interested…at least not if it's sprites."

"But where are they taking them….and for what? It's not like the old days when they were desperate for sailors."

"And then there's the other thing…" I looked at Hamble unsure of just what he meant.

"The other thing?"

"Well you've got to ask yourself, Humphrey…wherever they take these sprites…do they want them dead or alive?" The thought that I might have ended up as dead meat had never occurred to me and I confess I felt the slightest bit faint at the prospect. I knew that no one was ever going to pay me for this (this seemed to be becoming a habit) but it would be something I had to get to the bottom of. Hamble and I rolled Scuzzer into a nearby pile of old fish boxes and headed off for the last barge home. As we walked along the quiet damp quayside, I stopped Hamble in his tracks.

"We forgot about all that money."

Hamble smiled at me in the light of the dim streetlamps and held up the old leather wallet. "I don't know anything about myself, Humphrey Boggart, I don't know whether I am a good man or a bad man…but I do know that Scuzzer is definitely a bad man and that a lot of people have been hurt in order for him to get his hands on all this. At some point in time I will decide what the best thing to do with it is. Until that moment comes, I'll stick hold of it."

"You know what, Hamble Titchmarsh, I'm sure you will discover that you are indeed a good man." In the distance, the bright lights of the last barge to ThurMar pierced the gloom.

*

I guess the effects of the night before had taken their toll on me as I struggled to get out of my bed. I opened the door to the outer office and the first thing that I saw was a gun. Behind it was the beautiful Scarlett.

"Blood and sand, Scarlett! What are you doing with a gun?" Cowering on the pointy end of it was Hamble who had apparently been interrupted in mid-shave due to the white soapy beard that framed the rictus of fear on his face.

"I always carry one; a girl isn't safe these days. Anyway, never mind me, what are you going to do about him?" She thrust the gun in Hamble's direction and the old man shrank in terror.

"That's Hamble," I assured her as I eased the gun, not without some resistance, from her grasp. "He's a guest; I said he could stay here until he gets himself fixed up. I'm sorry; I guess I should have told you."

"You're not kidding, you should have told me; I could have shot him!" I noted the angry look on her pretty face and had to concede she was probably right. Make a mental note to tell Scarlett everything, I told myself. Hamble went back to finishing his shave after the briefest of introductions and Scarlett flounced on her chair and proceeded to start work.

"We'll begin with your diary, shall we?" she said pulling out a compact book from her bag.

"What do I need a diary for?"

"Well if someone comes looking for you, I can tell them where you are. So, where will you be today?"

"I don't know, I'm supposed to be looking for this mystery boggart but I also need to be out of town."

"Well what about you tell me what you're working on then perhaps I'll have some idea about what I need to do. So, what's the name of this boggart you're looking for?"

"I don't know!"

"What do you mean 'you don't know'?" Scarlett's face began to complement her name.

"I don't know his name because that's what I am trying to find out…his name! That's why I've been calling him the 'mystery boggart!'"

"OK…" I'll give Scarlett her due, she doesn't do flustered. "Who is it that has asked you to find out his name?"

"Er…Queen…er…Mrs King!"

"Right so we'll call that the Mrs King case, shall we?"

"If you want."

"Any more cases?"

"Well sort of…"

"What do you mean…sort of?"

"Well I don't really know; there are the disappearances and then there's Hamble and there's the rosebud man." Scarlett shot me a glance.

"Rosebud man?"

"Yeah…the guy who was shot in town the other day. His last word was…*Rosebud*."

"Oh…but really Mr Boggart, just who is going to pay for all these cases? I need to keep a record of our clients in order that they pay for your services. So, you've got the disappearances…of whom?"

"I don't know yet."

"Right, so you're trying to find someone called…"

"I don't know their name…names…yet". Scarlett sighed.

"And the client's name is?"

"Mr Scuzzer and Mr Tranter." I watched her right the names down in her book.

"And this…Hamble fellow…is he paying for his own case?" I looked over at Hamble more through exasperation than desperation and he nodded his head.

"That's Mr Titchmarsh to you, Scarlett." She gave a short glance at the old man who was combing the ring of hair that surrounded his bald head.

"So that just leaves this 'rosebud man'. Who is the client who wishes you to pursue this case?" She looked up at me with her beautiful green eyes. I cleared my throat.

"His name is…" I watched her with quill poised. "His name is Boggart, Humphrey Boggart." I expected a reaction but got none as she wrote the name into her book without looking up.

"Right…the diary…will you be available at all times today?"

"Er…no…"

"OK…"

"I'm going with Jonty…er Mr JT Thumb on a mission."

"So, shall I say you'll be out for the rest of the day?"

"Yes…I expect I will."

I felt guilty watching her write it down in the diary knowing full well I would be gone for a few days. It would be the first time I had gone back to the country since I had settled in ThurMar. I was not going back to my home but to Jonty's place of birth. The Guardians had released the rosebud man's body for burial and Jonty had found out that the man was to be buried at the village of Without. As his brother Plum Thumb was the village undertaker, Jonty had agreed to accompany the coffin back to the village. Somebody had paid for the man to be buried there but nobody knew just who it was. That in itself was interesting.

"Where is it that you are going?" asked Scarlett as she sucked on a pencil that she had sharpened to within an inch of its life. "Just in case someone asks…"

"And why would they?" I was getting angry with her now.

"Well…they might need to contact you and if I know exactly where you are then I can tell them can't I?" She gave me one of her special withering looks. "So…where are you going?" Her quill was once again poised over the book.

"I am going to the village of Without-the-Wall. Just outside the Wall of Thorns apparently."

Scarlett's reaction surprised me. "Why are you going there? It's miles away…you'll be gone for a day or two at least!" I guess that now she had a job, she didn't want to be alone here so soon.

"We're attending a funeral….for 'the Rosebud man'. Without is the only place he can be connected to. It was Jonty who saw him first…he said that it was almost as if he had come right through the Wall of Thorns. Then he stole Jonty's bike and disappeared until we saw him coming into the city."

"Did he say anything to Mr Thumb?"

"Not really, he just said he was sorry and then muttered something about getting the police."

"The police?"

"Yeah…we think it's a bit like The Guardians."

"So why are you and Mr Thumb going to the funeral?

"Well because we feel that somebody should; nobody should be alone at their funeral." Scarlett seemed satisfied with the answer and turned back to her work. Just at that moment, Hamble came in from the back room looking considerably smarter from the first time I had seen him.

"Humphrey... Miss Alewife!" I nodded my head at Hamble, while Scarlett returned to her paperwork and mumbled from beneath her striking red hair.

"All set for your first day at work, Hamble?" Jonty had been only too willing to give the old fellow a job after the loss of Sphagnum. "I've told him to go easy on you."

"I've never been frightened of hard work, Humphrey. At least I don't think I have..." he added as an afterthought.

"Come on, I'll take you round. And Scarlett...you'll be all right won't you? You've got enough work to be getting on with." Without lifting her head up from the page she was writing in, she said.

"Oh don't worry about me while you're off enjoying yourself in the countryside. I've got plenty to keep me occupied!" As I pulled the door behind me I just heard something that sounded like "I'll just carry on writing about" - bang went the door - "-ing hobbits, shall I?"

"Charming girl," said Hamble as we walked along the corridor towards Jonty's. "Is she local? It's just-" We knocked on Jonty's door and waited. I had told him all about Hamble and he seemed quite happy to help the poor fellow out. The door opened and the little man bustled us through to his office. He was just about to start telling Hamble what jobs he wanted doing when he stopped in his tracks.

"Do I know you from somewhere?" said Jonty. Hamble looked at a loss.

"Well you might do...but I'm not even sure if I know myself from somewhere." Jonty looked confused for a second until he remembered what I had told him about his new assistant.

"Oh yes...yes...I remember now. You've lost your memory, haven't you? It's just that I seem to know your face. I get the feeling that I've seen it somewhere prominent...but I can't for the life of me remember where?" Jonty snapped out of his reverie and proceeded to tell Hamble how he wanted a great pile of handbills counting, boxing and delivering to numerous addresses around the city. "There's a street map in the desk if you need it...but don't worry if you can't find any of the addresses as I've got a little ahead of myself with the work. They're not really due till next week." He stared once again at Hamble's face. "Extraordinary!" He shook his head in frustration. "Well, come on Humphrey, we'll never get to Without-the-Wall if we don't get a shift on."

Both Jonty and me stopped in the doorway as Hamble burst into song.

"*Some of them live without the wall and some of them live within. Those who stayed within the wall were never seen again*". When a sixty year old man starts singing a nursery rhyme for no reason, it kind of takes you by surprise. Jonty had a stupid look on his face.

"I haven't heard that since I was babe-in-arms!" he said. "My mother used to threaten me with it to make sure I came in at night." I looked at Hamble who was shaking his head as if he was trying to get rid of something.

"It's not a nursery rhyme that I remember." I said, hoping this might lead somewhere.

"That's because it was a song that was particular to the two villages", said Jonty. "Without-the-Wall and Within-the-Wall....just like the rhyme says. When the Wall of Thorns appeared and the Palace of Fotherghyll was...how shall we say...closed for business, well that was the end of the village of Within."

"Jonty, would you mind if Hamble came with us to Without?"

"No, like I said, the work I've given him isn't urgent. Why?"

"Don't you see? If Hamble knows the rhyme like you do, then perhaps he comes from Without as well."

"But surely if he came from Without, I would know him; we are about the same age."

"Good point," I conceded.

"Do you know of *any* Titchmarshes in Without?"

"Not off the top of my head...but the name does seem familiar."

"It's worth a shot, don't you think?" Both of us looked at Hamble who just sat in a chair with his head in his hands.

The way to the City's Charnel House was not unpleasant...for us three at least. We crossed the road and took a short cut through Caravan Park. Once we were in the park, I noticed a change come over Hamble. Jonty and I were chatting amiably as we walked but I couldn't help but notice that Hamble was dead-heading roses without breaking step. I thought it best not to say anything as Jonty clearly hadn't noticed it. As we left the rose garden and progressed along the side of a large herbaceous border, Hamble started to become agitated. His eyes kept darting to the various shrubs that lined the pathway. Jonty was busy blathering on about Sphagnum needing to borrow some bolt-cutters for something but I was intrigued as Hamble recited what seemed to be an unknown language.

"I think he's practising to be an escapologist. What do you think?" Jonty's question broke my concentration... "I said, 'what do you think?'"

"About what?"

"About Sphagnum being an escapologist. I was just saying he got himself fast in a set of chains and he needed bolt-cutters to get out of them."

"Oh...right...yeah...must be that then." Hamble was still reciting the gibberish as we reached the pride of Caravan Park, its beautiful golden bean arch. He stood there amazed by the glorious cascades of yellow blooms hanging from long walkway.

"It's beautiful!" he cried. "I've never seen it done like this before! They've obviously trained it over the archway. Just beautiful!" Jonty and I watched in amazement as Hamble fingered the plants with a tenderness that belied his thick calloused hands. He squatted on his haunches and grabbed a pinch of soil before tasting it and nodding his head in approval.

"He's a gardener, Jonty! Hamble's a gardener! That's what he was doing while you were rabbitting-on about Sphagnum…he was naming the plants in the border."

"Well I suppose he looks like he knows what he's doing," harrumphed Jonty. Intelligent men never like to be accused of rabbitting-on. "Anyway, shouldn't we be making tracks…we don't want to miss the barge."

At the City Charnel House, Jonty signed the papers in triplicate and the three of us waited while an ox-cart with the coffin on board came round to the front of the building. It had a dead man on the back and another seemed to be in the driving seat.

"Hop on, lads!" shouted the cadaverous old man charged with taking us all to the barge station.

"Blimey, do they know he's out!" I whispered to Jonty. The three of us climbed up onto the seat, switching positions when Jonty let it be known he didn't like sitting in the middle. We shuffled round on the bench before our driver chucked his ox into action. Jonty was excited about taking the coffin back on the canal to Without-the-Wall.

"I haven't been on the sleeper barge for some time. It's much quicker by stage-coach but not half as comfortable. It's a lovely journey, Humphrey, I'm sure you'll enjoy it. And there are all sorts of interesting architectural features along the way. It's a pity we have to get off before the Mile Tunnel. It's simply an outstanding piece of engineering..."

The progress was slow and I took advantage of our high position to look around. I turned in my seat and noticed something further up the street. A familiar figure wearing a long coat and a black brimmed hat was summoning an ox-cart over to the side of the road. Last time I had seen him it had been at the football ground just before he tried to assassinate the Massy Witch. He seemed to be gesturing that the driver follow us, which caused me some puzzlement...maybe I was being paranoid. After all we were just carrying a dead body to the barge station. What possible interest could he have in us?

Jonty continued to enthuse about the canal system beyond Without which we weren't going to be seeing anyway. "Every hundred yards or so there is a ventilation shaft to let the stale air out. I bet you don't know, Humphrey, why the Mile Tunnel isn't built in a straight line?" I shook my head before checking back over my shoulder to see if the second ox-cart was gaining on us. Jonty continued with the lesson. "When they had started building the tunnel, they decided to begin it at both ends. The idea was that both tunnels would meet up in the middle...when it became obvious that they wouldn't, they had to put a large bend in the tunnel!"

The ox-wagon was still keeping a steady pace behind us. When I mentioned this to Hamble he turned around and shrugged.

"Where else could it go?" he said, indicating the small side streets. I nodded at his reasoning but the whole situation didn't feel right. For the sake of my own satisfaction, I needed to check this man out.

Jonty was still going on about the wonders of canal architecture in the Fotherghyll region. "...they have to switch off the coal engines and 'leg' it through the tunnel..."

"Hmm," I added. Just then an old water sprite, who despite his arthritic knees, was keeping pace with our ox-cart, recognised Jonty and called across to him. Thankfully, while they were speaking to each other, it put an end to Jonty's interminable rambling about the canal system. Behind me I noticed that the trailing ox-cart had pulled up. It *was* following us! After a minute or so, I nudged Jonty in the ribs and asked what the old water sprite wanted.

"He's going to the barge station as well. I told him it's a pity we've no more room on the bench."

"Can't he hop on the back?"

Jonty laughed, "I suggested that but he said people might think he'd risen from the dead." As we approached the right turn onto the city's main thoroughfare Great Canal Street, I had an idea.

"Tell him when we get round the corner, he can take my place..." Jonty looked dumbfounded. "...provided he wears my hat." Jonty's level of dumbfounded-ness reached new peaks, so I put him out of his misery. "There's a guy who seems to be following us…it's too much of a coincidence…I think it's the assassin from the football match."

"Oh…I read about that in the paper" said Jonty. I sighed.

"I just need to know why he's following us. Don't worry about me, I'll see you in Without." After we had turned into Great Canal Street, I slipped off the cart and helped push the old water sprite into my seat. I threw him my hat and watched them move off. "And sit up a bit!" I shouted before slinking into the nearest shop which, ironically, turned out to be a hat shop.

As the ox-cart with my pursuer on board went past the window, I noted that he was intent on watching our progress along Great Canal Street. His black hat, like mine, was pulled down over his eyes and I couldn't clearly see his face. I decided to follow him…following me. I needed to look inconspicuous so I paid the hatter for the nearest thing he had to my own hat…which unfortunately happened to be pea green in colour. As I headed out onto the street, I saw my quarry jump carefully off the ox-cart and head down the pavement. I watched in horror as he pulled out a gun and took aim. The sound of the gun going off stopped everyone dead in the street and many of them dropped to the ground. In the distance I could see my beloved hat flying through the air as my companions hit the floor of the ox-cart. The assassin fled across the Silvergate Bridge, but as my first concern was for the old water sprite who had taken my place, I decided not to follow him. I ran down to the ox-cart and was relieved to see everyone was safe and sound, the cadaverous driver was still shaking and the old water sprite was slumped on the floor of the cart.

"Oh, my days! Are you all right, sir?" I shook him until he managed to turn round.

He grinned through multi-coloured teeth. "Frightened me so much I stood up straight for the first time in years. Only problem was my knees locked and I fell over. Sorry about your hat though, son. Shouldn't think you'd want it back now you got that nice new fancy one." Talking of the hat, it was Hamble who hurried back to the ox-cart holding it in his hand. His finger poked through the bullet hole in the crown.

"That was meant for you." Hamble was nothing if not to the point. "Did you see who did it?"

"Yeah, he was off like a whippet. Must have thought I'd bought it." Just at that moment the sound of the Guardians hand-bell could be heard in the distance. Within minutes they were at the scene. Six humourless hulks, the brightest and most decorated of which approached me.

"Excuse me, citizen. We have reason to believe a murder has been committed here. Could you show us where the body is?

When the Guardians had digested the information that there wasn't actually a body to cart off, except the one on the back of our cart...which they had only just given us in the first place, they disappeared as quickly as they had arrived.

"Might as well complete the journey together, then," said Jonty as he got back aboard the ox-cart.

"Oh, I suppose that means, I've lost my lift now," said the old water sprite. Just then something across the Great Canal caught my eye. There he was. As bold as a bear at a picnic, the assassin was on the other side of canal watching the proceedings. He had no reason to believe he wasn't successful as the place had been swarming with Guardians.

"He's over there," I whispered to Jonty and Hamble, "I've got to go after him. But how can I get across the canal?"

"I think I know," said Jonty and he turned to the old water sprite. "Your family have worked the ferries for years, Harrell. Can you get Mr Boggart over the canal?"

"No, but I know a man who can." He turned and gave a shrill whistle and three small red-hooded heads popped above the edge of the canal-side. "Stanli, get Mr Boggart over to the other side as sharp as you can." A young water sprite raised his thumb up in readiness.

Time was not on my side. "Jonty, you and Hamble will have to go to Without…er…without me. I'll make my own way there and…where can we meet up?"

"The Sleeping Beauty," said Jonty, "that's the name of the inn in Without. We'll meet you there." I nodded, grabbed my holed hat, ran across the road and shot down the quayside steps into the little boat. Stanli, who was wearing the traditional red hooded coat of the ThurMar ferrymen, took to the oars and started rowing.

119

"I suppose this must be a freebie if the old man wants me to do it. So don't expect me to sing as well." He rowed across the canal at quite an impressive speed and I could see the assassin walking down the far quay. He seemed confident that his work was done.

"Stanli, do you know the left bank well?"

"Like the back of my hand, mate."

"I wonder if you'd act as my guide over there."

"It'll cost you but..." he held out his hand, "put it there." And as he looked at his outstretched hand, he added, "Here, I've never noticed that wart on my knuckle before."

Just as we docked on the far side of The Great Canal, I spotted the assassin rounding a corner into what looked to be an open square. I dropped a few marks into Stanli's hand and stood by while he tied up his little boat. At the top of the stairs we had to wait for a gap in the horse-drawn traffic until we could scurry across the road.

"Which way did he go?" called Stanli as his little red coat fanned out behind him.

"He turned into that square...but after that...I don't know."

"Probably heading into The Ginnels...don't worry...I know that like-"

"Yeah, yeah...the back of your hand...I know. Come on." The two of us hared across the square and into one of the small lanes that ran off it. The Ginnels were a series of tight-knit alleys and small canals that had a dubious reputation. It was said that if you were ever lost in The Ginnels then the locals would treat you as one of their own…which meant that they would be quite happy to rob you of all your possessions and leave you for dead.

Once we had gone quite a way into The Ginnels, dark clouds gathered over the city and it started to rain. It was the sort of rain that made you long for a good all over wash as soon as you got home. Stanli pulled his hood over his head and burrowed further into narrow lanes.

"Stick close to me and you won't go wrong," he grinned.

At the next turn we made, both of us stopped dead as we saw someone crawling on their hands and knees across the cobbled lane. Stanli approached the man and asked him if he had a tall man wearing a large brimmed hat. The man looked up from the floor and when he saw me he scurried away to the shelter of a nearby wall. Stanli questioned him further. On the floor at my feet, I spotted a small bloodied object which the rain was in the process of cleaning up. At first I struggled to identify just what it was. So I bent down and picked it up.

"He thinks you've come back for the other one," said Stanli returning from the cowering man. "Apparently he confronted a man dressed similarly to yourself a few minutes ago. Thought he'd relieve him of a few things. The man brought out a knife and removed this gentleman's ear. That's what he was doing on the floor…looking for it." I handed Stanli the piece of gristle I had picked up.

Far from flinching, Stanli held the ear to his lips and whispered into it. "It's all right, my friend. We've found it." With that, a grin split his face and revealed a set of sharp green teeth. The whole incident made me wonder how safe I was with Stanli, never mind the ruthless assassin I was pursuing. My guide handed the man his ear back and beckoned me to follow him.

As we ran over a small bridge, I mused over why the man wanted his ear back in the first place. There was nothing he could do with it…perhaps he just didn't want anybody else to have it…maybe give it a decent burial or something. Stanli was a quick mover and as he scurried down the other side of the little canal bridge and flew down the next alley, I was finding it difficult to keep up with him. I watched him take the next right before being mystified when he then headed back across my path and towards the left direction. Heading after him, I relaxed a bit as he was now moving at hardly much more than a walk. I pulled him back by the shoulder to ask him a question. For my trouble I received a knife to my throat and an unfamiliar water sprite face scowling back at me.

"In these parts, stranger, men have died for less than grabbing my shoulder." I jabbered my apology, held my hands aloft and turned to run the other way. Not knowing which way to go I stood and listened to the rain tapping on the brim of my hat. Stanli was nowhere to be seen. I contemplated shouting out to him but realised this would only advertise to the locals that I was both lost and an easy target. It would also possibly alert the assassin. Convinced that my silence would be the surest way to get out of here alive, my stomach lurched as I heard Stanli's melodious voice calling out my name.

"Mr Bog-gart! Where are you?" His call echoed over the damp stone cobbles, possibly notifying the assassin that the man he had just supposedly killed was now alone in the dark

122

labyrinthine lanes. Despite Stanli's constant calling the sound played tricks on me and his voice seemed to get further and further away whenever I felt I was heading towards it. The mean-spirited buildings ahead, rain dripping off their edges like crocodile tears, seemed to be lying in wait for me. The further I ventured into the warren, the darker and more ominous my being there became. It was lunchtime but it felt like night. Stanli had obviously given up on me as I heard his voice no more. I thought about how I might extricate myself from this living drain and headed towards the nearest bridge in the hope that a passing boatman might take me back to the bright lights of The Great Canal. As if to compound my fear and misery, the rain began to fall with more determination than ever. The darkness intensified. I caught my breath for a second before a flash of lightning illuminated the moment for me. Like some kind of fairground attraction designed both to thrill and to terrify a tall figure in a damp long coat and wide-brimmed hat stood in a nearby doorway.

"Who are you?" I asked trying to hide the fear in my voice. He stepped from the doorway with a certain clumsiness and approached me. Like myself; his hat was pulled down over his eyes. As if by his command, the rain stopped.

"Good afternoon, Mr Boggart. I thought you were dead." Despite the presence of water all around us, his voice was as dry as dead leaves. "Now I shall have the renewed pleasure of killing you again." From his pocket he brought out a flick-knife and began to walk towards me. With no means of protecting myself, I turned to run and splashed towards a small bridge that arced over a small canal. As I ran I looked back and took brief comfort from the fact that my pursuer wasn't the fastest man in the world. I turned up onto the bridge and headed across to the darkness of the other side. Taking a right where the small canal branched into two I plunged deep into a covered alley, I headed into its unlit depths; the echo of my pursuer's plodding steps offered no clue to whether he had made the same choice as me. The small canal that had accompanied me along the alley had pulled up short in a high-walled courtyard. The place might have once been a busy loading point but its covered storage areas were now empty. I looked around for an exit but the pervasive darkness from the surrounding walls offered little in the way of hope. A scurrying noise above my head made me look up to the roofs that dipped down into the yard and I wondered about the possibility of climbing out of this dead end when I heard the sound of my pursuer entering the courtyard. A few lights went on in the upper windows as I began to shout for help, but this was The Ginnels and people knew better than to interfere in what happened outside their houses, even during the day. That was why they were still alive and I was about to meet my end.

"Really, Mr Boggart, why prolong the inevitable? I have been assigned to kill you; it was only a matter of time." My enemy stepped closer towards me and pulled a gun out of his coat. "This time I won't take any chances."

"But who are you?" He reached inside his trenchcoat and proffered me his card.

"Alaric Deadman", I read, "Contract killer *no job too small…weddings a speciality*"

"That's pronounced *Deed*man actually.

And who is it that wants me out of the way?"

124

"Too many questions, Mr Boggart. The answers to which are not really your concern anymore." He pointed the gun at my chest…

The scuttling noise on a nearby roof made both Deadman and me look up. A black shadow threw itself at my assassin's head and knocked it clean off his shoulders and into the canal cut-off. I stared with disbelief as the shadow morphed into a human shape and told me in a harsh whisper to "Move!" I stood my ground with a dumb look on my face.

"But you've just knocked his head off his shoulders!" The black-clothed person persisted with the command.

"Move! He's not dead!" Open-mouthed I watched as Deadman's headless body got to its feet and stumbled towards the canal in search of its head.

"Over here, you idiot!" said Deadman's head as it bobbed up and down in the dark waters as his decapitated body stretched out to reunite them. I gaped in disbelief and then turned to run. Following my black-clothed rescuer was not an option as they had vanished without trace. I turned and headed back the way I had come, racing down the damp, dark streets until I had put as many cobbles between me and the strange un-dead assassin. My fears of being alone in The Ginnels were secondary now as I knew that there were worse things walking the streets. Unsurprisingly, the inhabitants of the area seemed to know that now was not a good time to be out and about and I saw not another soul until I gleaned a flash of red up ahead. Was it Stanli or some other canal ferryman on their way to work? I decided I would take the risk and headed after him. A bridge was not a good place to stand talking when it could be viewed from further down the canal, so I let the red-hooded person descend down into the next alleyway before I called to them. The face that turned towards me was one that I recognised but it wasn't Stanli's.

"Hello, love. Would you like to play a little game with me?" Underneath her red hood was a girl I had once known back home.

"I need to get back to The Great Canal."

"Lost your way, have you, love? You should know better than stray from the path." A poignant look came over her eyes.

"Look, Red, if I take you to a tavern and buy you a few drinks, will you promise me you'll go home?"

"Ooh, you're trying to get me drunk so that you can take advantage of me, aren't you?" She grabbed my hand and together we walked through The Ginnels.

She noticed that I was looking over my shoulder all the time and commented on it. "What you scared of, love…the bogeyman?"

"Something like that." A sudden dawning came over Red's face.

"Here, how did you know my name?"

I raised my hat. "You obviously don't recognise me; I used to be the Lepping Stones Boggart back home." She stared hard at my face for a while and then the coin dropped.

"Of course I didn't flaming recognise you…you were invisible, weren't you?" She pushed my chest and laughed out loud. I clapped my hands over her mouth and for the first time she looked frightened.

"Red, listen to me. There is a cold-blooded killer walking The Ginnels at this very moment and we need to get out of here as quickly as we can. I released her and she took my hand. Together we ran up the street.

*

Spending time with a working girl in the Frog and Ferryman's Arms was just the sort of thing I was having to come to terms with since I'd become a private dick.

"So, Red, how long have you been on the game?"

"Since I came to the city…I just had to get away from the forest and all that. That thing with Grandma did my head in."

"Yeah, I suppose having a loved one eaten by a wolf isn't easy to live with."

"I don't know about that…it's seeing a wolf cut open and your frail old grandmother popping out that did for me. I could never hug her after that without smelling the whiff of meat about her. So I decided to come out here. I just drifted into the game." Red shuffled the cards like an expert and dealt seven cards to both of us. I knew I was in for a beating as I had heard that these girls were good.

"Deadman's Knock?" said Red.

"What?"

Red seemed unconcerned at my reaction as she carried on shuffling. "Nines are floating and one-eyed Jacks take all." I nodded; it had been a while since I had played this game. I took a slug of my whiskey and fanned out the cards. I figured staying in the tavern would be safe enough. Surely Deadman wouldn't risk killing me in the open?

"So, what are you doing in the big city?" said Red, "And dressed like I don't know what." I told her about my new job and she genuinely seemed happy for me. As I spent the rest of the damp afternoon being fleeced by an expert, I let my mind wander. The question that was uppermost in my thoughts was - who was the mystery person who came to my rescue…and why they had bothered in the first place?

*

Early next morning I had gone back across the city to the office. I had spent all of yesterday evening with Red and to her credit she had taken some of the pressure off me. She had also taken most of the contents of my wallet off me. When you come so close to dying it sharpens your senses to the point of discomfort…I was in need of a diversion and laughing at bygone days with an old friend was certainly that. When I arrived back at the office, I noticed that the door had been broken off its hinges. I reached for the base-ball bat I had picked up at a local market stall and prepared to meet my intruder. The reception room had been turned upside down and as I looked at all the damage I heard the slightest sound coming from the back room. I walked to the door and gently pushed it open. Then everything went dark.

When I came round, it was Scarlett who was pressing the damp cloth onto my swollen brow.

"I'm sorry, Humphrey, I thought it was the intruder coming back."

"What hit me?" I mumbled.

"Er...it was me...I did say I was sorry."

"Has anything been taken?"

"I don't think so...er...I think your book, the one about the hobbits, might have been stolen." I struggled to my feet with Scarlett's help and smiled.

"You don't get away with it that easily, my dear. I can see the book over there, sticking out of your bag." Scarlett turned to where I was pointing. I think I heard her swear.

"It was like this when I came in this morning. Have you any idea who might have done it?"

"I've a feeling someone has got it in for me. As you know I'm supposed to be away but...well let's just say something cropped up. I'm still going to Without-the-Wall today and I suggest you keep away from here until I get back."

"But what about the book?" Scarlett could do mock concern really well.

"I guess it can wait."

"I presume this is paid leave?"

"Yes…three days paid leave. I hope to be back before then, OK?" She kissed me on the forehead. I flinched.

"Oops…sorry…I forgot."

*

The barge station was really busy but, as it was seven o'clock, it was only to be expected. I kept glancing around to see if my nemesis was waiting for another chance. As I got my ticket for the 7.15 sleeper barge, I turned to face a row of open newspapers. Behind any one of them could be the man who was trying to kill me. The barge and trailer arrived on time, which was not unusual as there weren't any locks between the Fleetpool harbour and the main barge station. As the conductor showed me to my sleeping berth in the trailer, I asked him if there was anyone on board wearing a black brimmed hat and a long coat.

"What do you think?" he smirked. Just what I needed…a smart arse.

"Well if you see someone dressed like that would you let me know?"

"It'll cost you…" I gave him a five mark note and plumped up the pillow in my bed a little harder than necessary.

The steam-powered barge and sleeper trailer were about to set off so I walked back up the gangplank onto the quay and made my way along to check out the amenities on the steam barge. At the corresponding gangplank I looked behind me and there at the entrance to the sleeper barge was Deadman, complete with snarling head. We stood facing each other along the quay. The conductor blew his whistle. I hurried aboard the barge and Deadman mirrored my movement onto the sleeper. I ran back up the gangplank and Deadman was back standing on the quay. As I made to walk back on board Deadman was ready to do the same.

"Make up your bleeding mind!" said the barge hand who was about to pull up the gangway. At the sleeper barge another man was poised ready to pull up his plank. Deadman saw his chance and began to walk towards me, his hand moving to his pocket. As the barge pulled away, I threw myself at the receding hull and managed to scramble aboard as a bullet from Deadman's gun splintered the wood at my shoulder. People on the quayside screamed and fled like ripples in a pond away from the cold stone that was Deadman. Crawling on all fours I made my way up to the cabin and caught my breath alongside the coal store.

"You all right, mate?" A strong smell of onions overpowered me as I looked into the white-rimmed eyes of the barge pilot squatting down beside me.

"There's a guy on the quay who's trying to kill me!" I hollered above the sound of the engine.

"Where?" He stood up. The sound of gunfire was followed by him falling overboard. It went dark. I realised we were passing under the Grand Bridge and due to the numerous steps, both up and down the other side, I knew

Deadman would have fallen behind us for a little while. As we passed into the light beyond the bridge, the conductor arrived.

"Where's Pilot Mann?"

"Er...he's been shot. You know I said a man dressed like me was looking for me?" He nodded. "He's been shooting at me and he hit the Pilot." The conductor lost his assuredness.

"Where's is he now?"

"He fell overboard." The conductor's mouth gaped.

"What, Pilot Mann?"

"Fell overboard."

"Oh no, what are we going to do?"

"I suggest we notify The Guardians immediately." The conductor recovered somewhat.

"We can't be doing that? We've got a timetable to run to, you know?"

"But a man has been shot and probably killed...surely there's need to notify the authorities?"

"To be quite honest I don't think he'll be missed. Not a person you could get close to."

"Bit of a loner, was he?"

"No...too many cheese and onion sandwiches...his breath could strip paint."

133

The conductor's face blanched. "Oh my giddy aunt! There's nobody driving!"

"Can't *you* steer it to the side of the canal? Preferably that side." I pointed to the opposite bank to the one Deadman was on.

"No, I can not! I am a qualified conductor and as a fully paid up member of the Bargehands and Pilots Union (white collar branch) I am not qualified and my collar's not dirty enough to pilot this barge."

"Well is there anyone on board who can pilot it?"

"There's Pilot Bilsborrow."

"Thank the gods for that…go and get him!"

"I can't. It's more than my job's worth."

"What?" I screamed, half exasperated, half hysterical as I could see Deadman making his way back down the steps to the quay.

"He'll go berserk if I wake him. He's the night driver…he doesn't come on till 9.30. He's having a kip in the sleeper barge."

"Well I suggest you wake him up!"

"You *are* joking, he's about six foot five in his stockinged feet. I'm not waking him. He once threw a conductor in the canal just for sneezing as he walked past his berth. Can't *you* drive it?"

"What?"

"Can't you drive the barge? I'll not say anything if you don't. Bilsborrow will take over from you at 9.30. He's quite amenable when he's had a good sleep."

"But what about the pilot?"

"Oh somebody will fish him out."

Deadman was getting nearer and I realised that while he would never be the quickest person to chase after you, he was nothing if not relentless. I cursed the fact that the means of travel I had chosen was no quicker than walking. As the barge engine's idled and momentum was the only force propelling us forward I realised that the possibility of Deadman reaching the next bridge before us was a very real one. I raced to the pilot's cabin and screamed at the conductor.

"What do I have to do?"

"Just steer it and keep putting coal into that fire." I picked up a large lump of coal, threw it into the boiler and stood back.

"You'll be better using the shovel," said the conductor.

BARGE CHASE

I dozed in my berth dreaming of the endless shovelling of coal into thousands of pot-bellied stoves, the conductor came up to me and knocked on my curtains.

"You asked me to let you know if I saw anyone dressed in a long coat and big hat." I sat up and tried to focus on his face. "Well a taller version of you is stood at the front of a coal barge about half a mile or so behind us." I followed the conductor to the back of the sleeper barge and saw Deadman, bold as a duelling scar, standing on the prow of the following barge. He waved at me. A cough from the conductor prompted me to hand him another five mark note. I stared across at my enemy. It was obvious he was a hard man to shake off. I would need to use all of my training as a nasty, evil little boggart.

"Without Cut-Off!" announced the barge conductor, some minutes later, to his passengers. To me he said, "You get off here and take a smaller barge down to the village." As some of the passengers stood up to collect their various belongings, I tried to work out whether the coal barge would catch us up before we could get off again. I knew I couldn't risk getting out now. At some stage soon I would have to fool Deadman that I was still on the barge and now wasn't the time. I looked ahead and saw the mouth of the Mile Tunnel swallowing the waters of the canal. The conversation Jonty had with himself about the Mile Tunnel the other day came back to me. I was somewhat grateful when I noticed that the Pilot Bilsborrow had moored the barge so that no one could get past it. I handed the conductor a ten mark note and told him I was staying on board.

"Suit yourself," he said pocketing the note. The tunnel mouth lay up ahead and fortunately there was no build up of barges waiting to pass through it. Jonty had said that the tunnel worked a system where traffic could only go through in one direction for an hour at a time. Fortunately the barge company timed its journeys accordingly and I could clearly see the green lantern shining over the tunnel mouth indicating that we could proceed through. Of course the coal barge could go through as well but it would have to keep some kind of distance between us. We waited while the new passengers boarded and settled themselves down for their journey further up the canal. The coal barge was closing in on us but I felt relieved by the almost steely determination of our pilot that it would not get to the tunnel mouth before us. Before all of the new passengers had settled down they were rocked off their feet by the sudden lurch into the centre of the canal by our barge. Straightening up, the pilot negotiated the few hundred yards before the tunnel mouth. The conductor collected the fares of the new passengers before going round and switching all the lanterns on. Up ahead before the tunnel mouth there was a small platform that jutted out into the canal. This I was told was where the 'leggers' got on. Sure enough waiting for us on the platform were two sturdily-built young men who hopped on the barge without the need for it to slow down. Once aboard I watched them as they fastened two planks to either side of the barge and laid themselves down upon them. As the barge reached the black mouth of the tunnel, the pilot switched off the engine and let his craft slide slowly into the tunnel's mouth. Once inside, the darkness would have swallowed us but for the flickering lanterns by which I managed to see the two 'leggers' set about their task. Slowly they walked along the sides of the tunnel, their great hobnail boots pushing the barge along. Jonty had told me that these men were a necessity for passenger barges. Being aboard a steam-powered barge in a cramped tunnel wasn't the most pleasant of experiences despite the frequent ventilation tunnels that lined the route. So passenger vehicles were still 'legged' through the tunnel. I noticed that the speed of our journey had slowed down somewhat from when we were under steam power. I asked the conductor whether the coal barge under its own steam would catch us up now that we were in the tunnel. He shook his head and smiled in the pale light of a lantern.

"Canal Company regulations state that steam-driven commercial traffic has to respect public transport and follow at a reasonable distance so as not to make travel through the tunnel unpleasant for fare paying passengers. And he could hardly overtake us in here, could he now?" I noticed a bright light ahead of us.

"What's that?" I pointed up the tunnel. The conductor turned around and nodded his head.

"Ventilation shaft. The light is from the outside. You get them every hundred yards or so." As we approached the first of these shafts I started to formulate a plan. The last rung of an iron ladder hung down into the tunnel allowing a person to stand on top of the barge cabin and climb up the shaft. I knew that the sooner I made my escape the longer it would take Deadman to discover that I was gone, but I had to make sure that my pursuer didn't see me. Looking behind, I could clearly see the coal barge's pilot light in the distance. In front of it, the light from the receding shaft illuminated the area around so clearly that I knew Deadman would be able to see

138

me making my escape. Then I recalled something Jonty had said about the tunnel not being straight. Hadn't he said that they had to make a bend in it to join the two ends up? If his information was correct, then we must be close to where the bend started. I strained my head to look behind me and for the first time I couldn't see the coal barge's pilot lamp.

Seizing the opportunity, I headed towards the bow. I was grateful that Pilot Bilsborrow was optimising this period of inactivity by having a nap. Below me the 'leggers' were too busy moving the barge on to notice anyone climbing up towards the roof. There was very little headroom between the top of the cabin and the roof of the tunnel, so I could only pull myself up and lay face down. To grab the next ladder I needed to be on my back, so I flipped myself over. Now that the arched stone roof passed close by my face, I could smell the soot in the stonework. It was all I could do to stop myself from gagging.

Minutes passed and I lay there visualising what I needed to do. My plan was to grab the bottom rung of the next ladder that passed over my head. Then I would pull myself to my feet and climb up the shaft. The arrival of the light told me that the next shaft was approaching and I prepared myself. Quicker than I could react to, the ladder passed over my head and I reached up for it only to have it snatched out of my hands by the barge's deliberate progress. I had failed this time but I had to make sure that at my next attempt was successful. The wait for the next hundred yards to pass was eternal but this time I was more relaxed. I grabbed the bottom rung of the ladder and held on, letting the movement of the barge continue beneath me. I reached up for the next rung and found myself almost sitting on the cabin roof. Then, when that disappeared from beneath me I was left dangling in the gloom over the second class passengers. Hoisting myself up the ladder, I managed to get a purchase for my feet for the first time.

Despite the bend in the tunnel concealing my escape, I realised I had to get up the shaft before the coal barge passed underneath. If my pursuer was as good at his job as he seemed to be, I doubted he would miss the opportunity to look up each ventilation shaft as he passed beneath them.

Halfway up the shaft there was a refuge which allowed a person to rest awhile from climbing or descending. I managed to reach it just as the coal barge passed beneath me. A great plume of steam whooshed up the shaft and took my breath away for a few seconds. Coughing and spluttering I slumped down on the floor of the refuge. Only when I had got my breath back did I allow myself a smile.

Minutes later I was sitting on top of the ventilation shaft and gazing at the Wall of Thorns for the first time. Even though I felt I was looking down on it from the small hill, it seemed to go on without end concealing whatever lay behind it. I thought about the old tale of the sleeping princess and wondered whether it was true or not...still I suppose it made a good story. My next problem would be how to get down to the ground without breaking my legs. I walked around the top of the chimney and noticed a great clump of gorse; its bright yellow flowers making a mockery of the sharp thorns hidden beneath. Better a few scratches than broken bones, I thought and I hung down from the edge of the chimney before letting go.

After a painful half hour spent removing gorse thorns from my anatomy, I made my way, somewhat gingerly, down to the old track that skirted the Wall of Thorns. The country air was redolent with sweet scents that made me feel homesick for my spot by the river. Once a water boggart always a water boggart, I guess. I eased myself over the small wooden fence that divided the field from the track and headed back towards the village of Without. At the point that the old track headed through a small copse, I found my progress halted by a fallen tree. The cut at its base suggested it had been felled for timber but why had no one bothered to remove it? The tree itself crossed the path and plunged deep into the Wall of Thorns. Natural curiosity led me to take a closer look into the thorns to see just how impenetrable it was. A short walk along the trunk was soon halted by the brutal vegetation. It was then that I saw the man's leg.

THE GIANT INSECT

When I realised the tree trunk was lying on top of a man's body my first reaction was to jump off. My second told me not to. After all there was nowhere to go without shredding myself on the evil-looking thorns that surrounded me. The man was clearly dead and I squatted down to see if I could see his face but it was hidden from sight. The shredded sleeves revealed arms that still embraced the trunk, one of which bore a recognisable tattoo. I made my way back along the trunk and jumped onto the track. How might such a death have happened? Weighing up the options I decided that the man must have been climbing up the tree when it was cut down plunging him into the Wall of Thorns, but why was he up the tree in the first place and why did someone cut it down? It couldn't have been an accident because it obviously hadn't been reported. What seemed beyond doubt here was that this man had been murdered. Realising that there was little I could do about all this, I decided to head into the village, at least there I could report it to the Guardians.

I was about to start walking down the hill when I heard voices. My first reaction was to make sure I wasn't caught near the dead man, so I guess I just panicked. Before they came into sight I threw myself into the undergrowth at the side of the road. I caught my hip on something hard and sharp and had to bite my tongue to stop myself from crying out. After a minute or two I saw them…four of them. They were carrying guns of some sort so I assumed they were soldiers but they were unlike any soldier I had ever seen before. Their uniforms were not the bright and colourful ones we were used to seeing, instead they were wearing different shades of brown and green which made them hard to pick out against the background of the countryside. It was almost as if they didn't want to be seen. They were about fifty yards from me and obviously looking for something as they edged their way along the road. If I wasn't frightened before, I was when one of them fired his gun at some movement in the bushes. The report from the gun seemed to go on forever. I had never heard a sound like it. Bullet after bullet discharged into the bush. A minute or two later, the soldier came out dangling the bloodied carcass of what I could only presume had once been a rabbit. His colleagues' laughter was cut short when the lead soldier discovered the fallen tree and a moment later the dead body beneath it. They sprang into action and began to investigate. The lead soldier organised his men into a cordon around the incident. He then pulled something off his uniform and began talking into it.

"Hi Jimmy, it's Rob from the search party. Tell the gaffer that we've located a body. We've secured the area if he wants to check it out himself...he better bring chainsaws and perhaps some lifting gear...OK...will do. Over and out".

I knew from what I had seen that these men were ruthless but what were they doing around here? A small party of soldiers equipped with guns capable of killing a number of people in a matter of seconds could create havoc if they wanted to. I kept watch on them for almost fifteen minutes and as cramp began to set in I had to shift my position. Without thinking I put my hand on the hard thing I had caught my hip on when I first took refuge in the bushes. It was a piece of machinery that I had never seen before.

The bulk of it was a complication of metal that extended out into a long-toothed chain. I felt at it like a blind man as I feared to leave the soldiers out of my sight for a second. I must admit that I thought my credulity couldn't be stretched any further at that point but what I was next to see had me gasping for breath. At first I wasn't aware of the noise because the buzzing of insects was not high on my list of priorities at that moment. Then I saw it. There, in the distance, coming over the Wall of Thorns was what appeared to be a large winged insect flying towards us. Within its black body, the clear outline of a man could be seen. While I gaped in horror at what I was seeing, the soldiers seemed relatively unconcerned by its arrival. The noise it made got louder and louder until it was all around me and engulfing me in its sound. The leaves on the trees and bushes flapped as if trying to get away from the great wind created by its large wings. I wanted to run away so much but the strange mixture of fear and curiosity kept me grounded. The soldiers, who had stood guard minutes before, now ducked down in reverence, fearful of the wings of this strange beast. The insect landed and then I could see it was not a beast at all, its metal gleamed and from out of its belly stepped a man I had only ever seen before on wanted posters. The tattoo on the arm of the man under the tree would surely have brought him.

*

When I finally reached the village, I found Jonty and Hamble sat outside the local inn, The Sleeping Beauty. My friends were relieved to see that I had made it and excited to

144

tell me of *their* discovery. Their joint enthusiasm prevented me from telling them about my own adventure out by the Wall of Thorns. I would tell them later.

"You've got to see this!" said Jonty as he dragged me into the gloom of the inn. Once inside it took a while for my sight to get used to the darkness but Jonty guided me round the bar until I faced an old painting that stood by the entrance to the inn's garden. The dull use of colour made it fairly hard to distinguish it at first but there was no doubt who I was looking at. I turned to face Hamble, who understandably was also looking quite shocked. There in front of me was a painting that, given the style of clothing and age of the frame must have been over one hundred years old. I stared at the face in front of me before focusing in on the name plate at the portrait's base. It said...

HAMBLE TITCHMARSH

HEAD GARDENER

PALACE OF FOTHERGHYLL

"It must be your grandfather, Hamble!" was all I could think of to say.

The three of us walked into the square. The flag above the village hall was fluttering at half mast in a cool wind that suggested the weather was on the turn. The people of Without seemed to be going about their business as usual. Jonty led us both into the porch that fronted the village hall. Despite the soft light outside, the porch remained dark and in the centre of it, on two trestle tables, stood the coffin.

"They leave it here so that people can pay their last respects and all that," whispered Jonty more for the need to say something rather than anything else. The three of us stood in front of the coffin. I removed my hat and looked at the dead man for the first time since he died in my arms.

"Your brother has done quite a good job with the scratches."

"Plum's a professional make-up artist. He could even make a troll look good."

"All credit to him, Jonty, when we found him, he didn't look as if he'd ever look good again."

"Who do you think shot him then?" said Hamble.

"I don't rightly know," I replied, "someone must have been trying to stop him from getting somewhere…but who and where? Your guess is as good as mine."

"Maybe he knew something about me?" said Hamble. Both Jonty and I looked at him. Whatever was going on in Hamble's mind, he was obviously having a hard time coming to terms with his identity. The painting in the inn had given him a lot to think about.

Just then we heard a sniffing noise behind us. The porch was surrounded by bench seats which on a hot day would offer a shady respite from the sun. Someone was sat in the recess close to the door behind us. We turned as one and peered into the dark shadow.

"Who's there?" I called. No answer. I called again. Another sniff. The three of us walked towards the shadows. On seeing a woman clothed all in black, Jonty raised his hat to her.

"Who is it?" I hissed.

"Good morning, ma'am. How are you today?" said Jonty as the woman rose to her feet, screamed and ran out of the porch with her arms flailing wildly.

"Who the blazes was that?" I asked.

"Apparently, nobody knows, my dear Humphrey. She is being referred to as 'Miss Terry'…it's a little joke of Plum's. Do you see?" I nodded, eager to pre-empt the explanation. "She's a fine candidate to be the new village idiot according to him. Quite impressive, don't you think." The three of us stood in the porch doorway watching as what looked like a black, screaming windmill careered across the road in front of a brewer's dray and disappeared down a small alley.

"Almost theatrical," I mused

"According to Plum, she only appeared the other week but he said he hadn't seen her for a few days. Still, I really think she's got the balance right. Our Sphagnum was just plain stupid and too much 'in your face' with it...but don't tell him of course, you know how upset he gets." Almost on cue a heavy shower drove us back under the shelter of the porch. "No, I think 'Miss Terry' has cornered the market in village idiots. Sometimes she can be quite lucid, I'm told. She had quite a lengthy conversation with Plum the other day."

"Whatever about?" I asked.

"Death, apparently. Perhaps the disturbed look upon death as an escape route, I don't know. Plum felt she had an air of sadness about her...perhaps a young widow, he thought. "

At eleven o'clock precisely, much to the relief of the people assembled, the rain stopped. The village druid arrived and said a few words over the coffin before it undertook its final journey. A guard of honour made up of some of the village's less well known citizens (the more prominent ones were busy) lifted the coffin up onto their shoulders. The druid led the way while Plum slow marched behind him holding a large ceremonial axe in the air. The procession began the slow journey down to the graveyard accompanied by the sonorous beat of a bass drum. Bringing up the rear were the mourners, which consisted of nobody else but us three, unless you count the meanderings of 'Miss Terry' who had turned up with a huge spray of flowers. She cast petals into the air as she danced all around us.

Though nobody actually knew the man, the villagers paid their respects by lifting their caps or bowing their heads as the small cavalcade walked by. Slowly we left the village behind us and made our way up to a small stone graveyard that was dwarfed by the brooding presence of the Wall of Thorns. As we entered through the tired old gates the welcoming sight of sun greeted us from behind the clouds. In the distance I could see the two gravediggers leaning on their spades as they waited to get back to the reality of their lives. Our little entourage made its way to the prepared ground. The pall bearers lowered the coffin into the grave and then removed themselves. The druid said a few appropriate words. There wasn't much to say about this man as nobody knew who he was. We all picked up a handful of soil and threw it onto the coffin, then left wondering what to do next, everyone sort of drifted away from the grave. Jonty suggested we go back to the tavern for lunch but I told him I wanted to have a look around, it was surprising what you could pick up at funerals. Only 'Miss Terry' remained and as Hamble and Jonty stepped out through the graveyard gates, I watched her as she threw petals into the last resting place of the rosebud man. The impatient gravediggers had to chase her away so that they could get on with back-filling the sodden soil. She stood almost respectfully at a distance and watched them shovelling the loose earth back into the grave. I waited to see if anyone else turned up to pay their respects now that the 'crowd' had gone, but it seemed as if my time would be wasted. I had been there as long as it took the two men to back-fill the grave and tidy up the site. Surprisingly, when they had finished they seemed to take an exception to 'Miss Terry' still being there and the larger of the two started to shoo her away. From my vantage point behind a retaining wall, I wondered why the man seemed so desperate to remove her from the graveyard…a past history of grave-defiling or public nuisance, perhaps. The man made sure that she was halfway down the lane to the village before he ceased his threatening behaviour. I turned my attention to the other gravedigger who was collecting up all the tools of his trade and putting them into a wheelbarrow. He waited for the other to return before the both of them headed off towards the great stone monuments at the top end of the graveyard. As soon as they entered this section reserved for the great and the good of Without-the-Wall, I decided to follow them believing that from within these high standing graves and memorials I would be better placed to watch if the dead man's grave had any later visitors. The gates to this superior cemetery had been closed by the gravediggers so I opened them once more. They were well-maintained and made no sound at all. I took up a place which gave me a view through the gate to the newly-filled grave. Ten minutes passed and no one appeared. I decided to wander around and passed various memorials which impressed by both their height and their expense. As I rounded a corner near to the far wall I fully expected to bump into the two gravediggers but they were nowhere to be seen. I looked down and saw the muddied track left by the single wheel of their wheelbarrow. It stopped at the door of a large granite tomb. It was if the two men had disappeared completely.

As Jonty had already made arrangements to stay over at his sister's house, and Hamble was staying at The Sleeping Beauty, I decided to stay the night there myself. The innkeeper stared at Hamble for a beat or two.

"You know, I keep looking at you. I seem to know you from somewhere" he said.

"Head Gardener, Palace of Fotherghyll," said Hamble. The innkeeper smiled without understanding. "Painting near the entrance to the garden, it's me…apparently." The innkeeper blinked, still none the wiser. "Friend of Jonty's, I stayed here last night."

"That's it! So, what can I do for you both?" Hamble ordered our drinks and I asked if he had another room for the night.

"I'm sorry mate but we're fully booked. Your friend here got the last single room."

"He can have my room. I don't mind sleeping in the bar area," Hamble called out, "After all I've been doing that for the last few weeks anyway." Of course the innkeeper wasn't too pleased about having Hamble sleeping around his unguarded bar, so he came up with a compromise.

"Look, if you don't mind the dust-sheets you can have the Princess Suite. It's getting late anyway and it's the best room in the house, only I've got the decorators in at the moment. You'll have to get up quite early in the morning though as they start work at seven. They have their own access through the fire escape and I don't expect they'll take kindly to having to evict a snoring i-boggart. It's the best I can do; I'll have the bed made up for you if you like." I nodded my agreement and took the drinks back to the table.

We enjoyed a fine meal from the inn's kitchen and had a few drinks before Hamble decided he fancied going for a walk…as he'd not had chance last night; deciding to have an early night instead. What better way to finish off the night, I thought, than to take a stroll through a country village as the day neared its end? As Hamble savoured the last of his drink, I noticed the innkeeper busying himself by closing the internal shutters. Strange, I thought. When he locked and bolted the front door, I let curiosity get the better of me.

"Expecting a storm?" I said.

"Jack-in-Irons."

"Sorry?"

"You two being friends of Jonty Thumb's, I thought you'd have known about Jack-in-Irons."

"Never heard of him!"

"He used to be an old legend that people frightened the children with," said Hamble recovering another relic from the archaeological dig of his mind.

"Used to be?" said the innkeeper, "that's a laugh. He's back now and I'll tell you this much. He's a lot scarier now I'm an adult. I guess when I was little I didn't really believe in him…but now…well I've actually heard him!"

"Just what is he?"

"Well you wouldn't want to meet him on a dark night, that's for sure. The people round here make sure they're all indoors when nightfall comes. Jack-in-Irons is ten foot tall, he carries a huge spiked club and he's not frightened of using it. Around his waist is a huge metal belt, hanging from which are the severed heads of his victims. As he drags their heads up and down the streets, he moans as if he is in agony."

"Well you would, wouldn't you?" My quip met with a sneer from the innkeeper.

"Well you might think it's funny, mister, but the people of this village are trapped in their homes when night comes. My trade has dropped right off these last few weeks since he returned…my only customers at night are those staying at the inn. Not to mention the giant insects that have been seen over the Wall of Thorns…some of them with a body in their clutches."

"Giant insects?" mouthed Hamble implying that the innkeeper was one toadstool short of a piskey ring. I decided to keep my counsel on that one.

"Now…would you like another drink, gentlemen?" said the innkeeper. Hamble held his glass aloft and I fumbled for my wallet. I walked up to the bar as the innkeeper began pulling a pint of Futtock's Neckoil for Hamble.

"Another whiskey for me, please…oh and one for yourself." The innkeeper's grimace melted a little. "So, have you ever seen this Jack-in-Irons?"

"Wouldn't want to."

"Why not?"

"They say if he meets your eye he will never stop until he's got your head on the chain around his waist."

"*They* say?"

"Well you know…legend says. We all know the stories; we've heard them since we were children. Anyway, I've definitely heard him and you will do as well tonight, I expect."

At the end of the evening the innkeeper pushed open the door and I followed him in to the huge room. Though grand in scale, it was covered in decorators' sheets. The smell of fresh paint was overpowering as he went around lighting the various oil lamps in the room.

"It's the best room in the house…normally," he said. The view across to the river and canal is spectacular. The both of us looked at the shuttered and padlocked windows. "You'll see in the morning…perhaps…when the decorators get here." And with that he took his own lamp and wished me a good night before pulling the door closed behind him. I lay down on the bed and began to consider the strange events that had happened to me over the last few days. There had been an attempt to kill me and another to kidnap me…not to mention being sapped by my secretary.

Half dreams of Hamble's grandfather, dead bodies and great flying insects prevented me from having a restful sleep. In the darkest hours what seemed like the caterwauling of a couple of tomcats trading insults outside seemed to put the seal on my night but a second hearing got me out of bed and fumbling in my coat pocket for my tool kit. Once unwrapped on the bed I took out my lock-picks. Looking round the room I decided that the fire escape would be the best bet. After all if I saw something interesting out of a window I'd then have to pick another lock to get out. I set to work on the old mortise lock and within a few seconds had the door open. As quickly and as quietly as I could, I was out onto the fire escape. Further down the street I could hear the eerie howl of some creature that seemed to be in pain. The cause of the noise was still out of sight and all I could do was wait until whatever it was that was terrifying the village appeared in my vision. As I waited for the answer to my question a thought struck me. What if they were right...what if the legend was true? I could look down into the evil eye of Jack-in-Irons and from that moment on he wouldn't rest until my bashed head was hanging from his belt. Then I thought, after the day I've just had what difference does one more lunatic chasing you make? I braced myself for the confrontation. Laying flat on the landing of the staircase, I poked my head over the edge. After all, if I kept quiet enough why would Jack-in-Irons bother to look up anyway...I hoped and gulped.

At the point that the wailing noise reached the corner of the inn, I felt the hairs on the back of my neck rise. There below me in the small winding street was a giant carrying a huge spiked club. He was wailing and groaning to the best of his ability probably due to the number of chains draped around his huge body and worst of all...there they were, hanging from his belt...five or six green putrefying heads bobbing along with every giant step he took. As my mind tried to make sense of what I was seeing, a strong gust of wind blew the fire escape door shut behind me. Jack-in-Irons stopped his wailing and turned his great head towards me. Call it bravado...call it sheer stupidity...I met his gaze despite the contents of my bowels beginning to liquidize. Jack-in-Irons? A terrifying vision for most people without a doubt…but some of us are made of sterner stuff. For a second, I wondered if I had perhaps been mistaken as the slow upturn of his gaze found my eyes and held them for a beat. In that moment of sheer blind panic I cursed my folly until the raised hand of Jack-in-Irons personally wished me a good night. I waved back. What followed the giant would give me even more of a shock. As I continued to watch the procession that trailed him, I thought back to the old rhyme I was taught as a youngster

If you wake at dead of night, and hear the sound of feet,
Don't go drawing back the blind, or looking in the street,
Them that asks no questions will not be told a lie.
Watch the wall, my darling, while the Gentlemen go by!

Just like that rhyme that warned us all to turn a blind eye to the night-time deeds of smugglers as they brought in the cheap drink and tobacco to avoid paying tax on it. The suggestion was that if you didn't actually see the smugglers then you could deny their existence. Beneath me, in the streets of Without-the-Wall, trailing behind Jack-in-Irons, was another type of contraband. Only this contraband wasn't strong liquor or tobacco, it was a far worse commodity. Walking two by two and shackled together by their chains was a line of sprites. Elves, goblins, dwarves…both male and female, you name it; there was every type of person but mankind. Until they too arrived; walking alongside their contraband armed with clubs, swords and guns were the men…two of whom I recognised immediately. Scuzzer and Tranter…each of them carrying a particularly evil-looking club. I watched as the docile queue passed beneath me. Bringing up the rear I recognised the goblin who had been kidnapped

156

the other night in the tavern. I hurried back into my room and dressed. The procession of slaves was just about fifty yards away as I reached the bottom of the fire escape. I made my way through the shadows until I was quite close to the men at the back of the procession. Ahead in the distance I could hear my good friend Jack-in-Irons moaning to his heart's content. I trailed the procession out of the village which eventually took the road out towards the Wall of Thorns.

As the two men who brought up the rear of the party were talking, I tried to get nearer to them. With a little luck they might be discussing just what it was they were up to. We were now away from the village and I had lost the cover provided by the shadows of the buildings. I was finding it difficult to stay close. I recalled that a dry-stone wall up ahead would allow me the luxury of being able to skulk alongside this procession of misery. Unfortunately my clumsy attempt to climb over it alerted the trailing guards and I had to force myself into a dry ditch to avoid discovery. I snuggled deep into the pungent-smelling trench and waited. One of the guards popped his head over the wall and gave nothing more than a cursory glance at the darkness in which I was hiding. Once he had gone I followed the procession, hidden from its view by the dry-stone wall. After half a mile or so, I heard the sound of the large gates of the graveyard swinging open. I popped my head over the wall and watched as the sprites were herded inside. As soon as they all moved on, I vaulted the wall and scrambled into the graveyard, taking refuge behind a gravestone. Before I could get my breath, I became aware of a presence close by. A powerful smell enveloped me and I felt the clap of a huge hand on my shoulder.

"Hello, Mr Boggart. I thought it was you. I saw you earlier didn't I? You know, peeping over the fire escape. You waved back, didn't you?"

"Oh hi, Sphagnum!" The wave of relief on recognising my discoverer in the dark graveyard washed straight over Sphagnum's head. Let's face it that would need to be a big wave.

"Yes, I thought it was you. That's why I didn't hit you with my big club." He brandished it in front of me like it was a teddy bear. "You didn't want to be out and about round here at this time of night."

"I could say the same about you...and just what is that awful smell?"

Even in the dark, I just knew he was blushing. "Oh sorry about that...it's the cabbages, they're getting a bit ripe now. The other guys keep complaining; that's why they make me walk so far ahead."

"What do you need cabbages for?"

"They're supposed to look like heads that have been chopped off. Do you get it? Like as if I was really Jack-in-Irons. It's clever isn't it?" Sphagnum held up the putrid smelling sack just like a child might hold up a recently-used chamber pot. I gestured that he ditch the sack, so he put it back in the...er ditch. He pulled a goofy face as he wondered what to say next.

"You mention 'the other guys'?" I asked.

"Yeah, the guys I work with. They're quite nice really. There are six of us all together. It's just that they don't like the smell of my cabbages too much. That's why they make me take them home after I've finished my job…instead of going with them. They also make me use a separate coach."

"This job you have, Sphagnum…just what does it entail?" He just stared at me. After his second blink I added, "What do you do?"

"Oh right…well these two guys…"

"Scuzzer and Tranter?"

"That's right…so you know them? I suppose they won't mind me telling you then. You see they told me it had to be kept secret…all this business."

"What business?"

"You know…all this 'Jack-in-Irons' thingy. They told me that I had to pretend to be Jack-in-Irons so that nobody in the village would get jealous."

"Jealous?"

"Yeah…well the people we bring here are going to a lovely place where everybody enjoys themselves and plays all day…nobody has to work and one day Scuzzer and Tranter say I will be able to go because they've got a special job for me and the others there."

"I'll bet they have. Who are the others?"

"Well there's me, Tom, Dickon and Harry. Tom and Dickon are the gravediggers here. Anyhow, I'll have to ask you to leave now, Mr Boggart, because that is one of my jobs. I hope you don't mind me asking but the lads told me that if anyone comes spying round here I am supposed to whack them on the head with my club, tie them up and wait while Scuzzer and Tranter comes to deal with them."

"And what do you think they would do with them, Sphagnum?"

"I know because I asked them! They smiled and said they would take care of them which sounds like the right thing to do with someone who was just being a bit nosy after all's said and done, don't you think, Mr Boggart? So, if you don't mind that is what I am going to do with you." Sphagnum picked up his club and as I started to back away, he slung it over his shoulder. "Are you coming, Mr Boggart?"

"What if I said I wasn't coming...that I was going to stay here and find out just what was happening to those people?" Sphagnum grabbed me and threw me over his shoulder. "Hey put me down, you big oaf!"

"I'm just going to take you back to the inn where you'll be safe." I needed to think fast...surely it wouldn't be too hard to outwit Sphagnum.

"If you take me back to the inn...who'll be on guard here? Someone else might sneak into the graveyard while you're away with me." Sphagnum stopped dead. Slumped over his shoulder I could almost hear the cogs whirring in his head. He started towards the village again. "But what if someone else comes?" I was almost wheedling now as his iron grip strapped me to his broad shoulder.

"I've been guarding the graveyard for almost two months now and you're the first person to come a-spying. I don't suppose anybody else will come now…and tomorrow *is* the last day." I made a mental note that perhaps Sphagnum wasn't as dumb as he looked.

Snapping out of the mood of self-pity, I would have stopped in my tracks had I been able to make them in the first place.

"What do you mean…tomorrow is the last day?"

"Tomorrow…we are bringing in the last coach party and my job finishes."

"Aren't you sad about losing your job?"

"Not really because then I will go and take my place in the wonderful land." As we entered the village I started to struggle.

"Look, Sphagnum, just put me down for a second; I promise I won't run away or anything." The big lad did as he was told and I tried to look him in the eye…some hope! He picked me up and stood me on a garden wall.

"Don't you understand? These people are being taken against their will. That's why they put chains on their legs. Do you think if they were going to such a wonderful place that they would need to chain them up?" Sphagnum's huge brow furrowed as if a team of oxen had just ploughed it.

"But it's my job…if I didn't do it…someone else would."

"I don't see many other giants around here. There's your Dad…do you really think that he would do something like this?"

"But they never seem to complain. They always seem to have a smile on their face when I chain them up."

"Well perhaps they've been drugged…I don't know but what's even worse, Sphagnum, is that now you're telling me that it's you who chains them up."

"I'm only doing what I'm told. I have to collect them in Thursday Market, I chain them up and me and Harry bring them on the coach to Without. Scuzzer and Tranter go on their own horses on account of…"

"..your cabbages? Yeah, you said." Sphagnum nodded. "And what about the other two?"

"Tom and Dickon?"

"Yeah."

"They stay here and arrange to meet us outside the village." I realised I had to break Sphagnum's will somehow. He was not a bad lad at heart; I decided to play upon his conscience.

"And these people you chain up, Sphagnum, how do you think their loved ones feel about their husbands or wives being taken from them?" I watched him ruminating over this like a huge cow chewing a particularly large cud. "And you…when *you* go…what about your Uncle Jonty, Uncle Plum…Your Dad" I played the ace. "…and *your Mum*?" A change came over Sphagnum and I realised I had got him. The giant began to tremble.

162

"You're not going to tell my Mum, are you?" Amazing to think such a huge man was terrified of Jonty's sister…time to press home the advantage.

"Well surely you don't expect me to say nothing to your Uncle Jonty…after all you are his favourite nephew." A smile came over Sphagnum…bless him.

"Am I really his favourite nephew?"

"And I'm sure Uncle Jonty will want to tell his sister…*your Mum*. She worries about you." By this time Sphagnum was a shambling wreck.

"B-But she'll tell m-me off!"

"She has a right to know where her son is…don't you think? Even if he has gone to…a wonderful land." A spark of resilience came over Sphagnum…it didn't last long.

"She doesn't really care about me. If she did, she wouldn't shout at me so much."

"You know that isn't true. She only shouts at you because she cares. I bet she does things for you without you having to ask. That's what mothers do, Sphagnum. They do them because they love you…and you want to leave without telling her." I shook my head.

"I could write her a note telling her how much I loved her…and you could give it to her…after I've gone." Sphagnum threw me an encouraging look.

"I could…" I said, "but what if *I* want to go to this 'wonderful land' as you call it. Of course if I went, it probably wouldn't be a good idea to tell anybody else." Sphagnum's thoughts played hide and seek in his head. *100-99-98...*

"What do you mean?" *86-85-84...* "If *you* went..." *79-78-77...*

"I'd like to see this place, Sphagnum. It sounds marvellous." *63-62-61...* "I mean if it's you who chains these people up, I'm sure you could fit me in." *52-51-50...*

"But we always bring a dozen...the others will know if there are thirteen." *45-46-44...*

"Surely you can keep it from Harry. If I can manage to get on board the coach just before you arrive in Without, you can fasten me up when I get on board."

"But what about the other one...the one who won't be coming?" *36-35-34...*

"Just take care of him, Sphagnum. *29-28-27...*

"And you will take his place? You promise?" *18-17-16...*

"Brownies honour." *10-9-8-7-6-5-4-3-2-1...coming ready or not!*

"OK!" Sphagnum's whole demeanour changed and he shook me roughly by the hand although most of my body seemed to get involved. "The coach gets here at around eight o'clock. Where are you going to get on it?"

"I'll worry about that, you just make sure there are only eleven sprites who get on board." Happy now that his mother had been kept out of the equation, he clapped me on the

164

back and headed off down the street. After a few yards, he stopped and turned around.

"Hang on…I'm Uncle Jonty's *only* nephew!" But I was already halfway up the fire escape to my room.

*

From the top of the fire escape I watched as first light broke over the Wall of Thorns and began to light the little village. At the end of the street Sphagnum was making his way back to the graveyard. My body told me that I needed sleep and tomorrow was going to be a long day. I pulled open the door and stepped into the room. The pre-dawn gloom was only broken by the white of the dust sheets that covered the furniture. The room seemed different but the need for sleep drew me towards the comfortable bed. I lay on it and looked around me. Something *was* different. The picture that hung over the fireplace…a portrait. It had previously been covered with a sheet and now the subject stared at me through the murky light. I got off the bed and walked over to the painting. A good detective would have ignored the need to look at the painting. A good detective would have asked himself a different question such as…*but the painting drew me in…the likeness was amazing…*a question such as where is the dust sheet that covered the painting and who removed it. The answer was immediate.

"The Sleeping Beauty, Mr Boggart, quite unlike yourself." I swivelled round to see Deadman holding a gun in one hand and a dust sheet in the other. So, that was it…the *four*-piece suite, I should have known.

Even in the face of imminent death, the uncanny resemblance of the portrait drew me once more to look at 'The Sleeping Beauty'. Unless I could get out of this situation, all the questions I wanted to ask would go unanswered.

Deadman had the upper hand but I wasn't going to kiss his ring.

"You're no oil painting yourself, Deadman."

"That's pronounced *Deed*man and I was referring more to your nocturnal wanderings rather than your ease on the eye…although if the hat fits then you should no doubt wear it." He walked towards me and pushed me into one of the armchairs that made up the now three-piece suite. He sat on the chair opposite and pointed the gun at me. "You impress me Mr Boggart. Just how did you manage to evade me on the barge?

"I listen to everything people tell me. It's what a good detective does. You never know what information is important until you need it. If you don't mind, however, I'll keep it secret in case I ever need it again." Deadman laughed, a dry cackle that cried out for a throat lozenge.

"I very much doubt that the need will ever arise again, Mr Boggart, you seem to forget that you are just minutes from departing this life forever. Despite my admiration for your prowess at evasion, you must admit that your escape from my clutches in The Ginnels was somewhat fortunate.

Just who was your knight in black armour that evening, anyway? I feel that I owe them a visit. No one prevents Deadman from executing his duty."

"To be honest, Deadman, I haven't got a clue."

"Mispronouncing my name only appals my sense of decorum, Mr Boggart. What it doesn't do is make me angry and unstable. So please desist in your futile attempts to rile me. The only thing that matters at this point is that you will cease to exist in mere moments." The chiming of the town clock signalled to the both of us that it was seven. Deadman seemed to almost approve of the orderliness of it all. He cocked the firing pin and waited for the bell to finish. Five…six…the door burst open and a goblin carrying a large toolbag bundled into the room. Unaware of our presence he held the door open while a second goblin entered carrying a large plank over his shoulder. Systematically the first goblin set about unlocking the first of the external shutters before Deadman rose from his armchair and halted him in his tracks.

"Freeze, goblin!" On hearing Deadman's voice the second goblin spun around with the plank. Deadman's head was knocked clean off his shoulders and sent flying across the room into my lap. I picked the head up and screamed as Deadman sank his teeth into my right thumb. A hail of bullets flew around the room as the rest of Deadman fired indiscriminately.

"Over here, you fool!" shouted Deadman's head as his body turned round and aimed. The bullet flew close to my arm and sank into the armchair. "Higher, you idiot!" screamed Deadman as he realised that the bullet could have as easily hit him. The goblins dropped their tools and scrabbled out of the room and I contemplated dropping Deadman's head and high-tailing after them. "He's getting away, you idiot!" Deadman's head had a low opinion of the rest of his body. "Stop him! The blind headless body spread it's arms and thrashed around the room in an attempt to stop me leaving. Having Deadman's head as a witness wasn't helping my progress, so I tipped the goblin's tools out of the bag and threw the hissing head inside it. Muffled curses came out of the bag but at least he couldn't control the movements of his other half. I watched as the headless body swept the space in front of it. Disorientated by the lack of instruction from its managerial department, the body stopped thrashing and appeared to start to concentrate. It was apparent that the head and body were connected by something more than sensual signals. I left the toolbag on the floor by the window and moved across the room. The body seemed aware of where its head was and made its way towards the toolbag. It was now unconcerned about my movements and I circled the hulk like a sheepdog as it lumbered towards its target. I watched as it stood over the bag and at the very second it started to bend down I threw myself at it and pushed it out through the window. The sound of shattering glass filled the air and I peered out and saw the flailing body hit the ground with a thud. After a beat or two the body staggered to its feet and swivelled round in some attempt to get its bearings. I grabbed the bag and headed for the door out onto the fire escape. Scrambling down the wooden steps two or three at a time, I was uncaring of whether the bag in the head was banging against the rails. I hit the ground and dared a look around the corner of the building. The headless body was surrounded by early morning workers who blinked their unbelieving eyes at what they were seeing. When they realised just what it was they *were* seeing they fled in any direction they could just as long as it was away from Deadman. The body swung round indiscriminately, it was frantically seeking a signal from its own head. If ever a headless body could look at something, it looked at me and the bag swinging from my hand. I turned and started to race down the street knowing that the rest of Deadman was coming after me. After leaving two streets behind me I noticed that the sound of those footsteps seemed to be getting closer. Clearly Deadman without a head was a lot quicker than the one with. As I neared the crossroads I faltered. I needed to separate the head from the rest of the body by as many miles as possible. The barges on the canal didn't offer enough speed, they could easily be caught up by an enthusiastic pursuer…what I needed was…coming round the bend! The blast of a horn both startled me and answered my dilemma. Behind me the lumbering Deadman approached at speed and across my path, the stage-coach of The Fotherghyllshire Road Carriage Company pulled to halt in front of me. I stood there with a bag in my hand looking for all the world as if I was requesting that the coach should pick me up at the Without-the Wall stop off. The driver slowed to a halt and waited for me to get on. When I didn't, he managed to get a little uppity about it.

"Look, mate, are you getting on or not? Now if you want to stay in this fly-blown stink-hole then that's up to you, but…" He looked over my head and saw Deadman, minus his, lumbering down the road. "Blood and sand! I don't care whether you get on or not, mate, but he certainly isn't! Gooo-on!" He urged his beasts into action and the four horses responded. I jammed the toolbag containing Deadman's head into a gap in the baggage compartment at the back of the coach and stepped back. As the coach and four headed off, the headless body of Deadman reached me, stopped for a second and headed off in pursuit of the disappearing coach.

I decided the one thing I needed right now was sleep. My room would be buzzing with activity once the decorators had informed the innkeeper of what went on this morning. Deadman was off my trail for the time being so at least I knew I could get some shut-eye but where? I recalled the short time I spent in the dry ditch near the graveyard with some fondness. No one would disturb me there. The short walk up the road passed in a weary haze and, as I neared the graveyard, I saw Sphagnum's colleagues Tom and Dickon working there. But I was far too tired to bother with them now so I once more threw myself over the dry-stone wall and into the ditch.

Days had passed since JC had watched Jakob Grimm disappear into the Wall of Thorns. Whether he had ever caught the man he was chasing, she didn't know. What she did know was that the only way of getting through the Wall of Thorns was to hack your way through it. And there was the irony...the living wall could not be breached by anything magical...yet the awesome saw she had witnessed was powered by something beyond the ordinary.

Fruitless searching over the last few days had seen her scouring the Wall of Thorns for a weak spot but to no avail. Frustrated by her lack of progress, she had turned to her fellow sprites for an insight into how they arrived here. Her attempts to communicate with them led her to suspect that they were under some kind of spell. Deep down, JC knew that she was avoiding what ought to be her next course of action. She had put it off for long enough. The entrance must be within one of the palace buildings.

The palace itself was locked at night and JC had to fly up to the roof of the building before she could find a way in. She removed the dusty glass shards from a broken window. Inside, the attic room seemed as though it had been undisturbed long before the hundred-year curse had been placed upon it. The room was completely empty but for an old fallen curtain to one side of the window. Before she could be sure that this might be an ideal base she needed to explore the rest of the rooms on this floor. Making short work of the locked door with her tool kit, she gently closed it behind her and moved onto the next one. The pale moon shone through a row of skylights and illuminated the central corridor. Drifts of dust parted in her wake though no human could ever have seen the creature that disturbed them. One by one she checked out the other rooms; some were unlocked whilst others required the application of her toolkit. Coming to the last room she saw that it too was empty save for a solitary old spinning wheel by the window. JC made her way over to the wooden contraption. A sense of history almost overwhelmed her as she recalled the story of Fotherghyll Palace. Could this be the very spinning wheel that brought about the curse? It also begged the question that if all the spinning wheels had been banned from this kingdom, how come one was to be found, of all places, in the attic of the palace?

JC approached the spinning wheel with an air of almost reverence. She ran her hands over the dusty woodwork, gently turning the wheel that was redolent with history. She was almost smiling as she caressed the entire wooden machine with her hands.

Closing the door behind her, she was satisfied that the undisturbed attic would be a good base from which to begin her investigations of the palace buildings. She returned to the first room she had entered and decided to make herself comfortable for the night. Whatever the Grimms were up to in this place, she needed to see it during the day. She looked around for something comfortable to sleep on and sighed when the dust-covered curtains on the floor appeared to be the only option. As she approached the dark hump of material her soft tread alighted on a small wooden tube. Squatting down to pick it up she held it to the pale light coming through the window. It was a musical instrument of some kind, a flute. She blew the dust from it and the lightest of musical notes filled the air. Beneath her the heavy curtain stirred. JC reverted to her invisible state, placed the flute back on the floor and edged up against the wall.

Heaps of dust piled up on the floorboards as the dark curtain began to take shape. Amid much coughing and sneezing a tall thin man, dressed in a long coat, threw off the remnants of the ancient curtain. JC watched as he stretched, yawned and let out a huge great fart into the room.

The man turned and faced JC although he was not aware she was there. She looked at him and saw that he was not all human; his elfin ears betrayed the traces of sprite in his make up. This was no ironised sprite, this was a child of a sprite-human relationship. He stretched, smacked his lips and walked over to the window. JC moved quietly to the side of him and watched as he peered out, trying to make sense of what he saw. He screwed up his eyes to focus but the look of confusion remained etched on his face and it was at this point that JC realised. The dust covered curtains he was wrapped in; the lack of any discernible footprints…the clues were there. This young man had been asleep for quite some considerable time.

*

JC recalled the story of the curse of Fotherghyll Palace as she watched the young man. If he had been asleep for a hundred years or so; would he remember his last waking day? Could you remember something that happened so long ago?

She needed to snap herself out of such speculation. She wasn't being professional. The young man had appeared in the place she had believed would make a good base. She needed to either get him out of here, never to return. But what if he did return? Perhaps she needed to kill him? What would she do with the body? Light elves weren't blessed with physical strength and the thought of sharing her room with a rotting corpse over the next few weeks didn't bear thinking about.

Once the young man's eyes had become accustomed to the darkness in the room, she saw him pick up the flute. Like her he blew the dust off it and the ethereal note returned to haunt the room. Enough light allowed her to see him smile, his pointed elfin ears picked out by a passing moonbeam. When he put the flute to his lips, JC sprang. Within a second she was at the back of him, with her knife to his throat.

"Play a tune and you're dead!" she hissed into his ear.

After his initial shock, the young man croaked, "Everyone's a critic these days". Ignoring his attempt to lessen the tension, JC stayed in aggressive mode.

"And what would you know about these days?" Immediately she regretted her lack of tact.

"Look, I don't know who you are but I think you're over-reacting to the situation. OK, perhaps I shouldn't be here, but I was only sleeping in an attic room that looks like no one has cleaned for a hundred years." JC fought the urge to smile. "I mean, it's not as though I've slept in the King's bed or something."

"How did you get here?" asked JC. The young man gave this some thought before answering.

"I'm not even sure *where* I am." He tried to turn his head but JC pushed the knife into his skin, a trickle of blood ran down into his coat.

"Don't even think about it!"

"Look, can't we just talk?"

"OK," said JC. She reappeared and flew at high speed to the corner of the room. The man turned to look at her. She threw her knife and it juddered into the centre of the window frame, within a second she was upon it and had pulled it out. He tried to follow her speed of movement but she was back in her corner again before he could focus. There was no need for her to say anything. She was just marking his card. A few seconds passed before she continued.

"What is your name?"

"My name is…" Even in the darkness, JC could sense the confusion on his face. "I can't remember what my name is!" He reached out for the flute more for the comfort of the one thing that seemed familiar to him, but another of JC's knives thudded into the woodwork in warning. She was retrieving it from the wood and away in a split second. "I think I am a musician. Perhaps if you would let me play, it might help me?"

"And risk everyone knowing we're here!" JC's fury was apparent. The young man laughed in the darkness. "You find it funny, do you?"

"I can't believe I've just woken up in the attic of what seems to be a large house and I can't remember who I am. Last night must have been special. Just to top it all I find myself in the company of a mad knife-throwing elf. Of course I find it funny!" JC bit her tongue before replying. Be professional, she thought. If she was to be of any use tomorrow in her investigations she had to get some sleep, but the last thing she needed was to be alone with this...musician. She had to bite the bullet.

"Listen to me now, and listen carefully. I am going to tell you something that...", she needed to think about what she was about to say, "I'm going to tell you something that you will find difficult to understand. But I want to assure you that I am deadly serious in what I say." The young man nodded and made himself comfortable on the floor. "I have reason to believe; given the information I have that you have been asleep for..." Even now she couldn't bring herself to say it. "...for a very long time." She discerned the young man smiling.

"Musicians obviously need their sleep," he said. "I expect it is not the first time I've had a lie-in." JC's frustration was beginning to overwhelm her.

"Listen to me, whoever you are; you were locked in this place. See, there are no footprints in the dust and, by the way, have you ever seen so much dust? You were sleeping under an old curtain that shipped enough of it to fill a coffin. When I say you have been asleep for a long time, I'm not talking about a lie-in here. I'm talking about one hundred years!"

The young man's laugh betrayed his incomprehension. He thought about saying 'you're joking' but he had seen enough of JC to know that she wasn't the joking kind.

"But that's impossible…" He looked round at the evidence before him. How could he have contemplated sleeping in this dusty old room, beneath that old curtain if he had only arrived here last night? Why could he not even remember his name, let alone the night before? "But how?"

"We believe…"

"'We'? Who's 'we'?"

JC sighed, this wasn't easy. "'We' are The All-Seeing Eye…"

"Who *are*?"

"…an organisation who have been monitoring issues of state security now for…"

"Never heard of them!"

"…for almost seventy years now." The point was made. The young man resorted into a sulk. "The Palace of Fotherghyll, that's where we are now, was put under a curse some one hundred years ago…a curse that put all who were living here to sleep for a hundred years. The palace was protected from outsiders by a fast growing thorn which precludes the effect of magic upon or even above it. This so-called Wall of Thorns recovers faster than any person can cut through it. Because of this no one had been able to enter the palace grounds to investigate until yesterday when I managed to fly over it."

"You flew over it? I thought you said that magic wouldn't work over this Wall of Thorns?"

"My employers arranged for me to float down over it from a balloon…" JC could see a look of confusion on his face. "It's the latest way of flying." She failed to force the smugness from her voice.

"So you're a spy…a secret agent."

"My name is JC Bigg and my position at The Eye is that of Seer," said JC a little stiffly.

"So you're trying to tell me that I have been asleep for a hundred years!"

"Give or take," said JC.

"How do I know you haven't set this up?"

"Maybe I could have…if I had one good reason to do so!" JC's sympathies for the young man were beginning to wane. "Believe me. I *am* sorry for you. But this is not just about you. Estimates of old documentation indicate that there may be as many as two to three hundred people who were victims of this curse. And while we at The Eye are mindful of this fact there is something else going on here and that, primarily, is what I'm here for. No disrespect, but I haven't time to act as a counsellor." With a howl of exasperation, the young man hurled himself across the room at the door and began to sob. JC switched to full alert and back to standby in the time it took him to hit the door.

"I think perhaps you should calm down. You might attract somebody's attention." The young man, turned his face to JC and spat out his reply.

"This may be just a job for you, Seer or whatever you are…but if you are telling me the truth, and I think you are,

178

then everyone I ever knew in this world is dead!" The elf stared into his livid moist eyes, bit her lip and nodded.

JC watched the young man crying alone in the corner of the room. He was trying to come to terms with the torrent of conflicting thoughts that filled his head. He knew that everyone he had ever known must have died but, unable to identify himself, how could he possibly know who he had lost? JC recognised the irony of telling someone who had been asleep for a hundred years that the one thing they needed now to come to terms with everything was time. She excused herself in the twilight, unlocked the door and waited for a reaction from the young man. It was no surprise to her that none came.

A short sleep in another of the attic rooms was not as refreshing as it needed to be but she felt almost grateful for the arrival of the dawn. She was ready to start the job she had come here to do. The discovery of the young man had been a distraction but her first priority was to get some food for the both of them.

Inside the strange silver metallic kitchens, the like of which she has never seen before, JC watched as the various sprites were accorded tasks by human cooks. They undertook their work in silence. It was so different from the busy castle kitchens she had been in before. Her first directive of getting some food for the young man and herself was on schedule. A young goblin opened one of the many silver doors which revealed a vast quantity of food within. The accompanying blast of chill air surprised her as she scanned the silver cupboard for practical supplies. The goblin removed a pan of red sauce and shut the door.

"You got the salsa, Ramsay?"

"Yes, chef!" said the goblin with a new found enthusiasm.

"Then follow me and I'll show you what to do with it!" shouted the cook from across the kitchen. JC waited until the young goblin had left before opening the silver cupboard once again. The cold air caught her breath as she rummaged inside to find something to eat. Her hand settled on a large packet of square yellow things covered in a see-through material. She picked them up in wonderment.

"The cheese slices are floating out of the fridge" said an old elf who was staring at what JC's invisible hand was holding. She was worried that the elf's statement might bring about the cook's return. The sight of the old elf conversing with a floating packet of cheese might cause him problems.

"It's for him!" JC tapped the elf on the shoulder and, while he turned round with all the speed of a hibernating hedgehog, she was off, helping herself to a few of the small bread rolls that another elf had brought in on a tray. On her way out she noticed some bottles of what looked like a drink of some kind. Nothing familiar like ginger beer and sarsaparilla stood out. The strange names gave nothing away, although when she came across one called Doctor Pepper, she made her mind up. These were not drinks, they were medical supplies. It was then that she noticed a case of bottles that were labelled 'Sprite'. Perhaps this was the drink by which the humans kept their sprite slaves in their trance-like state? She removed a bottle from its see-through packaging. Further investigation revealed a case of spring water. Satisfied she had enough for the time being she was off and on her way out of the building.

She was more careful heading back to the palace. JC was aware that if her path crossed that of a human, the sight of bread, cheese slices and a couple of bottles floating along might draw unwanted attention. With a great deal of subterfuge, she made her way round the back of the palace and flew up to the roof. When she tapped on the window she was surprised to see a somewhat cheerier young musician waiting for her. His eyes betrayed the fact that his tears had not long dried up.

"I've remembered my name," he said, but his attention faltered as he fell on the bread, cheese and water.

"Save some for me!" said JC, feeling a little ungracious. After all, the young man hadn't eaten for a hundred years. He poured the water down his throat which enabled him to make room for more of the dry bread and cheese. When he had sated himself enough to speak, she asked him how he knew what his name was. The young man smiled.

"It's in my coat!" He showed the neatly sewn label inside the collar. JC was too far away to read it. "I remember my mother sewing it in. I remember my mother!"

"That's good!" said JC trying her hardest to be upbeat.

"I remember she died…before all this…" She was a lovely woman; a bit of a dreamer. She told me that my father used to say that. That's why he was attracted to her in the first place." The young man was getting tearful as he relived his mother's death once again.

"So, what's your name? I see that there is some sprite in you."

"My name is Presley." JC nodded.

"Elvish?"

"The ears are a giveaway, aren't they? The story is that my father, who was a king of the elves, found my mother singing in the woods and he charmed her away from her home for two years. When I was small my mother had asked if she could take me home to show to her family. My father said that she could go back for one day but she would have to be back at the entrance under the hill at midnight or she would be lost to him forever. When she returned to her family there was such joy at her homecoming that a big celebration was held in the village. Mother had a bit too much to drink and we never got back to our home under the hill."

JC smiled sadly. She recognised the scenario. Many a fanciful young woman had been courted by an elf and left in the family way. It was always easier for the mother to weave a fantasy around the child's arrival than it was to tell the truth. Still she supposed it was better than evoking storks and gooseberry bushes.

"Mother told me that my father was an accomplished musician. So I followed in his footsteps and became a musician of some note. That is why I am here at Fotherghyll, I remember I was commissioned to play here for some reason." Presley offered JC some of the food that was left which she accepted with little persuasion.

After they had both eaten, JC filled Presley in on what was happening at Fotherghyll. As far as she could see the people who had fallen under the witch's curse one hundred years ago had all been removed. Presley, locked away for some reason, had been an exception. Now the place was filled with sprites as some kind of slave workforce for whatever enterprise was being hatched.

"There must be someway out of here," said JC. "Records show that there were only a few sprites who lived at Fotherghyll prior to the curse being fulfilled. Whoever is running this place is getting them in here somehow and if there's a way in then there's a way out. I need to find that way out."

"Well, I'll be willing to help you in any way I can," said Presley. JC looked at him and smiled.

"I might have to ask you to make sacrifices."

"Bring it on!" said Presley

"Young man, you're going to have to get yourself a job!" If Presley's face was a picture, it would, no doubt, have been called 'The Scream'. A look of dismay clouded JC's face as she noted the empty 'Sprite' bottle at his side. Oh well, she thought, I suppose someone had to see how effective it is.

Once she was sure Presley was all right, JC decided that the large building in which she believed the sprites were being kept might be worth investigating. She mingled with the sprites hopeful of hearing some form of dissent against the position they found themselves in, but there was none. She

184

listened as so-called 'team-leaders', sprites who had been here the longest, tried hard to rally their troops for the day ahead. From what she could determine the information filtered through to the somewhat comatose sprites without registering the slightest interest. This characteristic was reserved for the sudden appearance of Rutger Grimm. The resultant scramble of her fellow sprites was an embarrassment for JC to witness, but it gave her the opportunity to become invisible without the human noticing. Rutger Grimm announced to the sprites that as soon as they had put on their uniforms they were to line up in fours outside the building where he would be waiting for them. JC waited until he had left before reappearing before the disinterested sprites. She watched as they put on the by now familiar red cap and green uniform which carried the name of this enterprise – DOMANIA. Each sprite had their own locker and nametag. JC rummaged through the cupboards around the changing room and found what she had been looking for. As the sprites hurried out of the building to do Rutger Grimm's bidding, JC did her best to find a Domania uniform that might fit Presley. The tunic and cap were not a problem but Presley's long legs would take some covering. She wrote his name on a name tag and was about to leave the room when she noticed that one of the team leaders had left their clipboard on a shelf. JC read and noticed that there was an instruction that a dwarf i-sprite was to be sent to work on the children's rides tomorrow morning. She ripped the note off the clipboard and hid it in the bottom of the open locker upon which she had written Presley's name.

Now that the building seemed empty she searched some of the other rooms, the majority of which seemed to be of a recent construction. As she left at the far end of the building, she noticed an old wall outside that didn't seem in keeping with the architecture that surrounded it. Within the wall was a large ornate door with a sophisticated lock that suggested something of importance lay beyond it. JC was sure that this was the door that was used to bring in the sprites. As she turned to go back into the sprite's building she trod in what was more than likely dog muck. Unable to risk leaving footprints, she stuffed Presley's uniform beneath her tunic, and flew back through the building.

In the yard outside, Rutger Grimm noticed the door open and watched as a nearby tuft of grass became misshapen and flattened for no reason. He paid scant attention to the sprites who lined up, each one waiting their turn to pass through a machine that sprayed them with something. JC, concentrating only on removing the dog dirt from her boots, was unaware that despite being invisible, someone was watching her. Behind him, the pack of elfhounds with their handlers had also registered an interest.

"You must be joking if you think I am going to wear these!" protested Presley. JC's professional veneer prevented her from laughing at the sight of him in trousers that finished halfway up his long thin calves.

"The tunic fits OK," she said.

"I know the tunic fits OK! But look at these trousers. I'm supposed to be a sprite. I am going to stand out like a sore thumb!"

"You'll be fine. I am going to protect you with an elfin glamour. Humans and ironised sprites will just see what they expect to see, a tall 'ironed out' elf. But remember that you must approach all humans you see and ask how you might help them." Just saying it made JC sick in her craw.

"But still…"

"This job you're going for tomorrow. They want you to work on the rides."

"Rides? I'm no good with horses."

"How about wooden ones?" Presley's eyebrows could have knitted a child's bootee at least. "I've had a good look around this place and it seems to be some sort of gigantic pleasure ground. There is a section that contains strange carousels and even longer conceits that involve a track, not unlike the railway that is being built back in Thursday Market." JC noted the blank look on Presley's face. "Oh…sorry, I forgot."

"So they want me to go and work on these carousels and such? But I don't know the first thing about them!"

"Ask yourself, Presley, how many sprites you know…knew…who could do this kind of job. Obviously they will show you what to do. The point I was trying to get to was that it seems from my investigations that the job very much entails working on your own. It'll just be you…it might give you time to do a bit of exploring…" Presley relaxed for the first time since the conversation began. Then, he began squirming in a quite alarming way. JC unlocked the door. "Is it the first time since you woke up?" Presley nodded as he wavered in the doorway. "It's the last door on your right."

*

Eager to see the outside world again after a hundred years, Presley accompanied the invisible JC down through the back staircase at the palace.

"Hardly anybody seems to use it," said JC in the way of conversation.

"This is weird," said Presley, "it's like I'm talking to myself."

"You're going to have to stay in the sprite's sleeping block from now on."

"What?"

"If you're not to arouse suspicion, there is no other way."

188

"Just think, you'll be able to play your flute again. And because your room-mates are drugged they probably won't complain."

"Very funny!" The two of them left the building at the back where no one could see Presley on his own.

"I'm off through the gardens…down to the railway," said JC. "You do what you like, but stay out of trouble. It might do you good to feel good about the protection of elfin glamour. Approach a few humans…the more confident you feel about yourself, the better it works. And don't forget you are a slave."

Presley set off one way and JC, well, once she had stopped talking, Presley hadn't the slightest idea where she was.

As she walked away, she turned to watch him make his way down towards the food halls. There was something about him that made her feel protective towards him. She shrugged off the feeling with difficulty and set off through the palace gardens. The sound of dogs barking in the distance did little to distract her.

*

JC had never been the gardening type. Elves liked their landscapes natural. Formal gardens were a human thing. Planting her invisible bottom on a wooden bench, JC unfolded the plans to the layout of the palace gardens. It appeared they had changed little in the last hundred years. The only thing missing was the huge ornamental lake, the dried up basin of which was to her right. In the distance, the gardens rolled out before her.

"It must have been some weeding job," she said out loud as she folded up the plans.

"It was! It took a crew of fifty gardeners to get this straight," said a voice from behind a bush. JC stuffed the plans back inside her jacket and stepped away from the bench. A small human gardener rounded the bush. "There's only me now. I've told them I don't know how they expect me…Oh!" The gardener lifted his cap and scratched his bronzed pate. JC flashed him an invisible smile before she carried on her way.

The old plans indicated that the boundary wall of the formal gardens edged up against parkland but on reaching the wall, JC was surprised by what she saw there. A small powered cart was making slow progress over the manicured grassland towards her. It's occupants she recognised as Wilkie and Hans-Christian Grimm. As they stopped the cart and got out, JC was unsure why they were there. The landscape they travelled in was hardly fit for hunting…unless they were hunting for her. Wilkie Grimm walked to the back of a cart and began to search through a large long bag. JC expected him to pull out a rifle, but was somewhat bemused when he extracted a long stick with a metal knob on the end. Now she was sure they weren't about to shoot her, JC climbed over the wall and stiffened when she dislodged a small rock onto the ground. Hans-Christian Grimm shot a look in her direction and held it for a beat. His brother swung the stick and hit a small ball a long way. Wilkie Grimm pushed the heavy glasses back up his nose and smiled, which was an unusual occurrence in itself and the two of them mounted the cart and set off on their way. The cart's speed made it easy for JC to follow them and marvel how they seemed to take such pleasure in hitting a small ball a long way. Near to where a small flag was fluttering in the wind, JC got close enough to hear them speak.

"The train will be in soon. Do you need to pick anything up?" said Wilkie.

"No, I'm fine. I believe Rutger is heading out this morning though…finalising the TV promotion for opening week. He's back tomorrow." Wilkie watched his brother tap the ball almost to the hole.

"What is that noise? Is it dogs I can hear?" said Wilkie.

"You know the little problem, I told you about?" said Hans-Christian. "Well, I decided to bring in the experts."

"The barking seems to be getting closer. I'm not a big lover of dogs."

"Oh there's no need for you to worry, my dear brother. They're elfhounds. It's only elves that need to be worried. Isn't it, my dear?" Doubting her invisibility for the first time, JC saw him turn around and look almost straight at her.

*

Across the strange landscape she could see them…three men, each with a handful of dogs. Elfhounds. She knew they had caught her scent, so she set off at a run. The laughter of Hans-Christian Grimm rang in her ears as she ran across the strange green landscape and hurdled the occasional sand trap they seemed to have set for her. JC felt the adrenalin rush as she made her way towards the line of crags in the distance. She was not scared because she had been professionally trained. This was the sort of thing she had joined The Eye to do. Making good speed, she was confident that she had put more yardage between herself and her pursuers. She kept the line of crags to her left-hand side and eventually arrived at what she assumed to be the railway track. About a hundred metres ahead she could see that the track split into two. One branch headed towards the crag and the other down towards a small building which, even at this distance, she could see was swathed in smoke and steam. The sound of the approaching elfhounds made the choice an easy one. If she headed to the crags there would be more places to hide but there was a distinct possibility that she would be the only sprite around. If she chose the steaming building, it would be more likely that there would be sprites slaving away and the elfhounds would lose her scent in amongst them.

JC saw her first ever railway engine leaving the way it had come. She watched as its immense power pulled three coaches out from the daylight and into what looked like a huge cave. For a while she was transfixed by the sight and the overpowering sound it produced. Sprites and humans filled the breach it left like worker ants seeing off an attack. It was almost as if they were clearing the area in the expectation of something else happening.

As the engine left, the vacuum of silence was filled with the howling of the approaching elfhounds and JC was startled into action. She knew from anecdotal evidence that you couldn't hide from an elfhound. Even invisibility could not confound them. Now she had other sprites around her she at least felt some security. Alone in the gardens and across the parkland, she had been an easy trail for the dogs to follow, but here, surrounded by others of her kind she felt safe. She watched sprites bundling the supplies that had come on the steam engine onto smaller vehicles ready to be driven back towards the centre of Domania.

The cave intrigued her. There was something about it that made the mind doubt itself. Approaching the edge of it she peered deep into its darkness. The track upon which the steam engine had left was clear to see. She stepped back again and was struck by the fact that the cave stood alone. It appeared to have no framework at all. Usually a cave appeared within the setting of a crag or a cliff, but here it was different. It was a cave in the middle of nothing. Wherever the darkness of the cave ended there was only sky beyond it. She walked to its very edge and peered around it. There was nothing there!

She looked back into the cave and back again at the fields and the Wall of Thorns in the distance. The depth she could perceive inside the cave was not here outside it. Perhaps it was an illusion, she thought. She came back round to the front of the cave and put her hand inside it. She could feel the rough walls and even walked into it for a yard or so. On the floor, her feet found the railway track heading away from her. Only minutes earlier she had seen a very solid railway engine going into it. This had to be some kind of trick.

Behind her the hounds came closer; two sprites manhandled a barrier into place that separated the station platform from the cave. JC's attention was startled by a hissing sound to her right. She looked but could see nothing.

Behind her the excited elfhounds sensed their quarry was nearby. Their handlers, knowing that she was close, prepared to let them off their leads. JC's proximity to the mouth of the cave meant that she failed to see that the entrance to the cave was disappearing. Accustomed to the hissing noise to her right and comfortable with the number of sprites around her, she failed to notice that the elfhounds were closing in on her...

*

From his perch on the fence, high above the road down to the station, a rather tall sprite put his flute to his lips and recalled a tune he hadn't played for a hundred years.

*

...JC, at last aware of the approaching commotion behind her, turned and saw a pack of elfhounds heading straight towards her. Her first reaction was one of surprise. The dogs would have been on her within seconds. She might have been ripped to pieces before she even thought about flying above their slobbering jaws, but for some reason they just stopped. Their floppy ears pricked as well as they could before their heads turned and they charged off up the hill past their bemused handlers.

Whereas most people who had survived such a situation might have sat down and thanked whatever god they believed in, JC got on with the job in hand. The hissing noise was getting closer and louder. She noticed that the cave to her right now seemed a lot darker than it had been. She ran back to the safety of the station platform and assessed the cave from there. It was disappearing. The entrance to the cave was closing. She had to make her mind up. Should she stay where she was or take the risk of finding out what lay at the end of that dark tunnel? She took the latter option. Within minutes the world behind her had disappeared. She was alone in the darkness.

Standing in the dark, JC was somewhat relieved when a mysterious lighting kicked in and illuminated all around her. She found herself alone in a great cavern, the roof of which disappeared into the darkness above her head. Her first instinct was to work out how to get back to where she had come from. Time spent in Domania had affirmed that the steam engine arrived everyday at the same hour but, as she walked back towards it, she still couldn't imagine that this wall, deep in some unknown rock separated her from the world she had always been familiar with. Making her way across it like a run-of-the-mill mime artist she marvelled at how smooth it was. It was man-made, that much she was sure of.

With no sign of any access back through the wall, JC decided to search the rest of the cavern. She knew little about this new concept of the railway but it was obvious to her that, in this new world, this cavern had once played a large part in its operation. Tracks were all around her and the rusting hulks of old engines sat in the furthest shadows of the cavern. She searched some of the old buildings, the majority of which were derelict and revealed little of interest to her. There was, however, one building that intrigued her. A small wooden shed was kitted out with a comfortable chair, a table and a small bed with a blue cover. Numerous books lined a shelf near to the chair. Immediately, JC was on her guard. She felt the chair and bed and took solace from the fact that they were both cold.

Now satisfied that she was the only person in the cavern, she set about walking along the tunnel. She left the light behind her and proceeded with care along the track. Not usually one for being fearful, JC found the lack of any light at the end of the tunnel somewhat disconcerting. She pressed on regardless, buoyed by the certainty that the steam engine must have gone somewhere. As her eyes became more accustomed to the light her usual confidence returned to her. She lengthened her stride and walked straight into a wall.

Some minutes later, she awoke to the sound of voices. Flicking herself into a state of invisibility, she soon realised that the voices came from beyond the obstruction that had pole-axed her. She reached for the wall and recoiled at the feel of iron. Outside the voices continued.

"Look, Dad, it's more than my job's worth."

"All I'm asking, Mike, is that you let me in for a quick shufti around. Who's going to know?"

"In two days, me, Tracey and the kids are going in there. Can't you just wait until we come back?"

"No…because I know things about Elphinstone Crag!"

"Oh not that again, Dad…"

"Don't look at me like that, son! The Crag holds a lot of secrets. Things have happened…even in my lifetime. My own great, great grandmother disappeared in there and was never seen again!"

"That's ancient history, Dad!"

"Oh it is, is it? You seem to forget, I've actually been in there and seen something myself…something unnatural. And despite all that, you're still intent on taking my grandchildren in there?"

"Your grandchildren *want* to go in there! They're delighted to be going in there! There are kids all around the country who want to go and see Domania. Your grandchildren are privileged, Dad, because I work for the company! And I want to work for the company for many more years so no; I am not letting you in the bloody tunnel!"

"Well, if you won't let me in…"

"I *can't* let you in!"

"…If you won't let me in, then I'll have to go in the way I went last time, won't I?"

"Don't be so silly, Dad! You're an old man…" JC could hear the older man marching away across the gravel. "…Dad!…Dad! Don't do anything stupid, Dad!" She chose that moment to bang on the steel wall.

"Help! Help! Let me out!" she shouted. Outside of the wall there was silence. So she repeated her cry.

"Who's there?" said Mike. JC could hear his father returning.

"Will you please let me out?"

"Don't you come any closer, Dad! I'm not opening this door until you're a hundred metres away." JC heard the older man trudging back away from the tunnel. When she heard Mike walking away, she cried out once again.

"Hang on!" he said. "I've got to go back into the box." Seconds passed before a loud grinding sound filled the tunnel. JC winced as searing daylight poured in around her. The metal door ground to a halt and the still invisible JC ducked underneath it. "Come on, miss. I'm sure you can get underneath that!" JC stood by the tunnel entrance and watched as Mike approached. He was a large man with dark hair and he fell to his haunches to look beneath the door. "Hello? Hello? Miss, are you there?" Mike's father started to approach the tunnel entrance. "Don't you come any closer, Dad!" JC smiled as the son ran back into the box and closed the metal door.

"Isn't there anybody there?" said the older man addressing the head of his son through the window of the security box.

"No. She must have gone back."

"Why would she go back?"

"I don't know!"

"That's your trouble…" said the older man under his breath as he looked around, "…no imagination." JC felt uneasy as he seemed to look right through her before addressing his son once again. "The both of us have just heard a young woman's voice coming from inside the tunnel. Aren't you the least bit curious about where she is?"

"Look…I opened the door and she didn't come out. She'll bang again if she wants to come out…I'm just doing my job, OK?"

"Well, seeing as you've been so unhelpful, son...I'm off to find another way into this...Domania." Mike shrugged from behind his desk. JC caught the look on his face as she passed his window. He was clearly shaken. But it was what the father had said that interested JC. She had a day to pass before she returned back through the time-gate. It might be interesting to follow this old man for a day.

*

The first six hours had been eventful for JC. The world she found herself in was far more advanced than her own. More of the metal travelling machines whizzed by on smooth roads that only had the occasional pot-hole in them. She followed the old man, who she soon discovered to be called Walter Coope, back to the house where he lived. She watched him cook himself lunch by placing a pre-packaged complete meal inside a small metal box. Three minutes later, a bell rang and Walter removed the meal which was now scalding hot. Watching him eat it reminded JC that she was hungry. When Walter left the room to go upstairs, she helped herself to the bread and jam that had been left out. She was sure he wouldn't miss the few gulps of milk she took from an unusual soft bottle.

Walter talked to himself a lot, which she found useful in her coming to terms with this strange world she found herself in. She followed him outside and watched as he opened up a small building to one side of the house. Inside JC could see there was a vibrant blue travelling machine similar to those she had seen dashing about on the streets of this town. Walter began polishing the bonnet with a gentle affection.

"The 1968 Mark Three Riley, Elf," is what JC thought Walter said; which shook her for a moment. Was he addressing her? Could he see her? Surely not, but this tendency to state out loud what he was doing was beginning to trouble her. Perhaps he was mentally unstable? She watched as the old man drove the vehicle out of the building and left it running before going back into the house. JC walked around the vehicle. She noticed that it had the name 'Riley' on the shiny grill-type thing at the front and was relieved to see the name 'Elf' on the back. She would have felt excited by the possibility of travelling in this machine, had it not been built almost entirely of metal. The sound of running water from the first floor of Walter's house allowed her to open what she thought to be the passenger's door. She took a seat in the vehicle and waited. Straight away she began to feel uncomfortable due to the proximity of the vehicle's iron frame. Her chance to escape was lost as Walter locked the front door behind him and climbed into the vehicle. He was now wearing leather gloves and had changed his flat cap for a newer one. JC's discomfort was short-lived as the two of them soon arrived at the centre of a town that she discovered was called Gilsland. Walter parked his machine amongst many others and while he was buying a ticket to place inside the car, JC got out. In a world that was completely alien to her she would later witness him arguing with the lady behind the counter at the Post Office about his car tax (apparently he had forgotten to bring his M.O.T. - whatever that was). Then she followed him to the Public Library.

"Map of Elphinstone Lead Mines," said Walter as he placed a small map on top of a large empty table. Minutes later he was back with another which he put down beside it. "Elphinstone Mine Branch Railway". She watched as he used a machine to make a copy of both maps. When he had the copies both neatly rolled up he took the maps back to the counter and thanked the librarian.

"Back to the car!" he said to no one in particular, and JC followed him back to what she now knew to be a car. As they approached it, conflicting emotions filled her mind. Physically repelled at the thought of getting back inside this iron box on wheels, JC let her professionalism dictate otherwise. Her biggest problem would be getting into the car without Walter becoming suspicious. This fear remained groundless as Walter opened the passenger door to put the rolled-up maps into the footwell and chose to leave it open while he muttered something about 'tyre pressure' and went away to check the wheel furthest away from the door. JC took her seat and waited.

They next visited a huge emporium on the edge of town that sold tools and equipment for all purposes. JC marvelled at the wide range of things that she could only begin to guess the use of. Walter filled a wire mesh trolley with items and took them to a disinterested woman who placed each one before some sort of magic eye that recorded the price.

"48 pounds 75," said the woman. JC was shocked when Walter placed a small stiff card into a machine, pressed a few buttons and walked out of the shop without paying for them. This was truly a strange world.

On the way back, she started to feel ill. She tried to concentrate on the new world racing by outside. Her head ached and she recognised the symptoms of ironisation.

Back at his house, Walter shot through the door and ran upstairs. JC almost kicked the door off its hinges to get out. With Walter emptying his bladder with glorious relief, he couldn't hear the sound of an elf being sick in his begonias.

THE HIGHWAYMAN

I woke with a start and stared into a huge mouth. A large tongue licked me and I was almost overcome with smell of wet grass. Country boys know to show no fear so I pushed the dun cow's head out of the way and tried to remove myself from the ditch. I looked at my watch. Almost one o'clock. I stretched and scratched my backside before hopping over the wall. I was about to set off back to town when I noticed that Tom and Dickon were still working in the graveyard. I decided to pay them a visit. As I neared them I noticed that they had dug four graves, the furthest away of which was almost double the length of the others.

"Afternoon, lads!" I pulled my hat well down over my face.

"All right." The bigger of the two answered.

"Blimey! Four graves in such a tiny village. What's happened here then? Has the plague returned?"

"We don't ask questions...we just obey our orders." Again it was the bigger guy who answered.

"Yeah, but four graves! Surely someone round here would know what had happened. And that one..." I pointed at the huge grave. "That must be for a giant. I mean the only giant round here is Jack Carn...oh and Sphagnum. I hope nothing's happened to either of them." At the mention of Sphagnum's name the two men shot me sharp looks. "Four graves...and one of them for a giant. I shall have to ask

204

Scuzzer and Tranter about that one. Bye now!" I started to walk away and the quiet one turned to the other.

"Here Tom…what does he mean by that? Does he know Scuzzer?"

"Shut up, you fool! Let me think!" It was just a matter of time. I had almost reached the graveyard gate when I heard the two men running up behind me. I turned to face them.

"What do you mean when you say you'll have to ask Scuzzer and Tranter?", said Tom.

"Well I presume it was them who asked you to dig the graves…seeing as nobody seems to have died in the village."

"It might have been," said Tom.

"It was them!" said Dickon who was becoming more animated by the minute.

"I was just wondering….now that the job's nearly finished why they should want four graves digging and one of them large enough to take a giant." By now Dickon was bouncing up and down in terror.

"They're for us Tom! Me, you, Harry and Big Sphagnum! They're for us! They want to keep us quiet. To keep the secret forev-" Dickon was cut off as Tom slapped him across the face.

"Shut up, you fool! That's just what this-" Obviously Dickon didn't take too kindly to having his face slapped as he threw himself at Tom and together they fell into the grave presumably reserved for Sphagnum. I left them to it. I had planted the seeds of doubt…six feet deeper than planned.

"Look I'm not happy about this," said Hamble from high upon his horse. Plum Thumb had leant us one of the black mares that pulled the hearse used for the more discerning dead people of Without. "I just get the feeling I've never ridden a horse before." I looked up at him as he balanced his rotund bulk nervously in the saddle.

"Look, Hamble, all you have to do is trot out into the middle of the road and shout 'Stand and Deliver!' While the driver is distracted, I'll sneak into the back of the coach and you can just ride away."

"Won't they think that's a bit strange…going to all that trouble to ride out here, stop the coach and then just ride away?"

"Look, the driver will be so relieved that he's safe, he's not going to ask too many questions. Trust me. Anyway, this seems like as good a place as any."

The silhouette of Hamble and his steed resembled an equestrian statue in the pale moonlight. Image is everything I thought as I saw that my hat and coat had transformed him into a gentleman of the highway. After a minute or so of silence, save for the chattering of Hamble's teeth, the distinct sound of horses' hooves could be heard in the distance. I grabbed the reins and pulled the horse and its skittish rider further into the forest. Tying the pair of them to a branch I made my way back to the road and waited while Scuzzer and Tranter cantered past on the road to Without-the-Wall. I made my way back to Hamble feeling somewhat naked without my accustomed hat and coat.

"Right, Hamble it's up to you now. The next thing that passes this way will be the coach with Sphagnum and the prisoners."

"And the driver."

"Hamble, I've seen this Harry and he's half your size. He'll be terrified when you come riding out of the forest."

"Riding?"

"Well…*sidling* out of the forest then. All you've got to do is create a diversion and the rest is up to me, OK?" Hamble tried to nod his head without creating any knock-on effect further down his body.

Nearly half an hour passed before the sound of the oncoming coach could be made out. I set Hamble up by the side of the road and explained just how he was to make the horse move. He seemed to have got the hang of it so I took up my place at the other side of the road. The coach was travelling at quite a speed and I gave Hamble the thumbs up before ducking out of the way.

The sound of the coach slowing down was plain enough. It was working. I heard "Stand and Deliver!" boom from Hamble's chest. The coach slowed to a halt and I scurried over to the door. In a second I was yanked inside the coach by a large arm and found myself sitting in a gloom that smelt somewhat of rancid cabbages. Sphagnum caught the wrinkle of my nose.

"Sorry, but seeing as it was the last day I didn't want to buy any more." I shook my head at Sphagnum and put my finger to my lips. I was puzzled to hear the driver getting down off the coach as Sphagnum manacled me with the rest of the prisoners. The scream that followed threw me. I had been expecting the sound of Hamble riding away being followed by a huge sigh of relief. The driver clumped back onto the coach and slowly we began to build up speed as we drove the last few miles into Without. I put my thumb up to Sphagnum and he just nodded.

"What did you do with the prisoner whose place I had taken?" I whispered.

"I left him next to Harry", said the giant. This puzzled me somewhat.

"Hang on, if you left him with Harry, who on earth is driving the coach?" Sphagnum shrugged.

"I don't know, he said he was replacing Harry as he wasn't very well." Unusual but fair enough, I thought. "Then when I laid the other prisoner in the bushes to make room for you, I saw Harry lying there and he *didn't* look very well."

"What do you mean he didn't look very well?"

"His face was purple and his tongue was sticking out."

"What do you mean? Dead?"

"Sshh!" said Sphagnum, "he'll hear you."

"What does *he* look like?" I pointed up above us to indicate the driver.

"He dresses a bit like you and he uses a lot of big words."

"Deadman!" I whispered.

"Oh I thought you meant what does the driver like. Harry was short and fat."

My mind was racing now. I thought I had got rid of Deadman but now his evil backside was just a plank's width away from my head. My only hope would be that he didn't recognise me without my clothes on...so to speak. The outfit I was wearing was practically inconspicuous and quite a good fit as it had been borrowed from the vast range of Plum's lost property box. It seemed the people who left them in his funeral parlour never bothered to come back for them. I had just to keep my head down and act dumb like the rest of the passengers.

As I became more accustomed to the flitting of the moon's light into the coach I tried to make out just who my fellow passengers were. The coach seated twelve comfortably, with a small open area down one side that allowed access to the banks of seating behind. Sphagnum, myself and a young male dwarf were sat facing the rest of our team. In the front row were two female goblins and a careworn-looking boggart. It was almost like looking in a mirror I thought as the moon's light lit up his face every now and again. The rest of the passengers were obscured by the shadows of the coach's interior. Each one of them had a vacant look on their face and a mouth that hung agape. I felt awkward as I practised the same look in the face of my doppelganger.

When the coach began to slow down as it arrived at Without-the-Wall, I nudged Sphagnum who incredibly had fallen asleep.

"Whatever you do, I don't want you to speak to me. Do you understand? I'm just like the others now, OK?" Sphagnum nodded. As the door opened I fixed the vacant look on my face and sunk back into the shadows.

JC sat on a chair by the window as Walter clattered around the house preparing for his expedition. He filled an old rucksack with apples, biscuits, chocolate and a large bottle of water, two long lengths of climbing rope, a crowbar, a torch and an old biscuit tin that had a red cross painted over it. He then tested the lamp of an old pit-helmet before strapping it to the rucksack.

"Oh, nearly forgot!" said Walter, as he left the room and returned minutes later clutching a solid wooden box. He wrapped a careworn towel around it and set about emptying the rucksack again. The old box was then given pride of place in the rucksack and everything else was stuffed back in around it. "Can't be too careful", he mused. He remembered the maps and poked them down into the top of the bag.

The last thing Walter did before leaving the house was to write a letter which he addressed to "To whom it may concern". It was written quickly and JC never got a chance to read it before the two of them made their way out of the house. Walter headed through his garden and struggled to climb over the fence that backed onto the countryside. JC floated over it and felt a pang of guilt. The pair of them made their way across a field until they reached the railway track.

"No trains at this time of night", said Walter as if to reassure himself. He put his head down and marched along the track towards the Elphinstone tunnel. The invisible elf flew along in his wake.

When the pair of them got close to the mouth of the tunnel, they could see the light burning in the security box. Above it a large sign proclaimed DOMANIA into the twilit sky. Walter looked for an unused path between a clump of nettles and made his way along it. The path climbed away from the tunnel and up the side of the crag for quite a distance. An old ruined building lay up ahead. Little of it survived and its grey stone walls looked like broken teeth. Walter stepped over a low wall and found a space to open up his map. Using his torch to see, he pointed out the old adit entrance to the mine before peering through the gloom to try and work out where it was. He folded up the map and hurried further up the incline. With his torch he checked behind the dark bushes searching for the elusive entrance.

"Aha!" shouted the exultant Walter. "Here it is!", and he turned as if he wished to share his discovery. He brushed the foliage to one side and forced his way into what looked like an old cave. Some way into the cave, Walter unpacked his rucksack and took out the crowbar. The entrance was barred with old wooden planks. With a tenacity that belied his age, he began attacking the wooden barrier with the crowbar until he had made a hole large enough for him to squeeze inside. Pulling his rucksack in after him, he untied the pit-helmet and set it on his head. The lamp was switched on and JC could clearly see through the remaining planking that the adit sloped down into the mine. Once Walter had set off on his way, JC climbed in through the gap in the planking and followed at a distance.

The old man had travelled barely fifty yards when JC heard his helmet scrape along the top of the adit. She knew she had to be careful and kept close to Walter so that she could see the lie of the rocks. Were she to crack her head and be knocked senseless, there would be no one to rescue her.

At the end of the adit, the pair of them walked into a small cavern. "This must be Brierley's Cavern!" announced Walter and his voice echoed around the ill-lit walls. He checked it against the map and walked to the far end, where a large dark space failed to be illuminated by the lamps. Walter looked into the void and sighed. "Nearly fifty years…where did it all go?"

JC watched as the old man looked down into the dark abyss below. She could see that he was wrestling with some inner demon but had nothing but admiration for him as he began the descent using the wooden steps that had been knocked into the rock. Walter was thankful that the light didn't show how far down he could fall as he drove himself down. Descending on crude wooden ladders, a full ten minutes had passed before Walter felt the relief of pressing his foot onto solid ground again. He pulled out the map from his rucksack to see where he needed to go next. Floating behind him JC could see that they were now in the First Gallery. Walter started to search for the place where he could descend to the next level. More wooden stairs beckoned him further down into the darkness where even the light seemed frightened to go. JC dreaded to think how the old man would cope if his lamp went out but she decided to put thoughts like that out of her mind. Walter was no professional, but she could see the old man had guts. It was slow going but the pair of them continued to descend through the different levels.

Halfway down the fifth descent, Walter felt for the next step with his foot and found nothing. Stretching his foot deep into the darkness he was once more hopeful of finding somewhere that might take his weight. He could feel nothing. The need to look down was weighing against the fear of the unknown. He had fought the constant fear of falling by refusing to look down at any time but now he had no choice. He angled his head back and down, hoping that the lamp on his helmet might illuminate the problem. The wooden steps seemed to have finished as the descent passed between two large outcrops of rock. Below that the darkness offered no clue on how a person should proceed. Walter took a grip of the step above him and tried to lean further out when his aging fingers slipped. Scrabbling in panic, he lost hold of the step and plunged into the darkness.

Walter plunged into the gap, his hands grasping at the rock face; the expectation of certain death was only fleeting as he soon felt his back come up against more rock. His rucksack had jammed him in between the two outcrops and the feel of his legs dangling in the air made him heave up the small amount of food he had within him. JC's heart had been in her mouth as she witnessed the old man fall. Unsure of what to do she was almost relieved when Walter took the initiative himself. Bringing his knees up and pushing hard against the rocks he forced himself high enough to free his rucksack. His lamp illuminated an iron hand grip hammered into the rock.

JC floated towards the old man and appeared before him. She was surprised when he didn't seem phased by her arrival.

"Oh, I wondered when you were going to introduce yourself!"

"You mean you knew I was with you?"

"You've been with me since you came out of the tunnel."

"But how…?"

"Oh I couldn't see you…but I know enough about fairies-"

"Elves!"

"…enough about elves to recognise the signs. I *know* the history of Elphinstone Crag. Why did you think I was talking out loud? Did you think I was mad?"

"Well, actually…"

"Leaving out the food and the car door open for you…I really thought you might have been smart enough to guess." JC tried to act professional and bit her tongue but old habits die hard.

"I might not be smart but I'm not the person whose legs are dangling over a bottomless pit."

"That's not usually a problem to someone who can fly. Now are you going to help me or what?"

"Give me your helmet!" Walter unstrapped the helmet and watched as JC placed it on her own head. The top of her face disappeared and Walter laughed.

"Perhaps it would be better if you carried it." JC snatched the helmet off her head and slowly disappeared out of Walter's vision. "There must be a way down. The miners would have passed this way; even I passed this way many years ago; I was a much fitter man back then."

JC's voice came back to him. "If you can ease yourself down between the two outcrops there are some footholds carved into the rock that you should be able to reach." A minute or so later, Walter's foot found the support of the ledge beneath him. Relief coursed through his body. He had reached what he hoped was the Grand Gallery. In near darkness, he watched as his helmet came floating back to him. He fastened it back onto his head and put JC back into his spotlight.

"Walter Coope!" he boomed as he thrust out his hand to JC.

"I know; I was with you when you were rude to the lady in the Post Office. My name is JC Bigg."

"So…you're an elf, are you?"

"Can we get on, Mr Coope?"

"Please, call me Walter."

"Can we get on, Walter?" Looking a little disappointed, Walter got on with the job of locating exactly where they were. He got down on his knees and opened up the map on the hard rock floor.

"This is where we are now. It is called the Grand Gallery and it was from here that the miners would branch out in their search for lead. As you can see from the map there are numerous other galleries that can be reached from this point." Walter pointed his finger at each in turn. See, that one is the Tapper's Gallery, Hobgoblin's Gallery, Boden's Gallery…that one is Our Lady's Gallery…we'll be passing that one. This is the one we're after!" JC followed Walter's crooked finger and saw that *Vision Gallery (closed)* was underlined in ink. Walter took some time to get to his feet before looking through his bag for the torch which he switched on and handed to JC. "Try and find the signpost!"

"What?"

"It's on the map! I saw it the last time I was down here. There was a stalagmite; the miners had nailed signs on it which pointed the way to all the galleries. I've seen it, JC! It's here somewhere!" The two of them wandered around the large gallery illuminating small sections at a time until JC shone her torch at what looked like a very wet wedding dress.

She raised the torch up along its ever-narrowing column and saw, with some disbelief, a signpost collared into the ever growing stalagmite.

"I've found it!" she cried and Walter hurried over. "The Our Lady's and the Vision Gallery are over that way." Walter turned and marched down a well-trodden path; JC floated after him. A hundred metres or so down the path, He dipped his head into what looked like a cave. Curious to see why he was smiling, JC came up close behind him and shone her torch into the cave. The sight of a woman standing there took her breath away.

"This is Our Lady's Gallery!" shouted Walter, his voice booming around the rocks. "It's just a statue carved out of a rock formation. The faded colours of her painted blue dress and scarf told the tale. "The miners used to take great comfort from the mother of Christ being down here with them." Walter looked at JC and realised she had no idea of what he was talking about.

They moved on and arrived at Vision Gallery. It was clear that this cave had at one time been boarded up. Some of the planking had been removed.

"Why was it closed?" asked JC.

"According to a book I read, the miners were so scared of what they saw in there that they would never go back in again." Walter began squeezing through the gap in the planking. "I'll tell you what JC; it was a lot easier getting through this gap last time I came here."

"What did the miners see...what did you see?"

218

"Just like they said – a vision; it was a land of sunshine, forest and fields, hundreds of feet down below Elphinstone Crag. Whatever it was, it wasn't right and I know that this Domania thing has something to do with it." JC shone her torch close enough to the old man's face to register the concern there. "My grandchildren are supposed to be visiting this place in a couple of days' time, and I don't like the idea very much. There's a history of disappearance around here…young men, children…even my own great-great-grandmother went into these caves and never, ever came out again. She left behind her son, my great-grandfather. He was only one year old."

JC already knew what 'the vision' was. The miners and Walter had seen a glimpse of the world JC had left behind only yesterday. She doubted whether it would be prudent to explain all this to Walter. Better to find out just what he intended to do before putting him in the big picture.

"It's just like a big picture…" said Walter, jolting JC out of her train of thought, "…that sort of fills the cave. It's sort of…interactive, I think they call it now…"

"What?" said JC trying to round up her thoughts.

"Well you can actually enter into the picture…if you can survive the fall."

"What do you mean?" JC was somewhat confused now. Walter looked at the dial of his luminous watch. "You'll see for yourself in about four hours, I expect.

"Where's Harry?" I recognised the voice as Tranter's.

"Unfortunately, Harry was a little inconvenienced, so they asked me to take his place." It *was* Deadman; my stomach churned.

"Who's they? There is no *they*!" This must have been Scuzzer I could hear.

"Just be gracious that your contraband has arrived safely. I expect that is the last I shall hear about it. Now if you don't mind, I have my own business to attend to. I bid you farewell, gentlemen."

"Now just a minute-" There was the sound of a scuffle then all we could hear was the erudite hiss of Deadman.

"Now look, I have tried being nice but it seems to have little effect on your dullard intellect. As arranged, your large companion and myself have successfully transported eleven 'passengers' to the village of Without-the-Wall. Now if that is all I shall overlook your pathetic attempt to bludgeon me and remove this knife from your throat."

"OK, OK!" spluttered Scuzzer.

"What do you mean eleven passengers?", said Tranter, "There are supposed to be twelve."

"I really don't think that's important at the moment," hissed Scuzzer as he was dragged towards us. The door next to me flew open and Deadman poked his head into the gloom of the coach like a lizard looking for woodlice. His head was inches away from mine as he tried to count the passengers. He turned towards Sphagnum and I could see his rancid breath vapourising in front of me

"You! I counted eleven passengers just before I set off. How many did you put on board?"

"Eleven-Twelve! I think", said Sphagnum clearly flustered.

"Well is that eleven or twelve? Quickly, man! I don't like mysteries."

"Twelve, yes it was twelve." Sphagnum recovered somewhat. "It's always twelve. Isn't it, Scuzzer?" With his head jammed hard against the coach door, Scuzzer could only manage to speak one word. It was probably 'yes'.

"Strange", said Deadman, catching sight of my doppelganger in the light of the moon. "Ah, a boggart." I tried to sink further back into the shadows. "Conveniently near the door." Deadman grabbed the boggart by the front of his tunic and pulled him out of the coach. "What is your name?" The boggart straightened up and stared into the distance.

"You won't get no response from him", said Tranter, "he's what you might call 'out of it'."

"Hmm, I wouldn't be too sure. You see, I was sure that there were eleven passengers and now there are twelve. I might have conceded an error on my part were it not for the strange occurrence that befell us on the way here. We were stopped by the most ineffectual highwayman I have ever seen. The man clearly couldn't ride a horse and fled at the

221

slightest provocation from me." Having now experienced Deadman close at hand, I suspect that both Scuzzer and Tranter would not have been surprised by the highwayman's reaction. For myself, if I hadn't been so worried about my own predicament, I might have spared a thought for Hamble.

Thrown onto the floor and away from Deadman's steely clutch, Scuzzer regained some of his previous bravado. "So? What's the problem with this boggart?"

"The boggart bears a passing resemblance to someone I know." He took off his large hat and placed it on the head of the supine boggart. "More than a passing resemblance." From the coach window I could only see the wispy hair that attempted to cover the large detachable head of Deadman. From the reaction of Tranter and Scuzzer, the front wasn't a pretty sight. Scuzzer, still prone, attempted to reach inside his coat but Deadman already had a gun pointing at him.

"I'm just checking his name on the list", stammered Scuzzer. Deadman moved towards him and watched as Scuzzer uncrumpled a piece of paper. "That's him there...the long name" said Scuzzer, pointing to name on the list. "We took him from a tavern in Fleetpool, about four or five days ago."

"Yeah", said Tranter, "he told us all about this lovely little dog he was getting. ...still he hadn't picked it up at that point...so we thought...well...no harm done. I mean, we're not heartless, you know." Deadman seemed somewhat mollified.

"Gentlemen now that I can see that your cup overflows with the milk of human kindness, I will leave you to get on with your own business and I shall attend mine." Maybe the likelihood that I was sat cradling a whiskey in the Sleeping Beauty Inn was a more pressing need. "If you have no objections?" Scuzzer looked deep down into the barrel of the gun pointing at him and slowly shook his head. It was Tranter who allowed himself the question that Scuzzer would only have asked if someone else was in the firing line.

"Who are you?"

"My name is of no import to you…and should you ever hear it from my lips…it will be the last thing that you do hear." The maniacal laugh that followed made me envy my fellow passengers. At least in their drug-addled state they would have been immune to the fear that Deadman inspired. Without a further word he swept away from us and headed towards the town.

"It's been a strange night", said Tranter as he helped Scuzzer to his feet. As last in line I was stood close enough to them as they discussed matters. "First Tom and Dickon don't show up and now this. You don't think the whole thing's falling apart on the last day do you?"

"Maybe Tom, Dickon and Harry are just smarter than we gave them credit for. Digging four even sized graves might have been a reasonable request but the extra-large one…" Scuzzer indicated Sphagnum with his head. "Perhaps they just put three and one together and got four." Sphagnum was busying himself with the prisoners further up the line. Their complicity made it easy to line them up one by one.

"What are we going to do with him?" said Tranter nodding towards Sphagnum.

"He's not a problem; we can sort him out once we get the cargo delivered. I'm sure Mr Grimm can spare us a couple of men to tidy things up. The sound of that name, linked with what I had been witness to out by the Wall of Thorns gave me even more cause for concern. When Sphagnum reached the end of the queue, he began to put on his Jack-in-Irons costume. Fastening the pungent belt of cabbages around his waist caused Scuzzer and Tranter to move away. He began to loop a long heavy chain around his broad body. As he bent down for the club, I tried to whisper a warning to him.

"What?" said Sphagnum. Scuzzer turned on hearing his voice.

"Who are you talking to, Sphagnum?" The giant's face reddened.

"I...er...I thought someone said something." Scuzzer sounded suspicious.

"Well Tranter and I didn't say anything...so it must have been one of the workers." He walked along the line looking at our faces which were empty canvasses waiting for some paint. "Which one of these lovely lads and lasses spoke to Sphagnum? Was it you?" He thrust his face hard in at one of the female goblins. Not a flinch. Next he chose the young dwarf...once again he was met with an impassive stare. As he headed down the queue, I felt him watching me as I gawped in front of me willing a dribble of saliva to fall out of my open mouth. I braced myself for the moment when I would need all my self-control not to blink or flinch. I didn't think I could do it. No doubt it took years of training to achieve such supreme body control. I felt Scuzzer come close to my ear. He whispered, "Was it you?" I summoned something from somewhere and presumably passed with flying colours. Scuzzer walked back along the line and signalled Sphagnum to move off. With Tranter behind us, Scuzzer halfway and Sphagnum a long way ahead, our chain-gang began its final part of the journey – through the village of Without and up to the graveyard.

Looking somewhat unusual with all its welcoming windows barred and shuttered, it was clear that the people of Without-the-Wall took no chance in attracting the evil eye of Jack-in-Irons. Our procession was like a cold wind blowing out the lamps and candles of the village. I wondered why our little party needed to pass through Without at all when the graveyard could be reached along the main road without venturing into the village. And then I realised that to prevent discovery of any kind the village needed to be locked up. It was almost like a bizarre reversal of prison where the good people are locked up to protect them from the bad ones who walk the streets. It seemed to have worked. Were it not for my own inquisitiveness, the secret would surely still have been safe. As we left the village and headed towards the graveyard, the black shape of the Wall of Thorns could be made out towering over it. It was a constant reminder to the people of this area that something strange had happened here all those years ago. The dark brooding shadow seemed overpowering but there, beyond it, a distinct glow in the sky was apparent. Some bright light was shining out from beyond the Wall of Thorns. I didn't know what it was I was heading for but it must have a gasometer all to itself.

Sphagnum stopped his wailing and opened up the gates of the graveyard. We passed the last resting places of ordinary folk, the solitary mound of the stranger who had died in my arms and the four empty graves that awaited Sphagnum and the others. It was these that reminded me I had to speak to Sphagnum and warn him of the consequences of staying around the graveyard tonight. He stood a long way in the front of the line and I was at the back. At the place where I had seen the gravediggers disappear only yesterday, Tranter lit a couple of flambeaux and stuck them into the conveniently placed sconces. He and Scuzzer were discussing something and left Sphagnum to his own devices as he began to take off his Jack-in-Irons regalia. The rest of us stood in line in placid accord. I was hoping that Sphagnum would make his way down to me so that I could get him to leave but he was busy hurling cabbages out of the graveyard. The light of the flambeaux lit up the large tombs at our side and I read the inscriptions eager that one of these tombs might provide a clue as to what lies beyond. When Sphagnum had finished he came back and checked the manacles that bound us together. Soon I would get the chance to warn him. He was only two sprites away from me when Scuzzer called him over.

"Sphagnum!" he beckoned the giant towards him, "As you know, tonight is the last night that you will have to guard the graveyard." Sphagnum looked a little disappointed.

"I thought I was going through with you tonight."

"No, you've got to stay here and Tranter and I will come back for you before dawn", said Scuzzer. The giant was obviously disappointed but nodded his head. "Right, let's get this lot through." Tranter removed the flambeau from a sconce before pulling it down. The door to the tomb swung open and Tranter began to usher the party inside. One by one we were shuffled into the tomb which was surprisingly well-lit by even more flambeaux. As my eyes adjusted to the brightness, I saw Scuzzer pick something up off an empty shelf. I recognised it as being one of those boxes that the soldier had used to communicate with the Grimm brother. He spoke into it and told whoever was listening that the party was ready for its escort. As Scuzzer and Tranter muttered to each other in the corner, Sphagnum started uncoupling the manacles that were around our ankles. Once again I had to wait as he started at the far end of our line. The docile prisoners once freed from their chains just stood around and awaited their fate. Part of me wanted to shout at them and wake them out of their stultifying reverie. When Sphagnum finally reached me, I whispered "You've got to get out of here; they are going to kill you."

"Don't be silly, Mr Boggart, Scuzzer and Tranter are my friends", whispered Sphagnum.

"You must believe me. There are four graves outside waiting for you, Tom Dickon and Harry." The giant just smiled and began undoing my chains. Scuzzer walked over and clapped his hand on Sphagnum's shoulder.

"Leave him, I'll sort that out. You take up your guard outside." A strange whining noise filled the tomb and I found it hard not to register surprise at what I saw. A tiny carriage made its way into the tomb but, like one of those cars I saw in *The Big Sleep*, it appeared not to be pulled or pushed by anything I could see. The tiny carriage pulled up in front of us and a party of soldiers, similar to those I had seen the other day, dismounted from the two trailers that it pulled. Each man carried the impressive guns I had bore witness to only the other day. Scuzzer, standing in the doorway of the tomb, turned and waved at the leader; Tranter moved alongside his friend and watched as the driver of the small carriage uncoupled it from the trailers and drove it forward. The three of us watched as the driver, who looked distinct with his black spectacles and shaggy brown hair, tried to turn his vehicle round in the short space that was available to him. It was a long process and the narrowness of the tunnel meant that he had to move the vehicle backwards and forwards numerous times in order to turn it around. I found myself sandwiched between Scuzzer and Tranter but it wasn't hard to feign impassiveness as I watched the cheerful driver persevere with his interminable task. Despite all this, I remained aware of the dire situation I was in. My feet were still encased in chains, but now that all the other prisoners had been unfettered and were being loaded onto the trailers, their chains were still attached to me. As the other prisoners were seated on the trailers and the driver finally manoeuvred his 'horseless' carriage back to the other end of the trailers. The leader shouted over to Scuzzer indicating that I wasn't aboard yet.

"Don't worry about this one, Mack! We'll bring him on ourselves!" The leader nodded and signalled for the train of prisoners to move off. I sensed that something might be wrong when Scuzzer came up close to my ear.

"It seems Deadman was right to be suspicious Mr Boggart. Tranter has a good memory for faces and you and the other boggart are dead ringers. Deadman suspected the wrong guy when he put his hat on your double. My suspicions were confirmed when Sphagnum kept hearing voices. I don't know if you are the reason Tom, Dickon and

228

Harry haven't shown but you are going to pay for it anyway."
I tried to remain impassive but clearly Scuzzer wasn't buying
it. "You can quit the act now, Boggart. You might as well die
with some dignity." Just as he pulled a gun out of his pocket,
Sphagnum pushed open the door of the tomb and held out a
piece of paper towards Scuzzer. "What's this for?" said
Scuzzer.

"It's a note from my Mum. I have to go home."

"What do you mean a note from your Mum?" Scuzzer
looked astounded.

"I've got to go!",said Sphagnum showing clear concern,
"You don't know my Mum."

"Why are you showing it to us now?" said Tranter
walking across the floor of the tomb. Sphagnum looked
behind him to the dark outside.

"I've only just been given it!"

"What do you mean you've only just been given it? Who
gave it to you? Is your mother outside?" Tranter and Scuzzer
looked aghast.

"No, it was the nice lady. OK? So I'll see you later.
Bye!" And with that Sphagnum turned and ran out of the
tomb.

"Wait! Sphagnum!" Scuzzer turned to Tranter. "Nice
Lady? Watch him, I'll go and see!" Tranter pointed his gun at
me. Behind him the last of the prisoners had disappeared
along the tunnel.

Minutes passed and Tranter started to twitch with uncertainty because of his friend's failure to return.

"Perhaps something's happened to him." I mentioned, greasing the wheels of his anxiety. Tranter looked down at the long line of manacles that were attached to my feet. The best he could come up with was…

"Don't move!" With that he bounded out of the tomb's door and went to look for his friend. My first thought was to get away, but the merest movement produced a caterwauling of chains that echoed along the tunnel. Curiosity got the better of me after a while and I decided to go and see what had happened to my captors. Dragging myself out of the tomb, I looked along the pathway that headed for the gate. I wasn't sure; it was dark, but I thought I saw what looked like a donkey with two heavy loads on its back…leading the creature was a slight figure. Whoever it was, it wasn't Sphagnum.

I dragged myself back into the entrance of the tomb and wondered what to do next. Looking down the long dark tunnel I wondered just how long it would take me to reach the other end carrying half a ton of iron. Only one way to find out, I thought. Gathering up the chains and manacles to the best of my ability, I started to walk. It was like trying to carry a dozen snakes as the chains found their way back to the ground no matter how hard I tried to keep them in my arms. In the end I just gave up and let them all fall to the floor. With a grim desperation borne of not knowing what else to do I just set off and let the chains drag behind me. The noise was incredible and after fifty yards or more I began to tire as the sharp edges of the manacles dug into the compacted earth of the tunnel's floor. By this point it was pitch black as the flickering light of the flambeaux in the tomb's entrance offered little in the way of illumination this far along the tunnel. I soldiered on. The manacles dug into my skin with every resistance the trailing chains met along the way. I was becoming weary with a mixture of pain and fatigue. When finally I succumbed to crawling on all fours, I moved at an even slower pace until I fell face down in the cold earth. I could have been there for minutes, hours even, when my head filled with what was both a strange but familiar noise. I pulled my head off the floor and saw a light far up the tunnel. It was coming towards me.

JC and Walter talked together in the darkness. He was telling her what he knew about Elphinstone Crag.

"It's all there in this book I have called *The History of the Elphinstone Mine and Branch Railway.* The introduction goes on about the history of the crag being a mystical site long before it became a lead mine. There had always been stories that beneath the crag lay 'the hollow hills' of the elfin kingdoms. The crag's name would indicate some sort of connection. In fact the owners of the lead mine had struggled to get locals to work there because of the strong belief that the hill belonged to 'the little people'. I'm just amazed that I'm sat in here, on a rock that will not do my piles any good at all, talking to a real live member of 'the little people'" If Walter could have seen JC's face he might have seen that the term 'the little people' did not meet with her approval.

"In the old days they just dug into the side of the crag to get lead. That long tunnel we found behind the bushes was an old adit mine and it produced enough for a few miners to make a living. Then when industrialisation came in, a mining company was formed and they started making exploratory surveys deep into the crag. What they found was a huge cavern that was surrounded by large deposits of lead. They called this the Minster Cavern on account of it being so vast..."

"I don't understand", said JC.

"...because it's as big as a Minster, a great church."

232

"What's a church?"

"It's a big building", said Walter somewhat deflated. "Anyway, this mining company spurred on by the vast profits they predicted, decided to build a railway track from the main line right into the cavern. It would save a fortune in transport costs. The Minster Cavern was ideal as the large space was big enough to accommodate all the pit head buildings that were needed for the mine to operate successfully. The only building they built outside the tunnel was the count house. That was the ruined building we passed before finding the adit."

"Why couldn't they put that in this Minster Cavern as well?"

"I can tell you're not from this world, my dear. It's all right for the ordinary working man to toil away underground, but you couldn't expect the men that run the mine to go underground as well."

"Why not?"

"You're probably asking the wrong person, JC. Then, when the mine was all worked out, they closed it. Boarded it all up and that was that. The men who had worked the mine, when in drink, would often tell stories of how it was haunted or that it was still guarded by 'the little people'. You saw for yourself that the names of the galleries seem to suggest as much."

"So when did they start this Domania thing?"

"It was about six or seven years ago. There was a piece in the *Gilsland Courier* about how they were going to build a

233

theme park beneath Elphinstone Crag. It would mean plenty of jobs for locals and they were going to re-lay the railway track and take people in on old steam engines. Most of us thought it was just a lot of hot air. People are always coming along with these pipe dreams and nothing ever comes of them. Slowly but surely, we started seeing the line being re-laid. Construction workers were taken on…everything was very hush-hush. Even those who were taken on as workers were sworn to secrecy. The pay was that good that they daren't risk breaking their vow of silence. My own son got a job as a security officer. The town seemed revitalised by it all. Mine was the only dissenting voice and who was going to take any notice of an old man spouting a fairy story?" JC coughed. "Sorry, no disrespect intended."

"Why were you so against it?"

"I've already told you. I've made a study of the history of Elphinstone Crag. Ever since I heard of the disappearance of my own great-great-grandmother, I've been sort of obsessed with it."

"What happened to her?"

"Apparently she was a very unusual woman for her time. My great-great grandfather, George, worked at the Elphinstone mine; he developed a sort of curiosity about the old mines that were no longer worked. He would often explore them in his spare time. Together he and his girlfriend, Dorothy Masters, who would later become his wife, would spend time down in these caves. They got married, had a son, my great grandfather, but still carried on with their interest in the caves. Most people thought they were mad. One weekend George and Dorothy left their son with his grandmother and set off into the caves. Two days later, George returned without Dorothy.

The papers were full of it at the time. George was distraught but the problem was that nobody believed his story about what had happened to her. If he had come back and said that Dorothy had fallen down a mine shaft, everyone would have believed him…tragic but plausible. George's story was so unbelievable that people started to forget they had been such a loving couple and speculated that George had gone mad in the darkness and the result had been the death of his wife."

"And what was the story of Dorothy's disappearance?"

"George said that the pair of them had broken into the Vision Gallery and whilst spending some time there, they had witnessed what might be described as a vision. Down in the depths of the crag, a new world had revealed itself to them. A land of fields and trees and blue skies was laid out beneath them. George said that they didn't know whether they dared to explore this new world but eventually they plucked up courage to let down some ropes off the rock shelf they now found themselves in. The two of them had almost reached the bottom when, looking up, they could see the opening they had come through was now beginning to close. They panicked, Dorothy screaming for her little son. George got back to the shelf and tried to pull his wife up but the closing of the rock sheared through Dorothy's rope and she fell back down into this other world. An official search was instigated through the caves and mines but the authorities declared that she must surely be dead. George would often go down the caves but he never saw the vision or his wife ever again. He took a long time to get over her disappearance but eventually he re-married. Tragedy was never far from his life. Some ten years later, his baby son disappeared from his cradle. On the same night, Jed Comstive, the local drunk told everybody that he had seen Dorothy, George's first wife walking through the town carrying a baby boy. There were those who just said he was a silly old drunk, but there were as many who said that Dorothy had returned for her revenge."

"Quite a story", said JC.

"Yes", said Walter, "now, are you going to tell me yours?"

"What do you want to know?"

"I would like to know what you are and why you are here. I do have some knowledge of what we called fairy lore, but most of it is insubstantial."

"As I told you before, I am not a fairy. I am an elf...a sprite with the ability to fly."

"And what is a sprite?"

"There are many types of sprite. I am an elf, but there are goblins, dwarves, piskies, boggarts, brownies..."

"Are there many more of you?"

"There is a whole world of us. As I suspect we are about to see. Undoubtedly, this other world that George and Dorothy saw; that you saw all those years ago, is the world that I come from...tt is the world that all sprites fled to when the domination of the Oppressors became too much many, many years ago."

"I see", said Walter, "and who are these Oppressors?"

"In the distant past, sprites and humans lived in harmony in this world. But there were humans who believed that sprites were no longer worthy to share it with them. A great wizard created a spell that rent the fabric of time and created a hole through which the sprites and those humans who were happy with their life as it once were, could escape."

In the darkness, Walter sighed. "This vision we are about to see is just such a hole, isn't it?"

"I think so", said JC, "and it is my job to seal it up. From what I have seen of your world, it is more developed than ours. Yes, there are people in our world who want to move it forward, but for sprites this is a dangerous concept. The powers that rule our world recognise that if we are to progress it needs to happen at a more natural pace. If people from your world can freely come into ours then they come at an advantage to the rest of us. Perhaps the Oppressors are still out to destroy us."

"Well, I can't say I've ever heard of anyone called that in this world."

"That was just our name for them. Who knows by what name they call themselves now. We are just hoping that they have nothing to do with this pleasure garden."

"Pleasure garden? Oh you mean the theme park, Domania. I get the feeling that it has been organised by somebody from your world."

"Why do you think that?"

"History, I suppose. Children have been stolen by the fai-, I mean sprites since time immemorial. This just seems to me like they're making a bulk order."

"I'll treat that remark with the contempt it deserves! History, as you are so fond of quoting, records that all the problems in our world are the work of human minds." The two of them sat in restrained silence for a few minutes. It was JC who was first to speak.

"Well, you've said what you think. What do you intend doing about it?" Walter maintained the silence for a few beats.

"Switch your torch on." JC duly complied and saw that Walter was bent over his rucksack struggling to remove and old wooden box. "Shine it on the floor so I don't trip over anything." He carefully placed the box on the rock floor and proceeded to open it. The lid was eased off and JC gasped at what she saw inside it.

"Is that what I think it is?" said JC. She moved the torch's beam from the dynamite in the box to Walter's grinning face. He looked almost maniacal as he nodded. "You see, that is yet another human invention of destruction. It has only just come to light in our world and the thoughtful money is on a crosser."

"What do you mean - a crosser?"

"That it was brought into our world through a time gate…by a human…one who crosses…from his world into ours. My main concern is what exactly are you going to do with that? I have been trained in its usage, quite recently as a matter of fact. But you are just a civilian…an old civilian."

"Don't be silly, flower, or quite so bloody patronising. I've been working with explosives since before your mother was born."

"I very much doubt it!"

"That's the Army for you…it taught me a trade, if nothing else."

"The trade of destruction."

"Look, if there's one thing we both agree on it's that this time gate needs blocking. I reckon if I can pack enough of this explosive around, I can make a bang that will cause the roof to fall down on the whole shebang!" JC lapsed into a thoughtful silence. "We'll get you back to your side and it'll prevent any of the children of my world, and my grandkids, ever disappearing again." As she watched Walter packing up the dynamite, she thought perhaps the old man had a point. He seemed somewhat over-excitable about his obsession with children being kidnapped by sprites but perhaps dynamite was the answer. But it would have to be used on her terms and not his.

From a corner of the cave, a faint glow appeared.

"What's that?" said JC. Walter's shrug was just visible to her. "It must be coming from the Minster cavern. What time is it?"

Walter shone a light on his watch. "About quarter to ten."

"The steam engine comes in around ten", said JC.

"It must be an emergency lighting system. For safety reasons, I expect." Walter made his way across the cave and found a small opening. "We can probably get through to the Minster Cavern." He set about moving some of the loose rock that had built up around the opening. JC came over to assist him.

To say the arrival of the 'vision' took Walter and JC by surprise was something of an understatement. Having spent the last few hours in almost total darkness, the appearance of a small tear of daylight behind them might have blinded them had they been looking straight at it. The sudden flood of light into the gallery from the top left corner of the wall cut short their examination of the passage through to the Minster Cavern. Two full minutes passed by before either of them felt capable of looking at the idyllic rural scene that had presented itself deep in the depths of Elphinstone Crag. With a pleasant stealth it began to fill the wall creating a cinematic effect for its only two viewers…the one standout difference from a big screen experience being that large sections of the image were broken up by the protrusion of rocks that stuck out beyond the presentation of the 'vision'.

"Now you understand why it was locked up all those years ago. The miners back then couldn't cope with what we are seeing. What am I saying? Even I couldn't cope with it when I was a much younger man. The miners decided that this was black magic and best left alone." Walter walked up to the 'vision'. "If the wall was perfectly flat, you know; then the image would be complete."

"It *is* flat where the steam engine goes through", said JC, "I felt it after it had closed up. They must have ground it down to perfection." A large enough space to crawl through appeared close to the floor of the cave.

"That must have been where my great-great-grandparents climbed down into your world", said Walter, picking up a fallen rock. He bowled it through the gap and it dropped down into the other world. Satisfied that it was safe to do so, he got down on his knees and stuck his head through. "It's quite a drop…and into brambles."

"That's the Wall of Thorns, a magical defence of the land you can see." She did a mental calculation in her head. "I suspect it wasn't there when your ancestors paid us a visit." Walter craned his head towards the right.

"There's a building over there!"

"That will be where the steam engine enters from your world.

241

"And some men working a pneumatic drill! Hello!" JC flew across and grabbed Walter's arm before he could wave it.

"I think it would be wise not to draw attention to ourselves."

Walter nodded. "Perhaps you're right."

"The time gate is travelling across us…from left to right. It will arrive at this Minster Cavern very soon." Motivated by this information, Walter moved across to where they had discovered the access to the cavern. He crouched down and began to slide the box of dynamite through the opening in the rock.

"What are you doing?" said JC. Walter stopped in his tracks.

"Well it's all right for you. All you have to do is fly out of this cave to get down there, I'm going to have to get through another way."

"I'm in the same boat as you. This cave opens out over the Wall of Thorns which is a magical creation and my powers of flight would fail miserably over it. I would just fall to my death." Despite telling Walter the truth, JC knew that she couldn't afford to let the dynamite out of her sight. In fact she knew at some stage she would have to separate him from it. Now was as good a time as any, she thought. "What we really need now, Walter, is a double line of attack…Now that you've seen what the problem is, I really think it would be a good idea if you alerted the authorities in your world about the matter."

"You are joking, aren't you? What do you think I've been trying to do for the last five years? They think I am some half-crazed madman. Even my own son doesn't believe me! Domania is the best thing that has happened to Gilsland since the arrival of the railway. Do you think anybody really wants to know that there's something not right about it?"

"But Walter, it's important that someone lets your world know what is going on down here. What if something happens to the both of us? No one will be any the wiser."

"I'm sorry, JC, but I'm in it for the long haul", said Walter with some conviction. He pushed the rucksack and the box of dynamite through the gap in the rocks before squeezing himself after them. Rather than being left contemplating his old white hairless legs, JC followed him, knowing full well that wherever that box of dynamite went, she would be sure to follow.

Once the two of them were clear of the passage, they found themselves on a rock shelf high in the Minster Cavern. Peering over the edge of the rock Walter gazed in wonderment at the scene below him.

"Minster Cavern! You can see why it was compared with a cathedral"

"I might…if I knew what one was", said JC, who was doing her best not to look impressed…when she had been in it before she was hemmed in by the darkness above her and had seen little of the cavern's vastness. From up here the emergency lighting picked out much more of its extent. It was massive and already the sound of the oncoming engine was filling its echoing vaults with clouds of steam. Arc lights clunked on as the engine pulled into the cavern, lighting up a huge flat wall.

"It looks like a large stone cinema screen!" said Walter, "Although I've never seen one that big". Already 'the vision' was beginning to appear across its stone face. "They must have had workmen grinding that down for months. It's a bloody work of art…as smooth as a baby's bum."

Beneath them the steam engine and its carriages slowed to a halt directly facing the stone screen.

"We've got to get down there!" shouted Walter over the noise. He pulled two coils of rope out of his rucksack and began tying them together.

"I'll make my own way down…" said JC, "…what about the dynamite?"

"Don't you worry yourself about that; I'll get it down there." He fashioned a loop in the rope and threw it over a large stalagmite before hauling on it to test its load-bearing capabilities. JC had to admire the old man as he packed the dynamite into his rucksack and fastened it to his back. She watched as he belied his age by easing himself over the edge of the rock shelf and set about lowering himself to the ground. Hovering beside him some hundred feet from the cold hard floor of the cavern, JC's concern was as much for the game old man as it was for the deadly cargo he carried with him. The next few minutes were a lifetime for her as Walter descended in his own time. When his feet met solid ground, he was so relieved to put an end to his ordeal that he almost threw his rucksack to the ground. JC grabbed hold of the bag

244

and gave him a nervous smile for his trouble. His sweat-beaded face gushed with pride as he looked back up to the shelf from which he had descended.

"Not bad for an old man, eh?" he grinned.

"Not bad at all", said JC surprising herself by actually meaning it.

Walter and JC had landed in one of the shadowy corners of the huge cavern. Ahead of them they could see that the big stone screen was half-full of the greenery that lay beyond it. The steam engine, perspiring like a cow in a winter field, waited as the crawling image of JC's world spread across its path. Walter approved as a matching pair of railway lines appeared in this 'other world'.

"Marvellous!" he gasped before turning himself to the job in hand. "It'll be a shame to destroy all this but you'll be all right, won't you, JC. You can just make yourself invisible and sneak back into your own world."

"What about the dynamite?"

"What about it?"

"Well they're not going to just let you walk up to the time gate and watch as you light the fuses." Walter thought about this for a second.

"I thought I'd do it after the gate had closed."

"Hmm."

"What?"

"Well how do you know it will work properly unless the gate is open?"

"I don't! I never had to blow up a time gate before, have I? Plus, I've got to make sure that I can get back to my own world or else I'll never see my grandchildren again anyway."

JC made a show of ruminating. "What you really need is a disguise…and I can't believe I didn't think of it before…"

"What?"

"Well…have you ever heard of 'the glamour'?"

"What, you mean 'fairy glamour'?"

JC sighed. "And you were doing so well, Walter."

"Sorry…tell me about 'the glamour'."

"If we could sneak you onto the train, I could place an enchantment over you that would make other humans see you as a sprite of some kind."

"Would it work?"

"Only if you totally believe in the transformation…and if you are up to the challenge."

"What's one more challenge to a man of my experience!" Walter grinned. "Go on, I'm up for it." He stood there, in the shadows of the cavern, with his arms and legs apart.

"Well", said JC, "what do you want to be?"

Walter thought about it for a while. "I'd like to be an elf, like you."

"Smart choice." JC made a few fluid gestures around Walter's outstretched body.

The old man waited for a second or two. "Is it finished? I don't feel any different."

"That is how it should be. Now you need to spend some time training your mind to believe that you will be perceived by humans to be an elf. This is an important part of the whole process. It's all about confidence. If you don't believe you look like an elf, then no one else will."

Walter looked bemused. "What do you think I should do?"

"I would suggest you spend the next few minutes by yourself…you need to think yourself elfin." JC couldn't believe she was saying all this. Walter, keen to take on his new persona, headed into the shadows of the cavern. Sure that he was out of sight, JC executed the next part of her plan.

The noise, amplified by the tunnel, intensified as the bright light approached me. Whatever was heading towards me was also oblivious to my presence. On and on it came at the same protracted speed. With nowhere for me to go; my only option was to press up against the tunnel sides and hope that it might not see me; might not obliterate me. I staggered to my feet. Had it seen me? I didn't know. I pulled up as many of the chains as I could out of its path. Once again, the cold metal taunted me as the more I gathered in, the more escaped from my grasp. The light was almost upon me now which meant I could see nothing. I turned my back on it and marked the irony of the last thing I would ever set eyes on…a glistening dank tunnel that led onward to the graveyard. It passed me. Whatever it was, it passed me. I opened my eyes and watched as it lurched to a halt and in the split-second it took to register my relief, I was yanked towards it…caught. Unaware whether through fear or confusion I felt nothing as I cannoned into the back of its cold angular frame. Lying face down on the earth, a strange voice washed over me.

"Are you all right, mate?" I opened my eyes and tried to focus on a man. He was short and thankfully concerned. He blinked at me through the thick lenses of his spectacles. "I didn't see you, I was reading a magazine." He held up the offending pamphlet and I groaned. "You see the tunnel is a perfect straight line and I get bored running up and down here so I point it in the right direction and read my magazine." He waited for a reaction; I was careful not to give him one. "Of course, you're not going to speak to me…

248

you're still under medication, aren't you? Blimey! I forgot. Here, you're still chained up an'all! *That's* why the cart stopped. The lads must have forgotten you." He busied himself by unravelling chains and tugging at the one's caught beneath the cart. With each pull a searing pain shot through my leg. A few minutes of agony passed before he pronounced we were clear.

"Let's get you up on the back and we can go and pick up Scuzzer and Tranter. You're lucky I was coming back for them or else you might have been stuck down here for days." The driver gathered all the chains up, threw them into the back of the cart and jumped back into his seat. Within a second we were off and moving. I looked about me, trying to work out what was powering this machine, as the entrance to the tomb got closer and closer. The thought that I might wrap a chain around the man's neck and strangle him crossed my mind but then I wasn't sure I could do something like that. At least I knew that Scuzzer and Tranter would not be making their appointment.

As soon as we reached the entrance to the tomb, the man hopped off the cart and lifted up a doormat that was behind the door. From beneath it he picked up a key and set about unlocking my leg-irons.

"There you go!" The man chatted to me without pause for all of the half-hour we waited for Scuzzer and Tranter to show.

"Well, it doesn't look like their coming my friend, so we best head on back up the tunnel." He looked me up and down for a second. "I wonder if you can understand me. It's just that…it'd be quicker if you gave me a hand to turn this cart round." I'd waited long enough. Without a word, I got up and went to the rear of the cart. He beamed a big smile from under his shaggy hair. "When I count to three, lift and head to your right."

Without chains and illuminated all the way, the journey to the end of the tunnel was a veritable pleasure. Austin, for that was the driver's name, prattled on about this and that before he actually told me something important.

"When I get back to the Palace, I'll put you into the holding bay with the other sprites. I'll let you in the side door and no one will know you got missed. I don't want anyone getting into trouble over this. They'll probably end up blaming me anyway." As we pulled up at an inconspicuous door, Austin jangled a few of the keys on his ring and selected the appropriate one. Within a few seconds I was inside the room and sitting on a shiny seat of the brightest orange colour. I looked round at my fellow prisoners and noticed that not one of them had acknowledged me. Austin came over, holding a board that he had taken off the table near the door.

"They'll start coming round in an hour or two, but before that the Chief Facilitator puts them...*you* through the Conditioning Process. I see the others all have their uniforms and name-tags so I'll give you yours." He rummaged through a few cupboards before handing me a uniform. "You best put it on, while I write out your name-tag." He peered at the board. "Which one are you, then?" he asked. "I know you can understand me, you get to know these things. You're a boggart, aren't you?" I nodded. "Is that you?" He pointed to a rather long name on the sheet. I shook my head. "Well we best put you on, hadn't we?" I told him a name. He wrote it on the sheet, gave me a name-tag and left.

250

*

It was the longest hour of my life. Me and eleven other sprites all waiting for something interesting to happen, except *they* weren't really all that interested. I tried to communicate with one or two of them but it was pointless. I made use of the time by itemising my fellow captives. Three goblins, four elves, three dwarves and one other boggart. I tried to provoke a reaction from the latter by calling his name. He just stared into the distance. I took his name tag and put it in my pocket. He didn't seem to mind.

After that, I started taking note of my surroundings. The room was lit by some means I was unfamiliar with…long thin glass bars that threw out a light brighter than I have ever seen inside a building. Austin had lit it by means of a small box on the wall. Perhaps a flint had been struck or something? I decided to think no more about it and concentrate on what I was going to do next.

Even though I was dreading the arrival of this Chief Facilitator, the sound of footsteps was almost a welcome distraction from the dead company that surrounded me. When the door opened, two men entered the room; one of them was wearing matching jacket and trousers that sparkled as he walked. The other I had last seen stepping out of a flying machine.

"Right, Mr Garlick, they're in here as usual." said the man who I suspected to be a Grimm brother.

"Please, call me Sven."

"Well…Sven…this group will be the last work you do for us."

"Oh, really? But you have my card, should any more work turn up?" Grimm nodded. "And I'll get paid later?"

"Yes, Sven, you'll receive your dues when the work is completed. Now, if I can leave you to proceed with this group alone, I can get on with something else." Grimm left the room and the unctuous Mr Garlick surveyed the sprites he had been left with. Unsure of what he was going to do with us, I made certain to move further away from him every minute his back was turned. I watched him as he set up two of the orange chairs to face each other. He grabbed the hands of one of the female goblins nearest to him and sat her down on one of the chairs.

Taking the seat opposite her, he made a mental note of her name tag and then he spoke to her.

"Hello, Nigella. Now I want you to just relax yourself completely…" So, that was his game…hypnosis. I watched his technique knowing that at some stage I would have to attempt to resist it. One by one he put the others under the spell but to what purpose? They all stood in a huddle by the door waiting for someone to tell them what to do.

When it was my turn, he walked across the room and tapped me on the shoulder. I responded as I had seen the others do and allowed him to guide me across the room. He sat me down in one of the chairs and took his place opposite me.

"Now then Randle, I want you to relax completely…" As he spoke I found it difficult to get the balance right. I wanted to look like I was doing what he was telling me, yet I had to fight the urge of being compelled to do it. My fear of losing control was the stimulus I needed to keep his suggestions at bay.

"Randle, you should be feeling totally relaxed now as though you were soaking in a long hot bath…long and hot with lovely soapy bubbles all around you." I don't know how this one worked on the other sprites because I had never had a hot bath in my life, let alone been surrounded by lovely soapy bubbles. "Now let yourself go even further…take a deep breath and every muscle in your body will relax, and as you become more relaxed you become even more absorbed in the experience. How do you feel, Randle?

"Fine", I answered.

"Good. I am going to suggest to you, Randle, that whenever you see a human being you will want to assist them in any way you can. You will ask them if there is anything you can do for them. And you will want to do anything a human asks you to. If another sprite has already volunteered to assist a human then you will allow them to do so. You may talk to other sprites but only if you need or can offer information. Remember at all times to be both polite and obedient to all humans you come into contact with."

He handed me a shiny smooth card which had five photographs on it. I looked at them in turn. These were the five Grimm Brothers…underneath each picture was their names. Hans-Christian, the one who had just left the room; Wilkie, Jakob, Rutger…and Arnie, these last two I had already met.

"Memorise these faces, Randle." Mr Garlick would have no worries on that score. "Above all else that I have asked of you, you must remember that a command from any of those five men is one that you must obey. Even if what they ask of you might harm another human being. Is that clear, Randle?" I nodded. Maybe at that moment he saw something in my eyes that made him unsure about me. For the first time he repeated a request. "Remember, that a command from any of the Grimm brothers over-rules any previous or future command by any other human. Do you understand that, Randle?"

"Yes", I answered. At that moment, Hans-Christian Grimm returned and as I was the slowest to react to his arrival, I stayed in my chair. He whispered into the ear of the goblin girl who was nearest to the door and handed her something.

"You all about done here, Sven?" called Hans-Christian Grimm. Without turning round, Mr Garlick answered.

"Yes, I think so", he answered giving me a look that suggested uncertainty. Over his shoulder I noticed Nigella the goblin approaching the pair of us. The sight of a long blade coming through the front of Mr Garlick's sparking jacket was probably more of a shock for him than it was for me, but I had it all on to stop myself from screaming.

A BRAVE NEW WORLD

Two dwarf i-sprites came in and removed Mr Garlick's prone body from the room. Five minutes later an elf with a mop and bucket arrived to clean up all the blood from the chair and floor. My attempt to attract his attention met with the same stony face that I had become accustomed to. As the elf left the room with a bucket full of bloodied water, the door was held open for him by the arriving Hans-Christian Grimm. Nigella the goblin was soon asking if there was anything she could do for him. Grimm smiled and shook his head. He picked up the board which held all of our names and checked it against her name tag.

"Ah, Nigella, you know who I am, don't you?"

"Yes, sir. You are Mr Hans-Christian Grimm. How may I help you?" He looked straight in her eyes and told her. "Nigella, I want you to report to the kitchens where you will be instructed in your new job." Despite having just murdered someone in cold blood, she beamed and left the room. One by one the sprites rose to the occasion, greeting Hans-Christian Grimm with a loving smile before heading off to the new jobs he had allocated them. I waited my turn knowing that I was last on the list.

"…And you, by means of deduction, must be…" He ran his sophisticated pencil down the page. "…Randle." He stared at me with his intense ice-blue eyes. From nowhere a strange tune filled the room. I did my best not to appear startled by this as he fumbled in the pocket of his short coat. Putting the small object to his ear he began to speak.

"Arnold...what do you want? Yes...yes...yes...I've got one here. I'll send him right now. Rides will have to make do with one less. Still, they won't have much to do once the children arrive", here he laughed, "OK...bye." He put his communicator away and stared at me once again as if looking for an opening into my mind. "Now then, Randle; I've got a special job for you."

*

It had come full circle. Hans-Christian Grimm sent me to work in the Old Gold Mine. Great! As a stranger to physical work, the prospect of having to graft as a miner was not a good one. Tipping people into the beck was more in my line but you could hardly call it physical. You could hardly call it work. The irony was that the last person I ever remember sending flying into the beck was about to become my new boss. I had been told to report to Arnie Grimm.

The bright sunshine hit my face as I went outside for the first time since I had arrived here. In my new role as a hypnotised, drugged sprite, I found it hard not to express the wonder of what greeted me when I eventually became accustomed to the glare. It was indeed another world. A world similar to that which I had seen in *The Big Sleep*. It was a world that might be lived in by a Humphrey Bogart with one 'g'...but this time it was filled with the natural colours of my world. I looked up and the first thing I saw were huge glass-fronted structures that defied the logic of the buildings I had seen in Thursday Market. Questions queued up in my head for answers. How did the buildings support their roofs when they seemed to be built of such insubstantial materials? What powered the small carts upon which uniformed human workers rode? Everywhere I looked there was light and noise emanating from the buildings. Strange music thumped out of boxes on the wall but I saw no evidence of any musicians. Where did it all come from? The shops that I saw bombarded me with images of strange and wonderful food. Things I never knew existed such as burgers, popcorn, kebabs, fries-to-go and pizza. My mouth started to water at the thought of food and I wandered into the place that sold these pizzas. A wonderful smell filled my nostrils as I approached the brightly-coloured counter. A young male elf, wearing a red, green and white uniform was spinning pastry in the air.

"Can I have one of your pizzas, please?" The elf stared at me for a beat before speaking.

"Sprites are supposed to eat in the staff canteen. Please leave the pizza parlour as you are not food staff." I nodded and dragged myself out of this 'parlour of pizza'. Just as I got to the door, I asked the elf for directions.

"How do I get to the Old Gold Mine?"

Now I was playing the game by asking for instruction, the young elf seemed more at ease with me. "The building facing you is the reception building. Pass it on the right, head on round the swimming pool and follow the railway track. You can't miss it." Before I could offer my thanks, he had returned to his pastry once more.

The swimming pool as he called it was a like a great man-made pond which had water bluer than any I had ever seen. It had chutes and fountains and as I passed, the water began to move in the same way that I had seen the sea move. Two humans were standing by a small pillar watching the progress of the water. It was almost as if they were controlling it themselves. The whole pool was framed by a fine-looking tiled surround. It was a thing of beauty.

I kept following the railway track and thought back to the piece I had read in the Thursday Market Barker about the railway back home. As of yet I had not seen a railway engine and I was excited about the possibility. To my left I saw towering structures that looked like railway lines in the sky. The one nearest to me was painted red and upon it a group of men were riding on a carriage of sorts. They travelled up and down at fantastic speeds. Just watching them career along this track made me feel almost sick myself. The carriage came to a standstill quite near to where I was passing. Two humans, both with huge grins on their faces, climbed out. They were wearing the uniform which bore the name Domania on the back.

"That's just great!" said the thinner of the two men. "Tell maintenance to oil the car and we can put that ride to bed."

"What about the other rides?" said the other.

"Somebody else must be doing them. They only told me to check on The RaptorCoaster."

"Jeez, what a name! Hey, Presley!" The stocky man shouted over what looked to be the tallest dwarf, I had ever seen. At the sound of his name he hurried over.

"Yes, Mr Finch. How may I help you?"

"Presley, I want you to lubricate the cars on the ride. OK?" The young dwarf nodded and headed back over to the track.

"What sort is *he*?" said the thin man. The other turned to watch the receding Presley.

"Er…apparently he's a dwarf. Yeah, that's it."

"A dwarf! Isn't he a little tall for a dwarf?" whispered the thin man.

"Hey, the Grimms said they were sending us a dwarf, so what do I know? He's got a beard and a funny hat, right? He's a dwarf! You've seen *Lord of the Rings*, haven't you?" The thin man shook his head gravely. Mr Finch just shrugged his shoulders. "Well pardon me if *I'm* not the expert! Come on, we've got a train to catch."

I headed over to where the young 'dwarf' was working. There was something 'not right' about him. It wasn't as if a tall dwarf was an impossibility; it was something in his manner, such as the odd surreptitious glance over his shoulder, that suggested he was not as conditioned as the other sprite slaves. I sidled up to him as he busied himself with a tub of grease.

"All right?" I said. Despite being somewhat startled he carried on applying grease to the runners. And there it was; I saw him in that split second of fear. Seeing through an elfin glamour disguise is nigh on impossible for a human, and when an ironised sprite loses his magic the ability to penetrate such disguise is lost as well. The glamour is held together by the wearer's confidence and the victim's indifference. By showing an interest and disrupting the control of the wearer it is possible on occasions to break through the disguise. For a split second I had seen a tall young man whose ears betrayed him to be the child of a human/sprite relationship. The tall dwarf returned but his unease seemed apparent. I broke the silence by asking the way to the Old Gold Mine and the chance to act normal by replying to my question seemed to galvanise him into life.

"Oh, right. Well, all you need to do really is follow the railway track. You can't miss it." He glanced at my name tag then, returning to his work, he muttered. "I must get on."

"OK, thanks. Oh and there's just one thing, Presley." I nodded towards his name tag.

"And what's that, Randle?"

"You're not really a dwarf, are you?"

"Just because I'm tall doesn't mean I'm not a dwarf", Presley replied. I nodded my head.

"True, but dwarves tend to wear the beard...as a statement, almost a badge of honour." Despite my interrogation, Presley didn't seem flustered.

"I've got a beard."

"Yes, you have now, but when I startled you a moment ago..."

Presley's composure returned in full force. "For the sake of argument, Randle, let's say that I am not a dwarf. Now what are *you* going to do about it? You see I am protected by a glamour that other human's cannot get past. When they see me they see a dwarf. OK, a rather tall dwarf but that is just what they see. If you go and report me to the humans that run this place, I will just play dumb and they won't get what you're saying. However, what they will find interesting is that you are noticing things that you shouldn't notice, you being drugged and hypnotised and all that. It seems to me, Randle, that you are the one who has the problem." He dropped to his haunches and started working on something. I took the hint and turned to go.

"Nice meeting you", I said.

"Yes, you too…keep in touch."

The discovery of someone who wasn't part of the Grimm brothers' set up gave me food for thought as I made my way up towards the gold mine. What was his motive for being here? Even more so, *how* did he get here? All thoughts of Presley the 'dwarf' were put out of my mind when I was presented with a dilemma. The railway track split into two different directions and there were no signs and no one to ask. Naturally, I chose the wrong track. After a further ten minutes of walking I arrived at a small building that resembled the barge station back in ThurMar except that it found itself stopping in the middle of nowhere. I could only presume it was some kind of station for the steam engine, but still I had yet to see one of these fantastic machines. There seemed to be no good reason why this line should end here in the middle of field that climbed up to the distant Wall of Thorns. What were they thinking of? It was almost as if they hadn't finished putting the track down. As I approached the station building itself, I could see that there were a lot of humans milling about. The two men who had been discussing Presley, the so-called dwarf, were there. Construction workers nursed the tools of their trade as they waited on benches. Numerous sprites busied themselves with their work, some cleaning, whilst others were hanging baskets of flowers from the station's canopy.

Not wanting to get into trouble with my new boss, I had turned to head back up the track. My eye was caught by a movement, high up above the nearby Wall of Thorns. A series of black irregular-shaped holes started to appear in the tree canopy just above the Wall of Thorns. They looked like ugly black grazes on a woodland painting. The holes began increasing in number but there seemed to be no logic to this unusual occurrence.

"What *is* that?" called a voice from behind me. I turned to see a pair of human workmen standing waist deep inside a hole. They were wearing strange bright blue hard hats with attachments that fit over their ears. "We saw it yesterday. Can't work out what it is", said the older of them.

"Hello, sirs. How may I help you?" The show must go on, I thought.

"Don't bother with all that crap, mate. Me and Rob are just here to do a job like you are. It's just that we noticed it yesterday...those black holes, and neither of us can explain them. Is that somebody waving, Rob?" I turned to look at it and all I could do was shrug my shoulders. "Oh well, best get on", said the man, "this job was supposed to be finished yesterday. OK, Rob!"

The noise they made had me jumping a full foot in the air. I turned round and saw that they were drilling in the hole with some kind of hand-held machine. A large flexible pipe connected it to a small carriage that had been rumbling away unnoticed. The workman caught me looking and tapped his mate on the shoulder to indicate that he stop.

"Here you don't want to hang round here too long." He pointed to his ear. "You'll go deaf."

I moved a short distance away and continued to observe the black holes high above the Wall of Thorns. The noise from the machine was still loud but I did not want to get too close to the station where my curiosity may attract unwanted attention. What seemed more fantastic was that no one waiting at the station had even noticed it. Perhaps they couldn't see it from where they were. Then an announcement was made at the small station and those waiting began rising to their feet; papers were folded, bags were picked up off the floor. I looked behind me to see if a steam engine was coming…nothing.

High on the Wall of Thorns, the holes, which now resembled a series of small caves, appeared in their entirety and hung there like black stains on the canopy of greenery. I began to worry that I had been standing still for too long (after all none of the other sprites had seemed to notice the caves) when something even more spectacular happened. There, half in the sky and half on the ground, a similar opening appeared. It was just like the caves but this time it was accompanied by more unfamiliar noises. This hole in the world (for what other way could I describe it?) got larger and larger and I headed down towards it wary that I must appear to have some job, lest a human queries why I am there. As I made my way down towards the station the incessant noise got louder. It was a slow process but the opening revealed a great metal monster, a thing of iron and steam. I got nearer to the action by grabbing a discarded broom and sweeping away for all I was worth. I would no doubt be in trouble with my new boss but this I had to see. This was special.

As the hole in the world got larger the steam engine roared into life and pulled itself into our world from…somewhere else. I was sure I was witnessing the opening of a gateway to another world. No wonder the Grimms wanted to keep it hidden behind the Wall of Thorns.

I hung around for a good hour as passengers got both on and off the steam engine and a crowd of sprites started to unload the supplies that had been brought in. What amazing things might they be bringing into this world? While all this activity went on, no one paid attention to a sprite listlessly sweeping the path up from the station, but I had to get back and find the Old Gold Mine. Still clutching the broom, which I hoped could justify my appearance anywhere; I started to walk back along the path until I reached the thunderous thrumming of the two workmen and their drilling machine once more. The senior workman saw me and tapped his mate once again. The noise abated.

"They're going now." The man pointed over my shoulder and I could see that he was right. The small caves over the Wall of Thorns were now starting to disappear in the same way that they had arrived, from right to left.

"You there! Boggart! Get on with your work!" I turned and the sight that beheld me turned my knees to jelly. A small self-powered carriage had slowed near to the track where I was standing! On it were two men, both wearing the traditional suits that those in authority wore. Hans-Christian Grimm and the man who I recognised as his brother Wilkie stood before me. I stared at them for perhaps a split second longer than I should have done

"Yes, sirs. How may I help you?"

"What are you doing here? I sent you over to the gold mine!" said Hans-Christian Grimm.

"Sir, I got lost. I think I followed the wrong track." Hans-Christian seemed somewhat mollified by my answer.

"Hmm, I told Arnold to get a sign put up! Is that boy good for anything? Right, well get yourself back up the line and hope to hell that my brother goes easy on you. Carry on, Wilkie. I don't want to keep my consignment of tropical fish waiting any longer."

"Hans, Hans, we can't have sprites doing just what they want. I think we need to get to the bottom of this", said Wilkie Grimm, who had been watching me intently through his spectacles all the while his brother was speaking. Hans-Christian sighed.

"Then you sort it, Wilkie. I've got better things to do!" He manoeuvred his brother out of the carriage before continuing his journey down towards the station.

Wilkie Grimm adjusted his suit before he looked down at me from the other side of the track.

"Right and you are?" Adjusting his spectacles he peered at my name tag. "Randle. So, why did you deliberately disobey an order…particularly one from a Grimm brother, Randle? Hmm?" I kept my head face down like an admonished child. "Look at me, sprite!" I lifted my head and caught the dark glare of his eyes full on.

"Well, sir, I didn't really disobey as much as manage to get lost. I was told to follow the railway track to find the Old Gold Mine but I seem to have followed the wrong track. When

265

I arrived here, I asked a human what I should do and I was allocated this broom." I held it up as if it was evidence.

"Hmm. A credible answer but it doesn't explain why you were stood watching the opening of a time gate instead of sweeping with your broom. By the way, you can put it down now." I did as I was bid. "Now whether you know it or not, my brothers and I are…let's say…not very nice to know. It's not our fault…blame the parent, I say. As for them, well for some reason they seem to think I'm over-cautious. I can't seem to let things drop. It's not a problem. I can live with it." His faced twitched like a guttering candle. "But we're not talking about me, are we, sprite?" I lowered my head fearful of what was coming.

"No, sir."

"Look at me, sprite! What my brothers fail to see is that dealing with the small problems cuts down the possibility of larger ones occurring. It's just like that old saying…'Watch the pennies and the marks will take care of themselves'…Your interest in what was going on around you implies that you have not been conditioned to the correct degree. This leads me to the possibility of two conclusions…firstly, that the conditioning didn't work or, secondly, that you were never conditioned in the first place. The first conclusion could be down to my brothers' generic inattention to detail. If, however, it is the second conclusion, then it raises the possibility of a totally different scenario. While my brothers seem to think that the threat arising from the escape of a fugitive through the Wall of Thorns was ended when he was shot in Thursday Market, I think differently. The amount of time that has passed between his escape and his death is ample for a great deal of information to have changed hands. I'm not one for playing the percentages, sprite. Taking chances is not in my nature. Worse case scenario? It would appear we have a spy in our midst." Behind him the drilling started up again but he hardly seemed affected by it. He continued to talk to me but I couldn't hear a word he was saying. I began to feel scared and willed the workmen to stop and take an interest in the pair of us. He continued to talk to me as behind him I could see the steam engine, now free of its carriages, coming up the line. I stepped further away from the track. Wilkie Grimm seemed almost impervious to the approaching noise. With the steam engine only a matter of yards away he pulled out a gun close to his chest. The remorseless drilling continued; the noise was overpowering and I couldn't believe that he was unaware of the oncoming train…until the moment that he stepped out in front of it.

Walter Coope was somewhat bemused that his elfin disguise had been seen through straight away. At first he put it down to his not having enough self-belief but when the Domania security guards opened his box of dynamite and found it to be filled with rocks he realised he'd been stitched up. Despite her deviousness, JC had never been able to hide the fact she was uneasy about the presence of his dynamite.

When he had returned from the shadows eager to be seen as an elf, JC had suggested he hide in the goods carriages at the back of the train. The last thing she did before he left her was hand Walter his box of dynamite. As the train pulled through the time gate into JC's world, Walter was at once swarmed by a number of elves, dwarves and goblins all eager to ask how they might help him. His popularity amongst the sprites had been quickly noticed by one of the security guards, a good friend of Mike, his son.

"Mr Coope! How the hell did you get on board the train? I hope your Mike had nothing to do with this." Walter assured the young man otherwise. "I'm sorry but I'll have to ask you what you have in the box." At least JC's subterfuge had spared him the discomfiture of seeming to be some kind of terrorist. The security guard believed Walter's explanation that Elphinstone was a veritable treasure trove of rare geological specimens. Fortunately the young man wasn't sharp enough to ask why Walter had actually brought the specimens *in* to the Minster Cavern. He was asked to remain seated in the goods van while the sprites set about the business of emptying it of all the supplies. The guard allowed him to look out of the window and see 'what all the fuss is about'.

"Marvellous, isn't it, Mr Coope? I don't know how they've done it, but you have to admit it's bloody marvellous." The security guard and Walter gazed out onto the pastoral scene and the gleaming theme park set in the distance. "I mean, how do they fit all this inside Elphinstone Crag? Some of the lads think it's done with-"

"Smoke and mirrors?" said a dejected Walter.

"-CGI…you know computers. I mean, look at that sky…it's seamless, like in that film – *The Truman Show*."

Walter already knew the secret of Domania so he found it hard to be as impressed as the young man. What was giving him more concern was that he felt let down by JC. He had trusted her and she had made him look a fool. The dynamite had gone. She had told him she knew how to use it. He could only hope she would finish off the job he had set out to do…for the sake of his grandchildren.

Walter sat for a good hour waiting to be returned to his own world. At one point the security guard shouted out of the door to find out what the hold up was. After a quick chat with one of his colleagues, the young man discovered that there had been an accident further up the line.

"Apparently someone stepped out in front of the engine when it was heading up to the turntable."

"Were they…?"

"Killed instantly…yeah." The two remained in silence until the sound of the engine returning sparked the young man into action. He leaned out of the window and began a conversation with the engine's driver. Some minutes passed before he pulled his head back into the carriage.

"Blimey...it was one of the bosses that got run over! I don't suppose that'll be the end of it. There like as not be an enquiry." Walter, still in a state of despondency, was at a loss for something to say. The guard continued, "Oh and I've arranged for the driver to stop just as we leave the tunnel. That way you'll not get into trouble and neither will I. He's cleared it with the security guard at the tunnel entrance. You'll be able to find your way home from there, won't you, Mr Coope?" Walter nodded.

When the train eventually lurched out of Domania station and into the half-light of Minster Cavern, Walter found himself comfortably seated in the one of the passenger carriages. He peered out of the window, eager to see if JC was still around, if only so that he could give her a disparaging look.

JC, having managed to stash the dynamite in a safe place, was feeling bad for having tricked Walter. As the time gate began to close, she knew he would now be waiting to be taken back to Gilsland. She felt she needed to at least assure him that she would do her best to make sure the children would be safe. Still in a state of invisibility, she made her way back towards the train as it began to pull out of Domania and into the tunnel. She took up a position close by to the little hut she had discovered when she had first set foot in the cavern. As Walter's mournful face gazed out into the half-light of the cavern, JC flickered into visibility just long enough for him to see her. Just long enough for her to mouth the word 'sorry' to him. And just long enough for Rutger Grimm to catch a glimpse of her from the window of his hut.

As the train made its way back into the tunnel, JC looked through the gap that separated it from the worker's hut to the land beyond. She was heading back there and she wouldn't care if she never saw Walter's world again. The noise from the engine made her indifferent to the clatter she was making on the stone chippings. No one would hear her and no one could see her as she made her way back to the place they were now calling Domania.

Rutger Grimm, despite wearing a dove grey designer suit, was lying on the ground in the shadow behind the shed. He watched as JC's invisible feet dislodged the stone chippings as she moved alongside the departing train. At the point that she passed by him, Rutger swept his arms around her invisible ankles. JC's body fell to the floor, her head hitting the ground. In an unconscious state she re-appeared in front of him. He looked at her face for a good while before bundling her up in the duvet cover from his shed and trussed her body at her feet and shoulders with a couple of belts.

Rutger left JC by the side of the line and returned to his shed. The frequent trips he made into the world he came from had caused him some concern. He knew from speaking to his brothers that there would come a time when making the journey back would not be pleasant. Wilkie's experience when they had brought back Carl had been an eye-opener to him. The risk of missing the time gate would become even greater as the years went by. He remembered his first visit back when he had stayed overnight at the Elphinstone Arms. A reckless night of overindulgence had led to him sleeping though the alarm. He missed the time gate and Mother wasn't at all pleased. Wilkie, ever eager to point out the worst, simply stated that if *he* had done that he would be a dead man now.

The point had been hammered home. Rutger wasn't prepared to take the risk anymore. He'd spotted the old shed on a routine check and decided that it wouldn't take much to create a little refuge for himself; a place where he could think; a place away from Mother and his brothers, but most of all a place where it would be impossible to miss the opening of the time gate.

He put his mobile phone and wallet on the table and stripped out of the soiled dove grey suit. Standing in his shirt and underpants he opened a large double locker that housed a fine array of alternatives. He chose a charcoal pinstripe and put it on, taking time to admire himself in the full-length mirror. His confident smile beamed back at him.

Rutger bent down close to the package containing JC and pulled out his mobile phone. "Hello, Mother. I suggest you send someone down to the railway station. I've got something you just might be interested in."

A BAD MEMORY RETURNS

Arnie Grimm sat in his office just inside the entrance to the Old Gold Mine. He was talking into the small device that I now knew to be a phone, similar to the one Bogart had used in *The Big Sleep*. It was how people communicated within the Palace grounds. I sat across from him as he chatted to his mother…

"Look, I don't know how it happened! We weren't there when it … but you know how he is – was – always bothered about silly little things…It was something and nothing, Mother…Hans-Christian said he had some issue with an i-sprite and, well you know how Wilkie was…What? Well he didn't always wear them…or if he did he'd switch them off…and there *was* a pneumatic drill going off right next to him…The sprite? Well, actually he's here with me now. He was supposed to be working for me but he got lost…I don't know, it's a big place, Mother, even I get lost!" Arnie Grimm stared across the table at me.

"Yes, of course he looks *all right*…much like they all do…OK, I will. Bye, Mother." He put down the phone and got up from the desk. "Mothers! Sometimes they drive you mad." I thought it best to keep my own counsel while I worked Arnie Grimm out. "You don't say much."

"Is there anything I can do, Mr Grimm?"

"Not really, Randle. My brothers only gave me this job *because* there's not much to do. I mean, how difficult is it to design a treasure hunt adventure for a group of stupid kids and monitor the meat refrigeration units…oh and throw the

273

odd 'problem' down the mine shaft. It's hardly rocket science, is it?" I nodded, although I hadn't really got a clue as to what he was talking about.

It was clear that Arnie Grimm hadn't recognised me. I guess without the clothes and hat I usually wore, I was just another i-sprite to him. The death of his brother had clearly shaken him up a bit. He was no longer the confident young man I recalled flying across the Lepping Stones some time ago.

"Can I ask you something, Randle?" he said. I nodded. "Did you actually see what happened to my brother?"

This time I shook my head. "I didn't see the accident. He'd called me a rude name for getting lost and then sent me up here to wait for you." A white lie, I thought. Witnessing the appalling death of a person, no matter how abhorrent they seemed, is not a nice thing to do. The steam engine had continued along the track and then come to a halt by a great circular machine that enabled it to turn around. When I reached the engine itself, I tried to look anywhere but at whatever remained of Wilkie Grimm. There were too many questions that remained unanswered for me…the biggest one being…why didn't he hear it coming?

"Mother spent all that money on hi-spec hearing aids but he never used them. He was profoundly deaf." I had my answer. "He must not have heard the train because of the pneumatic drill that was going off behind him. I doubt whether someone with perfect hearing would have heard it."

"He seemed to be able to hear me talking!"

"That's because he could lip-read, Randle." The young man looked decidedly sad. "As you can imagine, I don't feel like doing much today…I've lost two of my brothers in a few days…" The silence weighed heavy. "First Jacky…crushed under a tree and now poor Wilkie…I'm not really in the mood for working. You might as well take the rest of the day off. Go on." As I got up to leave the office, Arnie opened a drawer in his desk.

"Here, you're the only staff I've got. At least this way I can keep in contact with you." He handed me something. "It's a mobile phone. When the tune plays…press that button…then put it to your ear…you'll be able to hear me talking to you." I placed the phone in my pocket. Arnie Grimm closed the door behind me and I couldn't help feeling sorry for him.

As I made my way back down towards the station, I tried to make sense of what Domania was supposed to be. The Grimm brothers had created a place where people could enjoy themselves but which people? And it certainly wouldn't be much fun for us sprites. The jobs weren't too good back in Thursday Market but at least sprites were paid wages there. Here we were little more than slaves.

Having been given the rest of the day off, I wasn't sure what I should do with myself. Investigate, I suppose. I had made a point of retaining my broom as a vital prop in poking my nose where it wasn't wanted. The day had been an unpleasant one so far. I had witnessed firsthand the death of two men. As I rounded a bend near to the children's rides, I saw the only thing that could have made it worse. Walking towards me, as he struggled with a rather unwieldy bundle of cloth, was Alaric Deadman.

275

When she finally regained consciousness, JC's initial reaction was one of utter confusion. She tried to make sense of her last waking moment and failed. All she knew now that she was enveloped in some kind of stifling material and she needed to get out of there as soon as possible. Her feet were held firm by some kind of fastening but she felt the one around her shoulders could easily be moved with a little squirming on her part. Her first attempt to do so brought about increased pressure in other places. At that point someone shifted her centre of gravity. The material around her face was cleared and she found herself face-to-face with…

"Alaric Deadman!"

"Well, well, well…if it isn't Seer Bigg of the All-Seeing Eye…and the name is pronounced *Deedman* as well you know."

"What are you doing here?"

"As a matter of fact, Bigg, I was invited here. The question is…what are *you* doing here?"

"And who exactly was it who invited you here?"

Deadman smiled and somewhere a flower died. "You'll find out soon enough." He hoisted her cocooned body under his arm and marched off in the direction of the palace.

The journey through the realm of Domania would have been a comfortable one had JC chosen to remain still in her goose-feathered prison. It was only a matter of time before

276

Deadman lost his patience. He grabbed the bundle of elf/duvet cover with his left hand and held it straight out in front of him. Over his shoulder, JC caught sight of a boggart sweeping imaginary leaves along the road. It was the last thing she saw before Deadman punched her right in the face.

PRESLEY COMES CLEAN

It was fortunate that just at the moment Alaric Deadman was passing by me, the person he had trussed up inside that bundle of cloth had finally taken offence. His ensuing struggle allowed me to sweep myself past him as he tried to subdue his prisoner. A swift punch seemed to have done the trick for him and I watched him walking away from me with the limp bundle under his arm. I wondered just who that poor wretch might be and knowing that there was only me who could do anything to help, I was about to follow when a quiet voice said…

"A penny for them…" I feared for my trousers and began sweeping for all my worth when Presley stepped in front of me. "Rutger Grimm needs something moving. He asked me to get someone to help and come to the palace…will you assist me?" This time the voice was loud enough for others to hear.

"Only if it's in that direction." I pointed after Deadman and Presley nodded. The pair of us set off towards the palace.

"How's it going?" I asked without moving my lips.

"So-so. Have you worked this place out yet?"

"Not really…although I've just seen someone, I would rather I hadn't. Have you ever heard of Alaric Deadman?"

"Is he over a hundred years old?" Presley's question threw me.

"I don't know…he's an i-sprite…ex-boggart."

"No…the answer's no…I don't know him." An awkward moment passed. "Don't mind me; I get a bit bitter at times. It's nice just to have a conversation with another rational being." The two of us walked on, our stiff-lipped conversation flowing like a brick falling down steps. Presley, like me, seemed to be guarding his thoughts. "So…who is this Deadman fellow?"

"That's him up ahead…a nasty piece of work…a professional killer. He's tried to kill me once…well more than once actually."

"You're kidding?"

I shook my head. "He's got someone wrapped up in that quilt. It's someone small…a child or more likely a sprite." Presley shot a look at the tall figure of Deadman. "I'll let you into a secret. If you ever cross words or even swords with him…his head comes off."

"What?"

"It's true. I've seen it happen twice. He can just fix it back on again but the trick is to separate his head from his body…the further the better in my experience."

"You sure he has someone wrapped up in that bundle?"

"Well I saw him punch whoever it was to knock them out."

"So it's probably not a child then?"

"It *is* Alaric Deadman we're talking about. He'd punch his granny for the last biscuit in the tin. The strange thing is…since I've been here I've not seen any children or a sprite that hasn't been ironised."

Presley stroked his chin. "I have. I'm not sure I should be telling you this but I've seen an elf."

"Not ironised?"

"No, she's a light elf. You know…flies…makes herself invisible. She's the one who put the glamour on me. Goes by the name of JC…"

"Bigg?"

"Yes…do you know her?"

"We've had our moments…you think that might be her inside that bundle?"

"Like you said, I've not seen anyone else it could be."

Presley and I scurried to make up the distance as Deadman and his cargo disappeared into the main entrance of the palace. Once inside we could see him mounting the ornate marble staircase that dominated the entrance hall.

"Do you know where we're supposed to be going?" I asked.

"Not really, Rutger Grimm told me to come to the palace. I suppose that's a licence to roam…until somebody stops us."

"Ah! There you are…good!" Presley and I got no farther than the bottom step before the exuberant Rutger Grimm skipped down the staircase to meet us. Right…we're off to the railway station. We'll take the buggy", he said, bustling past us. Presley looked up as Deadman walked along the balcony with his bundle.

"We can't do anything now", I hissed under my breath. "If we don't do as we're told, we're dead anyway." Presley nodded and the two of us walked down to the waiting Rutger Grimm.

"Hop on the back!" he shouted and the two of us did just as we were told.

The journey to the railway station was a short one by buggy. Presley and I clung on to the bars that supported the flimsy roof. Once we were at the station, Rutger Grimm took us to a small shed that backed on to the station building. Inside he pointed to an old wooden box. On the side, the words DANGER and DYNAMITE had been stencilled.

"Right, you two. Can either of you read?" Both of us thought it wise to shake our heads. "Oh, well, never mind. The problem is that this box turned up the other day and it is dangerous…it's er…poisonous. As our guests, the children are arriving in a couple of days; we need to move it down the old mine until it can be disposed of properly. There's an old stretcher over there that the both of you can carry it on. Now whatever you do, don't drop it, OK?" Both us nodded our heads this time. The stretcher was laid on the ground and we placed the box on top of it. Pre-empting our attempt to lift it, Rutger Grimm stopped us. "Hang on! Wait till I'm gone, OK? You know where the old mine is, don't you?"

"I know, sir. It is my place of work."

"Oh, right…that's good. When you get there you should ask my brother Arnold where he wants it putting." I noticed that beads of sweat had started to form on his brow. "Well, I'll be off then…OK?" By the time we had answered he was gone. Presley gave me a rueful look before the two of us left the shed. Rutger Grimm and his buggy were already on the road back to the palace.

"I don't suppose you know what Dynamite is?" said Presley. I shrugged my shoulders and the box shook a little on the stretcher. "Careful! Grimm said that it was poisonous…we don't want to spill it!"

Seeing as I knew where I was going, Presley was happy for me to take the lead. The two of us made reasonable progress on the road until we reached the turn-off for the old mine. The path to the old mine was more uneven and we moved along at a much slower pace. Just at the point where the path rose up to the entrance to the mine, Presley tripped over a rock and the stretcher slithered to the ground. Both of us froze. An age passed as we waited for something to happen. Fortunately nothing did. Presley and I dared to take up the stretcher and walk the few hundred feet to the entrance of the mine.

Arriving at the mine office, Presley and I gently lowered the stretcher to the ground. I peered into the office and could see Arnie Grimm playing some kind of game on a picture box. As I pushed the door open I could hear his excited shouting.

"Eat laser you Xyglon scum! Yeah! Come on!"

"Excuse me, Mr Arnold." Arnie Grimm swivelled in his chair at the sound of my voice.

"Jeez, Randle! You frightened the life out of me there! Anyway, I thought I gave you the day off so I could mourn my brother's sad demise." I looked at the strange plastic button box he held in his hand. "Oh…it's the new Xyglon Battleground game…it just arrived on the train this morning. I'm test driving it for the kids. I'll show you how to play and we can have a game when things are on the quiet side."

"I'd like that very much, Mr Arnold."

"Please, just called me Arnie…well at least when Mother and my brother's aren't around. Right…what did you want me for?"

"Your brother, Mr Rutger, asked us to bring this box up to the mine…to keep it safe."

"Oh, yeah, he did mention it. What's in it?" Arnie stepped outside the office and nodded at Presley.

"This is Presley…he's a dwarf." Arnie eyed the tall figure in front of him.

"Right…pleased to meet you, Presley." He looked down at the box and went into reverse. "Whoah! Dynamite! What the hell is that doing here?"

"Mr Rutger told us it was poisonous", said Presley.

"Poisonous! Dynamite isn't poisonous it's highly explosive. I'm no expert but if that box is full then the slightest knock could blow the lot of us and a great deal of this mine to pieces!" Presley and I stepped away from the box as this new information began to sink in. "I don't know what my brother was thinking of when he asked you to bring it here. You two I suspect he's not too bothered about...no offence...but I'm supposed to be his brother!"

"What are we going to do with it?" I asked, before realising that this wasn't the sort of question a sprite was supposed to ask.

"Well to start with I suggest that the three of us look for somewhere safe where we can put it...then...er...the two of you can take it there. After all there's no point all three of us taking the risk and I am the man in charge down here so I'm delegating...that's what I'm doing I'm delegating. Come on..."

THE SEER'S TALE (cont.)

When she woke up, JC found herself still encased in the duvet cover and propped up in a leather armchair. The room she found herself in was well appointed and appeared to be an office of some sort. Voices could be heard from outside the room. Her restraints seem to have increased and struggling to escape them seemed futile now. More than anything else her face hurt. She struggled to see out of her left eye and the build up of dried blood and snot left her with the feeling that Deadman may have broken her nose.

As she tried to piece together what had happened to her in the last hour or so, the appearance of Deadman had been an eye-opener in one sense of the word. He was a known assassin to the ASE…his motives for killing were less well known.

"Ah…Seer Bigg, I see that Alaric has taken care of you." JC peered through her good eye and was surprised to see Doris Morris, Commander of the Guardians smiling benevolently at her. "I'm quite surprised that our illustrious leader, Avis Davies, failed to mention to me that she intended to infiltrate the Palace of Fotherghyll."

"I suspect Avis Davies's good reason for not informing you has now been justified, don't you, Commander?" The smile left Doris Morris's face for a second. "You must have been aware that there had been stories of 'goings on' behind the Wall of Thorns for years now. The curse was due to end later this year. If you knew a way to enter the Palace of Fotherghyll, why did you not enlighten the Massy Witch? But then I think I already know the answer to that question."

Doris Morris sat down behind the desk. "You see, Seer Bigg, I have found myself in a dilemma for some time now. When I first became a witch, I relished the power the position gave me...to see the fear in someone's eye when you look at them. It still gives me a thrill...that power...that fear. But when I meet someone like you, Seer Bigg, I don't see it. You are the product of your leader's age. Avis Davies is a good woman, she commands respect for the good she had done for society. She has made witches answerable to the people they govern; so much so that we hamstring ourselves by our obeisance to the Act of Self-Regulation."

"And rightly so", said JC, "otherwise there would be no stopping a power-crazed witch from imposing their will on everyone. The very fact that a self-inflicted spell using something as elemental as running water can curtail the activities of a power-hungry witch is testament to the trust arising between both witches and their people."

Doris Morris sighed. "Do you often quote the speeches of the Massy Witch, Seer Bigg?"

"I find them inspiring!" said JC, trying hard to conceal her embarrassment at actually having spoken the last sentence.

Doris Morris's laugh rang around the room. "The reason I created Domania here was because I crave the power I have been missing. In this world behind the Wall of Thorns, I can fashion an alternative vision...a different vision to Avis Davies', away from her and other like-minded disapproving eyes. It will be a world that once again lives in fear of the witch."

"But when the Wall of Thorns disappears on the hundredth anniversary of the curse, your world will be there for all to see."

"Never fear about that, Seer Bigg, the Wall will only disappear when I tell it to."

"At some point, the Massy Witch will find out, if not from me then from someone else…and then what will you do?"

"I will destroy her and her kind."

JC tried to smile but it hurt too much. "How?" she sneered. Her face seemed to manage sneering more easily than smiling.

"You have seen for yourself, that Domania has a time gate. I will destroy Avis Davies by means she cannot comprehend. To quote a phrase from the world beyond your own, 'I have the technology'. All the time you have been snooping in Domania you have seen things beyond your wit…guns, flying machines…improved communications. The Massy Witch will not know what has hit her."

"But you *have* power. The Massy Witch named you as Commander of the Guardians. To all intents and purposes you are the second most powerful person in the land." JC caught the look on Doris Morris's face. It was a look that said that second was never good enough. And JC had seen that look so many times in changing room mirrors to know that nothing she could say to Doris Morris would make the slightest difference. She tried anyway. "Do you really want the entire world to despise you?"

"Why should I care whether people despise me or not? Their feelings are unimportant. It is their fear that excites me. It is easier to make unpopular decisions when you care little for the people it affects. I shall show you how easy it is, Seer Bigg." Doris Morris clapped her hands and Alaric Deadman stepped into the office. "Ah, Alaric…Seer Bigg has been sent here to investigate the palace and its grounds. Make sure she gets a close look at the mineshaft…especially the bottom of it."

"I don't know where the mineshaft is, Commander", said Deadman.

"Hmm. Lock her away somewhere…I'm sure Hans-Christian will want to 'interview' her anyway. In the morning when he's finished with her you can take her up to Arnold for disposal. It seems we've managed to find something that he's good at, after all."

I suppose it was payback time. Having half a day off, while all the other sprites were working, meant that there was no case to argue when Arnie came a-calling. In Domania, there was never a case to argue if you were a sprite. Presley and I had stashed the dynamite where Arnie had told us to and, being given the rest of the day off; the pair of us had spent it in a fruitless attempt to find what had happened to JC Bigg.

The snoring of my room-mates in the Hall of Residence mocked my early rise as I wrestled with my clothing to find my mobile phone. I pressed the button as instructed and the horrific tune stopped.

"Hello?"

"Hi, Randle, it's Arnie. Sorry about the time but I've got a problem. We need to work together on this one."

"What do you want me to do?"

"There's a guy on his way from the refrigeration company and he's going to show you what you need to know to run the unit. He wants to get it done before he catches the train out of here. So, by the time Mother pops down later to check things out, I want you to be a refrigeration expert." The silence at my end of the phone was borne of confusion. I simply hadn't a clue about what he had just said to me.

"Hello? Randle?"

I thought I better start showing an interest. "Just what is a refrigeration unit?" I asked.

"Oh yeah, I forgot you sprites don't do electricity, do you? Well you know that everything here is powered by electricity…" He waited patiently for my recognition of this fact.

"Electricity?" I was still in the dark. Arnie started to panic.

"All these things…phones, lights…computers…they're all run by electricity."

"Where does it come from?"

"How should I know? Look, you just stick the plug into the socket and there it is!"

"OK." I needed him to calm down. "So what does a refrigeration unit do?"

"It keeps food cold…to stop it going off. If you freeze a hunk of meat until it's solid, you can keep it for ages…years, probably."

"But how do you eat it?"

"When you let it thaw out, it's as fresh as the day you froze it."

"Really?"

"Really!"

"So why do we need the refrigeration unit to be at the mine?" There was a pause on the line. I realised I had overstepped the mark for a sprite.

"I don't know yet. I suppose Mother will tell me today. The main thing is that we get the thing working."

"I'm on my way."

"For some reason it's really important to her."

When I arrived at Arnie's office, Mr Burgess, the man from the FridgiKing refrigeration company was already there. Arnie waved at me through the window and then ushered his guest out of the office.

"Bit of a strange place to put it, isn't it? Down an old mine", said Mr Burgess, chewing his lip.

"What do you mean?" said Arnie.

"Well, I'm asking myself - what is it for? You usually have them near the kitchens."

"Do you?" said Arnie, obviously unhappy with the situation. I let them get on with their discussion as I gazed into the darkness around us. The feeling that we were being watched was making me uneasy. The dark recesses above and below could have hidden a multitude of evils.

"What I can't understand is that you've got refrigeration units set up within the food halls. I know because I've just given them a clean bill of health. The capacity you have in those units far exceeds the needs that you have at present. But I can't see the point of this one, unless it isn't for catering purposes. You tell me. Do they need this sort of thing in a mine?"

"As far as I know there aren't any plans to mine down here", said Arnie

"There's always people interested in gold, Mr Grimm."

"Look, Mr Burgess, it isn't even a gold mine. It's a lead mine but we thought it might make it more exciting for the kids. I'm designing a treasure hunt trail for them", said Arnie.

"A bit dangerous, isn't it?" I mean, you haven't even issued *me* with a safety helmet." Arnie clapped his hands together in exasperation.

"I'm sorry…I forgot, look, I can go back and get them if you want." Mr Burgess frowned.

"Now we're here, it's as broad as it's long to me. Nobody bothered with safety helmets when I first cut my teeth in the world of on-site inspections."

A few hundred yards down the illuminated mine track the three of us rounded a bend and I got my first glimpse of what I supposed was a refrigeration unit. A huge silver box the size of the ground floor of a house stood in front of us; its appearance all the more incongruous because of the natural rock that surrounded it. Arnie opened the silver door with an agreeable ease. Popping his head around the door, Mr Burgess was dismayed by the darkness that greeted him. He chewed his lip once more and set off down one side of the huge metal box. A distinct click could be heard and the FrigiKing RU2100 burst into life, its comfortable rumbling noise filling the cavern.

"Power's good!" said Mr Burgess and he ushered us inside. The two of us watched him inspect the refrigeration unit to within an inch of its life.

"Well, I've got things to do…" said Arnie, "I'll leave you both to get on and head on back", but he hadn't bargained for the pernickety Mr Burgess.

"To be honest, Mr Grimm, I think it is prudent that more than one person is acquainted with running the FrigiKing RU2100. What if Mr…" Burgess looked at my nametag. "What if Randle here got locked inside?" The result was that Arnie and I spent the next hour being showed in the most intimate detail just how to run the RU2100.

When our endurance was finally ended, Mr Burgess said the strangest thing.

"Pit ponies!"

"Sorry?" said Arnie Grimm

"Do you still use pit ponies?"

"What for?" Arnie was nonplussed.

"For the gold mine!"

"Look, Mr Burgess, I have already told you that we have no plans to mine here."

"Well I noticed that the refrigeration unit is fitted with meat hooks so I wondered if maybe you were going to freeze any pit ponies that died down here. You know so that you don't have to take them up 'as and when' they die."

"What are you on about?" Two hours spent in the company of Mr Burgess had pushed Arnie to the brink.

"It seems Mr Burgess is interested in just what plans we have for his refrigeration unit, Arnold, my dear." The voice stopped us in our tracks. The three of us turned round and there in front of us was a woman I had seen before. The last time she had been dressed in the imposing black cloak of a witch; today she wore an impressive blue outfit cut to show off her figure. I prayed she wouldn't recognise me.

"Mother!" Arnie was just as shocked as us at the arrival of this glamorous woman so far down an old mine.

"I called in at your office, darling, you weren't there so I thought I'd come looking for you…just in case there was a problem." Mr Burgess approached Arnie's mother and held out his hand.

"If I may say so, this is no place for a beautiful woman; Hector Burgess at your service, ma'am. May I say that I find it hard to believe that you are this young gentleman's mother." The woman I recognised as the witch Doris Morris accepted Mr Burgess' hand with grace and held onto it for longer than necessary. I watched as his eyes began to screw up in an agony of disbelief as this beautiful woman filled his body with pain until he could take it no more. She let go of his hand and he collapsed into a lifeless heap at her feet. The witch turned and monitored my face for a reaction. I was getting good at playing the dumb sprite, I even remembered to blink.

"Get rid of the body, Arnold…but make sure it's somewhere deep I don't want any of the children to come across it."

After I had helped Arnie Grimm dispose of Mr Burgess' body down a nearby shaft, the two of us made our way back up the mine to the surface. I got the feeling that Arnie wasn't too happy about things, but I knew better than to ask him about it. Being a dumb sprite was all about reacting to situations, not creating them.

When we got back to the office, Doris Morris, the woman who Arnie referred to as 'Mother' was waiting there for us. He slumped down in the chair opposite her and I stood at the back of the room awaiting further instruction. Just blend into the back ground, I told myself. This could be a good opportunity to find out what was going on in this place. To my great relief, Doris Morris hadn't recognised me minus my brimmed hat and long coat.

"You're probably wondering why I came down to see you", said Doris Morris. Arnie shrugged like the stroppiest schoolboy. "You see, darling, I think it is time you took on a more adult role within our new venture. With Jakob and Wilkie gone, I'm going to need you to grow up just a bit. It's unfair on your two remaining brothers to have to cope with this all alone, especially after that unfortunate business with Carl. I had high hopes for him."

"Yes, I know you did, Mother. But he let you down, didn't he?"

"He did let me down, Arnold, but he had something which all the rest of you didn't have and that was an emotional attachment."

295

"He was your favourite of all of us. He was the only one whose name you didn't change."

"Now let's not be childish about this, darling. He remained Carl because the name suited him."

"And I suppose I didn't suit Wayne, did I?"

"As a matter of fact you didn't, darling. How anybody could have called their child after a hay cart is beyond me."

"My mother called me Wayne!"

"Your mother is dead, Arnold! Now don't make me think that the others were right."

"What do you mean?"

"Your brothers told me that it might not be a good idea to bring someone as young as you across from the other side but oh I knew different. 'What this place needs is a bit of youthful spirit, a bit of mischief', I said and look how I have paid for it since."

"Oh, here we go!" said Arnie

"Well, it wasn't Carl or Rutger who stole Avis Davies' broom now, was it?"

"Oh, not that again…when are you going to let that drop? Have I got an eternity of you going on about that ahead of me?"

"It gave her the opportunity to consider that which she had never considered before – that someone didn't like her very much. Nobody knew about this place including her till she started questioning you about why you stole her broom. You hadn't even the wit to tell her you took it because it was there."

"I stole that broom for you!" Arnie fought to suppress his tears. My proximity as the person responsible for Arnie being apprehended caused an earth-rendering shift in my bowels.

"Yes I know you did after I distinctly asked you not to draw any attention to yourself. You are and now unfortunately always will be impetuous. I brought you here too soon; I realise that now."

"Well what are you going to do about it? Are you going to kill me like you did Mr Burgess?" Doris Morris smiled at her 'son'.

"What I am going to do Arnold is to give you more responsibility and hope that you prove to me what I saw in you at first."

"What do you mean…more responsibility?"

"Look at you here." Doris Morris indicated the surroundings. "You're stuck in an office, tucked inside an old lead mine. Your only responsibility is to create a treasure hunt for a group of children…"

"And to run the refrigeration unit!"

"…and to run the refrigeration unit. The reason I didn't give you too much to do was because I thought you'd resent being tied down. But I can see now that you want to be a part of this venture. Circumstances have a way of making someone come of age. You'll always be my eighteen year old son but I know you can be so much more." The change in

Arnie's demeanour was further evidence of the hold Doris Morris had over him.

"I've already delegated someone to run the refrigeration units", said Arnie, indicating myself, "I suppose that frees me up to take on other projects." Arnie was really buying into this responsibility idea. Doris Morris turned to look at me and I must confess being in the spotlight of her gaze was not something I wanted to experience again."

"Are you sure he's capable, darling? I don't want this messing up."

"He knows more about it than I do." Hardly a ringing endorsement but I was on the brink of promotion here.

Doris Morris turned to face me. "Right then, sprite, I've a little job for you. Outside now!" This is it, I thought. She's recognised me and has got me booked for a one-way trip down the mineshaft. Pointing through the office window she indicated what looked like a great white maggot that lay on the floor outside. The person standing beside it only compounded my fears…fortunately Alaric Deadman had his back to us and was concentrating on his phone.

"I want you to take that charming bundle and throw it into the refrigeration unit. Make sure she can't get out."

I nodded my head before ducking out of the office. Not wanting the new arrival to see my face, I went straight to the matter in hand and bent down to lift what was probably the Seer JC Bigg, now placed in a muslin sack, soaked in water and tied up.

"Come in, Alaric", said Doris Morris. "Have you been waiting long?"

"Time is relative, is it not?" said Deadman. I could feel his gaze burning into my back. I hoisted the recumbent elf up onto my shoulder and set off away from them both as quickly as I could. "Where's he taking her?"

"To the refrigeration unit. She'll not last long. She's wet through already." Arnie came out of the office.

"Oh…hi Deadman!

"It's pronounced *Deed*man."

"Yeah, whatever", said Arnie Grimm, who was clearly not a fan of the evil i-sprite.

As I carried what I presumed to be the inert body of JC Bigg down towards the refrigeration unit, it dawned on me that I had just been asked to kill someone. As a drug-induced, hypnotised sprite I would not be expected to question the command. Earlier when I helped to tip Mr Burgess down the mineshaft, the poor man was already dead. The only crime I had assisted in was neglecting to give him a decent burial and I felt bad enough about that. Being told to kill someone was quite a different matter. With what I now knew about the refrigeration unit, I was sure that placing someone inside it for any length of time would not be conducive to their health…I needed to get JC away…somewhere safe.

A small rock fell from up above me in the cavern and I looked up. Once more the feeling that I was being watched came over me. I put it down to a Deadman-induced fevered imagination and carried on my journey. Once again I pondered the tricky situation I found myself in. In the course of my investigation into this apparent slave trade that Domania surely was I had worked myself into becoming the trusted servant (more likely slave) of Arnie Grimm. Even Doris Morris had not exactly taken against me. I knew that it had come to a parting of the ways. When I let JC go free, as I surely would, it would mean that I had taken sides and that I would at some point have to face the consequences. Then a quite fortunate thing happened to me. Someone hit me over the head with a rock.

JC woke in the dark to find a beautiful disembodied face floating in front of her. On seeing JC open her eyes its concerned features morphed into a smile that JC took comfort from.

"Hi", said the face.

"Who are you?" JC knew she was very weak. She was in no mood to offer resistance.

"My name is Rosebud. I live here." The young woman was dressed from head to toe in black. Her face was lit only by the light from the fire that crackled in the grate. "And who might you be?"

"I'm known as JC."

The elf struggled to keep the face in focus as the dark body moved around the room. Now she was becoming more accustomed to the light, JC could see mannequins clothed in luxuriant ball gowns displayed around the room.

"Where are we? Is this the palace?"

"This is a secret chamber. No-one knows about this room. Not even my governess…"

"Your governess?" JC's recall fought against the pain. She tried to get out of bed but all movement seemed to lead to further agony. Rosebud hurried to her side.

"You mustn't try to move around so much. Your wounds might reopen."

"Wounds…what wounds?"

"You don't know?" Rosebud's face became pained. "They cut off your wings. You were in a bad way when I rescued you." JC, coming to terms with her mutilation, didn't push for further details. Rosebud grasping at anything to fill the silent minutes to come; continued with her story. "Fortunately they'd left the disposal of your body in the hands of a solitary i-sprite at one stage and it wasn't much of a task to whack him over the head…"

JC wrestled with her memory. Her sluggish responses led her to believe that she might have been drugged at some point. Images of Hans-Christian Grimm, Doris Morris, Deadman, Presley and the old man Walter flitted in and out of her head. She wanted to get up and do something but the slightest movement drained her.

"You should rest now", said Rosebud, sensing her inner conflict, "it will soon be morning and I will have to put out the fire. This room might be a secret to all but me but a smoking chimney might raise questions. You must stay in the bed and keep warm. I will go and prepare you a hot drink and some food."

JC watched as Rosebud stripped out of her black clothing. Long tresses of auburn hair fell out from beneath an unravelled turban. A toned body revealed itself once divested of all its black encumbrances. JC sensed she was watching a fellow warrior…a sense that took an alarming turn for the bizarre when the beautiful young woman fitted herself beneath the folds and fripperies of a formal ball gown.

Rosebud sighed and turned to face JC. "It's the very least my governess expects of me. I think I'm part of the performance here. They've renamed my country Domania, you know? It is going to be a pleasure palace" The sarcasm in her voice betrayed her real feelings.

From deep within JC dredged up a story; the knowledge of which seemed to spring from another age. "You're the princess, aren't you? The princess who slept for…" JC couldn't quite bring herself to say it.

"…for a hundred years, yes. And I can't say I'm too happy about it!"

"You mentioned your governess…"

"Dorothy Garland…what of her?"

"So…she did put herself to sleep. What an amazing woman!"

"I suppose so."

"Well you must admit it showed a loyalty beyond the call of duty."

"She is a very powerful woman…and in no way a servant to me. Actually it's quite the reverse. In fact-"

Even in her weakened state, JC wasn't ready to hear about the faults of Dorothy Garland. "Still, her reappearance in society can only be a good thing. Witches of that stature come along only once in a while. What does she make of this Domania thing? Not too happy, I expect?" Rosebud, now wearing a pale green ball gown, flounced across the room. The caring face had now been replaced by one of frustration.

"I presume she is still a practising witch", continued JC. "She will need to be informed of the 1941 Naming of Witches Act…and the Act of Self-Regulation. She'll need to register and self-administer the Irrevocable Spell. Of course it'll mean her changing her name…to something that rhymes."

"She already has."

"Perhaps you can arrange it for me to meet her….what?"

"And you *have* already met her. She's now called Doris Morris." Rosebud let the information sink in.

"But that's impossible!"

"That's the trouble with heroes, JC…when you eventually meet them they invariably let you down."

"But I thought you said that Dorothy Garland had only just woken from the spell…like you."

For the first time since JC had met her, Rosebud looked confused. "What do you mean?"

"Well Doris Morris has been a Coven Council member for at least forty years." JC was a little surprised when Rosebud, a princess, brought up by a governess and a vision in sage said…

"The lying cow!"

"Randle? Are you all right?" The voice was familiar and I struggled to get the face of Arnie Grimm into focus. "What happened?"

"Someone hit me", was the best I could come up with.

"Who?"

"I don't know." I spoke because it was marginally easier than shrugging my shoulders. Arnie lifted me to my feet.

"I suppose the elf got away. Mother's not going to be happy." Arnie helped me over to a shelf of rock and sat down next to me. "Are you sure you're all right?"

"Yeah…the back of my head is a bit sore." Arnie took the sprite hat off my head and looked.

"It's been bleeding but it seems to have stopped now. Maybe we should get you over to the medical centre to get you checked out."

"I'll be fine." I reckoned the chances of me bumping into Alaric Deadman would increase if I left the shelter of the mine. Arnie placed my arm over his shoulder and the two of us set off up the incline.

"I wonder who did it?" he asked. This was going through my mind as well. I ruled out Deadman simply because if he had recognised me he would have done much more than knock me out. Who else did that leave? Presley? Surely not…another elf? Who?

When we got back to Arnie's office, I asked, "Why did your Mother want the elf putting in the refrigeration unit?" I knew I was crossing a boundary here. Sprites weren't supposed to ask questions. Arnie didn't seem too surprised though and his answer was quite candid.

"The elf was a Seer from All-Seeing Eye. She didn't like the idea of her snooping around." I daren't ask the obvious – why? I was grateful when Arnie carried on. "Mother has put a lot of time and money into this project. If the truth be told she's put a lot of time and money my way as well." I guess my eyes betrayed my interest in his story. "You sure you want to listen to this?"

"I'll be fine."

"I first met by brother-to-be, Rutger Grimm in 1985…back then I was known as Wayne Platt. I'd been summoned to appear at Gilsland magistrates court again." Arnie caught my puzzled look.

"Of course you've never heard of Gilsland, have you?"

"No."

"Well that's where the train comes from every morning. It's just about a mile from here though you wouldn't know it. Anyway, I was nicked for breaking and entering again and my solicitor had dredged up all the old stories about my broken childhood hoping for them to be taken as mitigating circumstances. Fortunately for me the judge was a soft touch but he told me if I ever appear here again then a custodial sentence would await a guilty verdict.

"Rutger was waiting for me outside the courthouse. We looked like the odd couple...him in his expensive suit and me in a fur-lined bomber jacket, white shirt and jeans. I remember I had a tie on...well you have to...if you're going to court. Anyway, this fellow was waiting outside for me and he suggested we go for a drink in the pub across the road. The Wig and Pen it was called. He bought me a drink and did what nobody else before had ever done. He actually listened to what I had to say. He listened while I raged on about being moved from one home to another, never knowing how long I would stay at any one place. He even listened to me when I told him how it felt to be frightened. That fear of not knowing whether you are safe or that the person who is supposed to be looking after you really cares about you at all. There were things that I didn't want to talk about; things that I will keep inside me forever. But now I was grown up, I didn't care anymore. I did what I liked and I told him I was never going to be scared again.

"Rutger finished his posh whisky and offered to get me another drink. When he came back he sat down in front of me and told me that a few years ago, he felt just the same. He was washed up and going nowhere...and because of that he was going to offer me a way out. He asked me how old I was and I told him eighteen...soon to be nineteen. Of course when he asked me that I got a bit suspicious; you see I thought he might be on the pick up or something. He assured me he wasn't. He said he was trying to find out if I was suitable for what he had in mind. 'How would you like to remain eighteen forever?' he said. Straight up, Randle that is what he said to me. 'Imagine it, you'll never grow old, never feel the pains of old age. You'll keep your looks...' Then I thought he's some kind of cosmetics salesman trying to flog me an expensive moisturiser or something. It was then I came right out and told him that he'd been OK, buying me a couple of drinks and listening to me and all that but now I told him that he was sort of giving me the creeps …"

"What did he say to that?", I asked.

"He told me about 'the brotherhood'"

"The brotherhood...what's that?"

"Well I'm thinking this is some sort of religious cult, but Rutger assured me it wasn't. He said if I join the brotherhood, I'll have everything I want; nobody will be on my back and best of all I will always be eighteen years old. He told me I'll be the youngest of the brothers as Mother had always recruited older men before."

"Mother being…Doris Morris?" Fortunately for me Arnie had forgotten he was talking to a supposedly-drugged sprite.

"You're not going to believe this, Randle. He told me she was 144 years old. And that back in 1872 *she* did what Rutger was asking *me* to do right now."

"And what did you do?"

"I got up and walked away. Rutger stopped me by the door and said, 'All I ask of you, Wayne, is to give us a chance. Meet me by the Elphinstone railway tunnel tomorrow morning at 9 o'clock. What have you got to lose? You could live forever.' I turned round and asked him how old *he* was. 'I'll always be 28 years old', he said. Yes, but how old are you really? I asked. And do you know what he said? It really cracked me up."

"No", I said.

"He said, 'I'm really thirty.'" I could only watch as Arnie cracked up once again.

THE CHILDREN ARRIVE

The revelation that young Arnie Grimm was really forty year old Wayne Platt from another world was not easy to take in. The crack on the head I'd taken yesterday meant that any kind of brow-furrowing was way beyond me. I hadn't even been able to make the most of my easy-going employer's offer of another half-day off. I had just been about to walk through the door when Arnie's phone made that strange sound.

"It appears they want all sprites to report to the main hall for extra conditioning. As you're an 'R', Randle, you'll be in the second group which means you've got thirty minutes to get there. Sorry about that, it looks like you've lost your day off."

At the main hall we were addressed by Hans-Christian Grimm. He told us that each of us would be allocated a family and it was important that we found time during our day to make sure that our family had everything it needed. The importance of providing the parents with plenty of food and drink was emphasised. As for the children, Hans-Christian was sure they would take care of themselves, but should any of them require pointing in the direction of the fast food and fizzy drinks available at the games centre then that is what we should do. After Hans-Christian Grimm had finished we were taken to the games centre where we were made to understand the importance of getting the children to play on these games machines. We were told that once the children were in the games centre they were able to get their own food and drink and would come to no harm as there were on-site facilitators to take care of them. The consequence of this was that it left us free to get on with our other duties. The idea certainly had my approval; I'd probably picked up the promotional jargon with more enthusiasm than the brainwashed goblin who sat next to me. Before we left the games centre each of us was shown information on the family we'd been chosen to care for.

So that was why the next day I found myself at the railway station waiting with a hundred other sprites for the train to arrive. I hadn't managed to talk to Presley yesterday even though we were in the same group for conditioning because he was at the other side of the room, but I did catch his eye on the platform. All around me my fellow sprites waited in trance-like composure whilst he and I did our best to sidle closer to each other without showing any sense of purpose. The hiss of the opening time gate meant that our conversation wouldn't be overheard.

"How's it going?" said Presley, whose ability to speak without moving his lips was becoming impressive.

"Have you ever thought of going on stage?" I replied through a cheesy grin; hoping against hope that a bottle of beer wouldn't arise in the conversation.

"I already *was* on stage but if I decide to develop the act I know where to come if I need a dummy." At that moment the time gate began to open up and an announcement was made.

"***Your children and families will soon be arriving so let's have a big smile and cheery welcome ready for them!***" A wave of cheerfulness began to fill the platform as the sprites girded their grins to meet the new arrivals. Presley and I took advantage and began to talk more freely.

"Have you found out anything about my elf?"

"So it wasn't you then?"

"What are you on about?"

"Yesterday, I was assigned the job of putting the elf in the cold storage. My intention was to let her go once I had got far enough away from her captors. Then someone parted my hair with a boulder. Not you then"

"Why would I do that?"

"I don't know, maybe you still don't trust me."

"I do trust you! So you don't know where she is?"

"No but whoever took her probably thought I was going to bump her off…so she should be in safe hands. All I know is that she wasn't in a very good state when I picked her up."

"What do you mean?"

"Well she was either unconscious or drugged. Whoever rescued her would have had to carry her."

The loudspeaker burst into life once again. "***Let's hear you all cheering for our visitors!***" The sprites took up the challenge and cheered their hearts out as the engine came into view. It was trimmed up with bunting and the sign 'DOMANIA EXPRESS' arced over the front of the engine. The sound of a brass band could be heard in the distance, its volume increasing as more and more of the train appeared.

When the time gate was open wide enough, the train pulled into the little station. Presley and I waved the Domania flags we had been given and cheered with the rest of the sprites. A brass band marched out of the goods carriage and lined up on the platform. Presley and I took it as our cue to separate.

Finding myself hemmed in by milling sprites all eager to be united with their 'families' was strange. I just wanted to get to get this 'meet and greet' situation over with so I frantically scanned all the arriving faces on the platform. Families poured off the steam train and fully briefed with Domania procedure were looking around for their 'family guides'. I looked down at my photograph of "Mike Coope, father" and then looked up again into the actual thing. It was almost as if Jonty had made me a copy from the photograph.

"Hi, I'm Mike Coope, I work for the company. You must be Randle?" He waited for a response; I didn't really give him one other than shaking his hand. "This is Tracey, my wife…and these two rascals are Tommy, my son and Kelsey, my daughter. Tommy is twelve and Kelsey is…" Mike Coope looked at his wife.

"Kelsey is six", said Tracey Coope.

"Hello and welcome to Domania. My name is Randle and I am your guide!" I tried to really sound that exclamation mark. I remembered to smile 'an extra smiley smile' at the children. The boy curled his lip and the girl screwed up her face.

"That's not a real fairy!" said little Kelsey. "He's too tall." She looked round her at all the other sprites. They're all too tall!" She folded her arms in disgust.

"Don't be silly, Kelsey", said Mike. "The brochure says you get a fairy guide. He must be a fairy. He's probably a different kind of fairy than you are used to. What kind of fairy are you, Randle?"

Tracey Coope stared at my face. "The make-up's *very* good."

"Tracey is actually a trained beautician. She knows a thing or two about make-up!" said Mike.

"Er…Kelsey is quite right. I am not a fairy. I am a boggart!"

"Ooh! Randle's a boggart, Kelsey!" His daughter was not impressed.

Eager to move things on, I continued. "And right now I would like to show you to your luxury accommodation!" These exclamation marks were playing havoc with my cheek muscles. The family duly followed me away from the station and onto the small railway carriages that stood waiting to take us into Domania itself. As the small train made its way up to the reception area I managed to keep the smile on my face as darling little Kelsey continued to point out that the goblins, dwarves and elves were all too tall to anyone who would listen to her. Her brother occasionally looked up from his small 'games box' to sneer at the rides, the swimming-pool and just about everything really. Mike and Tracey, the adults, were continually looking up at the sky.

"How do they do it, Randle?" asked Mike.

"Sorry?" Distracted by Kelsey repeatedly kicking me under the seat, I hadn't been listening.

"How do they make the sky look so real? We came here through a tunnel into a hillside which we've been around the back of. We know that this can't possibly exist so we must be underground. But look at it!"

"It's probably done with CGI?" Tommy surprised me by communicating before returning beneath his lop-sided fringe. After we picked up the keys from reception I took them to their apartment.

With their luggage waiting for them inside, Mike and Tracey began exploring their home for the week. I was dreading the next item on my agenda. I had to take the children to the games centre which allowed the parents some quality time on their own in which to unpack and explore their own part of the complex. A 'sumptuous platter of food' had been prepared for each parent couple.

"Come on then, Tommy, Kelsey…let's go and take a look at all the things you can do this week! And get ourselves some food!" Tommy handed his games player to his mother and Kelsey seemed to forget for a moment that I was too tall to be a fairy and took hold of my hand. Walking down to the games centre, I tried to initiate a conversation with Tommy to little effect. Kelsey was clinging onto my hand now and looking at all the other sprites that we passed.

"I'm glad we've got you now", she said. "I'm a bit scared of the goblins and dwarves. Are they like you as well but they've got better make-up?"

"Stop talking stupid, Kel", said Tommy. Blimey, we are honoured, I thought.

"The elves are quite nice", continued Kelsey, "but I don't trust them." I looked at her with renewed interest.

"Why do you think that, Kelsey?"

"Because Pop Coope knows a lot about the elves that live in here and he's told us stories about them."

"Pop Coope?"

"Our grandfather", explained Tommy in as few words as possible.

We arrived at the entrance to the games centre. Children were already making use of the 'hundreds of games systems all equipped with widescreen technology'.

"Cool", said Tommy. Within seconds he had availed himself of the first free seat and was sifting through 'the myriad games that are available'.

"One down, one to go", I muttered under my breath. Kelsey tightened her grip on my hand as if she had overheard.

"I don't like computer games", her look was almost a challenge. "What else is there?"

"Well, Kelsey…we've got a lovely pool which has all sorts of chutes and waves just like the real sea…" She didn't look too impressed. "…and we've got places to eat if you're hungry. You know you can just go up to the counter and ask for whatever you want. It's all free. We've got shops as well but you'll have to ask your mother and father for things out of there. We've got a 'massive jungle gym'…" I looked across at complex and saw the towering theme park rides. "Oh yes, I nearly forgot we've got some 'awesome rides for children of all ages'."

"I don't like rides that go too fast!"

"No…we've got nice gentle rides as well." After showing Kelsey, the swimming pool and assuring her that there were always people there who would look after her but that it might not be me, we made our way over to the rides. I was hoping to get a chance to speak to Presley whilst I was there but the ever present hand of Kelsey Coope wasn't going to make it easy for me. I took her onto one or two of the smaller children's rides and she seemed quite happy to tootle along on the back of a huge caterpillar or sit astride a dragonfly as it made its way interminably round in a circle. Presley saw me as I was just helping Kelsey onto a small train that had taken her some persuading to board. I waved to her each time the train went past. Presley wandered over under the pretence of wiping some oil off a gaily painted panel.

"All right, Randle? I managed to get rid of mine at the games centre. They were quite impressed by 'hundreds of games systems all equipped with widescreen technology'…whatever that is."

"I seem to be stuck with little 'miss whingey'. I'm going to see if I can talk her into returning to her parents. Then I can get on with finding out what's going on here."

"On the face of it, it seems to be a marvellous place for children", said Presley. Both of us waved as a pre-occupied Kelsey came into view from within the window of her carriage.

"What do you mean 'on the face of it'?"

"Well…actually. All these rides that you can see…" I looked about me at some of the complex theme park rides that dwarfed us. "None of them actually work."

"What do you mean?"

"Well I tell a lie because the RaptorCoaster works…that one…but all the other big rides are out of bounds to kids. I've had a bit of a potter round when no one's been looking and they look like they were never meant to work. It is almost as they have been put there just for show. As you can see all the little rides are OK." Kelsey came round again taking delight in returning our waves.

"Well what's the point of that?" I asked. Presley just shrugged his shoulders. Kelsey had finished her circular train journey and eager to try something else she ran off into the labyrinth of children's rides. "Oh no…where's she gone to now."

"Never fear", said Presley as he pulled out a small flute from his pocket. "Watch this." He started to play a tune on his flute.

"Yes, very good, Presley, but I really must get Kelsey back to her parents." I set off to run but the little girl was standing before me gazing intently at Presley…another three children were standing behind her. "Kelsey, there you are!" Presley stopped playing and the little girl and her followers came to life again. "Come on; let's see what your Mum and Dad are up to. She took my hand as I glanced at Presley who had popped his flute back into his pocket. He tilted his head on one side and returned to polishing the panel.

Kelsey and I made our way back to her parents apartment and were surprised to see they were about to have company. Rutger Grimm, a young woman dressed in a ball gown and Doris Morris herself, were climbing up the steps to The Coope's apartment. I put my finger to my lips and faced Kelsey.

"You've got to be very quiet but your Mummy and Daddy are being visited by the beautiful princess and the wicked witch. Kelsey's eyes widened to the size of mark pieces. She was close to tears. "Don't worry, they're only pretending." I was intrigued as to why Doris Morris would want to speak to Mike and Tracey Coope personally.

"Are you sure the witch isn't going to kill Mummy and Daddy?" Little Kelsey was quite beside herself with fear.

I had to reassure her. "I know the witch isn't going to kill your Mummy and Daddy because this is a place built specially for people like you and Tommy and your Mummy and Daddy to enjoy themselves."

"Who told you that? The wicked witch? Well she would, wouldn't she? Pop Coope was right…we shouldn't have come here. I'm going in." Before I could stop her, Kelsey was across the road, up the stairs and into the apartment. I didn't relish coming into contact with Doris Morris again but I suppose I had a legitimate excuse. As soon as Kelsey had entered the apartment I chased after her in dumb sprite mode.

"Kelsey! You should go down to the games centre! There are games for children of all ages", I called after her. As I crossed the threshold I was stopped dead by an icy stare from Doris Morris. "Sorry, ma'am", I said, with a metaphorical tug of

319

my forelock. Mick and Tracey Coope, both wearing an inane grin, seemed happy enough.

Doris Morris gazed at Kelsey and gave her a most endearing smile. "Hello, little girl and what is your name?" Kelsey ran and grabbed her mother's hand.

"Her name is Kelsey, ma'am." I answered eager not to offend. Kelsey shot me a look that said 'traitor'.

"Well, Kelsey, darling. Would you like to meet a real princess?" For a second, her defences were breached and the little girl looked up at her mother before nodding. "Allow me to introduce Princess Rosebud!" The young woman, resplendent in her pale green ball gown had her back to me as she curtseyed to Kelsey. This was Princess Rosebud, her auburn hair piled high above her pale neck. I recalled the painting from The Sleeping Beauty Inn and the likeness it had to someone I knew. Little Kelsey appeared awestruck by Princess Rosebud and when Doris Morris suggested that the princess accompany the little girl to the games centre while the grown-ups finished their chat, Kelsey was mesmerised into agreement.

Hand in hand with the little girl, Princess Rosebud turned to leave and, on seeing me in the doorway, struggled to contain her surprise.

"And you, boggart...who seems to turn up everywhere...you may leave as well", said Doris Morris. I turned in front of Kelsey and the Princess and marched down the steps. Outside I waited until Princess Rosebud and Kelsey had caught up with me. Side by side the three of us walked down towards the games centre.

"How are the hobbits coming on, Scarlett?" I asked, feeling a little peeved by the arrival of my secretary in Domania.

"There doing just fine, Humphrey. How's your head?"

"He's not called Humphrey…his name is Randle!" said Kelsey.

As six year old Kelsey Coope swung on the arms of the princess and boggart that accompanied her, Scarlett and I argued like an old married couple.

"Couldn't you have just asked me to hand over the elf? I was going to let her go anyway", I said.

Scarlett let out an infuriated sigh. "It had to look real. How would you have explained it to Doris Morris, eh?" She had a point but as sure as eggs were eggs I wasn't going to admit it. "Besides you couldn't have just let her go she needed caring for properly."

For the sake of the elf, I took her point. "Well where is she, then?"

"She's safe where Doris Morris won't find her."

"She'd better be all right?"

"She is…but she's not in good health. She's had her wings amputated." For a few seconds the verbal hostilities between us ceased.

"Oh…still…they do grow back, I'm told. Not that it's any comfort to her…at the moment. But she's safe…that's the main thing." It didn't take long for those hostilities to resume again.

"Exactly, and you are complaining about a little bump on the head."

"A little bump on the head! Are you kidding? I was out cold for hours! *And* it was the second time you've done it in a week!"

"Look I made sure I hit you on the other side of your head from last time and I hung around until Arnie Grimm came to your rescue."

"Thanks for nothing!"

"Well I had to really…I needed to wait until it got dark before I could smuggle JC into the palace."

"You know I've a good mind to sack you. You've been nothing but trouble since I took you on."

"You think you had a say in the matter? Anyway you can't sack me because I resign!"

"Good! It's not as though you've been of any practical use to me."

"Oh you think so, do you? It's funny you should say that…"

"Oh it is, is it?"

"Yeah, it is." Kelsey was still swinging happily between us. "Well just you think back, Humphrey Boggart…do you remember Sphagnum bringing a note from his mother?" I stopped in my tracks causing Kelsey's swing to go awry.

"What about it?"

"That was me…I gave him the note…"

"Right…so?"

"And it was me who disposed of Scuzzer and Tranter."

"What…you killed them?"

Scarlett shook her head. "Locked up for a long while, I should think."

"That was you…with the donkey?" I mumbled my thanks.

"Sorry…did you say something?"

"I'm sorry…thanks."

"Pardon? Do you have some kind of speech defect?"

"OK, I said I was sorry! And thank you for coming to my aid! I suppose that makes up for cracking me over the head. OK! Are you happy now?"

Scarlett flashed me a look of extreme dismay. "But you haven't thanked me for the other time I saved your miserable backside." She was the disappointed princess with a pout that could cut a cake in half. Despite the presence of a small child between us, my anger began to rise again.

"What are you on abou- ?" Then it hit me. The black-clad figure that saved me from Deadman in The Ginnels. "That was you?" Scarlett fought hard to keep the smugness from her face. "Well I thank you for that as well." I said with a degree of calm. "It seems that I do indeed owe you one."

"Don't mention it, kind sir." It was the false concern that really got to me.

"You really are an annoying-"

"Stop it, you two!" It was little Kelsey who brought our bickering to a halt. "You're just like children." The three of us walked on until we reached the games centre. Kelsey caught sight of her brother who was engrossed in playing a game. He acknowledged her presence with a grunt; only stopping to do a double take on seeing me in the company of a princess in a ball gown. He nodded at the pair of us before resuming his game. I led Kelsey over to where a group of elves wearing badges indicated that they were Child Facilitators. They were watching over some of the younger children. One of their number took Kelsey by the hand and over to a games console that seemed to have a lot of ponies and pink in it. Scarlett and I left the games centre and walked together towards the palace. Despite all the attention she got from young girls wanting to meet a real live princess she managed to tell me what had happened to her since she had woken up that century.

"I remember waking up and the first thing I felt was this burning desire to kill the person who woke me. There was this man who I had never met before and I just attacked him for no reason…"

"You didn't hit him over the head with a rock, did you?" I asked. Scarlett mugged a smile before continuing.

"I would have done if I could have got hold of one. I really wanted to kill him. The man fled for his life and Dorothy, my governess, you probably know her better as Doris Morris…she gave me a gun…"

"Wait a minute…you say Doris Morris is your governess?"

"She has been since I was a little baby over one hundred years ago." Scarlett could see me making the mental calculations in my head.

"Surely she can't have been alive for that length of time?"

"JC says she's been in the public eye for forty years."

"Yet she doesn't look a day over thirty. She's a better witch than I gave her credit for. So what happened to the man you were trying to kill?"

"I'd never even fired a gun before but within seconds I was outside the palace shooting at this man who had dared to wake me up."

"Did you kill him?"

"No. This other man came and told me he would deal with it. I left him to it."

"Did *he* kill him?"

"No...they brought him back in something called a body bag. He had cut his way through the Wall of Thorns with some sort of sawing machine. His name was Jakob Grimm."

"Yeah, I saw his body and the sawing machine...did you get to the other guy?"

"That was why I came to Thursday Market."

"To finish him off?"

"No...the urge to kill him sort of wore off. I suspect I was under some kind of spell. I felt I ought to go and apologise to this man so I left the palace."

"You can get out of here?"

"Yes, I used the same way as you got in I expect…through the tunnel. You forget I spent my childhood in this palace and I know all about its little secrets. It wasn't difficult for me. I spent some time in Without trying to find what happened to the man I had tried to kill. I stayed there for a few days." A lovely smile came over Scarlett's face. "Seen any mad women lately, Humphrey?"

My mind went back to the woman we first saw in the porch of the village hall. "You're not 'Miss Terry'…the village idiot?"

Scarlett grinned with pride. "Yes…that was me! Miss *who*?" Then the penny dropped. "Oh, Humphrey that's awful."

"Hmm, I know. Don't blame me. You seem to have a thing about wearing black."

"Don't knock it…princesses only get to wear it at state funerals."

"Yeah, I keep forgetting you're a princess. So what was with all this Scarlett Alewife business?" Scarlett gave me a look. "Yeah, I suppose it was a dumb question. I'm hardly going to take on a princess as my secretary without asking a few questions. Anyway, should I be calling you your highness…or Rosebud?"

"Stick with Scarlett, if you don't mind. I've always thought Rosebud was a bit soppy."

"I take it you never found the man?"

"No, I heard that he'd been killed. Doris Morris had taken care of business."

"I know, I saw him die. She even turned up personally to take the body away. I'm surprised she bothered to have him buried."

"That was down to me. I sort of insisted. She lets me have my way every now and again. She thinks it helps if I still believe I'm in charge."

"Now that you know she hasn't been asleep for a hundred years, unlike yourself, how does that make you feel?"

"Dorothy had been my governess all my life. It was her who helped me come to terms with what had happened to me. Finding that your mother and father have died over eighty years ago is not an easy concept to grasp. I was inconsolable but Dorothy helped a great deal in getting my life back together. She made sure I was protected..."

"Look, it sounds to me that all this is a set up..."

"What do you mean?"

"The train comes through a portal to another world. This makes Fotherghyll land very valuable...any contact with this other world and the possibility of trade means there is money to be made. We've seen how far advanced this other world is just by the things that surround us. We've seen flying machines...electricity...mobile phones and what's worse I have seen guns that fire twenty bullets a second. Think of the power that can be gained from being in possession of all these things."

"So what are you saying?"

"That somehow Doris Morris, or Dorothy Garland that was, has engineered all this. She's got rid of everyone who ever lived here-"

"Except me."

I nodded. "Behind the Wall of Thorns she's built herself a little power base. She's brought in sprite slaves…"

"But your argument falls down there, Humphrey. The sprites have been brought in just to entertain and look after the children. They've not been used to build a huge monument to the greatness of Doris Morris, have they?"

"That is the only thing I just don't get. Domania could be so much more but she has created an amusement park for children. Why?" The ringing of a small bell caused the both of us to look up. Coming down towards us balanced precariously on a bicycle was Presley. I put my hand out more in a gesture to stop him falling off it than anything else. As he didn't know Scarlett, he played the part of dumb sprite very well.

"It's OK, Presley. Scarlett…sorry…Princess Rosebud is with us. She has good news about JC."

Presley's eyes brightened. "How is she?"

"She could be better", said Scarlett, "She's been through a lot. I'll make sure she's OK." Heartened by that, Presley smiled.

"Anyway, what are you doing on a bicycle?" I asked.

"Is that what they call it? I've never seen one before. I was told that I could ride one…so I guess I had to."

"What about the rides?"

"Oh, I've been taken off that now." My puzzled look brought an explanation from Presley, "They've closed all the rides on health and safety grounds."

"What? Why?" I asked. Presley shrugged. "Even the little ones?"

"Even the little ones", he said. "Most of the big ones weren't working to start with. You knew that."

"I know but this is a place for children. You'd think they would make the effort to get everything working."

Presley nodded. "They've got me delivering these pizzas now. For the parents…I quite like it. It's my job to box them, put on the special sauce and then deliver them on my trusty metal steed."

"What's the special sauce?" asked Scarlett.

"They only put it on the adult's orders for some reason. Maybe it has alcohol in it or something…I don't know. I tried it…didn't appeal. Anyway, is there any chance that I can I see JC?" I looked at Scarlett but she shook her head. It'll be hard enough getting you in without anyone seeing us." Presley looked disappointed.

"Give her my best wishes and tell her that the elfhounds liked my music so much they've all decided to leave." I gave Presley a look. "She'll know what I mean. I'd better go; I've more pizzas to deliver." With that he hopped on his bicycle and the pair of us watched as he freewheeled crazily down the path.

"I seem to know his face from somewhere", said Scarlett, "JC neglected to mention him to me but I can understand that. She hasn't had much choice in having to trust me. Come on." The two of us reached the back of the palace buildings and Scarlett went on ahead. A few seconds later she was back.

"Right, it's all clear. Get on your hands and knees!"

"What?"

"Hurry up! Before somebody comes!" Scarlett raised her eyes skyward. "You'll have to travel beneath my skirts." It was my turn to roll my eyes but I did as I was bid. While Scarlett sauntered into the palace I was scurrying like a snakehound beneath her numerous petticoats. It wouldn't have been too bad if Scarlett's secret hideaway hadn't been on the first floor. The stairs were a killer for my knees. From inside her dress I visualised all the people of the palace watching this strange young girl who had been asleep for a hundred years making slow progress across the polished marble. After the torture of the stairs, Scarlett stopped by treading on my fingers. Outside her dress I could hear some sort of mechanism being activated. We moved on.

"You can come out now", said Scarlett. I brushed aside the folds of her dress like a comic actor arriving on stage. The two of us were alone in a dusty corridor. My attempt to stand up straight was almost mechanical. Scarlett pushed open a door and we found ourselves inside a room peopled with dressmaker's dummies, each one wearing a ball gown similar to that which Scarlett was wearing. On the far side of the room was a bed and rising from it was JC Bigg, Seer of the All-Seeing Eye.

"You, OK, Kid Gloves?"

"Are you going to persist with that stupid nickname?"

"What do you think?"

"Do you find him as annoying as I do, Scarlett?" The princess nodded.

"Cold in here, isn't it?" I was referring more to JC's demeanour than the temperature.

"We can't have a fire during the day", said Scarlett, "they've installed electric heating in the rest of the building. A smoking chimney would attract-"

I interrupted Scarlett, "This electricity stuff, it powers everything here, doesn't it? Where does it come from?"

"What do you mean?" asked Scarlett.

"Well I sort of understand how steam power works…you burn the coal, boil the water and the steam makes enough pressure to do things. This electricity doesn't seem to come from anywhere."

"All I know is that it comes through the time gate while it is open", said JC. "When I first came here I watched this team of humans who sprang into action every time the gate opened. They took this tube, I think they called it a cable, and connected it to one that came up from the railway tunnel. Whatever electricity is, they pumped it in while the time gate was open."

"But they must keep it somewhere…like the steam…they must have somewhere to store it."

JC continued, "I followed the cable and it goes underground but I did discover a strange building that had lots of these cables coming out of it. The place has danger warnings plastered all over it. I assume that is where this electricity is kept. What are you getting at?"

"Well if we destroyed this electricity storage place then nothing here would work. The children and the parents would want to go home. It could be the beginning of the end for Domania." JC seemed to mull over my idea.

"But how would we destroy it?" said Scarlett.

"Has anybody heard of something called dynamite?" I said.

JC shot me a look. "What do you know about dynamite?"

"I know where there is some? The Grimm brothers had me and Presley move some that they had found."

"At the back of the railway station?" JC was becoming more animated despite the obvious pain she was in. I nodded.

"Could you find it again?"

"Yes."

"That's good." JC seemed reassured. "Your idea about destroying the electricity is a good one. However I was hoping to use that dynamite to blow up the time gate itself. That remains the primary objective of my mission…but I'm sure we could spare a stick or two to take out the electricity storage point. It is just that I am not well enough to undertake such a mission yet and dynamite is too dangerous to be used by untrained hands. Do you think you could get me a couple of sticks from the box?"

I nodded.

"...and there are some primer charges and lengths of fuse in the attic here."

"I could get those", said Scarlett. JC slumped back onto the bed, exhausted by her own enthusiasm. Scarlett and I watched her and reverting to type like any hospital visit, we were soon at a loss for something to say until Scarlett broke the silence.

"What was that message that Presley had for JC?"

"Is he all right?" JC perked up once more on hearing Presley's name. Embarrassed by her sudden change of character she offered something by way of explanation. "I was the first person he saw when he woke up..." She looked at Scarlett. "Like you, he's been asleep for a hundred years."

"You want to think yourself lucky, he didn't take the same attitude as the lovely Princess Rosebud here", I said, despite the intensity of Scarlett's glare.

"That might explain why I seem to know him from somewhere", she growled.

"He's a musician, I think. He said to tell you that 'the elfhounds liked his music so much they've all decided to leave'.

"That's certainly good news", said JC. "Things are starting to look up. Avis Davies should be here anytime soon.

"How do you know that?" I asked.

It was Scarlett who answered. "When I got back to Without with Scuzzer and Tranter, I met with your friend Jonty who took it upon himself to notify the Massy Witch. It turns out he knows her."

"I know that.

"Jonty Thumb is the main reason I managed to infiltrate Domania" said JC.

"Well he wasn't much use when it came to getting me in here!"

"As one of the top scientists at The Eye…he has priorities. Helping a half-baked investigation by an amateur detective is not one of them."

"Well I seem to be doing better than you are at the moment." I instantly regretted what I had said. "I'm sorry…I shouldn't have said that."

JC, surprisingly didn't react. Suitably chastened, I decided to move the conversation on.

"So what's Avis Davies going to do when she gets here?"

"Sort this thing out", said JC.

THE RAID

Before reporting to Arnie to help him set up the children's treasure hunt, I thought I would check in on the Coope family to see that they were comfortable. On the way I passed the Games Centre, so I went in on the off chance that Tommy Coope was an early riser. Since arriving in Domania the boy had spent every waking hour in this place; so it was no surprise to me when I recognised the top of his tousled head sticking out over the back of a comfy chair. The large screen in front of him filled with the words *COMING SOON TO DOMANIA – XYGLON BATTLEGROUND.*

"You're up early, Tommy." Face full of concentration he ignored me while he watched the screens. "I said, 'You're up early, Tommy'"

"What time is it?" he said in a single word of three syllables.

"Ten past eight."

"At night...or morning?" I looked into his tired eyes and worked it out.

"Have you been in here all night?"

He shrugged. "Came in here after I got something to eat."

"What about your Mum and Dad? Haven't they been looking for you?" Tommy rubbed his eyes and blinked into the harsh light above. He shrugged again.

"Is the burger place open yet? I'm starving. Will you get me one? I'm just starting a new level."

"I'm not your slave, Tommy!"

"I'll think you'll find that you are! All the other kids have got servants!" Tommy was making a scene so I needed to ease the situation. People were beginning to take notice.

"Don't you think you'd be better going back to your apartment to freshen up and to check in with your Mum and Dad? Come on, I'm going round that way myself." I reached out for Tommy's hand. Big mistake…he snatched it away from me.

"I'm not a baby! I'm cool, all right." I watched him walk away from me and thought that maybe I was approaching this from the wrong angle. Maybe I would be better seeing his parents first. I looked round the Games Centre. It was so early in the morning and yet every screen was being used. Some children were asleep in the chairs that went by the name of the Chillout Space. By the look of some of them in here, Tommy wasn't the only one who had spent all night saving the world from monsters.

When I arrived at the Coope's apartment, I was a little surprised to find both parents fast asleep. Kelsey, however, was wide awake and in the process of trying to make herself a cup of hot chocolate. I managed to intercept her before she got to the steaming kettle.

"Seeing as your Mum and Dad are still asleep, I'll leave them a note and take you down to the food hall for your breakfast."

"Yaaay!" shouted Kelsey as she jumped up and down.

"What would you like?"

"Burger and chips!" she continued with her jumping. It seemed to be the choice of most children down there. "Come on, then." Kelsey grabbed my outstretched hand and the pair of us headed off for the food halls.

As we walked past him, Tommy grudgingly acknowledged our presence while tucking in to his own burger and chips. Kelsey's idea of sharing her brother's breakfast table met with a churlish grunt which suggested the likelihood would be over his dead body.

"Yes, miss, how may I help you?" The elf behind the counter ignored me so I stood back to let Kelsey order her burger and chips. In the contrary manner of most young children, Kelsey asked if she could have some cereal and an apple.

"We're not serving that any more", said the elf. "There's just burger and chips; egg, beans and chips, sausage and chips...chicken nuggets, fish fingers are available but are really a lunchtime option."

"All served with chips?" I asked. The elf nodded.

Kelsey sighed. "Just the burger and chips then…" I whispered in her ear. "…and a cup of tea for my friend", she added.

"I don't do drinks you'll have to get that from Zelda at the end." I looked down the end of the line and saw a goblin sat staring into space. "She makes the tea." The elf gave us his brightest smile and headed back to the kitchen. I moved the tray down towards the till where Zelda lay waiting when a movement outside the Games Centre windows caught my eye.

"Just go and sit with your brother, Kelsey. I just need to go and see someone." The little girl looked imploringly at me. I sighed, picked up the tray and headed quickly over to Tommy's table. Before he could grunt, I told him…"Look after your sister a minute." …and I was off outside and standing in the doorway.

It was the sudden arrival of the men I had witnessed obliterating a rabbit outside the Wall of Thorns that had grabbed my attention. My discovery of Jakob Grimm's body and their subsequent removal of it seemed so long ago now. I watched as the soldiers, still in their unusual mottled green uniforms took up positions outside the Games Centre as if they were expecting trouble. Their appearance was now enhanced by large helmets and padded vests. By now, one or two of the children had noticed the events unfolding as well. The soldier who seemed to be in charge of the situation took up a position quite near where I was standing.

Hans-Christian Grimm's arrival on the scene came as a surprise…more so for the fact that he was now also attired in the same way as the soldiers. He scurried over to the commanding officer and asked for a progress report.

"Nothing to report yet, sir", said the soldier. "My men are in position. All we can do is wait until the enemy break cover." Whispers around the Games Centre had brought more children to the windows. "If you don't mind me saying, sir", continued the soldier, "I have some concern about the presence of so many children at the scene. I could let the enemy come out of the building and engage them elsewhere but we would lose the element of surprise and risk the possibility of a hostage situation arising."

Hans-Christian Grimm nodded his head despite looking a little annoyed. "Leave it to me." He popped his head through the glass door of the Games Centre and got my attention. "You, sprite!"

"Yes, Mr Grimm, how may I be of service?"

"Get the children away from the windows! Quickly now!" Eager not to miss any of the action, I relayed Grimm's request to the Child Facilitators. With the kids out of the way, I took up a position out of the eye line of Hans-Christian Grimm and prepared to watch events unfold.

Random shots were heard coming from the building and the waiting soldiers tensed themselves as they took up their battle stations. Minutes passed without anything happening. I realised that the building they had under surveillance was the one by which I had first arrived in Domania. Whoever it was that the soldiers were waiting for, they were entering by means of the tunnel from the graveyard in Without-the-Wall. Just as I was wondering who the new arrivals might be, the door of the building slowly opened.

340

A group of red-coated soldiers rushed out with fixed bayonets. Numerous sharp bursts of fire from Grimm's small army cut the advance party to shreds in no time at all. The poor blighters never even got the chance to fire a bullet in anger. Those that followed showed a little more caution but they too were shown little mercy by the killing machines that were trained on them.

A brief respite was afforded by the appearance of Avis Davies. The Massy Witch came out of the building protected by an air spell shield. Using her for cover, the remains of her troops tried to find positions from which they could attack their enemy. Grimm's soldiers, realising that they could not pierce the cover of the Massy Witch, threw hand grenades over her defences. One by one her small army was picked off until the witch stood alone protected only by her magical shield. Hans-Christian Grimm urged his soldiers to surround her.

"She can't touch you…the second she drops her shield…shoot her!" Avis Davies with an almost regal calm walked back towards the building she had come from. "Shut the door!" shouted Hans-Christian Grimm. One of his soldiers intercepted her and closed the only escape route Avis Davies had been left with. The Massy Witch realised she had nowhere left to go. To use her magic on her enemy she had to drop the protection of her magical shield. As soon as she dropped the shield, their automatic weapons would cut her to ribbons.

Hans-Christian Grimm was now talking on his mobile phone. Children, drawn by the sound of gunfire to the Games Centre windows, were drooling over the carnage now in front of them.

"Cool!" said Tommy Coope.

"It's so realistic!" said another as Child Facilitator sprites were doing their best to peel them from the windows.

"Get those children away from here!" barked Hans-Christian Grimm as more of them filled the doorway and some even started to venture outside to look at the corpses. As I did my best to round up the more curious of the children I managed to catch the eye of Avis Davies. Trapped within her magical shield she acknowledged my look, although deep down I suppose she wondered what help an ironised sprite could give her in this dire situation. She seemed almost transfixed by her predicament.

Once the children were all safely rounded up and moved back into the Games Centre, domestic sprites began clearing up the dead bodies. Sawdust was sprinkled over the pools of spilled blood and all the detritus of the battle was removed out of harm's way.

Summoned, no doubt by their brother, it was not long before Rutger and Arnie Grimm both arrived to survey the scene.

"We can't get at her until she drops her defences", said Hans-Christian, eager to finish off his objective.

"Surely she'll fall asleep at some point", said Rutger.

"The spell can be held throughout sleep by a powerful witch", said a voice from behind them. Doris Morris cut through her three remaining sons and made a little wave at the Massy Witch. She approached the shimmering shield of Avis Davies. "And Avis Davies is certainly a very powerful witch!" Doris Morris fired a magical charge at the shield but it had little effect. "See what I mean?" She walked all around the

Massy Witch as though she was searching for a weak spot. "The only way to bring down a powerful witch is by natural causes. Even a witch as mighty as the esteemed Avis Davies has got to eat sometime. Bullets may not be able to get through her shield but by the same token neither can bread nor water." She addressed her next sentence directly to Avis Davies. "For the sake of the children and the men who will have to guard you, perhaps you would like to accompany me to the palace?" It was unclear whether Avis Davies could hear anyone from within her protective shield but she stayed where she was.

"Don't worry, Mother", said Rutger Grimm, "If she wants to stay there she can. I'll have a sign made saying that she is the Wicked Witch who is being guarded by the soldiers. The kids'll love that sort of thing. She wanted to know what was going on in Domania…we'll make her part of it until the time comes when she finally breaks. Then the soldiers will be waiting for her."

"I need to speak to you, Rutger", said Doris Morris. Arnie tapped me on the shoulder and indicated with a nod of his head that he wanted me to accompany him to the old mine.

"Arnold!" said Hans-Christian Grimm. "Mother wants a meeting at the palace."

"Always the last to know", muttered Arnie under his breath. He turned to me and said, "I'll phone you when I've finished." I glanced across at Avis Davies, who now resembled a gift shop doll in a display case. She returned my look and I gleaned some reassurance from her eyes.

By now Kelsey Coope had re-attached herself to my side. Fearing for her safety on her own, I returned her smile.

Something strange was happening here. Her own parents seemed to be in some kind of lethargy from which they didn't want to escape. Then again it wasn't only the Coope's children who were running wild around the place. Surely all the other children's parents weren't as irresponsible as Mike and Tracey Coope? As the days had passed the Games Centre was always filled to capacity with boys and girls who were more than happy to spend all their time playing various console games. Tommy Coope had become a dishevelled urchin who had marked out his territory in the Games Centre with chocolate bar wrappers stuffed down the side of his armchair. The centre itself was kept clean by an army of sprites, one of whom removed a discarded burger tray as I tried to get a grunt out of Tommy. I asked him when the last time he'd been back to his apartment was. True to form, he shrugged and picked up his game controller.

Kelsey and I headed back to see if her mum and dad were up yet. The sudden frequency of sprites riding bicycles up and down the roads of Domania indicated that the parents were all being fed by delivery. Our arrival at Mike and Tracey's apartment found them both slumped on the sofa with a vacant look on their faces. They were not the cheerful, curious people who I met only a few days before. It had become apparent that they were being drugged. The mountain of food delivery cartons stacked on every available surface gave me a pretty good idea just how the drug was being administered. The question was how to broach the subject without provoking a reaction. I couldn't afford to take the chance of being found out myself so I just went along with things and made everybody a cup of tea. Someone knocked at the door and Kelsey went to answer it. Through the window I could see Presley clutching a pizza box. I waved him inside. Unsure of the company he nodded his head in acknowledgement. Kelsey had already taken the pizza off him and was putting it on plates for her mum and dad who struggled to stir into life on the sofa.

"Look at them, Presley", I said. "It has got to be that special sauce you put on all the adult meals."

Presley nodded. "But what can I do about it? Even if I neglected to put in on their meals, there are almost twenty of us preparing and delivering them." Behind him, Kelsey was just about to eat some of the pizza. I was about to stop her when Mike Coope came alive.

"Kelsey! That is mine and your mother's food! You get yours down at the food hall." The little girl was quite shocked by her father's sudden animation and dropped the plate on the floor. "You stupid girl!" continued her father, "Now look what you've done!" He hurried over to where the shattered plate was, picked up the pizza off the floor and began to eat it.

Eager to make the most of Mike Coope's unexpected lucidity, I spoke to him. "You do know your son is spending his nights in the games centre."

"Who?" said Mike as he savoured his pizza.

"Your son, Tommy. He wasn't here in the apartment with you last night and when I came round I had to stop Kelsey making a hot drink for herself." Mike looked up from his meal.

"Look...?"

"Randle."

"Look, Randle. We're having our dinner at the moment...can't we sort this out later, OK? I looked at Presley in despair and the pair of us left the Coopes to their meal.

"We've got to do something about this 'special sauce'." I said. For some reason, Doris Morris doesn't want the parents to be…"

"Like parents?" said Presley. I was just about to agree when my mobile phone rang. It was Arnie. He needed to talk to somebody…now.

THE PRICE TO PAY

When I got to Arnie's office at the head of the mine, I knew he had been crying. His red-ringed eyes looked up as I pushed open the door to the office. I asked if he was all right. He shook his head.

"Not really, Randle. There's something very big going on down here and I'm not happy about it at all. The fact is…it's doing my head in." I needed to push him further.

"If I can help you in anyway, Mr Grimm, I will." A complete lie but if you couldn't lie to the Grimms who could you lie to?

"I suppose I can talk to you, Randle. You're a dumb sprite; you aren't going to ask questions." If I hadn't been a dumb sprite, I'd have rolled my eyes.

"Everything's changed, Randle. It's Mother…she killed Rutger, my brother."

"What? Why? How?"

Arnie answered the last question first. "She did what she did to Mr Burgess. He couldn't do what she asked of him." It all came gushing out as he retold the scene he had been party to. "You see, Domania is not what it seems, Randle. It's not even what I thought it was. When Mother first told me about her idea, I thought…sounds great. It was the sort of place I'd have liked to go to when I was younger…if I'd have had the chance. I thought my chance had come when Rutger came along and made me the offer I couldn't refuse…staying eighteen forever…loads of money…plus the ultimate get-out clause. Yeah…you can always get out of trouble when your

Mum is the Chief of Police…or Commander of the Guardians as they call it here. When I got the call from Mother…I had nothing to lose. That's the type of person she likes…no attachments. That's why Carl had to die?"

"Carl?" I was pushing it here, I know.

"Mother needed Carl to build Domania. He's done a good job but he had the one thing the rest of my brothers didn't have – responsibilities, emotional ties…call it what you will. You see he had a brother who he thought he would never see again and a private detective found out where he was. He was delighted but Mother wouldn't have it. She had made Carl a very wealthy man in the other world…but it was now time to come and live in this world. That's the problem with Mother…there's always a price to pay. Sometimes it's just too much." Rather than unburdening himself to me Arnie withdrew and sank into a dark mood. It was time to forget about playing the dumb sprite.

"What did she ask you and Rutger to do?"

"Nothing."

"Nothing?"

"She just wanted us to sit back and do nothing. Rutger said he couldn't, so she killed him. She just spoke into his ear and he threw himself off the balcony. It's Domania, Randle, it's not about making money, like me, Rutger and Carl thought. It's much worse than that. Mother's older sons were fine about it. Hans-Christian, Jakob and Wilkie had too much to lose if they didn't go along with it. If she makes them go back to the other world they would just crumble up and die. They daren't stand up to her"

348

"What do you mean…'crumble up and die'?"

"They were born in the other world so when they came into this world for the first time they stayed the age they were. Rutger and me are different. We arrived here some twenty years ago. Even if I had to go back…I'd be about forty and Rutger would have been about fifty. What the older ones don't understand is that we can't live with what she wants to do. I see the children running around in Domania and I can remember when I did the same things. Hans-Christian is nearly 130 years old. He cannot even remember being a child. Why should he care what happens to them if it means he can live forever?"

"And what is going to happen to them?" There was no point pretending any more.

"They're going to be left here on their own."

"What do you mean?"

"At some point she's going to send the parents back without their children."

"But why…and what about the children? What does she plan to do with them?

"That's what the refrigeration unit is for. She's wants to eat them."

"When you said 'eat them', what exactly did you mean?" Arnie looked at me as if I was stupid.

"What do you *think* I mean?"

"You mean she actually wants to eat…children?" I still couldn't take it in.

"Domania is going to be a child farm and she's fattening them up. That's what the refrigeration unit is for. The kids are just going to eat rubbish food, sit around on their fat backsides playing video games until Doris Morris comes around and says I'll have that one…with a side salad and a nice Chianti."

"But…" I was still dumbfounded.

"You're a sprite in *this* world, Randle, surely you've heard of wicked witches who eat children."

"Well, yes but it was all outlawed years and years ago. In 941 when The Naming of Witches Act was passed."

"Yeah, well it *never* happened in my world. Witches were only ever heard of in stories you were told as a kid. And in those stories they ate kids…that's why they were wicked."

"I know, but…"

"She's done it before you know…although she was desperate at the time. She told us her story once over a few bottles of wine one night. Rutger and me were almost sick."

"What happened?"

"Back then she was called Dorothy…"

"Dorothy Garland…yes I know."

"…and she first discovered this world by accident. She had been exploring some old mines with her husband when the time gate opened. As you can imagine they were eager to explore the new land they had discovered but when the time gate started to close they tried to scramble back up their ropes and the closing of the gate sheared through Dorothy's and she fell back to the ground. I suppose the people in the other world presumed she was dead. They wouldn't have known that the time gate opens at the same time every day. The thing that cut her up most was that she had left behind a baby son.

The fall from the time gate was a long one and she lay there with a broken leg for a day or two before she was discovered by an evil fat old witch called Peg Thatcher."

"I've heard stories about her", I said. "There was a chant that children used to sing in the schoolyard… 'Peg Thatcher Child Snatcher!'"

"Well Peg lived deep in the woods and she nursed Dorothy back to health only so that she could make her a slave. She spent months in a state of near starvation living off the scraps that Peg left her until one day, after the fat, old witch had caught and killed a passing child, Dorothy was so hungry she gnawed on the cast off bones."

"So that was when she first got the taste for eating children?" I asked.

"She told us that hunger drives people to do extraordinary things and despite her initial remorse, she could never quite lose the taste for the food that had kept her alive. Dorothy stayed with Peg for ten years and during that time, the witch noticed that the young woman hadn't aged a day since she first found her. Peg wasn't getting any younger and her health was failing. She reckoned that the prospect of living forever at her present age far outweighed growing old and dying in this world. So she asked Dorothy if she could find her way back home if the both of them could get up to the time gate cave. Eager to see her husband and son once again, Dorothy was naïve enough to think Peg was doing it out of the goodness of her heart but she readily agreed.

Once the time gate had opened, the pair of them flew on Peg's broomstick into the open time gate. Dorothy began to lead Peg back through the cave system knowing full well that the witch would be far too big to get through a certain opening in one of the caves."

"Smart woman", I said.

Arnie nodded before carrying on with his story. "But when Dorothy returned to her own world she discovered that things would never be the same for her. Her husband was still living in the same house. Dorothy looked through the window and saw that he was now much older. Her son was no longer a baby; he was a handsome young teenage boy. Then she noticed another child asleep in a small crib and when a young woman walked into the room and kissed Dorothy's husband, she realised that there was no going back. The comprehension that her husband had given her up as lost and married again pushed Dorothy over the edge. While walking through the town, she caught her reflection in a mirror and saw that she too had started to age. Feeling that there was nothing left for her in this world she realised that her chances would be better in the world she had just escaped from. Her reasoning lost, she returned to find that a despondent Peg had taken to her bed. The old witch was dying but in return for Dorothy caring for her she would teach her how to be a witch."

"And that's how she became a witch."

"Yeah, but she told us she was much better at public relations that Peg ever was. Bear in mind that all this was over one hundred years ago. Making full use of the expertise from living in 19th century England, she began to make herself indispensable to the local king. She even saved his daughter from death."

"Princess Rosebud? I'm not even sure about that…"

"What do you mean?" said Arnie.

"Think about it, she controls a palace that has its own personal time gate…its own private army making use of weapons that this world cannot compete with. Isn't it possible she meant to do this all along?" I realised I had crossed a line here. Arnie lifted his head and looked hard at me. He picked up his mobile phone and looked at it.

"What are you doing?

I asked.

"You're not like the other sprites, are you, Randle? If you had taken the medication that they receive we would not be having this conversation. I guess, because I needed to talk to someone, I never questioned it." Arnie started to punch in a number on his phone.

"No, I am not like the other sprites, Arnie, and I know that you are not like the other 'sons' of Doris Morris. That is why I have been able to talk to you."

"Rutger wasn't like the others…" The phone was up against his ear now.

"That's why she killed him, Arnie. And if you don't do as she tells you…she'll kill you too. Think of all of those children who are going to die. Not only die but Doris Morris intends to freeze their bodies in the refrigeration unit…and then eat them. Do you want that on your conscience?"

"I don't have a conscience." A voice could be heard on his phone. "Mother, I need to know something…do you love me?" From across the desk I could hear the pause before she answered. "Of course, I'm all right", said Arnie, "but you still haven't answered my question." Another squiggle of sound; a trace of a smile on his face. "And I love you too, Mother."

My insides lurched. I hadn't even noticed that he'd switched off the phone.

Arnie continued. "That evening, after she told us her story, Rutger and me talked about how we could live with such knowledge. We decided that it all happened a long time ago and it was nothing to do with us. Like her, we needed to get on with our life."

"Yes but now she wants to do it all again…with your help!" I was out in the open here with no way to hide. "She is going to eat the children of these people who have come from your world. They may be the children of people you know; people you went to school with."

"I don't care a damn about the people I went to school with! I was picked on from the moment I arrived to the day that I left." My words, ill-chosen, had failed me. It was Arnie himself who saved the day. "If I'm doing it for anyone it's for the kids. Because I know what it is like to be scared and at some stage in Mother's plan those children will be scared. And do you know what, Randle? It's the ones who tell you they love you that you should be most afraid of."

VISITING TIME

If we were going to save the children of Gilsland then we needed some kind of plan. Our little group had arranged to meet in Scarlett's secret chamber and with the number of hostile Grimm brother's down to one and Doris Morris back in ThurMar there was little need for journeys spent crawling under Scarlet's petticoats.

I was pleased to see a change in JC's appearance. She was clearly not one hundred percent fit but I had managed to catch her doing press ups at the side of her sick bed when I made my entrance. Her first concern, however, had not been for herself but for the health of Avis Davies. I assured her that her boss was holding up her own despite the presence of the three soldiers who guarded her.

JC continued to punish herself with stretching exercises as we waited for the others. The room was dimly lit and I found myself heading into the darker corners to pass the time. She was clearly not happy about Arnie Grimm's involvement. Her hostility towards him meant that I had to spend a good deal of time convincing her that he had never really been a bad person as much as a misguided one. A fresh burst of exercise allowed her to think over what I had just told her.

"Our biggest problem is Doris Morris", gasped JC as she came to the end of a count of fifty."

"I wouldn't know where to start. Perhaps if we could rescue Avis Davies…"

"You leave that to me…but even then I couldn't be sure of destroying her. The only certain way we have is by running water."

"You mean that spell…what's it called?"

"The Irrevocable Spell."

"That's it…but how is it irrevocable? Surely if you put it on yourself…you can take it off?"

"Apparently the spell contains a memory wipe. You can only inflict it on yourself and the process makes it impossible for you to ever remember those words again."

"Even if you saw them written down?"

"It's beyond me…but it's something to do with being unable to see the combination of words if ever presented with them." JC had busied herself once more with a series of pull-ups on the top rail of the four-poster bed.

"You want to be careful you don't overdo it", I said as my eye caught a series of paintings at the far end of the room. They showed the Palace of Fotherghyll in happier times and I marvelled at the beautiful formal gardens. I wondered whether they were the work of Hamble Titchmarsh. I confess I hadn't given my friend too much thought over the last few days. The last time I had seen him he had found himself astride a horse for the first time in his life. I wondered where he was now. As I stood in front of another painting of the gardens, a delightful watercolour of the ornamental lake and fountains, I finally realised that Hamble, like Scarlett had slept for a hundred years. Unlike Scarlett, he and the many others that worked at

Fotherghyll Palace had been removed and left to fend for themselves when they woke up in another part of the country

"The problem is", continued JC as she slumped onto the bed, "that there doesn't seem to be any running water in the palace grounds."

"There must be…what about the plumbing?"

"It must come from a subterranean lake or something…but we could only harness it in a hose pipe and I don't think that it would be enough."

"It's a pity Fotherghyll still hasn't got these." I looked into the painting in front of me.

"What?" JC slid off the bed and came to my side.

"There used to be an ornamental lake and a long series of fountains. Look…in this painting!"

"That's it!" said JC heading across the room. The plans I have showed a lake at the back of the palace…the lake bed is still there but for some reason the water has been turned off. Look at those fountains!" JC pointed at them; row after row of powerful jets of water arced across the long rectangular lake. "If only we could get Doris Morris into the middle of that lake bed."

The arrival of Presley broke our chain of concentration. He nodded to me and then rushed across to JC.

"I'm so glad to see that you are well." He attempted to give her a hug but the coming together of a six foot beanpole and a four foot high elf with two wounds in her back wasn't ever going to be easy. She winced and he slumped down into an overstuffed armchair. He pulled his flute out from his pocket and started to play a tune. JC and I both grimaced and were thankful when the close arrival of Scarlett and Arnie put an end to his musical offering.

One good thing about Arnie Grimm's participation was that we now had the inside information we needed. It was through him that we knew that Doris Morris had returned to Thursday Market to invite some like-minded witches to sample the delights of Domania. Arnie had been told that his mother wasn't the only witch who dreamt of power. Doris Morris had let it be known that she was working on ways to remove the Irrevocable Spell and naturally any self-respecting power-crazed witch would be curious to test the water…so to speak.

"Mother's going to be away until tomorrow morning. I expect she'll be back in time for lunch." said Arnie, without any irony, after Scarlett had personally escorted him into her secret chamber.

"It might be a good idea to get the parents and their children out while she is away, said Presley."

"Easier said than done", said Scarlett. "The parents seem past caring."

Arnie nodded. "There's not a lot we can do about that. Hans-Christian is in charge of their medication. From what he says they will still be under its influence for a few days even after they stop taking it. We haven't time to wait for it to wear off."

All the time Arnie was speaking JC stared at him as though she was searching for flaws. From the look in her eyes, she still wasn't about to give him the benefit of the doubt.

"I'm still not clear why you wish to help us", said JC, now sat on the edge of her bed. "What's in it for you?" I was about to say something in Arnie's defence but JC lifted her hand to stop me. "Let him answer for himself."

"Whatever you think I am, I am not inhuman." JC raised her eyebrows; no doubt she thought the word a contradiction in terms. Arnie continued. "I know that if I stay here, I couldn't live with myself knowing what Mother…what Doris Morris plans to do with the children. But rather than stay here, I will go back. I will help the children return to their home. I owe them that much. Doris Morris is fond of saying that there is always a price to pay."

"And just what is this price that you will pay?" JC was still not willing to ease up on him. Arnie looked at Scarlett and me as if to say 'doesn't she know?'

"If I go back to the world I came from I will age by over twenty years. Isn't twenty years of my life enough of a guarantee for you?" JC shrugged her shoulders and winced with the pain.

I thought she was being harsh and I told her so. "If he stays here he will live for ever…just like Doris Morris. Just like Hans-Christian Grimm. Both of them have lived over a hundred years. Arnie is willing to give immortality up rather than let those children suffer. I think that shows just how human he is."

"Is this true?" JC turned to Scarlett.

"We know that Doris Morris was my governess before I fell asleep...and now look at her!" JC didn't need long to ponder on this.

"So she couldn't possibly go through the time-gate herself? She'd just revert to her proper age."

"Crumble up and die", said Arnie.

JC let this information sink in for a while. "Arnie, what are we fighting against here?"

"Well, now that Mother is away for the day, there is just Hans-Christian and the ten soldiers who make up his army."

"And three of them are guarding Avis Davies at all times?"

"Yeah, Mother doesn't trust her with anything less."

"So that means there are seven of them active somewhere else in Domania".

"Er...probably not...Hans-Christian lets them rest most of the time...provided they are ready whenever he needs them.

"So we're not likely to come across them by accident?"

"No. They'll probably be holed up in the palace bedrooms", said Arnie.

JC climbed off the bed and gestured that we all sit around the table. Presley attempted to help her across to the chair but she shrugged off his attentions. Scarlett hurried over with a couple of cushions to help JC ease herself down into the chair. A pained look came over her face as she sat back.

"Right! Things we need to do before Doris Morris returns tomorrow morning. When the time gate opens we need to get all the parents and children down to the railway station. Any ideas?"

"We need to create a diversion." I suggested. "I was wondering about the place where the electricity is stored. If we can blow that up then Hans-Christian and his men will be as far away from the railway station as possible."

"That's a good idea. I'll need to train somebody up to do that job…we need Scarlett and Humphrey to round the parents and children up and then they've got a bigger fish to fry…"

Scarlett looked across at me. "I'll tell you later", I said with a wink.

"Hang on" said Presley …who's Humphrey?"

"Yeah, I was just thinking that!" said Arnie.

I raised my hand. "Sorry you guys, but I've been working here under an assumed name…my real name isn't Randle…it's Humphrey…Humphrey Boggart."

JC muttered under her breath, "That's not what I heard."

"Oh, I've heard of you," said Arnie, "Isn't mother trying to kill you?"

"Yeah…" I replied.

"She's got Deadman after you, hasn't she?"

"It's pronounced Deedman!"

"Oh…you've met him. Cool. Yeah…he really does hate it being mispronounced, doesn't he? I'm always winding him up about it. Well if you've met him and you're still with us…you must be good, Humphrey Boggart!"

"I've met him a few times, Arnie." The youngest Grimm brother whistled in appreciation. "Now can we get on?"

"…Arnie", continued JC, "I've got other plans for you…so that leaves Presley. Do you think you could manage that?" She smiled at the tall young man and he nodded his head. "Arnie, it is up to you to destroy the railway tunnel so that no-one else can ever use it again."

"And just how am I going to do that?"

"Have you ever heard of dynamite?" said JC. Arnie's face turned white.

"B-but I've never used it before!"

"That's not a problem. Stay after class with Presley and I'll show the both of you."

"What about Avis Davies?" I asked.

"Leave her to me.", said JC.

THE END OF THE ELECTRICITY

It all happened so fast. The next morning I had already met up with Scarlett when I got a call from an excitable Arnie.

"The parents are leaving today. Hans-Christian has got the soldiers rounding them up at this very moment."

"But what is he going to do with them?"

"There's a special train been chartered. It's a through train to London."

"I don't know this place."

"It's a great city over a hundred miles away. When they get off the train they will not know who they are, where they are or why they are there." I realised that if all the parents were in the same state as Mike and Tracey Coope then it wouldn't be difficult to pull this off.

"Why are they sending them to this… London?"

"To buy time, Ran- sorry, Humphrey. It will take a day or two before anyone in their world will know what is going on. By then the time gate will be closed for good."

"And the kids wlll be trapped in this world… we need to reunite them with their parents at the station. Hans-Christian and his men will not be able to do anything to stop them surely."

"I wouldn't be too sure. The man is ruthless… his soldiers are paid a lot of money not to have a conscience. Most of the children are at the Games Centre. Those that aren't are being escorted there by sprites. I've got to go down to the station to organise things at that end. If I don't, Hans-Christian will know something is up."

"We can make this work for us, Arnie. Hans-Christian has done the hard part for us. All we need to do now is to get the children there. When Presley blows up the electricity, the soldiers will be sent up to investigate. If the parents are presented with their crying children…surely something will register with them. We're going to have to wing it but it might just work."

*

Scarlett and I breezed past the soldiers who were guarding Avis Davies on our way to the Games Centre. The Massy Witch, weakened by hunger, was still asleep beneath her protective shield. We hoped she would not have long to wait. Despite the ominous task that awaited us later, Scarlett and I were feeling optimistic about our first challenge. All we had to do was tell the kids in the Games Centre that their parents were leaving them behind in Domania. Then we'd just have to stand back and watch them rush down to the railway station.

Our announcement fell on deaf ears. One or two of the children looked up to see what the commotion was. I approached Tommy Coope, who was reluctant to talk at all.

"Can't you see I'm busy!" he snapped. "It's the new release of *Xyglon Battleground*." He gestured to the screen with his open hand.

"But your Mum and Dad are leaving Domania!"

"So? They know where I am, don't they? We only live a couple of miles away. It's not as if they can't come and get me whenever they want!" I don't know whether I was more staggered with Tommy's reaction than I was with the fact that he had actually spoken so many words in one go. Scarlett reported back that she was having no luck in moving the children.

"One kid told me that it was much better here as he didn't have to eat pukey vegetables all the time. Another told me he hated school and would be quite happy to stay here for the rest of his life. I just can't believe it. Perhaps we should tell them about Doris Morris' plans for them?"

"I don't know...we don't want to scare them but we have to get them out of here somehow." I stood up on one of the tables and started clapping my hands. Scarlett, in full ball gown, climbed up beside me. "Now listen, everyone!" I said. "The reason your parents are leaving Domania is that they have been drugged over the past few days. They don't realise that they are leaving you behind. Think about it. If your mums and dads were in full control of their senses, do you really think they would be getting on that train?"

Scarlett, seeing that my announcement was having little effect, decided I needed the more direct approach. "The reason your parents have been drugged and sent home is that there is a wicked witch who wants to EAT YOU ALL!" It

366

seemed to work as most of the children stopped what they were doing.

"We know that!" shouted a tall blonde girl from the back. "She's outside with the soldiers watching her. As soon as she lets her guard down they're going to shoot her."

"Yeah…we don't want to miss that!" shouted a small spiky-haired boy who was standing near the window with a half-eaten burger in his hand. Yells of agreement from the other children indicated which way the wind was blowing for us.

Scarlett wasn't going to give up though. "The witch outside is a good witch who came here to rescue you. The bad witch is the one who owns this place."

"But you came round with that witch to welcome our parents to Domania. Why would you do that if she was as bad as you say she is?" said an annoyingly eloquent young boy who stood before us.

"But I didn't know that then!" Scarlett's answer seemed lame and was greeted by jeers from the children.

I looked at the clock on the wall. "We're running out of time, Scarlett. The time gate will be closing for good soon." The children were all back playing on the games machines as if nothing had happened. Scarlett and I could only look on in misery. Up till now the pair of us had seemingly drawn the easy straw at the meeting yesterday. JC had to rescue Avis Davies; Arnie had to blow up the rail tunnel and Presley…

The explosion was loud enough for everyone to hear. The plunge from light to semi-darkness brought a hushed reaction from the children. Now without games to occupy them they turned to us for an explanation.

"How long will the screens be down for?" asked one child.

"Is someone coming to fix it?" asked another.

"What are we going to do now?" was the general consensus of the rest.

It should have been an opportunity for us to pull the situation round. Blessed by the closure of the all-engaging machines, we assumed we had the children's full attention at last. Once again we exhorted them to go down to the railway station and at least 'say goodbye to their parents'. The children of Kelsey and Tommy Coope's world have little fear. When something goes wrong…they are sure that someone will come along to fix it. Within seconds the rumour that someone *was* coming to mend the machines was so loud we overheard it and almost believed it ourselves. Both of us stood transfixed as we wondered what to do next. The children were not coming to the railway station. Then a man came who said he could fix it…for us.

PLAN B

"You should always have a 'Plan B'", said Presley. He was dripping with sweat having run all the way from the electricity store. "I was going to mention it before but you seemed to know what you were doing. I told JC yesterday, after everyone else had gone. It was her idea that I get myself down here as soon as I'd lit the fuse…just in case.

"But what are you going to do?" I said, desperate to hope that somebody might do something. Presley put his flute to his lips and began to play a simple tune.

Scarlett, not used to being tainted by the whiff of failure, was more scathing. "What is it going to be, Presley? You're going to Morris dance them up to the station?"

"Something like that…that'd be quite appropriate, don't you think?" said Presley taking his flute from his mouth. "Watch this!" Once more he started playing and as one the children turned to look at him. The tune continued and Presley began walking out of the doors and left towards the station. We watched open-mouthed as children rose from armchairs, pushed aside their food and abandoned their blank screens to follow him. Scarlett and I held open the large glass doors as the children, entranced by the tune, skipped out of the Games Centre and along the road behind him. A big stupid smile filled my face as I looked across at Scarlett. She shrugged her shoulders. We hurried after the merry band as they made their way alongside the railway track. For the first time since he had arrived in Domania, Tommy Coope was grinning like a gargoyle. He was holding his sister's hand as they skipped along in time to Presley's music.

*

At first we thought it fortunate that there was no sign of Hans-Christian and his soldiers when we arrived at the railway station. A worried-looking Arnie was waiting for us.

"It's too late, Humphrey. The parents have gone...the train left just after the explosion. Hans-Christian made sure it was on its way before he dispatched his soldiers up to the substation." As Presley ceased playing the crowd of thirty to forty children stopped and looked somewhat bewildered.

"Not to worry" said Presley, "we just carry on." I looked at Arnie.

"The time gate is still open...there's no reason we couldn't walk along the tunnel anyway", he said. I looked at him and at Presley. "This will be the last time I ever see the both of you." I shook Presley by the hand. "It's a different world through there...you sure you know what you're doing?"

The musician grinned at me. "I just hope that this world is ready for a musician like me?"

"Maybe so but a word of advice...I'd change the name...it doesn't sound very...showbiz!" He flashed me a smile and the flute was back at his lips. The children, entranced once more, could do nothing but dance after him.

I turned to Arnie. "You OK with this?" He opened his jacket and showed me the sticks of dynamite.

"JC has shown me what to do. She's been in the tunnel and has estimated how long the fuses need to be. So, yes I'm

OK with that. In a few hours time I'll be a middle-aged man. I'm not so sure about that part of it." The two of us hugged each other and I whispered in his ear.

"I've got a confession to make." Arnie's sweat-beaded brow furrowed. "You remember the day you stole Avis Davies' broom…when you fell in the river?" A look of bemusement crossed his face. "Well I'm the reason you fell in the river. I caught you by the ankle…I was the boggart of the beck!" The bemusement gone, a big grin took its place.

"I never did understand how those two country bumpkins managed to get the best of me." He made a face of false anger. "I owe you one, Humphrey Boggart!" But the big grin soon returned. It was the look that I first saw on that fateful day by the beck; the look that made me change my mind and my life. He clapped me on the shoulder and turned after the dancing children.

*

We had left the station well behind us before we heard the first sounds of gunfire. In the distance we could see Hans-Christian Grimm send his men down into the tunnel. In less than a minute, the first of a series of explosions could be heard, each one less impressive than the one before it. The cloud of dust and smoke that spewed out from the tunnel took a long time to clear…and we didn't have the luxury of time on our side. The two of us took a short cut through the pristine remains of the children's rides and the now-deserted apartments. We needed to get to the palace. Scarlett and I had a trap to set and I was destined to be the bait.

"ninety-nine…one hundred!" JC dropped off the rail of the four poster bed and landed with her feet splayed on the floor. "Coming ready or not!" It was now or never. The pre-operation exercises were done more in the way of convincing JC that she was fit enough to pull this off. She was not used to worrying about herself and it played on her mind. The missing ability of flight was another nagging concern.

It had been half an hour ago exactly when JC heard the explosion from the electricity substation through the labyrinthine walls of the palace. If all had gone to plan, Presley would have hared down to the Games Centre and helped Scarlett and Humphrey to move the children. She had a feeling his particular skill would have come in useful. Never having been a parent herself, through choice, she regarded children with the same cynicism that she employed on adult members of society. Basically she didn't trust them.

By now Presley and the children should have gone through the time gate. She felt a little sad that she would never see him again…perhaps in a different life…another world? No…she was being weak. Be professional, she told herself.

Scarlett had instructed JC in the intricacies of the secret door and she checked through the mirrored spy-hole to see that the corridor was empty. Assuming once again the mantle of invisibility she pulled the archaic lever. The door had closed behind her and she ventured down the corridor. Before long she was outside for what seemed like the first time in ages. She bent down and pocketed a handful of stones before filling her lungs with fresh air and jogging off across the gravelled driveway.

Scarlett had told her that Avis Davies was still trapped within her own self-created prison where she was protected from all her enemies, except starvation. JC slowed to a stop just short of the Sprites Hall of Residence and peeked around the corner of the building. Sure enough, the bizarre sight of the Massy Witch, seated on the floor in the company of three soldiers, was a difficult one to take. Everything about the person JC so admired looked vulnerable, so powerless, that it made her question her own ability to succeed.

Before she had decided what to do, the tableau in front of her was animated by the arrival of Hans-Christian Grimm in one of the self-powered carts that JC had still not become used to. Grimm was clearly agitated as he screamed at one of the three soldiers to accompany him.

"The chopper, Jameson! I need you now!"

"Yes, sir!", barked the soldier as he stamped to attention.

"Sir?" said another soldier. "Is anything the matter?"

"The electricity has gone, your colleagues are gone, the tunnel has gone and the children are gone…but apart from that everything's bloody fine!" roared Hans-Christian Grimm. Jameson! Are you getting on this buggy or what?" The three soldiers exchanged looks before Jameson did as he was told and hopped onto the buggy. JC took the opportunity of moving one building nearer in the apparent confusion and was shocked by what she saw. Avis Davies, despite everything that had happened around her in the last minute or two, was still asleep.

JC's was finding it difficult for the first time in her life. Doubts were creeping in to her head. She had hoped for some co-operation from her mentor but now she knew she was all alone. She was disabled, feeling fragile…she looked at the two remaining soldiers…they were proper soldiers.

Her mind was flung back into focus by the arrival of Doris Morris and her guests from out of the tunnel building. JC shrunk behind the corner as the party walked up the road to witness the demise of the great Avis Davies. She could hear their jocular remarks and the accompanying laughter. For the first time in a long time she felt like crying. The merriment was soon halted when Doris Morris noticed something.

"Why are there only two soldiers guarding the prisoner?"

"Ma'am, one of the guards has been requisitioned by General Grimm!"

Doris Morris laughed. "Is that what he's calling himself now? My expressed orders have been contravened. Why is that?"

"Ma'am, General Grimm said 'the electricity has gone, our colleagues are gone, the tunnel has gone and the children are gone'"

"What?" The roar of anger that emanated from Doris Morris seemed to make the area reverberate. Daring to peek around the corner, she saw Doris Morris and the other witches heading off towards the palace.

The two soldiers flashed a look at each other before returning to their duties. JC was under no allusions about their abilities, these guards were not the stiff, bored, ceremonial types that were a pushover to disarm. These were mercenaries and the big money people paid them for their services meant that they were the best. They stood easy, eyes alive with expectation, their sophisticated machine guns primed for action. Humphrey had warned her of the gun's killing potential. She was yet to see them in action and couldn't even begin to imagine their power.

As she walked down the road towards where Avis Davies and her two guards were waiting, she realised she didn't have a plan. This was so unprofessional of her and the sight of Avis Davies slumped in defeat was not helping matters. Treading carefully so as not to make a sound, JC knew that the ability to fly was probably more valuable to her in this situation than was her invisibility...as a Seer, JC spent large amounts of her time in a state of invisibility but she never failed to recognise that, like the glamour, it only worked through the beholder's lack of attention and the wearer's complete confidence. It had been days since she had last been invisible and much to her discomfort she began to question her ability to hold the state. She was within fifty metres of Avis Davies when the soldier saw her.

*

The burst of machine gun fire cut through the air where JC had been standing only a moment ago. The elf had rolled to safety and now found herself struggling to catch her breath behind one of the smaller buildings. She cursed her weakness, as the pain from the wounds on her back ate at her strength. Around the corner she could hear that one of the soldiers was running up the road towards her. JC hared down the alleyway between two buildings and was almost knocked off her feet when a goblin pushing a small trolley came out of a side door. She brushed past him and was behind the open door when the soldier rounded the corner. The goblin was hoisted off his feet by the cascade of bullets and dead before his body hit the ground. JC didn't have time to gasp in wonder.

Around the next corner, she shinned up a drain pipe and was on the roof of the building before the soldier came into sight. With the adrenalin beginning to kick in, JC had forgotten the pain of her wounded wing stumps. This was what she was created for. Alive and alert now, the confidence surged back into her body. Free from the uncertainty, she once more reverted back to her invisible state and continued over the roof. There beneath her, the lone remaining soldier guarded the Massy Witch.

She cast a stone to the other side of the road and might have been shocked by the explosion of bullets that came from the gun if she had not already been travelling through the air. JC wrapped herself around his head before one flash of her knife dispatched him from both the worlds he had lived in. She hated herself for doing it but like any soldier she killed from necessity. It was kill or be killed. The world would be a better place without this man.

His colleague burst out from the back of the building and was shocked by what he saw…nothing, apart from the slumbering Avis Davies and the body of his dead colleague. Stood with her back against a nearby wall, JC enjoyed the discomfort of his uncertainty. So high was she on herself that she wouldn't even consider that the roles had now reversed. It was now the soldier who doubted his own ability and JC who moved with the speed and certainty of a consummate professional. Not for her the sentimentality of a disarming knock on the head. An enemy needed to be removed from the picture a.s.a.p. End of.

She stepped over the prostrate corpse and tapped on Avis Davies' protective shield with the hilt of her knife. An age passed before the Massy Witch opened her eyes. Without even looking round, the shield was down. Avis Davies held out her arms to JC.

"You're far too big for me to carry, Ma'am…but I think I know where there's a trolley."

THE RETURN OF THE LAKE

"You sure this is it?" I asked as Scarlett revealed the stop-cock that controlled the water supply to the ornamental lake and fountains.

"We can test it if you want to be sure."

"No, we don't want to give the game away. If Doris Morris sees even a small puddle she might just work out what we're up to." I glanced up at the balcony that overlooked the lake's dry bed and gulped. "I suppose there's no other way to do this?"

Scarlett shook her head. "At least we've got these. We could do some damage with these." The two machine guns lay on the floor at our feet. We had come across the dead bodies of the soldiers...at least we could assume that JC had succeeded in rescuing Avis Davies.

"We don't even know how to fire them...we could blow ourselves up.", I said.

"Still, it's a good way of getting her down here." She was right. Me standing in the middle of a dry lake bed would look a little suspicious, but me trying to work out how to use a gun quite near to a lakebed might just work.

"OK, you stay here by the stop-cock and I'll try and attract a bit of attention."

"It'll not be the first time." Scarlett gave me a peck on the cheek. Before the blush could arrive I was heading towards the lakebed.

"Let's hope it's not the last", I muttered under my breath. When I reached the side of the lake, I pointed the gun out in front of me. I was too frightened to exert the slightest pressure on the trigger. I tried again and this time a terrific sound filled my ears as I struggled to hold onto the spitting gun. Up on the palace balcony, a glass door opened. Doris Morris, dressed in the black garb of a witch appeared and gazed down at me. She was soon joined by a whole coven of her companions.

"Here goes nothing!" I aimed the gun at the balcony and pulled the trigger. The resulting destruction of the windows surprised me more than it did the witches who dropped to the floor. Buoyed by my success, I scurried into the middle of the dry lakebed and offered Doris Morris out.

"It ends here, Doris Morris!" I couldn't believe I was saying this as my legs struggled to hold up my trembling body. The gun was a comfort as I saw the black-hooded face of Doris Morris rise above the parapet.

"Who are you who dares to challenge me?" her voice carried to some effect.

"I go by the name of Humphrey Boggart." A second or two passed as she made the connection.

"You have constantly been a thorn in the side of my family!"

"I'm a private detective. I right wrongs…it's what I do."

"Not for much longer, boggart!" screamed the witch as she flew off the balcony and landed thirty yards in front of me on the edge of the lakebed. I fired the gun but she had protected herself in the same way that Avis Davies had done and the bullets ricocheted off her shield. Turning, she beckoned down the other witches and one by one they landed at her side. I released the trigger once again but her shield was strong enough to protect them all. Glancing across at where Scarlett was poised to release the water, I backed further into the centre of the lake. Safe behind their shield, Doris Morris and the other witches began to walk towards me. I was scared now but fearful of drawing attention to Scarlett, I fought the urge to look over to where I hoped she was releasing the water.

Doris Morris must have dropped the shield for a second as a flash of light knocked the gun out of my hands and sent it skittering across the cement floor. I hurried over to it and picked it up barely avoiding a further blast from the witch…still no water. Another blast and I was on my backside. I scrambled to my feet and pulled the trigger. Nothing happened. I tried again and the hideous laughter of Doris Morris filled the air.

"It doesn't work anymore, boggart. Now what are you going to do?" As she began to come for me, I saw she was now level with the line of spouts which made up part of the ornamental fountain. Close behind her the gang of witches were readying themselves for the coming sport. As I back-pedalled away from them, I thought about turning and running but I needed to keep them between the water-spouts. I looked across at to where Scarlett was spreading her arms in frustration.

"Run, Humphrey! I can't get the water to turn on!" she screamed before letting loose a volley of machine gun fire which took out at least three of the witches.

Doris Morris spun around; for the first time she was aware of what we were trying to do. She let out a hideous laugh of triumph and came towards me.

"The wheel won't turn!" shouted Scarlett. I looked at Scarlett for probably the last time in my life when I noticed a familiar figure closing in on her. A large old man, eased Scarlett out of the way and began fiddling with the stop-cock.

Driven by her rage, Doris Morris was almost on top of me when a great gush of water knocked her clean off her feet. I tried to get away but avoiding the powerful jets of water was impossible and before I knew it I was floundering on my hands and knees in the swirling water. Close by I could see that Doris Morris's heavy cloak was making it difficult for her to stand up. A long thin hand stretched out from beneath her sodden cloak and pointed at me. Above the rush of the water I could hear her curse.

"When I get out of here, boggart…you are dead!"

With the hundreds of lead spouts all spewing water high into the air, the lake began to foam and swirl. Soon we were up to our waists and that was enough for me to swim. I was born underwater and even though I was no longer as comfortable in it as when I was a river sprite, I let myself go with the flow. Doris Morris fought the water with her every sinew, thrashing in her rage until she lost her footing and was gone. The other witches seemed less able to fight against the power of the water and were soon dragged under its swirling current. I swam beneath the surface, careful to avoid the desperate claws of the drowning witches.

It must have been an hour later before Scarlett and Hamble pulled me dripping from the lake. I shook my old friend's hand and he presented me with a package.

"It's your coat and hat, Humphrey! Don't think I'll be holding any coaches up again. That feller damn nearly scared me to death when he pulled his head off his shoulders." I unravelled the package and popped the hat on my head.

"That's better! I feel like a detective again." I turned to Scarlett. "What happened with the stop-cock?"

"You've got Hamble to thank for that."

"It wouldn't have worked without the head-gardener's key!" said Hamble. He pulled out the old key that had accompanied him throughout his 'second life'. "The times I thought of throwing this away but I knew that one day I would discover what it was used for. And now I do thanks to you, Humphrey Boggart."

"It's a good job you arrived or else…" It didn't bear thinking about. "How did you get here, Hamble?

"I wanted to come through with Avis Davies, but she didn't want the responsibility of looking after civilians. She said the mission was very dangerous and her men were trained", said Hamble.

"It's a good job you didn't come with her, not one of her men survived."

"And I wouldn't have been there to release the wheel with the key!" laughed Hamble.

Scarlett looked across the churning lake. "Do you think she's dead?" she asked.

"She will have succumbed to the Irrevocable Spell", I said. "All witches had to sign up to it. She was the first witch to accept the spell. JC had seen her name in the register."

The three of us walked around the edge of the lake in the hope that we might find the remains of the sodden witch. Deep down I guessed that we would have been happier if we never saw the woman again. The lake was huge and she could have ended up on the other side. Someone would find her. What we needed to do now was to make sure that Arnie had destroyed the tunnel. The three of us had to get to the railway station before the time gate closed for the day.

As we headed over the manicured fields with their small numbered flags fluttering, I asked Scarlett what she would be doing with Domania now that Doris Morris was gone.

"I was wondering if you still needed a gardener. I might be over a hundred and fifty but I can still wheel a barrow", laughed Hamble.

"Do you know, I haven't really given it any thought...I've lived here all my life..."

"And some!" I said.

"...but if I'm honest, I've really enjoyed these last few weeks. It's been the most exciting thing I've ever done...apart from those hobbits!"

"Yeah...yeah...I get the message."

Scarlett continued. "I don't think I want to be a princess anymore. It's much more fun being a private detective."

"You mean a private detective's *secretary*..."

"I do believe I resigned from that job."

"You were sacked, as I remember."

Hamble decided to break up our squabbling. "So you won't be needing a gardener then?"

"Well someone will have to look after the palace grounds!" I put in. "You've got a responsibility, Scarlett."

"You're just saying that so I don't go into competition with you in ThurMar."

"Oh, it's competition, is it now?"

"Look, you two", said Hamble, "surely it would be better for you to work together...as a team...if that is at all possible."

"Hmm...Boggart and Alewife does have a ring to it."

"Alewife and Boggart sounds better *and* it's alphabetical!"

"Alewife isn't even your real name!" Hamble shook his head as the two of us bickered all the way to the railway station.

*

The time gate was still fully open when the three of us reached the platform. Dust and smoke still filled the air as Hamble scratched his bald head, trying to make sense of what he was seeing.

"This is what all the fuss is about, is it?"

"It's the entrance to another world", I said.

"If it is anything like the things I have seen in the short time I have been here then it will be a sight worth seeing", said Hamble. The three of us grabbed a lantern each from a nearby shelf and proceeded to light them.

"If Arnie has done his job properly then we shall not be able to see it." Scarlett led the way as we stepped inside the large cave.

"JC said if we follow the railway lines we should reach the tunnel that leads to the outside." We hadn't gone far along the dark tunnel when we reached the point where it was blocked. A huge pile of broken rock climbed up to the tunnel roof. The twisted railway lines, sprained by the weight of the fallen rock, were a testament to the fact that no trains would ever come this way again.

"Job done!" I said. Scarlett and Hamble nodded in agreement. "We best get back to Fotherghyll Palace and begin the clear up." Heading back the short distance to the time gate, we took comfort from the blue sky and green fields we could see in the distance. The sound of the time gate starting to close gave us only a momentary cause for concern as we knew we had time enough to pass through it. It was the figure that suddenly appeared there in silhouette that set our hearts pounding.

Steam rose off the damp clothes of Doris Morris as she stood in the bright sunlight beyond the darkness of the tunnel. Her hideous laughter echoed around the dark cavern. To one side of her the time gate hissed, ever nearer to closure for the day.

"Hurry up, you lot! I'm waiting!" shouted Doris Morris. The three of us stood our ground with no intention of going any nearer.

"Don't worry; I'm not going to kill you now. It would be far too quick and painless.

"How did you survive the Irrevocable Spell?" I asked.

Doris Morris laughed. "I invented the Irrevocable Spell…you don't think I'd be stupid enough to subscribe to it, do you? When I saw which way the world was going, I needed to have one ace up my sleeve. I instigated the idea and set an example by being the first to undertake it. Finding a witch stupid enough to think I had self-administered the spell wasn't difficult. After that I was proactive in getting all the other witches to sign up to it which did me no harm in my so-called superiors' eyes. But why I am bothering to explain myself to you, I don't know. Now are you coming back before the time gate closes?"

"Why should we?" I asked.

"For the old man, I promise a painless death. I don't even know who he is. For you and the princess, I make no promises. Because of you almost all my sons are dead and my grand scheme to harvest children is in ruins."

"You killed Rutger, yourself!" said Scarlett.

"And Arnie escaped through the tunnel.

"Then he is more of a fool than I thought he was!" Dismayed by the lack of progress, Doris Morris continued. "The time gate is almost closed. If you miss your opportunity today, don't worry. I'll be here at the same time every day until you have no choice but to return. Remember, thanks to your meddling, you have nowhere else to go and I can wait. As you know…I can wait forever!"

Avis Davies would live. She was severely dehydrated but JC had managed to get a little water down her throat. When the Massy Witch was finally asleep in Scarlett's secret chamber, JC decided it was safe to leave her.

She needed to get down to the time gate to check that it had been closed for good. As she came round the side of the palace, she was surprised when she saw the huge lake resplendent with its gushing fountains in front of her. A smile left its mark on her face. Could it have worked? She had devised the plan with Humphrey and Scarlett but a small part of her doubted that it would ever have succeeded and for that she felt somewhat ashamed. The events of the last few weeks had proven to her that sometimes you have to rely on the abilities of others. If it had been just down to her she would have failed in her task. She had to hand it to Humphrey, Scarlett and Presley…even Arnold Grimm; they had proved to be quite a team.

The appearance of the lake now meant that JC would have to get to the station via the gardens and the golf course. Domania seemed strangely quiet now. Embracing the solitude, she set off running. Despite the punishment her body had taken recently she was feeling quite good and she covered the ground in easy strides. Stopping every now and again to examine the washed-up corpses of witches, some familiar, some not, JC was heading over the golf course and down towards the station.

On hearing the strange drone behind her, JC looked round. Rising from behind the palace of Fotherghyll was a black helicopter. Leaning out of it with a machine gun was Hans-Christian Grimm. The spray of bullets cut up the turf to one side of her. JC assumed her invisible state and veered off at a right angle to her present course. Hans-Christian roared with anger as she disappeared from view. He let off a random volley of bullets, one of which caught JC in the shoulder. She crashed to the floor in agony.

Up in the air, Hans-Christian cursed the elf's ability to become invisible.

"Why don't you use the heat-sensitive equipment?" said Jameson.

"What?" said Hans-Christian.

"The heat-sensitive equipment…it finds people by the difference of their body temperature to their surroundings. Here…" Jameson handed Hans-Christian the heat-sensitive goggles. The helicopter circled the area where JC was recovering and Hans-Christian was amazed to see the elf appear as a rainbow-coloured shape sitting near the flag on the eighth green. He unleashed another spray of bullets which missed the recumbent elf by inches.

JC sprang to her feet and began running across the green. 'How did he know where I was?' was the question that banged around her head.

Above her, Hans-Christian watched as the multi-coloured vision ran ahead of him. The helicopter hovered above JC, poised for the kill. Hans-Christian took off the heat-sensitivity goggles and looked at his pilot. Jameson sensed that he was being stared at and turned his head. He recognised the fury on the face of his commanding officer.

"Sir?"

"If you knew that we could spot an invisible elf with this heat-sensitive equipment, why did you not suggest it to me before?"

"Never thought, sir. Out of sight, out of mind, I suppose...sir."

"Take us higher, Jameson." Below them they watched as JC headed towards the station. The helicopter soared up into the sky. Hans-Christian tapped Jameson on the shoulder.

"Sir?"

"You see all that below you, Jameson? Domania."

"Yes, sir!"

"It's ruined...all because you 'never thought'." Hans-Christian turned in his seat and pushed Jameson out of the helicopter with his foot. The man's screams died in the air. "Out of sight, out of mind, Jameson!" Hans-Christian took control of the helicopter and it swooped back down towards the golf course.

Below him, JC's running was laboured now. The day's events were beginning to take their toll. When her feet hit the hard concrete of the platform, she could see the time gate was almost closed now. Hopeful to at least see what had been achieved in her absence, she ran on. The sight of a black figure, standing before the dark depths of the cave had almost escaped her notice, but the maniacal laughter was unmistakable. Without wings for the first time in her life, JC flew through the air and hit her target hard in the centre of her back.

THE HOMECOMING

When Doris Morris was interrupted mid-laughter and knocked through the time gate just before it closed for the day, a knowing look of horror came over her. The whys and wherefores of how she came to be here were unimportant as she picked herself up and began to claw at the spot where the time gate had been only seconds before.

"Noooo-oooo!" she cried as a quick fire blast of magical charges failed to do anything but fill the cave with more dust. Then it came. With a furious look on her face, Doris Morris rounded on the lot of us. Her stare alighted on me.

"You!" she spat. "I warned you not to meddle…" The stare moved to Scarlett. "And you, I expected better from. After all I did for you. You will all die painfully!"

It was Scarlett who spoke. "And so will you…very soon…I expect." The witch put her hands up to her face. Already she was beginning to change. "After all, in this world you are probably almost 170 years old." Doris Morris raised her hand in a last act of defiance and clicked her finger. It fell to the floor. From one side a cough broke the silence and we all turned to see an old man standing in the doorway of a nearby shed.

"Who are you?" I asked.

"My name is Walter Coope. I have returned because I wanted to make sure that the children of Gilsland would never be threatened again. From what I have just heard, I know I can return back to my own world. However, if you wouldn't mind I would like to introduce myself to Dorothy Garland before she...leaves us." Now in a state of decrepitude, Doris Morris was finding it a struggle to stay on her feet.

"Who are you?" she asked in her cracked voice. All fight had left her now.

"I was once proud to be your great-great grandson" said Walter. "A descendant of your first born son, Gilbert Garland." Walter held a photograph up to the witch's face; her eyes betrayed a sadness within a face which now resembled a desiccated fig. "I have always believed the story that George, your husband, told about another world...so much so that I begged my son not to take his children into Domania" If there was a desire to weep, the lack of moisture within Doris Morris' crumbling body denied it. "I wish you to know that my own grandchildren, your descendants would have probably been victims of your evil had not these kind people..." Walter turned to us, "...laid their own lives on the line for them." Behind him Doris Morris' legs broke and she fell to the floor. Her body slowly imploded in a cloud of dust.

Walter walked towards us with an outstretched hand and introduced himself formerly. "Is JC all right?" Scarlett and I looked at each other.

"She's fine...I think", said Scarlett.

"But surely you are trapped in our world now", I said. "Now that the tunnel is destroyed..."

Walter tapped his nose. "There is still a way back to my world, but rest assured..." He held up a stick of dynamite. "I will make sure that even that avenue will be closed forever."

THE ASSASSIN REMEMBERS

And so it ends, thought Alaric Deadman as he witnessed the demise of his mistress. The time gate had closed up and from what she had told him, she would be dead in a matter of minutes. He thought about the unfinished business. If he killed the boggart, she wasn't going to pay him. In his hardest of hard hearts, two flints clashed against each other, for a second it was warm. There were other scores to settle.

The elf, Seer Bigg was not in a good way. He could see from here that she was carrying a bullet wound in her shoulder. She would probably die without help. Of course that was no concern of his. He bore her no grudge but equally so, he didn't care too much whether she lived or died. It was the helicopter that interested him. He watched as it landed in a field of buttercups where seconds before a huge cave had yawned its way into another world. Hans-Christian Grimm stepped out of the flying machine and strapped on the heat-sensitive goggles. Alaric slowly turned his head to where Seer Bigg had been. The elf had staggered off and would now be invisible to most but Hans-Christian Grimm could see exactly where she was going. Alaric pondered the irony. Had Hans-Christian Grimm not removed Alaric's head from his ironising body all those years ago, he too would be unable to see the elf moving away from the station. Thanks to the first 'son' of Dorothy Garland, Alaric's head remained pure sprite. It could live forever…but his body, alas, that was the body of an ironised sprite…this time. And when this one dies…what then? An amusing idea entered Alaric's mind…

He watched as Hans-Christian closed the gap between him and Seer Bigg. The elf was struggling now as she tried to make her way towards the old mine. Weary of the chase, Hans-Christian put a bullet into the elf's thigh and she fell to the floor. Alaric watched as JC, panting with exhaustion, rolled onto her back and waited for her fate to be sealed.

Above her, Hans-Christian peered through heat sensitive vision. "It might be better if you became visible again", he said, "If you want an easy death." As JC reappeared once more, Hans-Christian threw off his goggles.

"You might be finishing me off, Grimm…but all this…" JC spread her arms. …Domania…is finished and you're finished…"

Hans-Christian pointed the gun at JC when a noise behind him made him turn. "You? What do you want?" For the first time in a long while a look of fear found a place on the head of Hans-Christian Grimm. It remained there as the bullet lodged in his forehead. Alaric Deadman wasn't too concerned…he didn't need the head.

AFTERWARDS

"Not much of a castle, is it?" said Scarlett retaining the princess on at least one level. "I do think that banners are a little old hat these days... although they can be used to cover up a multitude of sins."

"I'm not sure I've ever seen so much pink in an armorial bearing", I said. I hadn't wanted to point out that, as someone who has been asleep the last hundred years, Scarlett was hardly the voice of fashion authority.

On dismounting from the ox-cart we were welcomed by some minion of Mrs King's who proceeded to walk us through the castle, pointing out some of the innovative features, the new queen had presided over.

Scarlett and I had found ourselves making the short journey to the Royal Kingdom of... the name escapes me already... which turned out to be much as I expected - a castle... a village and an attitude problem. I had been invited by the lady known to me as Mrs King to conclude the business regarding the claim on her 'baby', Barry the bull terrier, by an un-named boggart. Yeah, I know, I'd almost forgotten about it too what with everything happening.

The pair of us had made use of Mrs King's royal ox-cart and the progress had been slow. Scarlett wanted to be introduced to her as the new partner in the Boggart & Alewife Detective Agency. That was the name we had settled on despite Scarlett's initial reservations about the protocol. She had originally argued that if her name took preference we would then be the first name to appear in the Jelly's Directory under detective agencies. When I pointed out to her that we were the *only* detective agency in ThurMar, she then accused me of lacking vision. Even when she conceded that, as the senior partner and the person who came up with the idea in the first place, I deserved to be the first name on the door, she still couldn't resist tinkering. The journey to Mrs King's castle had brought about another example of Scarlett's so-called progressive thinking.

"Initials!" she crowed as the royal ox-cart trundled within sight of the castle. "How about the BAD Agency?"

"What?"

"Well initials are the coming thing, so I've heard. They're talking about calling The All-Seeing Eye... the ASE! What do you think, Humphrey? We could be the BAD Agency. An even better idea..." I looked out of the window at a herdsman who was trying to pull his cow through an open gateway.

"Annoying cow?" I shouted over to him. He nodded through gritted teeth. I left it at that as Scarlett continued.

"...would be to take away the Agency bit, I think it sounds a bit stuffy...how about we go with something like 'Associates'? That would give the name a more friendly feel. BAD Associates! What do you think?"

"I can see problems."

*

"This is so vulgar", hissed Scarlett into my ear.

Me, being nearer to the minion, opted for polite. "She likes mirrors, doesn't she?"

The pair of us entered a large, let's say, reflective room and greeted Mrs King.

"Please, Mr Boggart, take a seat."

"Mrs King." Scarlett and I sat in the chairs that were strategically lower than the desk behind which Mrs King sat.

"Let's not be so formal… 'your majesty' will suffice", said Mrs King. "And who is your acquaintance?"

"Allow me to introduce, my new partner, Her Majesty Princess Rosebud, daughter of the late King Cole of the Kingdom of Fotherghyll…she is soon to be crowned Queen, in her own right, although you can call her Scarlett, seeing as we're being so informal." Mrs King looked a little taken aback and being a queen by marriage rather than by direct line was technically Scarlett's inferior. Thankfully she recognised the fact, curtseyed and agreed that informality might be the best way to continue.

"I asked you to come here, Mr Boggart…to be present when the er…strange-looking man…"

"I think we've ascertained that he is, in fact, a boggart."

"…yes, the boggart who I owe my dog to will arrive to claim him should I not be able to guess his name."

"Well you need worry no more, Mrs King as the Boggart & Alewife Detective Agency have successfully recovered the aforesaid name." I put my hand into my inside pocket and began to pull out a…"

"Really? Oh…well…er…" said Mrs King.

I had expected a little more in the way of gratitude but I was new at this game.

"Well let's just wait for his arrival, shall we?" continued Mrs King, "I have been reading a little about your remarkable discoveries in…er…Scarlett's kingdom. It must have been very dangerous for you?"

"All in a day's work, Mrs King." The papers had carried the story of the reappearance of Fotherghyll Palace after all these years, but the All-Seeing Eye had made sure by the use of magic that there was little else to tell.

"There is a rumour that says you discovered another world. Is this true?" Scarlett flashed me a look. Avis Davies had demanded we keep the lid on the time-gate thing. An effective way of closing it for good had yet to be discovered. All-Seeing Eye seers had reported that Walter Coope had fulfilled his promise about destroying the access to the smaller time-gate.

"Scarlett and I discovered a large cave that appeared every day at a set time. In fact we got trapped inside it for a full day."

"And what did you find in there?"

"Nothing…after the lanterns ran out we had to sit in total darkness the rest of the time", said Scarlett, feeling as if the conversation required her input. "Although when the cave opened next day, we did find a severed head on the ground."

Mrs King thrust a fine lace handkerchief to her mouth in response to Scarlett's gory titbit. Hans-Christian Grimm had come to a nasty end. His body had never been found, more through lack of interest than anything else. The plight of counselling and repatriating a great number of bewildered sprites had become our immediate priority in the aftermath of the fall of Domania, but I'm sure Mrs King would not find that at all interesting.

The impending arrival of the un-named boggart was announced by the now-familiar minion who was called over by Mrs King. She whispered something in his ear and he left through a door at the back of the room. The double doors opened behind us and the familiar face of the un-named boggart came into the room. I say familiar because I had deduced that the boggart who I had shared that terrifying coach ride with at the hands of Alaric Deadman was the one who was hoping to claim possession of Barry, Mrs King's dearly-loved bull terrier. A seat was placed at one side of us and the un-named boggart was beckoned towards it. The swagger that Mrs King had led us to believe this boggart possessed had clearly gone. Once more I felt in my coat pocket for the piece of evidence that would thwart his claim to Barry.

A fanfare was played and into the room walked a tall, rugged and handsome young man with a large muscle-bound dog on a lead. Barry the bull terrier, once a carefree little puppy, was now a burglar's nightmare. Mrs King beckoned the young man over to the seat that now had been placed beside her. As the young man took his place, Mrs King cleared her throat.

"Firstly, I would like to introduce my husband-to-be, Redfern Frogmore. Redfern and I were childhood sweethearts until he left to serve the King. He recently returned to the area and took up a position as a local woodsman and we have since been reunited, soon to be married.

"Congratulations!" from me.

"Really, a woodcutter…how clichéd!" in a whisper from Scarlett. If only she knew the half of it! As the happy couple took delight in their joy, I noticed that Barry had made a point of greeting the un-named boggart. I watched as the sprite made quite a fuss over the barrel-chested dog. It was my turn for throat-clearing. Mrs King extricated herself from her betrothed and adjusted her clothing.

"Right…sorry…er un-named boggart…I have something to say to you", said Mrs King. The sprite sat up in his chair and the dog jumped up onto his lap. I decided that this was the opportunity to step in and reveal my findings.

"If I might be allowed, Mrs King?" A flutter of her hand was all the permission I needed. I addressed the boggart-with-no-name to his face. "Sir, some time ago I was retained by Mrs King to ascertain the name of the boggart who laid claim to ownership of her pet dog, Barry." The bull-terrier on hearing its name turned on the boggart's lap to face me; it wagged its tail quite happily. "You are the aforesaid boggart?"

The boggart nodded.

"It is my understanding that you helped Mrs King to weave straw into gold on three occasions when she was set such a task by her late husband."

"Sort of…"

"And was it not so that, Mrs King paid you something of value for the first two occasions you came to her assistance but on the third instance she had nothing to pay you with so you demanded that she forfeit her first born child as payment. You even brought a small contract with you for her to sign. Is that not so? Just a minute…..what do you mean…'sort of'?" There was silence in the great room.

"Well I didn't actually weave the straw into gold and I didn't actually ask for her first born. You see I knew that the old King would remain childless…her majesty here had been his sixth wife. None of them had borne fruit, so to speak."

"You say you knew that the King would remain childless. This would indicate a certain familiarity with the royal household. My enquiries over the last few weeks have revealed that-"

"Well I did actually work for him…"

"Aha!" The man had stolen my thunder but I had my trump card at the ready.

"Yeah, I worked in the King's strong-room, I am an accountant by trade and I kept the records of the King's gold. How else do you think I managed to produce all that gold for her majesty? Me, and a few of the lads, just did a bit of creative accounting and a bit of old-fashioned hands-on gold haulage. The old king didn't know if he was coming or going most of the time. As long as he had plenty of gold to gaze upon he was happy. We were working one night, doing a stock check when we heard her majesty here crying. The two lads I worked with knew a bit about the miller's daughter and said she was a bit full of herself…begging your pardon, your majesty. I didn't know you at that time." Mrs King nodded with practiced grace. "The two other chaps claimed that they had once asked you out, your majesty, and you had snubbed them. They asked me to 'play the lead', so to speak because her majesty did not know me. They came out of it with a pearl necklace and a ruby ring. For me, I didn't know what to ask for. One of the other guys suggested I should ask for her first born child… 'just to see how desperate she was'. I knew her majesty would never be blest with a child because of the old King's form in this area so I added a little footnote to the contract…more out of self-interest than anything else."

"Aha!" I shouted. "So you set her challenge whereby she had to guess your name before you would release her of her forfeit?"

"Indeed. But I am far from proud of myself for doing it", the boggart continued. "When the old King died, her majesty here had no need for accounting staff. Her new spending policy meant that the gold reserves took a big hit and the number of accountants was reduced. I was last in, first out."

"That's right", said Mrs King, "I was more interested in spending. As you may have noticed, I have introduced a number of modernisations to the castle. The last thing I needed was someone telling me to go steady."

The boggart carried on with his tale. "With my job gone, I was at a loss at what to do. The Royal Housekeeper felt sorry for me and she used to give me odd jobs to do about the place in exchange for somewhere to sleep and a bite to eat. One of the jobs she gave me was to take Barry here for his walkies." The bull terrier's ears pricked up on the mention of 'walkies' and began running round in an excitable circle. "I never saw

404

her majesty again, my position kept me in the castle's nether regions. Barry passed through a few hands before he actually got to me. I became very attached to the little dog and because her majesty had removed me from my position without even telling me to my face, I decided that taking Barry from her would be some compensation."

It had taken the boggart a while to get around to the nitty-gritty of the case. Once more I felt in my pocket for the trump card with which I would save the day. It was my turn now…

"I first recognised you when we shared a coach on our way to the village of Without-the-Wall. You were under the influence of a drug and were incapable of anything but breathing. Inside the land of Domania, you were given a uniform and a nametag, upon which was written your name. I have here the self-same nametag and I proudly pronounce that your name is…" I don't know why I waited so long. Dramatic effect I expect but before I got to announce the boggart's name. Mrs King said…

"I feel awful about the whole thing now, especially in light of recent events."

"…the boggart's name is…"

This time it was Scarlett who interrupted. "So what have you been doing in the meantime?"

The boggart replied. "The Royal Housekeeper told me that I shouldn't dwell on what had happened. She thought it might be a good idea if I started over…maybe go to Thursday Market and start a new life for myself."

And there it was…my life in a nutshell. This boggart had been hit hard by circumstances and had decided to do something about it. Just like me. I let the evidence fall once more to the bottom of my pocket. Why shouldn't he have the dog? Mrs King had done all right for herself; she was rich and happy with the new man in her life. What had this boggart got?...

"And then I won the Windblown Lottery!" laughed the boggart.

"Let's put an end to this charade!" I shouted. "Here is the nametag that you were issued with at your last place of employment." I couldn't stop myself; my hand just grabbed the identity badge and thrust it out into the air. "Your name is…"

"Stop!" shouted Mrs King, "I have no wish to know the name of this gentleman in such a manner. When I made him redundant, I did it without thought as to how a person might make a living and hearing his story makes me deeply ashamed of myself. I had decided, prior to hearing all this, that if Mr…" I held up the name-tag once more but nobody was interested. "…if this gentleman could promise to give Barry a good home then I would be happy to fulfil my part of the bargain. I can see from watching him and Barry that he clearly has a deep affection for the dog. So, Mr who-ever-you-are, if you would hand over to me the contract, then I would be glad to let you become the legal owner of Barry." Mrs King strode over to the dog and began to make a final fuss over him. The boggart pulled a crumpled contract from out of his pocket and handed it to Mrs King. Holding it in front of herself, she watched as Redfern struck a match and set fire to it. "You can have Barry. He obviously likes you more than he does me. I've got Redfern to take care of me now. On cue, the young man kissed Mrs King's neck.

Keen to leave, the boggart fastened a lead onto Barry's jewelled collar and the pair of them left the hall of mirrors and set out for a life together. Scarlett and I waited for something to happen. Mrs King obliged.

"Mr Boggart, Miss Alewife, here is your payment for the case. I would like to wish you both good day."

"I still can't believe you don't want to know the boggart's name!" I said, frustrated by not being allowed to close the case in the way I would like.

"Mr Boggart, I found out two weeks ago that I am expecting my first child. If letting Barry go would safeguard the future for Redfern, myself and our child then so be it. The contract is destroyed; I have you and Miss Alewife as witnesses. Let that be an end of the matter."

And so it was.

Outside, by the steps of the castle, a fast coach was waiting for us. Avis Davies had summoned us to The Druid's Palace to be formally thanked for our involvement in the strange happenings at Fotherghyll Palace.

"How did she know we were here?" asked Scarlett in all innocence.

"She's in charge of the All-Seeing Eye", I said, "why wouldn't she know?"

Scarlett and I left The Druid's Palace and stepped aboard the small ferry boat which would take us back to the mainland. Avis Davies had presented us both with medals but confessed that the real reason we were here was to be debriefed about what she was now calling The Fotherghyll Situation. All those that knew about what had really happened behind the Wall of Thorns had been sworn to secrecy. It was inevitable that some stories would get out but no mention was to be made of the existence of another world. In the interests of society it was necessary to guard against and to close down any further instances of time-gates. JC Bigg had been appointed as commander of the department entrusted with the monitoring and subsequent closure of all time-gate anomalies.

The All-Seeing Eye was happy by Scarlett's idea that Fotherghyll Palace should become a tourist attraction famous for its gardens and water features. A head-gardener had already been appointed, a certain Hamble Titchmarsh, who would oversee the project. Now that the Wall of Thorns was no more, plans were being put forward to rebuild the lost village of Within-the-Wall. The stone wall that originally separated the two villages was being restored to highlight the curiosity for the purposes of further tourism potential. Of course before all this could happen a lot of changes had to be made. All vestiges of the other world that had infiltrated Fotherghyll Palace and its grounds would have to be removed, including the time-gates. The story of the Sleeping Beauty was too big to hold back, those people who once lived at the palace were now undergoing counselling and had been offered work at Fotherghyll should they want it. Their old identities had been discovered from castle documents and everything possible would be undertaken to help them become themselves again.

As for those sprites that had been kidnapped and enslaved by Doris Morris and the Grimm brothers; well that was another problem. Brought out of their hypnotic state and withdrawn from the drugs they were given; they were now free to return to the life they had lived before. Reports, so far, had indicated that they had retained nothing from their experiences in Domania

Scarlett was still admiring her medal, the Order of the Four Leaf Clover. As the boat bobbed upon the blue sea, she put it back inside its velvet-lined presentation case and basked in the warm morning sun. I was tempted to throw mine overboard.

"I mean what is the point? What is the point in presenting me with the same medal twice?"

"It's the first time I've ever really had an achievement recognised. When I was a princess I was presented with something every week…but it was just because of who I was…I never actually earned anything…"

"You'd think they'd have a higher level of a medal…you know for someone who had 'taken action above and beyond the call of duty'…twice. You know, like a higher grade or something…"

"It was nice to see JC looking well. Her wings are almost back to normal. When we found her the next day, I didn't think she would make it. She's a very resilient person. She certainly deserves her promotion."

"…or maybe even a title", I continued "…perhaps I deserve some kind of title?"

"Seal Burger! Getchyour See-al Burger!" came a cry across the water.

The two of us climbed out of the boat and walked along the quay past a number of small booths selling souvenir trinkets and food for the tourists.

"They could have an Order of the Four Leaf Clover with…

"Extra fries?" called a big goblin who was serving a customer. I spun on my heel and caught sight of his booth with the newly-painted BURGER GOBLIN sign on the top. "Get the latest craze in fast food! Try our new Burgers!" he bawled at the crowd. Further along, another sign was being painted in bold green, white and red colours, prior to being lifted into place. The sign said PIZZADOMANIA. I asked the sign-writer which booth the sign was for and he pointed us further down the quay to a garish stall which was manned by a familiar face. There in front of me, slicing up his wares with a wheel cutter was the elf who had refused to serve me in the pizza parlour at what was now Fotherghyll Palace. I took off my hat and asked him for a slice of his four seasons pizza.

"That'll be two marks, sir." He flashed a big joyful smile at me before asking… "You want special sauce with that?"

GRAY LIGHTFOOT is a writer and performance poet who lives in the old Kingdom of Cornwall (that's the pointy bit that sticks out a the bottom of Great Britain) with Wendy and a one-eyed black cat called Licky (it's short for Liquorice). Along with most other writers he doesn't earn enough to make a living, so he drives buses around the Cornish peninsula to pay the bills...but he's happy...and that, to all intents and purposes, is the main thing.

He has now written two novels THE MALTHOUSE FALCON and BIGG'S LEAP (in the Humphrey Boggart comic fantasy series) and one book of poetry called A VIEW FROM A CAB (the poetry and musings of a bus driver in Cornwall)

Check out his website at www.graylightfoot.co.uk

www.ingramcontent.com/pod-product-compliance
Lightning Source LLC
Chambersburg PA
CBHW060141260626
47160CB00001B/67